Spurn the Moon

Kelsie Engen

Printed in the United States of America

First Printing, Dec 2017

ISBN: 0-998499412

ISBN-13: 978-0-9984994-1-3

Litera Scripta Manet

PO Box 10845

Fairbanks, AK 99710

To him whom I love.

Author's Note

I've long wanted to write a book set in England, but waited for the story that felt right being set there. In college, I was given the opportunity to live in England and attend school for a brief semester. There, I was blessed with the chance to add to my travel around England and fall in love with the beautiful city of York, England. But, I must admit, London comes in a close second to York. I used to say that I loved London the best, for there is no end to things to do in the city. However, after my most recent trip to England during the writing of Spurn the Moon, I have come to the conclusion that York unwittingly stole my heart.

One of my favorite things about writing this book was the ability to live vicariously in England through Adrienne, her family, and friends. And since I couldn't decide between London and York, I used both.

I know I've taken a few liberties with my setting, and I hope you'll forgive them and manage to enjoy the story nonetheless. As an author, I'll simply claim "artistic license" to make my story the best it can be.

I hope you enjoy Adrienne's story, the good and the bad. I've spent so long with her that I know it's time to let her finally go.

Kelsie Engen

Spurn the Moon

Chapter One
On the Doorstep

THE BLACK LIMO PAUSED BEFORE the iron gates, abandoning me on the pavement before my mother's London flat with my suitcases. I wanted to call it back, to rip open the back door and dive inside its relative safety, instead of trembling on my mother's doorstep, feeling like a petulant coward.

Instead, as the gates swung open and the rustle of rushing traffic rose into the air around me, I lifted my chin into the air and dug past my discomfort to find my courage. The white brick building yawned before me, a many-mouthed monster waiting to devour me with half a dozen windows searching out the plaza I stood in. I scanned them, but no faces appeared; no one to check that I stood unattended on their private sidewalk filled with bright potted plants and fences adorned in trimmed ivy.

The car slipped out of the gate, the gate locked behind it, and it merged into traffic to disappear down the street before I faced the lion knocker. The white door was immaculately clean, as though no street dared defile the door of its owner.

After a minute or two, I tightened my grip on the suitcase handle and climbed the stairs. A million scenarios of how my mother would greet me ran through my head like sprinters out of the starting blocks. Before I stopped myself—consciously or unconsciously—I raised my hand and lifted the knocker. My fingers released it, it gave one solid clang, and I stood waiting, wishing that everything was different: that my head wasn't throbbing from the stitches the doctor had just finished tying off, that I hadn't had to call my estranged mother to watch me for the next day, and that it had never come to me dreading to see her in the first place.

The door swept open with a suction upon the atmosphere that stole the air from my lungs.

She always looked perfect, as though a photoshoot was imminent. I could count on one hand the times I had seen her look normal. Violet eyes, bright against porcelain skin, and charcoal hair and lashes made her face one to be stared at. Despite my resemblance to her, I always paled in comparison. I was the moon to her sun, the night sky against her stars. Always her shadow, her echo, her backdrop.

"Adrienne." One word was all it took to erase all hope that she would welcome me with kindness.

Mustering my strength, I drew breath into my lungs and held it, shuddering under her scrutiny. "Victoria." My attempt at nonchalance echoed oddly even to my own ears.

"I wasn't expecting you."

My eyebrows lifted and my stitches reminded me of their presence with a flash of pain. Hand to my head, I said, "I called—"

"No, no, no," she answered impatiently. "Of course you did; the doctor made you. I meant, today. Earlier. When you called."

"Well, I know . . ." I shifted my weight to the other foot, glancing at my most comfortable pair of retired running shoes. My mother forgot how easily and deeply she had hurt others. She lived in her own little world of movies and A-listers, paparazzi and magazine interviews; I lived in a world where family meant everything. She never understood why I'd walked out, and even less why I refused to come back. I wiggled my toes underneath the breathable mesh on top of my shoes. And yet here I was, on her doorstep in London, begging for a place to stay.

"Why'd you call?"

Her words jostled my sluggish brain. "What? I need a place to stay— someone to supervise me. Make sure I wake up."

"Is that all?" Her head tilted casually to the side, her straightened dark hair brushing the tops of her shoulders as gently as a kiss.

Spurn the Moon

I bit my lip as blood pounded through my body, making my head ache with the effort. "And my hotel lost my reservation."

A slow smile lifted the corners of her lips, one of triumph, a sight I had not forgotten.

"Come on," Victoria said with false concern. "It looks like rain. We'd better get you in off the street."

It wasn't a welcome, and it was hardly an invitation, really, but it was the only one I could expect. So I tightened my grip on my luggage and trudged past the lion knocker into the marble decked interior.

Evidently, Victoria Talbot had had a pay increase since my last visit. It was easy for me to forget and lose track of her life. Almost eagerly, I had sheltered myself four thousand miles away at home in Alaska. Now, faced with her new flat, which she happily described to me as a home of three thousand square feet on three levels that spilled out into a private garden behind the white-marble chef's kitchen, I couldn't live in denial any longer.

My feet stuttered in the hallway at the lines of professional photos artistically arranged on the walls. In most, my mother stood alongside famous people I recognized as actors but couldn't name. At the end of the hallway, though, under the cover of the only shadow from the staircase, hung a picture of my twin sisters and me. Their grinning faces, the same faces I had left at home, stirred in me a deep and surprising homesickness.

Victoria led me into the sitting room, where tea was delivered by a housekeeper-slash-cook with a promptness that made me blink in surprise.

"Milk? Sugar?" the woman asked.

"No, thank you," I answered, sitting forward on my chair and watching her pour the strong, dark tea into the white cup. "Actually, do you have honey?"

"Of course, miss," the woman replied. She was an older woman, with a deeply lined face indicative of much time spent in the sun, as if she had lived her life in the Florida Keys rather than the tempestuous British Isles. She wore a plain, button-up white shirt above black pants.

When she disappeared, silence set in between Victoria and me, so I examined the room, glancing from the floor to ceiling bookcases, the cherry colored hardwood floor, to the pile of scripts lying on the side table next to Victoria. My gaze stuttered on a book-sized box with a heart-shaped lock. Funny the things she'd held on to, as I didn't recognize another thing in the room, not even a familiar picture, but I remembered this locked box. When I was only three, my curiosity had gotten a hold of me. I'd taken the key, which my mother had then worn around her neck, and had it in the lock, half turned when she found me. Victoria left us soon after that, and I never saw the box again. Until now.

The hired woman returned with a honey pot, and placed it beside my china teacup and saucer.

"Thank you . . ." I trailed off in question. "I'm sorry, I didn't catch your name," I said when she didn't supply it.

Her weathered face split into a gentle smile. "Oh, it's Mary."

"Mary?" I smiled up at her while the honey dripped off the wand and into my tea. "Thank you for the tea."

"Yes, thank you," Victoria added as an afterthought, tapping her spoon against her cup's rim without looking at Mary. Instead, she fixed her gaze on me, as though I were a small child she found endearing and cute to watch. "I've forgotten how absolutely darling you are."

My face grew hot. When was the last time my mother had embarrassed me like this? Usually my embarrassment was far-removed, as when my mother involved herself in a rather sexy movie or something that made my friends act like the young adults they were: guys suddenly impressed and interested in me, while girls became catty and sullen.

Now, I forced myself to watch Mary leave the room and close the door behind her, aware of Victoria's lingering amusement as she slouched forward and put her spoon on her saucer. Her slim-legged black trousers and her floaty, floral tank reminded me of a model. Even now, relaxed in her own home, she wore slipper flats that were street worthy.

She never relaxed, not truly. Her entire life was a stage, down to this display for me.

"So I talked to James after you called."

"You called Dad? It's 3 A.M. at home." I had landed many hours before, at a time when it might have been decent to call him, but I'd been knocked unconscious by a falling suitcase on the plane, and transported via ambulance to the hospital I'd woken up in. I'd only called my mother two hours ago. It had been a mess—still was, I admitted as I probed my stitches with a fingertip.

Victoria shrugged, somehow making the action delicate despite her insensitivity. "I wanted to make sure this wasn't some impulsive trip of yours. Co-parenting and all that." A pretty, ironic smile flashed upon the edges of her lips.

I blinked at her, remembering belatedly to shut my mouth. "Since when have I been impulsive?" The words stabbed me with regret as soon as they left my mouth, for my last exit from London could have been construed as just that.

The irony wasn't lost upon Victoria, for her perfectly shaped eyebrows lifted in a practiced expression of disbelief. "You really don't know yourself at all, do you?" She gave a tinkling little laugh that scratched like glass against my spine.

Tea scalded my lips when I tried to hide my frustration behind a drink. This meeting wasn't going as planned. I was here simply for a place to crash tonight, nothing more. As soon as I slept the night through—and didn't die from complications caused by my concussion—I'd be on my way, and we could return to not speaking to one another, like we had for the past three years. Flustered, I bumped the cup down against its saucer and reached for a cloth napkin. I blotted it against my lips. Yes, that was the way it had to be. It wasn't like I could expect Victoria Richie-Talbot to ever be sorry for what she had done to me.

"So to what do I *really* owe this pleasure?" Victoria's voice had gone from amused to bored. Every syllable of every word suggested that she had far better things to do with her time than spend it with her eldest daughter.

"I told you on the phone. The doctor says my concussion was too severe to be alone. I needed someone to monitor me tonight, in case it's worse than they thought."

She exhaled a slight puff of air from her nose in distaste. "I must say I'm surprised you called me and not Kat."

"Kat?" I shifted in my seat, buying myself some time. Unlike my mother, I wasn't a good liar. I wasn't even a liar. If I'd had Kat's number, I would have called her first—even though she was another remnant of a life I'd fled three years ago. Brushing a hand across my cheek to swipe away a strand of hair, I smiled in what I hoped was a polite way. "I didn't have her number. I only had yours."

Her smile grew catlike. "Always the honest little girl, aren't you?" She shook her head down at her tea. "Don't you worry people won't like you when you speak the truth?"

"No more than someone who lies worries that people won't like them when all their deceptions are discovered," I retorted, thinking of some of the lies she'd told me.

She laughed easily, casting me a look that managed to be both appraising and scornful all at once. "My little girl . . . all grown up, it appears. But still needs her mummy."

"On occasion," I muttered.

"But aren't you a doctor? Shouldn't there be some way around you needing . . . *me*?"

"No, I'm pre-med, remember? I'm over here for med school at Oxford, so give me a few years. I'm only twenty-two."

"Is that all?" She gave a little scoff. "Seems like only yesterday you were a wailing baby . . ."

Flushing, I dropped my gaze to my honeyed tea, and her voice washed over me as if she had taken the remaining honey and drenched her words with it.

My head took that opportunity to pound violently, stealing away any possible response. Concussion mingled with jet lag was my new worst enemy—even worse than my mother. "I graduated from my college in three years, *magna cum laude*. I'm going into cancer research. Hopefully." I dared a glance up at her, disappointed that all I had managed to do was offer her information, instead of return her to her place.

"Darling, of course you will." Victoria set her cup and saucer on the table beside her with a clink. "But you must be exhausted; why don't you just go up to the guest room and nap now?"

Following suit and putting my cup down next to hers, I caught the tail end of her glance at her watch.

She flashed me an almost apologetic smile and smoothed her hands down her thighs.

"Is someone going to be here, or am I just going to drift off into oblivion?" The wryness in my tone earned me a laugh.

"Of course someone will be here, darling." She cast a glance toward the living room door, through which the hired help had disappeared earlier. "Mary or I—or both of us—will be here."

"I can't sleep right now anyway." It was not quite one in the afternoon here, so not quite four in the morning back home. "I should message people at home and let them know I arrived all right." I brought a hand to my head to touch my stitches, but didn't mention them.

"Of course." Victoria's tone and manner were cooling the longer she sat, as though she had things to do that didn't involve me. I recognized it immediately; fortunately she wasn't the actress in her personal life she was in her professional life.

Of course, having an Oscar to your name is likely to do that, to make you think your act can smooth over any situation. Only I knew her act to be false, I knew her truths. And those truths would forever haunt me.

☽

Nearly as soon as I walked upstairs, the limo that had picked me up at the hospital appeared in the courtyard, and Victoria disappeared out the front door, while I watched from the guest room's bay window.

As she was driven away, probably by Charles, the same driver who had driven me here, I recalculated the nine-hour difference in time between my home in Alaska and Greenwich Mean Time. Still too early to call.

My twin sisters Margot and Sophie, younger by 4 years, would murder me if I called before nine. Dad's worth a shot though.

I dialed his cell number, just in case he was sleeping, and listened as his voicemail answered. He had a rule that if it were an emergency, we called the house phone—and everyone knew it, even the volunteers at his campaign office—otherwise, we called his cell and left a message. "Hey, Dad, it's me: your favorite daughter. Hope all is well there. I landed in London . . . a little less than safely, but safely enough. Apparently you heard about it from Victoria. But I'm okay . . . just have a bit of a headache. And a concussion. But I'll heal. I miss you and hope I'll get to talk with you soon. Love you."

Ending the call, I gazed out the window a little longer. The paved courtyard was empty now, except for the little square of grass in the middle, which housed a small statue of a person on a horse. I yawned and turned around, leaving the curtains wide open. Oddly for London, there was no one close enough for even this wilderness girl to feel like she was being watched.

Somehow, the absence of my mother made it easier for me to entertain the idea of a nap, and I lay down, intending on a short rest. I woke in all of my clothes atop the black and white chevron duvet to a dark room despite the open blinds. Warmth encircled me, and I blinked in confusion at the ornate ceiling, trying to figure out if it was the heat that had stirred me. After a few discombobulated moments, a rumble underneath my room alerted me to what I must have heard: voices.

Victoria must have a guest in the house, and not her housekeeper, for I couldn't imagine her holding a detailed conversation—complete with laughter—with the hired help.

I sat up, waited for the room to stop spinning, then rose and moved to the window. This room overlooked the front stoop, and I half expected to see a car parked outside, but there were none—not even a neighbor's. Frowning, I realized there must be a garage for this block of flats, a privilege allowed to few in a city like London. Here, Ferraris and Lamborghinis crouched alongside Toyotas and Nissans on traffic-laden streets, their owners having afforded the car, but still reduced to searching for a parking spot like anyone else.

My glance lifted to the heavens in an automatic search for the stars, but the steady glow of London's lights prevented my seeing much of anything.

The voices rose underneath me again, the male's rising to interrupt Victoria's tinkling laughter. Her laugh had always reminded me of a bird singing in the trees, higher than I could reach and utterly indecipherable. It had once tempted a smile from me, a desire to echo her laughter, but somewhere along the way, I had lost any amusement once found in her. I should have accepted sooner that there was no changing her, only accepting her. Then perhaps my amusement could continue, without the bitterness that welled up in me every time I heard that damnable laugh.

Shaking the irritation off my shoulders, I crouched to untie my tennis shoes. Getting comfortable in her house was not something I welcomed, and I had resisted it even through my slumber. Now, though, curiosity and discomfort outweighed any other emotion.

I slipped my sweaty, travel-stinking feet from their confines and peeled off my socks. I needed a long shower and a change of clothes. And a good run to stretch my legs. At the moment, though, a low, long chuckle returned my curiosity. In my sticky, bare feet I abandoned my post at the window and crossed to the door, every creak of floorboards burdening me with unfulfilled anticipation.

The door opened silently, inviting the voices inside along with a clink of ice against glasses. I paused at the top of the stairs, waiting for the voices to resume. A low murmur, words running into one another, drifted up the painted white banister and to my ears.

Solid stairs beneath my feet did not betray me with a sound, and I hesitated at the bottom, wondering if I should leave Victoria and her guest to their giggling privacy, when a phone rang.

I jumped, then crept forward and craned my ears to listen to the one-sided conversation that ensued.

"It is? That's unfortunate," a British voice said. "Yes . . . I understand. I'll let her know. Ring me with an update as soon as you . . . Yes. Thanks." Footsteps muffled by the Persian rug ebbed and flowed, and a chair creaked softly under someone's weight. "That was—"

"Ouch!" In the dark, I had not seen a white table nestled against the white wall, but my toe had found it, rivaling the pain in my head for several seconds. As I hopped on one foot, holding my toe, the door to the living room unceremoniously flew open.

Victoria stood behind a tall man in an Oxford shirt and dark slacks with loafer-clad feet. Oddly, I focused on his feet, thinking he must not have been here long if he hadn't got comfortable either. If the situation had been more comical, I would have appreciated his good looks more. As it was, his straight, thick eyebrows nearly touched in the middle as he frowned at me in confusion.

"You're not the housekeeper . . ." He trailed off with a half-glance back to Victoria, his brows separating slightly in understanding.

He was trim in a normal, middle-aged way, which meant he wasn't likely to be a movie-star friend of Victoria's, nor a model, nor sports player. None of which I would recognize even if it hadn't been the middle of the night, if my toe and head hadn't both been throbbing, and if his face hadn't been cast into half-shadow.

"No. I'm not," I managed.

"You—you're Adrienne, aren't you? Or Sophie? Margot?" He seemed to be guessing now, thrown off balance when I didn't immediately respond.

Lowering my toe and balancing on both feet again, I faced him squarely, confused. "Have we met?"

"No no no," he answered, running the words together and stepping back to open the door wider as if for me to enter the room with them. "We've not met, but I've been asking to meet you."

"Edmund." Victoria's voice was a gentle warning, the honey thickening as it cooled in my presence.

He didn't look back at her this time, but extended a hand to me. "I'm Edmund Chadwick, your mother's fiancé."

Chapter Two
The Fiancé

SOMEHOW I FOUND MY HAND enclosed by Edmund Chadwick's in a firm but gentle grip. His smile displayed teeth that were unusually straight and white for an older Englishman, and although two lower teeth remained crooked, they didn't mar the congenial effect. My breath steadied under his smile, but his name played over again in my mind on repeat, echoing softer and softer each time, as though slipping out of reach.

"Are you all right?"

His voice pulled me out of my reverie and I blinked at him. "Why do I know your name?"

He withdrew a little in surprise, his smile disappearing only to flash back on his lips with confidence I hadn't noticed before. "Do you follow politics, Adrienne?"

With his words, understanding and memory washed over my fogginess. "Politics." I met Victoria's disinterested stare over his shoulder. "Politics?" A memory from my childhood descended upon me, one wherein my mother had announced that she had left my father because he had chosen a career as a politician.

Victoria responded with a silent smile and head tilt, challenging me to speak my mind.

I didn't move, not to speak, and not to enter the room. "Engaged, huh?" I didn't know why the news surprised me so much, except that I had that deeply romantic streak in me, longing for a Hollywood ending. Ironic, since I knew Hollywood endings never happened in real life, and the people who played Cinderella never got their Prince Charming in the real world.

"Yes. We're planning an April wedding," Victoria answered, walking up beside Edmund and snaking her hand into the crook of his elbow. My gaze flicked down upon her hand, this time studying the large diamond ring with suspicion.

"Great. That's great." My voice sounded disembodied to my ears; words continued from my mouth, although I couldn't explain why. "I'm running the London Marathon in April." My eyes stuck on the glinting ring. She seemed to know it, for she adjusted her hand so I could better see the crystal-clear stone, and I recognized its high quality even from three feet away. "I'm going to get some painkillers. Kitchen?" Victoria gave a little shake of her head before nodding agreement. "Thanks."

I left them there, arm in arm, and disappeared through the white swinging door into the kitchen, grateful when it swung shut behind me. At the oven, I paused, straining my ears to hear approaching footsteps, and when I didn't, I let my shoulders slump.

How had I never expected this? How had I never expected my mother, a beautiful, vivacious, interesting—*rich*—woman, to remarry? It seemed foolish, now that I considered it, now that I was faced with it. But Victoria Talbot had never been seriously linked with a man. Her dating life—unlike the rest of her life—had been utterly hidden from the public eye. All else she had displayed for her fans, going to premieres, beaches, movies, parties, all with the expectation that the media and her fans' ever-watchful eyes would tag along. It was only her dating life which had remained her own. Now, I realized that, but until a few minutes before, I had never given much thought to her dating at all. It wouldn't have been any more shocking had my father showed up with a fiancée the day I left Alaska.

Confused more than I wanted to admit, I removed two tablets from their jar and swallowed them with a palmful of water from the tap. At the swinging door, I paused, gathering my will to return and trying to bend it into submission before I went in.

Edmund's voice, low and insistent, reached me before I reentered.

"She should know."

"No, not yet," Victoria answered, an undercurrent of ice chilling her voice. "Nothing has happened—there's nothing to tell."

"Darling," he began.

"She's my daughter, not yours." A sternness I had rarely heard in Victoria's voice had captured it and held strong. "You will not say anything."

Several seconds ticked by, but neither spoke again. With my palm on the door, I pushed it open. Victoria sat upon the couch again, while Edmund stood at the bar, only his profile visible. My gaze lingered on my future stepfather, his vacant, downcast stare betraying his descent into deep thought.

Even if I had not heard part of their conversation a moment before, Victoria would have betrayed how it regarded me. Not in poor acting, but in the simple fact that she met my gaze and gave me what anyone would have assumed was an honest, interested smile. My breath caught at the realization, and with it, the irrepressible urge to escape the smile she aimed my way.

"My head is pretty painful. I'm going to go back to bed," I told them before conversation resumed. "Edmund, it was lovely to meet you. I'm sorry it's been so short."

Before either responded, other than a slight frown, I slipped from the room and dashed up the stairs.

$$\mathbb{D}$$

Back in the safety of my room, I tried to keep my pacing to a minimum; they could probably hear my every footstep down below. But my thoughts raced and my feet wished to match them. Never had I longed for the ability to run my thoughts into place like I always had at home—even at minus forty.

Did Sophie and Margot know about this? Did Dad? Was I the only one left in the dark? I sighed. Of course I couldn't blame them for not filling me in on Victoria's life, as I seldom wished to hear about it. Gritting my teeth, I raked a hand through my hair and flinched at the tenderness of my head.

At a pause in my relentless pacing, I heard Edmund's calm, deep voice murmur again. Footsteps tapped a tattoo against the wooden floor below.

"I'll see you in the morning?" Victoria's words carried up the stairs and through the crack in my door. I shuffled across the smooth floor to listen.

"We'll see. I hope it won't be necessary." Edmund's response seemed distracted, almost cold. He seemed to realize it, for he added, "I hope the media decides to honor my request, that's all. But even if they do, I'll be busy with meetings most of the day. I'm sorry."

"I know. It's just . . . I miss you when you aren't around."

"I miss you, too."

Victoria did not answer, and I suspected they were sharing an embrace or a kiss. In silence, I shut the door and pressed my aching head against it for a long moment. Then I straightened and headed to bed. I sat down and debated just a moment before picking up the phone.

Only when the phone on the other end had rung three times did my gaze flick to the clock on the bedside table, doing the quick math. Six o'clock P.M. yesterday at home, the perfect time to call my sisters.

The phone rang through to voicemail. "Hi, you've reached Sophie. Leave a message, and I'll call you back as soon as possible."

Muttering to myself, I hung up the phone and dialed again. "Come on, Margot . . . Sophie . . . I need to talk to you."

At the third ring this time, the phone line went silent. Then, several belated seconds after: "Hello?"

"Margot."

"Hey! About time you called." Margot paused, waiting for me to respond. When I didn't, she added, "Adrienne?"

"Yes."

"Everything okay?"

I took my time in answering. Was everything okay? "I'm staying with Victoria. So . . . no."

"What's wrong?" An alert wariness was entering her voice, which I read even across an ocean. "Why are you there?"

"What's going on?" Another voice crackled through the line. "Is that Adrienne?"

"Put me on speaker phone," I requested of Margot. "That way I can talk to both of you at once."

"Sure." There was a pause. "Okay, we're both here. What's going on? Are you okay?" Margot asked.

A sixth sense began to dawn on me as Sophie remained quiet. My blood began to pulse in my ears at their ominous silence.

"Adrienne?" Margot urged.

"I'm staying with our mother. Because a suitcase knocked me out when

I landed in London."

"What?"

"Yeah. Someone popped the bin open and a suitcase clocked me. I have stitches."

"Oh my gosh. Are you okay?" one of the twins asked, probably Sophie.

"Yeah. I'm fine. I'll be fine." Tenderly, I touched my fingers to my head, where a huge knot had formed around the rough stitches. "But that's why I'm staying with Victoria in her brand new, gigantic flat in Kensington."

"Ohh. Sounds nice and cushy," Sophie said through her giggles.

"Nicer than your hotel?" Margot asked, her tone more subdued. So often, it was only by their tones that I could tell them apart on the phone. Sophie was always laughing, her subject often leaning toward finding a boyfriend, while Margot managed to have a decent talk before being lulled over into Sophie's universe.

Now, I wasn't amused by either of them, not with having just met our future stepfather. "Did you know?" My words came out quiet but forceful.

"Know what?" Margot asked.

"Sophie? Did you know?" I demanded.

She sighed. "All right, yes. We knew."

"And you let me come over here without any warning?" Instead of allowing my voice to rise, I forced it lower, furious at their secrecy.

"What are you—" Margot was unusually slow on the uptake right now.

"Couldn't you have at least mentioned that our mother was engaged to be married?"

A pair of hands clapped over the line. "Engaged?" Sophie squealed. "I did *not* know that!"

"Sophie! You didn't tell her?" Margot gasped.

"No. Neither of you told me that our mother was dating someone— nor that she was dating a politician."

"What does it matter if she's dating a politician?" Sophie scoffed.

"She said she hated them," Margot answered for me.

"Yes. All of them," I added, grateful that at least Margot had remembered that statement as well, and that it wasn't just me making things up.

"Well that's a stupid thing to hold her to," Sophie said dismissively.

Her words jolted me from my self-pity, and I bit back a laugh at the truth in her statement.

"She probably said that when she was mad at Daddy for going into politics."

"Of course she did," I said, "that's not my point."

"What is your point then?" Margot asked with the patience of our father.

"You know, she's the only mother you'll ever have," Sophie said in the lull as I organized my thoughts. "You'd better make it work."

I held my breath as I looked skyward. My sisters could get under my skin the way only my mother could. They were the three people in the world who could do so. For my mother it was clearly an innate skill, perfected without practice. As for my sisters, they had learned over the years how to push my every button.

"My point is she didn't tell me. Neither did you, come to think of it." I paused to allow them a moment of embarrassment I doubted they felt. Then I continued, "It wouldn't have been too hard to say, 'Hey, Adrienne, you know our mother is dating someone?' before I left for England."

Someone sighed. "Yes, you're right." It was Margot. "I should have said something. I shouldn't have left it to anyone else to tell you."

Her admitting it didn't make me feel any better. Instead it awoke a squirm in my stomach, as though I had put a guilt trip on her when she didn't deserve it. "Margot—"

"No, you're right. I should have made sure you were told. To be honest, I was surprised when you never mentioned it to me, but . . . I was too chicken to bring it up. I thought that it would make you not leave. And I thought it was important that you get out of here."

"I had to leave for school anyway," I muttered.

"You didn't have to. You *chose* to," Margot corrected softly. "You definitely didn't have to go to *England* for school—practically any school in the world would take you." She paused, and there was a shuffle in the background, one I imagined to be Sophie settling into bed. "But you chose England, Adrienne, and that's what I didn't want to ruin."

"You didn't ruin it." The words were reluctant even to my ears.

"Well, I'm sorry." Margot sighed. "I should have told you."

"Yeah."

"Hey, are you going to look up Kat while you're there?" Sophie asked from a distance.

"Kat?" Margot sounded as if she didn't know who that was.

"Yeah, Adrienne's friend."

I could picture Sophie's grin at the jab that I only had one friend.

"Isn't she still there in London?"

"I'm not sure. I don't think she lives here anymore. She might live up north again. I don't have her number anyway. Believe me, I thought about calling her a lot lately."

"Well you should. She's awesome," Sophie said, as if that answered any question I might have had about the matter.

Despite my irritation with my sisters, I laughed. "You're too much. We only hung out for a couple of summers together. Why should I look her up?"

"Well an awesome sister deserves an awesome friend. And she's awesome."

I rolled my eyes. They had always liked Kat, even though they'd only met her a few times. I think they believed it was good for me to have a close friend, one that was a little wilder than me, one that would be outgoing where I was reserved. "What are you doing tonight? Nice quiet night in?"

The twins laughed, and the subject transitioned to their plans for the evening. Although at home I would be dodging their parties, I was here instead, with homesickness washing over me at being so far away.

"Where's Dad? At work?"

"Yeah," Sophie said at the same time as Margot answered, "No."

I laughed. "Yes? No? Where is he?"

"He's gone up to the bush."

"What? Where?" I frowned, trying to remember any plans Dad had mentioned about going north.

"Yeah, someone backed out of the mission trip last minute at church," Sophie continued.

"Galena or somewhere around there, I think," Margot added.

"He wouldn't take no for an answer and insisted on going up to help build homes or something," Sophie said, as if exasperated.

"He's helping rebuild a school that burned down," Margot corrected.

"Oh." I sat down on the edge of my bed. "So . . . I can't talk to him? When did all this happen?"

"A few hours after you left. You took your sweet time calling, you know."

"Yeah, I was in the hospital," I muttered. "I have an excuse. You could have called—let me know, you know."

"Yeah, yeah," Sophie dismissed. "Of course it was the dead of night here."

"And since when has that bothered you?" I replied, amused.

Sophie laughed. "Okay, fine. I should have messaged you."

"Yeah. Thanks." I picked at a thread on the sheets. "So when does he get back? Or does he have his cell? Can I call him?"

"I don't know," Sophie replied, clearly unconcerned about her lack of knowledge.

"Margot?" I prompted.

"He's got his cell, but I'm not sure about service there; you know how spotty service can be up there."

"Right." Travel within Alaska had many dead spots, and Dad didn't carry a satellite phone unless he was going hunting.

"But he said he'd call as soon as he got a chance. I know they made it up safely, so . . . Don't worry, Adrienne. We'll keep you informed."

I scoffed.

"I promise. I'll send you regular updates." This came from Margot.

"Right. Okay." I pulled the thread free from the sheets and wrapped it around my finger. "And how long will he be gone?"

"Two or three weeks."

"*Weeks*?" I felt suddenly as though I was eighteen again and moving off to college.

Hanging up a few minutes later, I tossed the phone on the bed, mulling over our conversation. No matter which way I turned it, I was being a self-centered drama queen. Somehow, I'd taken a leaf out of my sisters' book, and I didn't like that at all. "I'll do better tomorrow," I told myself. "Today, I mean."

When I finally fell asleep again, aided by doctor-prescribed painkillers, I had disjointed dreams of starting school and failing miserably, only to be pulled out of class by Edmund, who grounded me for failing an anatomy exam. I woke confused, certain I was a freshman in college, only to remember that I was freshly arrived in London for medical school, and staying at my mother's flat.

I scrutinized the room, touched my head to check I hadn't dreamed everything—my stitches were still there, and pounding—then I swallowed another couple of pills and fell back into sleep, this time dreamless.

Chapter Three
The Daughter

WHEN I FINALLY DRAGGED MYSELF out of bed with my head aching, the sun hung high in the sky, peeking out from behind heavy gray clouds. Downstairs, a crowd of strangers bustled through the kitchen with their arms full of white objects. Before I could ask what was going on, a voice from the table nearby rang out.

"You must be Adrienne!" The honest, pure enthusiasm in the voice halted my steps and almost pleased me with its distraction. At the table I found a plump girl, a couple of years younger than the twins, sitting in front of a huge plate of scones.

"I am. You are . . . ?"

Her lips turned up in a wide, snaggle-toothed grin as charming in its imperfection as in its warmth. Pretty in a youthful way, she'd turn her share of heads. "I'm Sydney Chadwick. Your future stepsister."

Her words chased away all other thoughts. This ringing headache must be making me hallucinate. "My what?"

"Future stepsister," she repeated. "Scone?" She lifted the plate up toward me a few inches.

"No, thanks." Finding the kettle on the stove hot, I helped myself to a mug from the cabinet and a tea bag from the box on the counter. When I turned back to Sydney, her eyes dropped down to scrutinize me.

"Hmm. On a diet because of your training?"

"What? No." I frowned, growing more confused by the second. "What?"

"Training for a marathon, right?" She gave me an expectant look as her knife dripped jam onto the plate underneath it.

"Yes, but . . . how did you know?" I sank down across from her at the table.

She shrugged, now spreading clotted cream on half a scone. "Margot said something about it."

"Margot? You've spoken to Margot?"

"And Sophie. Mmm-hmm." She nodded eagerly, a crumb dangling off her bottom lip until she licked it with the tip of her tongue.

"When? How long have you known them?"

Her eyebrows lifted, prematurely wrinkling her smooth forehead. "Oh weeks ago. As soon as Daddy and Victoria got engaged."

Sinking back against the chair, I shook my head. A group of chattering people waltzed through the kitchen on their way out to the back garden, creating a buzz of noise that distracted me again from my thoughts. "You told them our parents were engaged?"

"Of course! I love your sisters. I couldn't wait to meet you, too, but Sophie said you never talk on the phone."

"Did she?" I shook my head. "Of course she did." What was a little white lie when it meant keeping me uninformed?

"Well." Sydney polished off the last scone and pushed back the plate. "I guess we should start getting ready."

I blinked. "Get ready for what?"

She rubbed a crumb off the corner of her plush lips. "For the engagement party."

"It's still morning though. When is the party?"

"Six," Sydney said as though that shouldn't have any bearing on what we were doing now.

I laughed. "No. I'm not going."

"You have to."

"Why?"

"It's your mum."

I squirmed and put a hand to my forehead. I heard my sisters' voices in my head telling me the same thing. "I haven't been invited."

"Really?" She frowned and stood up. "We'll have to fix that."

"No—don't. Please."

The clock above the kitchen sink chimed eleven. Plenty of time to get out of attending. And plenty of time to call back my sisters and . . . what? Demand they admit they lied? I sighed, shoulders sinking. I wouldn't bother. We'd walked that path too often. They'd apologize and do the same thing next time.

Sydney's frown deepened, like it antagonized her. "Why don't you go up and shower—I'll come find you."

"Shower?" I patted my head to check if it was greasy, making her grin.

"Yeah. Shower."

Bemused, I watched her slip out the back door, letting in a surge of noise.

"No peeking," she threw over her shoulder. "You should let it be a surprise."

Any desire to peek was far from my mind as I sipped the final draught of my tea. When I finished and rose to put the cup in the sink, the garden door opened and I glanced over, thinking it was Sydney. But a man about my age entered, turquoise eyes gleaming as they fell on me.

"Hi." He raked a hand through his surfer-blond hair. He seemed as though he could be straight off the beach in California, although his dress and speech were obviously British, with his skinny jeans and collared Oxford.

"Hello." I tore my gaze away, but found my eyes drifting back to him after I set the cup in the top rack of the dishwasher.

"You must be Adrienne." He approached, holding out the same hand he'd brushed his hair back with.

"Yes . . . how did you—?"

"I'm Jake. Jake Benson. I work with your mum." He had an accent that sounded vaguely Scottish to me.

"Oh. Okay. With her or for her?" I glanced at the door he'd just walked through, which Sydney had also disappeared through.

His lips flicked up in what was quickly becoming a familiar grin. It made my heart flop, beating to life in a manner I hadn't experienced in years. My cheeks burned as I realized that, in a few seconds, I was developing a crush. With a shake of my head, I calmed my heart. *He's hot.* I groaned inwardly. I was acting like Sophie. There was so much more to life than being attractive.

His grin had widened, almost cocky now. "No? You don't believe me?"

"I'm sorry—what?" He must have spoken while I was chastising myself for being such a teenage girl. "You're an actor?"

"Uh, no, not exactly." He grimaced. "I'm trying to become one, that is. Your mum is helping me with that."

"Oh. Like, getting you auditions?" Of course I'd have to crush on an actor, of all professions. He was absolutely, one-hundred-percent off limits.

"Yeah, things like that." He shrugged and leaned his slender hips against the marble counter's edge.

I nodded as I began to plan my escape. A crush on anyone my mother knew was a bad idea, and it was best to exit this little scenario immediately. "Nice. Well . . . I need to get going. Nice to . . ."—I glanced at him despite myself—". . . meet you." And, grabbing a water from the refrigerator on my way, I slipped out the door before I could get to know Jake any better.

$$\smallint$$

A knock on the door shattered my dreamless sleep.

Disoriented, I inspected the clock beside my bed with bleary eyes. Four P.M. Whoa. My quick nap had been anything but that.

I stumbled to the door and swung it open. Sydney stood in front of me, cheeks flushed with blush, her eyelids a gentle smoky gray that deepened her gray eyes and matured her face. Eyeliner made her slightly too small eyes wide and alarmed, her lips were blood red, and her sandy brown hair was smoothed up, puffy on top.

"You're not ready at all. You haven't showered," she reproached.

"No." As I stepped back to allow her inside, my stomach dropped to my feet, where Sydney trod on it with her trainers. Despite her face and hair being done, she wore yoga pants and a soft white tee. Over one arm she had draped a garment bag, and in that hand carried a small bag.

"Good thing I got my makeup. We'll have you ready in a snap." Her cheerfulness, had it not been regarding readying me for my mother's engagement party, might have otherwise been catching.

I closed the door after her, biting back my sigh and reminding myself that this was her father's engagement party as well; she was allowed to be excited.

"How long has your father been . . . single?" I asked as I turned back to her, trying to make my question as inoffensive as possible.

To my relief, Sydney hardly seemed aware that my question could have been offensive at all. "My mum died when I was born," she answered matter-of-factly. "Dad never seriously dated a woman until meeting Victoria."

"Really? That's . . ." I trailed off, not willing to say anything that would complete that sentence in front of Sydney. "So . . . when and where did they meet? And how?"

Sydney smiled at my tone of incredulity. "Your mum was at a fundraiser my dad was having . . . back in December?" She thought for a moment. "Yes, I think it was December. Maybe November. But your mum had donated a lot of money to the project, a house for disabled kids in the city, and they were dedicating the building. Your mum was one of the guests of honor, and she and Daddy . . ." Sydney trailed off with a little shrug.

"Right. They hit it off."

"Yeah." Sydney unzipped her garment bag and slipped it off the dress. A red, rather gauzy dress appeared, one which I hoped wasn't for me; frills and ruffles were never my thing. She shook it out and carried it to the wardrobe in the corner, hanging it from the top and smoothing out the wrinkles with her hands.

"They dated right away?"

Sydney stepped back from the dress and tilted her head at it, frowning. "No, not right away, I don't think. I heard about it a month later."

"Does your dad confide in you about things like this?"

"Oh, always. He tells me whenever he's fancying someone." Sydney put her hands on her hips and faced me. "Now, where's your dress?"

"I don't have one," I said without concern. "So you and your dad are close then?"

"Yeah, yeah. He tells me everything he can. What do you mean you don't have a dress? Didn't your mum give you one?"

"About when I got an invitation," I said dryly.

"Oh!" She brightened and dug in her Coach bag, pulling out a crumpled, ivory invitation. "Here it is."

"You have a dress in there too then?" The modern block lettering on the invitation was broken by the script of Edmund and Victoria's names. Nothing on it surprised me—now. A few hours ago, I would have been shocked by every word.

"Come on. We've got lots to do." Sydney was still talking, bustling out of the room to gather more bags that she'd left in the hallway.

I tossed the invitation aside and followed her, accepting a pair of bags while she dragged a couple of shirts off the banister and over her arm. "So, how long did they date before they got engaged?" I wasn't going to let her out of this conversation so easily.

"Oh they just got engaged a few weeks ago."

My heart clenched somewhere above my navel. "That recently?" And that long ago? I wanted to add.

"Yes. I've got to talk to Victoria about your dress . . . I thought for sure it would have been delivered by now."

"We have time."

"No, we don't. We only have two hours until guests arrive."

"Oh, well . . ." I couldn't break it to her that I had no desire to attend this party, not even out of curiosity. "Isn't that a little early for a party to start?"

"It's a dinner party," she muttered into a bag. "Five course meal."

"Oh. Nice."

"The caterer is excellent," she agreed. "Now, I've got to find Victoria. Do—" She cast an appraising look over me, frowning at my tired jeans and T-shirt. "Shower. Please."

Laughing, I faced the bathroom with its marble floor and majestic fixtures. "Okay. I'll shower."

"Thank God."

Without answering except for a smile, I shut the door between us.

A hot shower later, I emerged a bit more human, and a bit more tolerant of the expectations everyone seemed to have of me since I'd gotten here. Sydney seemed to expect a big sister, Edmund a mature, level-headed daughter, Victoria . . . well, I never knew what she expected, but it was never the real me.

With a towel tied off under one armpit, I patted another over my hair, carefully avoiding my stitches while trying to dry it rapidly so it could be styled. Any effort on my hair was mostly useless anyway, as it was too silky to hold a style for long.

"Adrienne? I've got a dress for you now." Sydney's voice broke through my thoughts as I stared at my shower-flushed face in the mirror.

A shudder and a sigh played a game of chicken down my spine. Dresses didn't excite me. If she had said a new set of running clothes, or a new pair of running shoes, then I might have charged out of the bathroom before she took them away.

"Adrienne," Sydney called again. "Did you drown?"

"No. I'm coming." Squeezing the ends of my hair in the towel, I opened the bathroom door.

Sydney had commandeered the room. She'd gone so far as to rearrange the furniture, to take advantage of the light flooding in from the front window. The vanity had been angled so it sat in a sunbeam, the chair angled away from the mirror for someone else to administer the makeup to the seated person. Half a dozen pairs of heels, all black, lined the floor in front of the wardrobe, and alongside Sydney's fluffy dress hung two others, both red.

"It looked like you have Victoria-sized feet," she said, motioning to the shoes. "But I grabbed a few pairs depending on which dress you pick."

My attempt at a smile felt like a grimace, cracking the skin across my face. "Great."

"Sit down so I can get started," she said, her face alight with anticipation.

While Sydney began painting my fingernails, I sat in front of the brand-new vanity mirror, with my back to the brand-new dresses and brand-new shoes that littered the too-perfect bedroom in this too-perfect life my mother had built for herself. No antiques for my mother, nothing that suggested a previous owner or previous life. She wanted the best, but she liked her things new, with no past.

Now Sydney hovered over my shoulder in the mirror, drawing my attention to her. Edmund would be perfect for my mother: a sixteen-year widower with a daughter who had never met her mother. Sydney would have an easier time befriending my mother than I ever would. For their sakes, I hoped neither Edmund nor Sydney had any baggage.

"We only have an hour to get you dressed and downstairs; Dad will murder me if I'm late."

She worked fast, fingers dabbing and brushes swirling. "Close your eyes." She dabbed a brush on my eyelid. "What happened to your head? Why do you have stitches? Don't open your eyes."

"Sorry. Uh . . ." Briefly, I told her about my flight over and how I'd ended up staying here. "It was a bad trip over," I finished, daring to open one eye since she hadn't touched my face with a brush for the past two minutes. With a wry smile, I added, "It's almost funny, if it weren't so painful."

Mouth open slightly, Sydney stared at me, until finally a smile tugged at her lips. "It *is* rather funny. So much happened on your trip over . . ." She giggled. "It's almost hard to believe."

"Worst trip ever. By far."

She dabbed blush on my cheeks, her smile remaining. "But it's a good thing you arrived in time for tonight. I wasn't sure any of Victoria's family would make it."

"Oh?"

"It would have been sad if she hadn't had anyone from her family here," Sydney murmured. "Close your eyes again."

I obeyed, although it left me blind to interpreting that look upon her face, the deep thoughtfulness unusual in a teenage girl. "Did she say she wanted us here?"

Silence stretched out between us while Sydney drew an eyeliner pencil along my eyelashes.

Then, "She never says anything about missing you."

The touch on my eyelashes halted, but I didn't dare open my eyes.

"But she doesn't have to. I can tell she does."

"How?"

"Oh, every now and then she gets this faraway look in her eyes, so sad, as if she's missing out on something. It's usually after someone mentions one of you, or when she sees a picture of you."

"She has pictures of us?" I couldn't keep the skepticism from my voice as Sydney worked on my other eye.

"Of course." The touch withdrew again, and this time I opened my eyes to find her gray ones soft and thoughtful. "She really loves you, you know."

I shook my head from side to side in a minuscule disagreement. That was not something I would say about my mother.

She handed me a tube of mascara. "Here. Can I trust you to put this on yourself?"

Taking it, I shrugged. "Sure."

"While you do, I'm going to get dressed." She glanced at her watch. "And then I'll do your hair." In the vanity's mirror, I watched her walk to the wardrobe and pull down her dress. "And you can pick out which dress and shoes you'll wear tonight."

After she disappeared into the bathroom, I sat there, rolling the mascara tube over my palm, confused. Staring at myself in the mirror didn't offer illumination, so I sat with numb thoughts while Sydney changed. Only when I heard her hand on the doorknob did I hastily unscrew the tube and begin applying it.

"Aren't you done yet?" Sydney's reflection appeared over my shoulder in the mirror, resplendent in her red ruffles which added another inch to her flat chest and smoothed out her plump waist. "Did you pick out your dress?"

Mascara wand hovering at my eyelashes, I stared unabashedly at her in the mirror. The dress added another five years to her age, so she appeared in her early to mid-twenties, mature and elegant despite the potential childishness of ruffles.

"Well?"

"No. No, I did not pick out my dress." I dragged the wand against my lashes. "Haven't even looked."

"I'll choose for you, then?" She stepped toward the wardrobe, her low heels clicking on the floor.

"Sure." I replaced the wand into the tube of mascara and surveyed Sydney's work in the mirror. She'd done an excellent job, bringing out the violet of my eyes so they even distracted me. I pressed my lips together, watching them disappear. She'd left them nude, but I doubted she would leave them alone—I was certain one of the red lipsticks she had lined up on the vanity was for me.

"All right." Sydney slipped one of the dresses off its hanger and held it up.

Seeing it in the mirror, I laughed. "No. No way."

A knowing smile appeared above the neck of the dress Sydney lifted in front of her. Its neckline plunged far below what hers did, but it was the lace and nude covering which made me shudder.

"I cannot wear that." I stood and faced her, abandoning the mirror and all pretense. "If that's my only choice, then I'm staying up here."

Sydney wrinkled her nose. "Well, you do have another choice." She tossed the dress she held onto the bed, then slipped the second from its hanger as she had done the first.

"That's better," I said immediately.

An irrepressible smile tugged on one corner of Sydney's lips as I crossed the room to examine the dress more closely.

"Wha—why are you smiling like that?"

"No reason."

"No reason?" I questioned, tilting my head at her and smiling knowingly.

"You're just so . . . predictable."

I laughed at that. "Oh? You know me so well already?"

"Well, I knew you wouldn't wear the first dress I offered. And you'll look better in this one anyway."

With a mock frown, I asked, "So you manipulated me?"

"Manip—? Oh no." Sydney's lower lip fell in a silent gasp, appalled. "No. I don't manipulate."

"It's okay. I'd rather wear this one, if these are my only two choices." Smiling at the younger girl, I swept the dress from her hands and disappeared into the bathroom.

Chapter Four
The Preparations

IN FRONT OF THE LARGE bathroom mirror, I almost changed my mind. The other dress might have been better. This one left little to the imagination—even to me.

It was a sheath of red, with straps across the exposed back that kept the dress pasted on. Either I was built a little differently from my mother, or this dress was designed to expose flesh that had never seen the sun. I wondered if there was any two-sided tape I could use to keep it in place —before certain parts of my anatomy slipped out and created one more way to embarrass me.

"Adrienne? Come on, we need to go downstairs in a few minutes, and I need to fix your hair still!"

With a grimace at the mirror, I turned my back on the image. It wouldn't do to fixate on things I couldn't change.

When I emerged from the bathroom, Sydney gasped and covered her mouth with both hands. "You're gorgeous."

I grimaced again. "Thanks, but . . . are you sure these are my only two dresses to choose from?"

"Oh, you pull that dress off better than your mum could!"

I shook my head, but didn't bother to argue. Comparison between my mother and me was not a topic ever worth entering.

"Well, sit down; I need to do your hair."

At that, I held up a hand. "No. Not with these stitches. Can't I just brush it?"

Sydney's aghast expression made me almost laugh again. "No! Everyone will have their hair done—you have to also!"

With a sigh, I sank into the chair before the mirror. "All right. Just . . . be gentle."

"Of course." She picked up a brush and, clenching a fistful of hair in her hand, brushed out the bottom strands to avoid pulling at my scalp.

"Do you miss your mom?" I blurted out.

"Miss her?" Sydney seemed as surprised by the question as I was. "I hardly remember her. So . . . not really. I suppose I miss the idea of her more than anything. Why?"

The scarlet red on my fingernails matched the silk dress exactly, so my fingertips all but disappeared into the fabric. "I guess mother-daughter relationships interest me." Lifting my chin, I flashed her a smile in the mirror. "I've never had a traditional one, myself."

"Ah. Me neither. But it's never bothered me."

"No?"

"No. Sure, it was lonely at times, but . . ." She shrugged and held half my hair up on top of my head, mouth pursed in contemplation, then dropped it so the strands brushed my shoulder blades. Her touch was surprisingly gentle, so, despite my stitches, I might not have known she played with it except for my reflection, and perhaps the ache starting in my upper neck warning me that this would be a long night.

"But I had friends," she continued. "And, even though they had both their parents, they weren't often around, and it was just as lonely for them. Eventually I figured having one present parent was better than two absent parents."

Her unexpected wisdom silenced me, so I watched her twist sections of my hair into braids instead.

In what seemed like five minutes, she tamed my thick, yet silky hair into a loose braid, and when I twisted to inspect the back, I saw tiny braids decorating the larger braid. She inserted some pearl pins in spots, and I debated asking whether they were real pearls or fakes. I supposed it didn't matter, in the end. Real jewels in my hair would make me nervous, while fakes would make me seem like what I was.

A quick glance at the clock on the bedside table showed me that the party began in less than five minutes. We were cutting it close.

Sydney followed my gaze, her own gaze narrowing while her lips tightened. "All right. I think you're good. Here's your lipstick—"

A wry smile pulled at my lips. "No chance."

Hand on her hip, she rolled her eyes. "You have to. Really. It'll look odd without."

She attacked me with the lipstick while I hesitated, and after the first jab, there was no point in fighting it. She smoothed on a thick layer, handed me a napkin to blot, then made me stand and twirl.

Nodding her approval, she set the lipstick at the end of the line with the five other shades she'd brought. "I think we're ready."

A flash of fading light coming through the windowpane caught my eye, a twinkle of the reddish sun descending through the clouds outside my window. The pinkish light somehow made the dress I wore seem redder, standing out against the paleness of the light that filtered through the window from the courtyard outside.

At times I could hardly believe I was standing in London, inside my mother's flat. It seemed as if no time had passed between my last visit and now, except that everything was different: my reason for being here, my future, even my past.

"Ready?" Sydney repeated from behind me.

"Uh, no. I need to use the bathroom." Turning, I just caught her rolling her eyes again, in the universal epitome of teenage annoyance. "You go ahead. I'll catch up."

"Are you sure?"

"Yes. My mother won't care if I'm late—and I'm sure your father will care if you are."

Her nose wrinkled. "Exactly. I'll see you there, then?"

"Yes."

Making no move, I watched her grow smaller in the mirror and disappear through the door. When she closed the door behind her, I contemplated sinking back down in the chair, but decided against it. Silk wrinkled.

Now, without an audience, I allowed the image before me to sink in. Even for prom, I had never looked so . . . Hollywood. With the hair finished, the lipstick on, mascara layered, blush glowing, I looked . . . like my mother.

Spurn the Moon

Except somehow not.

I frowned, and the girl in the mirror did the same.

My worry about sitting forgotten, I dropped into the chair and put my elbows on the vanity, resting my head in my hands. I didn't have enough energy for a party, especially one where I knew precisely three people: my mother, my future stepfather, and my future stepsister.

I picked up my cell phone instead, turning it over in my hands, unlocking it with my shiny, red painted fingertips. My fingers located the contacts list, and pressed down on my father's name.

Phone to my ear, I listened as the phone on the other end rang and rang and rang. Finally the voicemail picked up. After the familiar message, I left one of my own, trying to sound cheerful and as if everything was going great. But when I hung up, reality closed in on me again. *I can handle a party. That's all this is; pretend it's a political gala, like one of Dad's.*

I pushed myself back to my feet. I could do that. I'd been to dozens of his parties, conducted myself well enough to both blend into the background and stand out as the perfect politician's daughter. Now I just had to become the perfect actress' daughter, something under a bit more pressure and spotlight. That was all.

☽

At the top of the stairs, I smoothed the skirt down over my thighs and gathered my breath. I bit my lip and immediately let go, remembering the shocking red lipstick. Only teeth marks through it could draw more attention than the color itself.

Halfway down the stairs, I paused at the sound of the lion knocker echoing through the foyer. In my bedroom, I hadn't paid attention to the sounds of guests arriving, and so far, no one had noticed me in bright red. How long could I keep it that way? Was it possible all the guests would be in red?

A man in a black suit and tie stepped forward to sweep open the door.

"Evening," the guest said, holding out a square card as he entered, which I assumed to be his invitation.

At his recognizable face, I froze, inhaled sharply through my nose, and held my breath, hoping he hadn't heard. I didn't keep up with the movies, and actors didn't make it onto my radar often, but this face was the one that the twins had plastered to their walls since they were twelve: Damien Kerr. Handsome enough, with his deep blue eyes and black hair, and a stocky yet trim build, but certainly not enough to tempt me. No, apparently I was tempted by pale hair and Californian surfer looks, and men that played well with my mother. I grimaced, then smoothed my face over as he glanced up the stairs. A wrinkle flashed across his forehead before something down the hallway snagged his attention. His eyes widened then narrowed as if in disbelief chased by disgust.

"Good evening." A cheery voice answered his unspoken question. "Damien."

Chin set, Damien Kerr nodded a stiff greeting to the newcomer, who swept his gaze up the stairs as if he had been waiting for me. Jake's grin flashed up at me, dimmed only by the appreciation in his gaze. "Adrienne, you look gorgeous."

My heart stuttered at being thrust into the spotlight. "Uh . . . Thanks."

"Victoria and Edmund sent me to get you," Jake continued.

My gaze slid back to Damien again, who was glaring coldly at Jake.

Glancing up at me, he gave a curt nod, fashioning his lips into something passing for a smile. He then turned without a word and followed the man, whom I could only call a butler, down the hallway and out to the garden. Their feet tapped unevenly on the Brazilian wood floor as they strode away.

Not sure what to make of this entire exchange, I continued down the stairs, figuring I might as well get one answer from Jake.

"What was that?" I waited until I stood on even footing with him to ask.

His grin was quick and inviting, a relief after the unexpected arrival and the cold stare of Damien Kerr. "I have no idea." Hands in the air and eyes widening at my skepticism, he added, "Honest."

"Right. So why did my mother send you for me?"

A dimple flashed in his left cheek as he offered me an arm I didn't accept. "I suppose I looked bored."

At that, a smile broke through the frost on my lips, but instead of answering, I followed Damien's course with my eyes. He had already disappeared, probably walking as fast as he could to distance himself from whatever he didn't like about Jake. Still skeptical, I examined my escort again.

"What?" His eyebrows lifted in an expression of innocence, but one he seemed aware wasn't believable. He raised his elbow further. "May I?"

Reluctant to accept, but not sure how I might politely refuse—and what friction refusing might create with my mother—I opted for the path of least resistance.

)

"So you said you're an actor?" I asked as Jake led me away from the front entrance.

He grinned. "I'm trying to become one. Your mum is helping me with that. And helping me with my current job."

"Ah." I pressed my lips together. With his face and that grin, how could he fail? "Anything on the horizon?"

He shrugged. "Right now I'm doing some freelancing for my other business. But I hope I can land a big role soon." He nodded at someone standing guard in the living room on our way into the rear garden, and then we were in a masterpiece of an event, making me forget what else I was going to ask. A crew had come and gone while I wasn't paying attention, transforming the green and flowery English garden into something like a magical fairy forest, but with more forest and less fantasy.

The sight stopped me short in the doorway. "Wow."

"Did you not look before?" he asked at my surprise.

"No, I . . . never got the chance." How had I napped through this decorating frenzy?

White tents sprawled all across the grounds; Victoria was taking no chances that rain would ruin her engagement party. Thousands of white Christmas lights hung from both the interior and exterior of the tents, joined by what had to be hundreds of yards of tulle.

Throughout the garden of white, splashes of green leapt from the garden itself, accented by bright red patches. A few were women in dresses, but most were table toppers and roses. Hundreds of roses. The entire garden was littered with them, so many it was almost obnoxious. Red roses everywhere, joined by dark green foliage, and the whitest lilies I'd ever seen.

Jake led me down a red carpet lined with twinkling lights and deposited me in front of my mother.

She glanced at me once, her classic Victoria Talbot smile in rare form, and turned back to her guest. Then, as if something had just registered, she refocused her gaze on me, smile faltering.

"Adrienne?"

All I could do was smile a pained smile.

She recovered herself quickly, returning to her warm and welcoming self. With a laugh, she said, "I almost didn't recognize you—it's been so long since I've seen you so presentable." Turning to the guest I had interrupted her conversation with, she added, "Bill, this is my eldest daughter, Adrienne. She's so much more comfortable in her running clothes, I nearly didn't recognize her tonight."

Bill, a ruddy Brit with a glass of champagne already in hand, raised it and laughed a greeting in response, before moving off to mingle and refresh his drink.

"It's your dress," I murmured as he moved away.

"It is?" Victoria's frown sliced through me. "Hmm. Must have been a gift from some designer I hated. I told Sydney to pick from the surplus closet." With a wave of dismissal, she turned to the next guest approaching with a gift bag in her hand.

As I faked a smile for a woman I vaguely recognized, I didn't know whether to be insulted or flattered that she'd offered me dresses she hated. Whether this was her style at all was debatable now. Now it was a dress that someone thought my mother might like—but not one she liked enough to wear. Or maybe it had been thrown into the surplus closet along with a thousand other dresses, and forgotten about until someone like me needed one. It could be ten years out of fashion for all I knew.

Victoria laughed at something her guest said and kissed the man's cheek. On her other side, Sydney stood a little ways back from her father, who stood behind Victoria as though he were the man to thank for her greatness. The old cliché of a woman standing behind her man was quite the opposite here, I thought, looking at him as he beamed over her shoulder.

Jake swept a full champagne glass from a server's passing tray and pressed it into my hand. I sipped the drink for something to do, already wondering when this party would end, or when I could slip away, unnoticed.

"Jake, why don't you introduce Adrienne to some people?" Victoria swept dismissively to the mingling crowds.

"Oh, of course," Jake agreed, taking my free hand in his.

Even though I hadn't held hands with a man in three years, it felt somehow natural for Jake to hold mine, pulling me into the crowd with a grin flashing over his shoulder at me.

"See anyone worth knowing?" he whispered conversationally.

A laugh bubbled over my lips before I could stop it. "Um . . . not at the moment." Brightly clad women and classically suited men mingled in the space between tables, sipping on their drinks. A curvaceous, middle-aged woman helped herself to a fresh glass of wine, her dress seeming to cover less than a napkin would. I barely hid a grimace. "Anyone I should know then?"

He pursed his bottom lip out in consideration. "Let's try this direction." He angled us away from the house and toward a long table laden with flowers and appetizers.

A bright pink head, which clashed with the red roses around it, caught my eye. Curious, I gazed at the face beneath the hair piled on top of the woman's head. As if she felt my stare, she turned and focused on me, her large, hazel eyes illuminated by dark kohl liner. Her mouth, rosebud and lush, opened in a laugh as our gazes met, and my past collided with the present.

"Kat?" I asked incredulously.

Her laugh faded as if filmed in slow motion. I dropped Jake's hand and stepped toward her, having never expected to find her here in my mother's garden.

"Adrienne?" Her voice was just as I remembered, slightly husky as though she were a smoker, but, to my knowledge, she had never smoked a cigarette in her life.

"Oh my gosh. Kat?" I halted a few steps away from her, my jaw slack as words failed me.

"You . . ." Sweeping her hand through the air from my scalp to my toes, she shook her head, words apparently failing her as they did me. She gave a husky little laugh. "I should have expected to see you back here."

The moment in which it would be natural to greet her with a hug had passed, and I stood before her, growing more awkward by the second. "Yeah, well, I wouldn't have thought it either. But . . . here I am."

"Yes. It's . . ." Her lined eyes softened. "It's good to see you. What brings you into . . ." She glanced over my shoulder and faltered. "Into . . . London?" After only a second, Kat's lips curved upward as she waited for my answer.

"Well, I'm taking the summer to settle in and enjoy some travel before I head to Oxford for school."

"Travel? In London?" Kat's expressive eyes widened in excitement.

"Really? I just rented a new flat. You must stay with me. I'm looking for a flatmate."

"Are you?" For the first time, I examined Kat. Three years ago, I'd said my last good-bye to her, and she'd filled out since then: growing out of her juvenile slender-hipped, flat-chested frame, and shaping into an hourglass. "That would be . . . perfect. But I may be doing some travel . . ."

"Well it'd be great to live with you. I told my—" Kat's attention flicked to the side of my head. "I said I could find a flatmate, but . . ." she trailed off.

I frowned, waiting for her to continue.

"Adrienne." A finger tapped my shoulder, and I met Jake's turquoise gaze when I looked over it. "Your mother wants you."

With an apologetic grimace at Kat, I said, "What's your number? I'll call you and we can figure out a time to meet?"

"Yeah." Kat was already turning away, dismissive. With disappointment turning my mouth bitter, I accepted that I wouldn't see my only friend in London again anytime soon.

Chapter Five
Off Script

MY MOTHER'S ASSISTANT, CHARITY HARPER, stood beside the wedding party table, sheathed in a dress of spun gold. If she had been wearing a happier expression, she could have stolen my mother's spotlight. Instead, she scowled at me and pointed at a seat. "You're there."

Two men already sat where she pointed, two men I could only assume to be the groomsmen.

Their heads were bent together, one talking into the other's ear, as I approached. The one talking, a man in his mid-fifties, stood, gave me a nod, and walked away, while the other man half turned in my direction. My stomach knotted. Damien Kerr was a groomsman. His gaze flickered down my face to my toes, sweeping quickly and dismissively, then he pulled out his phone.

When I turned to look behind me, Jake had vanished again, abandoning me to Damien's mercy, whatever I could find of it.

"Hello," I said, trying to forget the awkward semi-meeting we'd had when he'd arrived.

"Hi." One word, clipped and tight, was all he offered.

"I'm Adrienne Talbot, Victoria's daughter." I set my champagne flute on the table.

He drank deeply from his water glass, eyes unreadable.

"You're . . ." When he didn't show any inclination for answering, I supplied, "Damien Kerr?"

Solemn, stormy blue eyes greeted my introduction from under his lock of wavy black hair, and he nodded just the once in answer.

"So . . ." The fork to the left of my plate was slightly crooked, and I straightened it. "You're a groomsman?" I wrinkled my nose at myself. I should have started with the weather. Every Brit would talk weather.

"Yes."

I blinked. He had this manner of staring straight ahead, ignoring every word I spoke with an expression of utter boredom, so his answer, despite it being only one word, wasn't what I expected.

"I really should stop asking closed-end questions," I muttered, racking my brain for small talk ideas. "How do you know my mother? Or Edmund?"

His chest rose with an intake of breath, remaining stationary for a long moment, until he released the breath in a long sigh, smoothing his napkin on his lap as if to cover up his exasperation. "Edmund is an old family friend."

"Oh." Well, that was more than I'd gotten out of him before. I shouldn't have bothered trying, but there was something in his closed expression that made me curious. A curiosity piqued by that strange interchange with Jake. Not that it was any of my business; but achieving conversation with Damien was such a chore that getting him to open up concerning Jake would be another matter entirely. "How old?" I asked. At his frown, I amended, "I mean, how long have you known him?"

"My entire life." A slight, quizzical narrowing of his eyes accompanied his answer.

"Which would be?"

He tilted his head at me, champagne glass half raised.

"I'm asking how old you are," I supplied when he drank instead of answered again. Irritation rippled under my skin, and I fought to suppress it. I would get nowhere being rude. "Twenty? Thirty? Not *forty*?"

A small smile rewarded me for my teasing audacity. "Twenty-eight."

"Really? Wow."

"Is that too old or too young?" The barest hint of amusement laced his words.

"Neither." I shrugged. "But isn't it a little old for Hollywood?" I couldn't resist the dig at his profession.

Over Damien's shoulder, Jake's attention flicked to me, his eyes narrowing into pinpricks of turquoise, and I smiled but dropped my gaze to the table.

He leaned back, considering me, and I thought for a moment that he was relaxing. But his fingertips whitened around the stem of his glass. "Twenty-eight is only old if you're a woman," he answered in his soft, upper class British accent.

"Hmm." I smoothed a wrinkle out of the white tablecloth and readjusted my spoon when it touched my knife. Next to our water glasses, a single red rose adorned each place setting, and a large bouquet of roses, lilies, and greenery squatted in the center of the table where Edmund and Victoria would sit. For now their seats were empty. "I suppose my mother must be well on her way out then."

"There are some who would agree with that." His words offered no judgment, simple fact, and gave me no indication as to his true thoughts on the subject. He was infuriating.

And yet I found myself wanting to keep him talking.

"And you? You still have plenty of long years left in acting?"

One shoulder rose in a shrug as careless as it was graceful. "We'll see; a few, at least."

A bug buzzed in my right ear and I slapped at it, accidentally brushing against my stitches. Wincing, I rubbed my fingertips over my forehead, grateful when the surge of pain dissipated quickly.

Damien shot me a glance, then pointedly turned away as the waiters began to serve the first course. We ate our meal in silence.

 ☽

Even before Victoria and Edmund seated themselves, it was the most awkward meal I had ever attended.

I was almost relieved when the toasts began. Something to break up the monotony of carefully judging each item of food before pushing it aside on my plate. My stomach grumbled. *When had I last eaten?*

"Something wrong with your food?" Damien's reluctant curiosity made me jump, as I hadn't been paying attention.

"Oh, no." My cheeks grew hot. "Well, I think so. I'm allergic to milk."

Understanding dawned on his face, and his gaze fell to my plate of lamb and potatoes.

Shrugging at my plate, I speared a small bite of lamb and dared to put it in my mouth. The rich flavors exploded across my tongue, and I closed my eyes in delight. "That's good."

Opening my eyes, I found Damien studying me, amusement flickering in his dark blue eyes. "How allergic are you, exactly?"

I took another bite, considering how to answer. "I've never gone into anaphylaxis," I began, "but I do tend to break out in hives and get pretty itchy."

His brows furrowed, but before he could add anything, Edmund rose from his seat, tapping a knife against his champagne glass to get the guests' attention.

"We've been blessed with such wonderful family and friends," Edmund began, raising his flute at the waiters standing around.

They jumped to attention with their champagne bottles, refilling glasses and delivering flutes to those who hadn't claimed one before. In their black and white uniforms, they reminded me of penguins waddling through a zoo exhibit, but these penguins replenished drinks and whisked away empty dishes. Earlier I had asked one about any dairy in the meal, and he said that everything had been cooked in olive oil; as my stomach roared, I dared a bite of the potatoes.

"And that blessing extends here today as we are able to share our joy with all of you." Edmund smiled out at his audience. "We are grateful for each one of you and that you would care enough to come and celebrate with us tonight. And now, I want to turn it over to our best man and maid of honor."

He toasted his glass in the direction of Damien and me, and the attention of every audience member shifted while the world tilted underneath me. My stomach clenched and groaned at the spotlight.

Damien, apparently expecting the attention, rose, buttoning his jacket with manicured hands before leaning down and picking up his glass with the tiniest glance at me. His gaze swept over my face so fast my lips reacted with an automatic smile too late, as he'd already faced the audience again.

"When Edmund asked me to be his best man, I was both honored and surprised. Edmund has been a second father to me over the years, and it gives me a great deal of pleasure to see him so happy."

When Damien faced the groom, I had a sudden vision of Damien at Edmund's age, as distinguished and refined, but perhaps a bit more handsome. At the thought, my throat tickled. I cleared it quietly, grabbing my glass and taking a gulp of water.

"We have had our ups and downs, Lord knows," Damien continued with a congenial nod. "But you've always been there when I've needed you, and even when I haven't known I needed you. I wish you the happiest marriage anyone can imagine."

On Edmund and Victoria's other side, Sydney beamed, her gray eyes so bright that they lit up her entire face.

Damien shifted to face Victoria. "Victoria, I know you realize what a good man you have. I look forward to knowing you better." He raised his glass. "So, Edmund, Victoria, today I am grateful. I am grateful that you two have found each other, and that true love does, in fact, exist. To the happy couple."

A hundred arms at the surrounding tables raised their glasses and drank with Damien. Belatedly, I grabbed my champagne and followed suit, as he sat and replaced his at the top of his plate.

A hand touched my shoulder. "It's your turn," said a voice in my ear.

Face on fire, I turned to Charity. "What?"

Pushing an index card at me with a grim smile, she said, "Your turn to give a toast."

"A—?" The index card between my fingertips, I glanced down the table at my mother, who smiled sweetly at me. My jaw set. This was one of her little challenges, like the ones she'd always liked to throw at me to "build character" or "to see what I was made of." My face burned; my throat was quickly becoming dry, almost scratchy.

Someone pulled at my chair from behind me, prompting me to stand. Time crawled while I smoothed the lines of my borrowed dress; my mother surveyed the waiting audience with a warm, almost queenly gaze, and she leaned over to Edmund, saying something which brought a smile to his face.

While public speaking had never bothered me, I rarely had to speak without a moment's warning. However, I had been witness to hundreds of my father's, and I knew how to pull off an impromptu speech: always begin and end with great sentences. With this reminder, I set the index card upon my plate. Damien's head turned toward it, the corner of his mouth twitching.

Considering what I should open and close with, I concentrated on making my motions graceful as I lifted my champagne flute. I swallowed again, trying to fight away the heat in my face. *It's just a speech. Not a big deal. Not even any cameras allowed in here right now, so it won't show up in the news or anything.*

Edmund cleared his throat, interrupting my inner pep talk. The wait had gone on long enough.

"There are few things more honorable or pure than taking vows to love one person for the rest of your life," I began. My tongue seemed as though it didn't want to say these words, but I forced it to behave and demanded a smile from my lips. Victoria's smile faltered.

"Few things are better than a wedding, and when it's one of your parents vowing to love and honor another, it makes the event especially important, especially memorable."

Damien shifted, his chin tilting up to examine me. He pressed his lips together.

"Although this engagement caught me by surprise, I could not be happier for you both."

Victoria faced me, her expression frozen. As I lifted my flute to her, her surprise traveled across the table and landed on me as if a bird had landed on my shoulder. I cleared my throat, tempted to take another drink to soothe it. *Why does my tongue feel so funny?* "I eagerly a—" I cleared my throat again, "excuse me. I eagerly await the years ahead, the holidays, the special events, with the new members of my family." Edmund's lips tugged upward. "Edmund, Sydney,"—I bobbed my glass to them each in turn—"here's an—an advance . . . welcome to the family."

The champagne tasted bitter in my mouth, twisting my lips down at the edges before I could stop them. Everyone drank, as they had for Damien's toast, but some of the guests at the closer tables were frowning at each other. Even Edmund's gaze was drawing together now. *Had I said something wrong?*

Flushing, but trying to stay calm and collected, I reached for my chair. Victoria touched Edmund's arm and said something, him leaning close to hear, and with another glance at me that seemed almost alarmed, he rose.

"Adrienne, come with me." Damien was suddenly there, taking my elbow in his hand and whisking me away from the table.

"What? What's going on?"

"Can you breathe all right?"

"What? What are you talking about?" My face burned at this attention.

Most of the guests had already resumed their chatting and laughing; waiters refilled glasses and served dessert. In the garden, which Damien rapidly pulled me through, beautiful faces mingled together, and vaguely recognizable faces jumbled with those of complete strangers. I had never been in touch with Victoria's life, but now it was clear: everyone was a stranger. Not even a family friend that I recognized—none but Kat. I had always considered family of the utmost importance to me, including my distant, uninterested mother, until that day three years ago. Regret's bony hands choked me so that it was hard to swallow.

"Adrienne! Talk to me. Do you need an EpiPen?" Damien's urgent voice cut through my distractions.

Itchy throat. Hard to swallow. Hard to breathe. My eyes widened as realization enveloped me. *The lamb and potatoes!* I wanted to curse my stupidity, but this wasn't the time for that. Instead, as I stared down at my body, I found hives popping up on my chest. Surely my face was swollen with them, and as Damien hurried me into the house, hives rose on my arms, like hundreds of little insect bites.

"I'll be fine," I said as he rushed me into the—thankfully empty—living room, and lowered me onto the sofa my mother had sat on earlier. "I'm fine. I just—"

"What do you need?"

Damien's mouth had opened, but it was Jake's voice from the doorway that spoke.

I glanced between them, two faces riveted on me. "Just an antihistamine. I should be fine. I've never gone into anaphylaxis before." Although my face still burned, I sensed it to be mostly from embarrassment rather than the milk I'd ingested. "It couldn't have been that much milk, and it was cooked," I explained weakly to Damien, who stood there watching me with large eyes and a grim mouth, "so it was probably the added stress from giving a speech." Already my throat was calming, but my arms and chest itched as though I'd suffered a thousand mosquito bites. I clenched my hands to prevent myself from scratching them.

Concern darkening his face, Damien stepped back and sank into the chair I had occupied earlier. He didn't speak, and I fell silent.

I rubbed my clenched fist over an itch on my thigh.

"Here." Jake returned, carrying a bottle of what I assumed were antihistamines, and an unopened bottle of water. "I didn't know how many—"

"No, it's fine." I smiled at him, trying to reassure him, for concern had folded his face in upon itself. "I'll be fine. It's just uncomfortable." Before handing me either bottle, he unscrewed them, fumbling with the lids so both ended up on the floor. Damien glanced at them but didn't bend to retrieve them. I swallowed the highest recommended amount of antihistamine with a gulp of water.

"Do you need anything else?" Damien's voice was gruff. "Should we call an ambulance?"

"No, I'll be fine." My gaze flickered between the two men. Men hated to be helpless. Perhaps he just wanted something to do. "Perhaps an ice pack?" When Damien's forehead wrinkled, I added, "It helps with the itch and swelling."

For a long moment, neither of them moved, and I began to say, "Never —"

"I'll get it," Jake said shortly.

Damien did not react, but continued to stare at me with such intensity that my cheeks burned hotter.

We sat in silence until Jake returned from the kitchen, a familiar blue gel ice pack in his hands. "This do?"

"Perfect."

Jake handed it over with a warm smile that put me immediately at ease.

For nearly a quarter of an hour, I sat in the room with both Jake and Damien, enduring the awkward tension between them and watching the hives on my skin flare and begin to ebb.

"Well? Everything all right in here?" For once, I was thankful for my mother's interruption.

"Yes." I sat forward, pulling the ice pack from my arm, where I had pressed it over the worst patch of hives. "I'm fine."

"Great." She pasted a smile on her face. "Damien? Someone was asking for you."

"Who?" he asked without moving.

"Your sister."

Damien appeared to hesitate for the briefest of moments, then nodded and rose. Without a good-bye, he disappeared through the kitchen.

"You're really all right?" Victoria asked me, showing a surprising amount of concern.

I dipped my head into a nod. "Just embarrassment now."

"Right. Well, I'd avoid the dessert."

"Right. Thanks." Biting my lower lip, I watched her disappear in the same direction Damien had.

"I guess that means we can get out of here, then." Jake flashed his grin at me. "Let's go on a walk."

Relief sent a cool breeze over my angry skin. "That sounds perfect."

)

"How long have you known my mother?" I asked Jake as we walked along a gravel path at the edge of a park, ignoring the rustle of the wind through the leaves. The breeze rushed over us, raising the skin on my arms and pulling at my hair with restless fingers.

"How long?" he repeated. "Oh, I met her about three years ago?" He almost seemed to be asking me.

Shivering under another icy caress of the wind, I continued, "And how did you meet her? Through a film?"

"Yes, but I was working as a hand with the horses at the time."

"You worked with horses?"

"Why so surprised?" His lips quirked up into a half grin.

"Nothing. I'm not," I added quickly. "What did you do with the horses? You have a lot of experience with them?"

"Oh yeah, I practically grew up in the stable. My dad worked as a stable manager up in Yorkshire."

"Oh? Is that why your accent is a little more northern?" Despite my jacket, which I'd grabbed from my room before sneaking out with Jake, I was shivering.

"You have a good ear, if you caught that. I've tried for years to get rid of my northern accent."

With the toe of my tennis shoes, which I'd exchanged my borrowed heels for, I nudged a rock out of my path and watched as it skittered across the beam of a lamp and out the other side. "It's only now and then when I hear it."

"I took lessons to get rid of it, so you'll have to tell me when it shows up."

I cast him a smile. "It's more in your intonations than anything."

He nodded solemnly. "Well, I only know from your mother where you're from. But what I really want to know is why on earth you'd come to London."

"Why?" Above us, the trees shook their leaves at us, and I glanced up, trying to see the stars through the murky London sky and the thick canopy of leaves. All I managed to catch was a glimpse of stainless steel clouds against a navy blue curtain. "Because it's London. Why would I not want to come here?"

"Yeah, but . . . aren't you from Alaska? It must be amazing to grow up there. It's so . . . exotic."

I'd heard all of Jake's words before—simply from other mouths. All the television shows about Alaska had built it up as some exotic place where everyone lived off the grid and off the land. "Not for most of us who live there. It's just life. And most of us don't have dogsled teams, no one lives in an igloo, and we don't have moose for pets."

Jake's eyes widened briefly, then he laughed, hearty and surprised. "Good to know. Although I would have guessed about the igloo. Not about the moose . . ."

At my questioning glance, he winked. Shaking my head, I smiled and reluctantly let the conversation fade.

Jake's shoulder brushed mine, and I shivered, but this time, it wasn't from the cold. My mind raced ahead, searching for subjects to talk about. The closed gates of a park loomed to our left, and I glanced at them absently. Although I supposed I should have been ill at ease walking on a city street late at night, with Jake, I felt perfectly safe.

"Come on," Jake said.

"What?"

With his wry grin, he grabbed my hand and pulled me toward the locked gates. Glancing around, he took hold of the gate and pulled at it. When it didn't budge, he stepped back to look at it, then interlocked his fingers together and motioned me over with a jerk of his head. "Come on then."

I stared at him, his intentions sinking in. "You're going to get me in trouble, aren't you?"

His grin widened, catching the light of the lamp and giving him an impish glow.

Already regretting it, I stepped forward and, with a glance around of my own, put my foot in his hands. In a few moments, I scrambled over the top of the gate, and waited as Jake pulled himself over with surprising grace.

"This way," he said, pointing straight ahead of us.

Spurn the Moon

The silence of the park settled around us, cars left behind as we distanced ourselves from the streets.

"So you're here for uni? A bit early, aren't you?"

I lifted a shoulder. "Yeah, well . . . I was ready to leave home."

"Any particular reason?"

We passed a thicket of bushes on one side, and I stared into their darkness, wondering what could be hiding in there. I bit my lip. "Well, there was someone coming back home I wanted to avoid." I flashed him a quick smile. "So I thought I'd come earlier, travel a bit, get settled in Oxford."

"See your mum maybe?" he added.

"Eh." I grimaced. "Hadn't been the plan." Three years *was* a long time to hold a grudge. Perhaps God was telling me it was time to let it go. Or at least address it.

"No?"

"It's a long story." One I had no desire to get into right now—or possibly ever. "We've never been on the best of terms. And . . . last time I saw her . . . " I trailed off, not wanting to tell the truth, but unwilling to lie.

Jake nodded as if I had said something reasonable. "My dad and I never got on. One row after another 'til I left home."

Rain began dripping from the sky in England's typical capricious weather. I had missed London, but until now, with its evening arms wrapped around me, I hadn't realized how much.

"Do you still see him?"

"He died."

"I'm sorry."

Pursing his lips together, he shook his head in dismissal of my apology. "No. It's been a decade."

"I'm sorry," I repeated. "I can't imagine what it's like to lose a parent. Especially when you're young."

The wind gusted over us, whistling through the leaves of the trees as we followed the park path in the direction we'd come. A car raced by on the streets outside the park, finding us over the wall. Shrugging my shoulders up against the increasing rain, I opened my mouth to speak, but Jake beat me to it.

"What are you studying?"

"Medical school. I want to be a doctor."

"Really?"

"Yes, I hope to go into research of some kind, I—" As I spoke, a large rock caught my toe, and I nearly fell.

"All right?" He caught me by the arm and supported my weight.

"Yeah. Thanks. Must be the champagne."

He didn't let go, tucking my hand into his elbow as he had when he'd led me to the party. "I'll hang on to you then."

A chuckle shook my ribs while butterflies raced through me. "Okay."

Jake glanced at his watch. "We should probably get back before someone notices our absence."

Heart sinking to my stomach, I nodded. "Sure."

"There's another gate up here."

I sighed, thinking of the courtyard of Victoria's new home waiting for us, one filled with lush trees and cobblestones, where the only cars admitted entered through a guarded gate, like a prison—not hers, but mine. A sigh wrenched its way through my chest. As I exhaled, my head gave a weak pound as if to remind me that I'd put my body through a lot today, and I should be resting. The cool skin along with the antihistamines and ice pack had soothed my itching hives, but at the thought, the desire to scratch returned.

In order to distract myself, I talked about my plans to enter into medical research; a plan I knew full well might change after a year or two at school.

At the gate, I went over first like before, landing with a synthetic tap on the pavement. A couple strolling by glanced at me with wry smiles as I waited for Jake to vault over.

The attention brought back my itch, and as Jake landed beside me with a heavy thump of his dress shoes and a grunt, I squirmed inside my jacket.

Jake stood, his face going still, and reached for my hand. "What's going on?"

"What?" When I followed his gaze across the street, my stomach dropped out from under me. I hadn't noticed the crowd at first, but before the gates to the courtyard a group of people with video cameras and microphones milled around, chatting to each other, voices rising and falling, indecipherable from one another, sounding like the audience at a concert.

"I don't know . . ." I muttered. "Is there another way in?"

"Uh . . . not that I know of." Jake's hand clenched over mine. "Let's hurry. Before they all recognize us."

Recognize us? How would they? I wanted to ask, but we were across the street from them. It was already too late.

"There she is!" someone screamed. The voice broke the stillness of the night and sent a jolt through my skin, jarring into my bones.

"Go!" Jake let go of my hand and curled his arm around my waist, pulling me toward the gate, into the crowd. I stumbled, my toes catching on the hem of my dress until I yanked the fabric up to my shins.

"Adrienne!" My name littered the air as the people descended on me. "Adrienne, just a quick interview?"

The crowd closed around us, and I gripped Jake's arm, terrified as questions swirled in my brain and panic overtook reasonable thought.

"Just a few questions," another voice begged.

All I could do was shake my head.

"Adrienne, what do you have to say about—?"

Jake banged on the gate, awakening the guard to our presence. He climbed out of his guard shack with aching slowness as a pushy reporter pressed himself against me.

"What do you have to say about this?" He thrust a folded newspaper at me.

"What?" Confusion rippled over me. I clung to Jake, yet at the newspaper before me, I lifted a hand. A clinking of keys against metal, then Jake fell out from behind me. At the pressing of the crowd before me, I stumbled backward. Jake caught me, pulling me through the gate with him. Vaguely I registered him exchanging words with the guard, angry words, but the man with the paper came through the gate behind me, slamming it shut after him.

The expression on his face, hungry and shadowed, sent shudders to my toes.

Chapter Six
The Scandal

"HEY, MATE," THE GUARD BEGAN, arm outreached.

The reporter dodged it as I lurched backward.

"Just a question," he insisted, raising the newspaper again. "What do you think about this, Adrienne?" He reached out and grabbed my upper arm with a grip stronger than a vice, shoving the paper into my face.

With a growl, Jake ripped me from the man's grasp. But my gaze had locked on the newspaper that the reporter held.

"Wait!" Yanking my arm back from Jake, I lunged for the newspaper. "That has my picture!"

"Adrienne—" Jake grabbed my waist, his breath breaking ragged over me. "Get out of here. Come on." As he tugged at me, the skies broke open. But the urgency in his tone sent a shiver down my spine that had nothing to do with the sudden deluge of rain.

Jake pulled at me. The guard pushed the reporter back to the gate. The cacophony of screaming voices washed over me thicker than rain. Microphones, recorders, phones, all hovered in the air at me hoping to catch a sound bite. Jake's arm tugged on me.

"Adrienne. Come on."

With another tug, Jake drew me from the madness of paparazzi, but all I could see was that paper thrust in my face, and my smiling college graduation picture, the same one I'd used as class president. A large fist grabbed my lungs and squeezed, the air rushing out in the one word I could manage to get past my lips.

I wanted to go back and wrench the paper from that man's hands, but Jake was pulling me away from them, away from any answers, across the courtyard, pushing me faster whenever I slowed. "Come on."

We both inspected the shadows as he rushed me to the door with the lion knocker.

Somehow, the door opened at his touch. He pushed me inside and peered out before shutting the door. Silent, trembling, I watched, aware of my hands shaking an inch from side to side. When he turned to me, eyes locked on my face, I quickly crossed my arms to still the shakes.

It didn't fool him. Mutely, he closed the gap between us and pulled me against himself. One arm crossed my back and pressed me urgently into him, his other holding my head against his chest like I was a child.

But my shakes intensified, until I worked my hands out and wrapped them around him, too, gripping his crisp white shirt with my fists as I fought the tears threatening to spill from my lashes.

"Look, it's okay. They can't hurt you in here."

"There," I muttered into his shirt.

"What?"

"That's where your accent comes through, when you say 'look.' It sounds like 'luck.'"

His chest shuddered with laughter. "Right."

A closed door separated us and the crowd of cameras and reporters and crazies, but the newspaper had answers—answers I wanted. Fury began to replace my fear, tapping through my tremors with tiny fingers, prising it open and inserting itself like lava through rock.

I dropped my arms from him and inserted them between us, pushing him away. "I need that paper." Hand outstretched for the door handle, I turned.

"Are you mad?" Jake stepped between the door and me. "You're not going out there."

"Are you going to stop me?" I challenged. "I *need* that paper. My picture is on it!"

Stubbornness darkening his features, he gripped my upper arms with both hands, leaning down to be eye level with me.

"Let me go." I forced calm into my voice. "I need it."

"Calm down." Despite the angry flush on his cheeks, his grasp betrayed no heat of anger. "We'll just check on our phones."

"I—oh." A shudder captured my spine. I hugged my arms around my ribs. "Right."

With a concerned frown at me, Jake pulled out his phone and unlocked it.

At the window beside the door, I moved aside the gauzy fabric and peered outside. The crowd milled at the distant gate, as if they were the ones caged and not the spectators at a zoo.

"Did you catch the title?"

"Yeah." That icy hand traced my spine again. That picture was one of my better ones, with my hair done smooth and subtle makeup the twins had put on for me bringing out the violet of my eyes. The indignation of exploitation began to bubble in my stomach again.

"What was it?" Jake prompted.

"'VICTORIA TALBOT CAUGHT IN AFFAIR'? Something like that."

A moment later, he said, "I've got it here." He extended his phone, the words I had just spoken taking up much of the screen.

"Adrienne?" Edmund's steady voice called out from the hallway.

I met his gaze over my shoulder, his dark gaze kind and concerned, yet formal and insistent.

"I need to speak with you." Edmund did not ask, he demanded. One way or another, he would get what he wanted.

"Sure," I said, but scrolled down Jake's phone instead of following him into the sitting room. I needed information first.

My picture and my mother's next to it were the highlights of the article, and this online story had several of both of us—including a childhood photo taken in Alaska shortly before she left us. The story was made mostly of pictures, the article itself only a few hundred words at most.

At age seventeen, Victoria Richie became an overnight movie star. And at age eighteen, she was a mother to her first daughter, Adrienne Grace Talbot. But this daughter was more than just an unexpected addition to her world—this daughter was the product of an illicit affair, one that she used to climb the Hollywood ladder.

Fury entered the back of my throat. Even if she *had* slept with someone to climb the ladder—something I had no doubt she had done—

my father had nothing to do with it. My father was James Talbot, a Senator of Alaska. It was obvious; I was just like him. Gathering my breath, I continued reading.

An anonymous source close to the family shares with us. "What's really amazing is how well this has been kept secret, considering how many people know. I guess when you've won an Oscar, people don't mind covering things up for you. But I'm not afraid; I think it's time that the truth came out." Adrienne Talbot is a recent graduate from the University of Alaska Fairbanks, where she was valedictorian and class president, graduating in three years magna cum laude. *She is taking a year off to "travel the world" according to the family friend. She is currently relocating to England for medical school at Oxford.*

The story's abrupt ending had me scrolling up and down for more, but all I found was: *Check back later for any updates.* How did they know all this? I clenched the phone tightly. Most of it wasn't even true—but my plans, who told them that? They had a real source. Too bad the gist of the story was built on lies.

Hands shaking in anger, I held out Jake's phone to him. Taking it, he nodded toward the living room where Edmund waited.

I set my jaw. "Did you know about this?"

"What?" Jake's eyes narrowed. "The article?"

"Yes. Before now. Did you know?" I searched him carefully for hint of a lie; his expression was open, innocent.

"No. Nothing."

Fury heated my face and chest. I unzipped my jacket, but glancing down at my dress and splotchy skin, I refrained from ripping it off. "I hate secrets," I muttered, glaring in the direction Edmund had gone. "Hate them."

Jake took my hot hand in his cool one and offered a small smile. "Let's go find out the truth then."

☽

"So who is going to fill me in?" I asked from the doorway of the living room.

"Please, sit." Edmund motioned to the sofa as though welcoming me into his home for an interview.

"I'm fine." I folded my arms tightly over my chest. Next to him, my mother perched herself carefully on the edge of the armchair and examined her nails as though nothing important had happened, as though my world hadn't just been rocked. *Don't overreact,* I told myself, *if you do, she'll never tell you the truth about anything.*

Jake positioned himself at the window, periodically peering through the curtains.

The conversation I'd overheard the night before came back to me, how Edmund had wanted to tell me something and my mother had refused.

"Well?" I prompted when no one spoke. "Is anyone going to fill me in?" On the coffee table between me and them sprawled the newspaper the reporter had shown me, my smiling face on the front.

Victoria sighed, but Edmund fixed me with a compassionate stare before glancing at my mother. I tightened my grip on my ribs, digging in my fingers.

"I think I deserve to know why I wasn't given a heads up, when you clearly knew something was going on."

At these words, Victoria raised her gaze to mine. Edmund's mouth parted, then closed without speaking.

"You two knew about this, didn't you? Knew it was a possibility."

"Yes, well—" Edmund began, but Victoria sliced the end of his sentence with the beginning of her own.

"Were you eavesdropping? I should have known."

"You were the two having the conversation while I was in the kitchen," I retorted childishly. "If you knew about this, you should have told me. I'm an adult—and it directly concerns me."

"Don't give yourself a bigger part than you have." Victoria stood and ran her hands down her thighs. "This scandal concerns me. You're just a casualty."

I inhaled sharply and held it. Only my mother could cut me down so quickly and carelessly. There was the sting to her honeyed tones, the honesty beneath the façade.

Blinking away tears, I gave a tight smile. "Well." I managed to keep my voice steady. "As a 'casualty,' I think I deserve some sort of 'settlement.'"

She frowned, not following.

"I'll settle for information." I pointed to the article on the coffee table, and everyone's attention fell on it. "That's a pretty nasty accusation about you."

Victoria waved a dismissive hand and smoothed her already smooth dress.

"I apologize for not forewarning you, Adrienne," Edmund said, his gentle brown eyes fixed on me, both apologetic and formal. "But we weren't certain of when—or even if—this would break, and we didn't wish to unnecessarily worry you."

I couldn't believe him for a second, but any argument evaporated on my tongue. Disagreeing with Edmund felt like disagreeing with authority.

I sighed. Edmund was right, at least partly; he couldn't control the papers. "Is this even a reputable newspaper?"

Victoria shrugged. "It's a tabloid. Where did you expect something sordid like this to break?"

"A tabloid." I nodded, my muscles relaxing the barest amount. That meant their "authority" was suspect. *But they knew enough about me to make it real. And yet, that's easily discovered if they looked . . .*

"Next time," I said to her, "please worry me."

Victoria lifted a brow in surprise. "Next time?"

Sarcastically, I tilted my head at her. "You forget how well I know you. You're rarely scandal free. There's always something that captures the spotlight, be it a new movie, be it relationships, whatever." I narrowed my eyes. "I don't care what they are. I've learned to live with them and ignore them. As long as they aren't about me, you can let them be your little . . . surprises. But in the future, if it's about me, please let me know in advance."

A small smile tugged at my mother's shocked mouth. She had straightened as I spoke, wonder lighting up her face as though I had risen to a challenge placed in front of me.

I turned to leave when her words drew me back.

"Don't you want to know if there's any truth to this?"

Slowly, I looked over my shoulder at her. "Come on. A tabloid? You forget whom I've been living with for the past twenty years. A politician," I prompted at her blank expression. "Half of what's printed in the papers isn't true. And probably ninety-five percent of what's printed in a *tabloid* isn't true."

Her eyes narrowed almost imperceptibly, then her lips curved into a smile. "You're right." She re-smoothed her dress, then held out her hand to Edmund. "I have misjudged you. Next time, I'll let you know."

Empty words. I forced a nod and attempted a grateful smile that ended up feeling like a grimace.

"Wait." A thought hit me. "Does Dad know about this?" He would need to be told. A scandal of Victoria's meant a possible scandal for him —especially if his paternity was called into question.

She tilted her head, but her eyes were hooded this time, unreadable as if she had entered actress mode. "I haven't told anyone anything."

My inner lie detector went off, and blood rushed to my cheeks.

"In the meantime," she continued, with a considering glance above my head, "I'm glad to see you find your bodyguard so . . . appealing."

I turned and Jake, standing sentry at the window, met my gaze with an apologetic grimace.

"My what?"

She scoffed. "Why do you think I've had him babysit you all evening? Edmund and I hired him for the sole purpose of keeping *you* out of trouble."

))

The revelation that Jake had been hired to protect me—actually paid to be around me all evening—shocked me exactly as much as my mother hoped it would.

After I stormed out, my two options occurred to me; neither sounded appealing. I could either hide out in my room and make confrontations with everyone more difficult when they came around in the morning, or I could return to the party as though nothing had happened, hives and scandal ignored.

So after a quick phone call to Dad, where I again reached his voicemail, I left a message telling him to call me—urgently—then I emailed him a link to what I'd found online and explained that I didn't know much more than that. Then I returned to the party.

Now, guests danced under the large tent before me, laughed and drank at the tables, stood in groups chatting avidly, all enjoying each other's company. Freshly filled champagne flute in hand, I dawdled by the gifts table, running a finger along the bags and their ribbons, wondering what people gifted a movie star and an English lord.

The diverting thoughts didn't last long. Anger made my head ache and my skin itch—or maybe the drugs had worn off, or the champagne's buzz dissipated. At the end of the table, I paused, squinting out over the dance floor.

I had never felt quite so alone. I had come to London with hopes for a fresh start, and nothing was going as planned. Nothing. Ever since leaving home, things had gone wrong. Tears brimmed on my lower lashes and I inhaled a shaky breath. I refused to cry. This wasn't irreversible; everything could be fixed.

Spurn the Moon

So far.

The negativity of my thoughts dragged a tear from my lashes, and I dashed it away with hasty fingers.

"Adrienne?"

The familiar soft, yet husky voice drew me out of my miserable reverie. Dashing two fingers under my lashes, I turned to find Kat examining me, her hip slightly cocked to one side as though posing for a picture.

"What?" The word came out slightly defensive, almost aggressive.

Her eyes widened, but her lips turned up in amusement. "Has she got to you already?" Her wry words brought a reluctant smile to my lips.

"No. I mean—sorry." I wanted to rake my hands through my hair, do something to release this pent up energy inside me, but my hair was shellacked with hair spray and it would make my head ache more. The gown I wore constricted me, tightening its fabric around my ribs, and lacing itself around my legs.

Kat laughed, a low, throaty laugh, which filled my mind with memories of us riding on horseback through parks in London. We would bring a picnic lunch with us and dismount at a random tree, then recline atop a blanket and people-watch. Kat would make snarky comments about people's fashion, and I would defend them, then she'd turn her comments on me, and we'd laugh together about ourselves. She stepped closer, claiming my viewpoint to examine the dancing crowd. "Ugh. Look at that one."

I followed her gaze to the woman I had noticed earlier, who wore a mere handkerchief to cover an area the size of Texas. A smile turned up my lips despite my desire to suppress it. The grin quickly overpowered my resistance, and I turned away, thinking someone might be watching. I had to think someone was always watching now.

"You're not looking," she said, a frown turning her plump lips down.

"I saw," I managed to say without staring at the unfortunate sight.

Kat tilted her head at me as if to say more.

"What?" I shifted my weight under her stare. It was different from those reporters, Edmund, and my mother. Not only was it honest, it saw me. It wasn't a random stranger trying to get a picture from a street corner so that they could put whatever caption they wanted underneath it in tomorrow's news. It was a familiar examination, a reading.

"You've changed." Those two simple words sent a weary shudder down my spine.

"So have you." My answer felt cliché, as though it were the response I was supposed to give to a friend I hadn't seen in three years. But for us, it was true. In three years I still knew my mother just as well, but in those same three years, Kat and I were virtual strangers. All our familiarity had already been exhausted; it existed in memories.

I fixed her with a sidelong stare, my amusement at the woman in the handkerchief long gone now. "Do you really need a flatmate?"

She grimaced at her almost empty champagne glass. The old Kat had hated alcohol, hated its stench, its appearance, its image. "I do, actually. A bit low on funds, especially to be living in London on my own."

"Would the two of us be able to afford it?"

"Oh, sure. I only need one." Kat shrugged, her sky blue dress shimmering with the movement. "Are you wanting to share a flat?"

"Maybe. Just for the summer. I didn't really come to London with a plan." My scoff had a bitter edge to it. "Apparently it wouldn't have mattered if I did. Everything's changed anyway. Landing in London with a concussion wasn't exactly a storybook entrance."

"Maybe it was." Kat grinned and shifted closer, holding her glass in front of her lips. "I heard about the crowd out front."

"You did?" I scanned her face for clues, but she was oddly inexpressive as she watched the guests dance.

She nodded. "My friend let me know. Thought I'd want to leave early." She lifted a shoulder in a shrug and scoffed as if the crowd hadn't changed anything. "They won't be looking for me. And you're staying with Victoria, right?"

Following her example, I nodded at the twirling crowd. A laughing man dipped his partner, who threw back her head, exposing her throat and smiling. "Yes. For a little while longer, at least."

"I think, under the circumstances, that might be wise." She drained her glass, her swan's neck arched back to reveal the hint of a tattoo under the hair against her neck. She slipped the glass onto the tray of a passing waiter, exchanging it for another with a practiced move, then turned back to me. "When you want to get away from her, just ring. We have a lot of catching up to do."

Chapter Seven
A Sensible Girl

WHEN THE LAST GUEST LEFT, the sky was turning golden over the plaza. From my window, I watched the crowd milling at the gate as they aimed telephoto lenses at the guests entering their cars. For all of their wild clamor, the media didn't force their way in through the gate as cars left.

The soft light filtered through gray clouds, promising an overcast morning. My head throbbed from the intense evening. I thought of my pain pills, but didn't move to take another. Instead, I stood at the window in my borrowed dress, the champagne's buzz long having abandoned me to my tumultuous thoughts. When the last car had pulled away and the lure of pain pills became too much, I closed the curtain and turned my back on the media.

I stripped down to nothing but hairpins and popped a couple pills, then crawled under the duvet and tried to sleep.

As soon as I dragged the covers over my head, faces and newspaper articles trickled through my mind, each battling with the other for my attention.

While the house settled into silence around me, my mind wandered back to the article. It wasn't the worst of it, not really. The worst was that my mother knew about it coming, and hadn't bothered to tell me.

A truck rumbled by in the distance. I rolled over, dragging the pillow over my head as I flattened my face into the mattress, only to wince and pull back when my head throbbed. The day swirled around me and came back to Jake. Why hadn't he told me Victoria had hired him to guard me? Everyone had known *some*thing except me. Even Kat knew about the article within minutes. Jake had snuck me out of the party, walked me through the park, made me feel special, and he had been lying the entire time. I clenched the pillowcase in my fists, trying to drown out my thoughts.

Mind whirling, I tossed myself onto my back again and stared up at the ceiling. What I wouldn't have given to run through the streets, dodging tourists and commuters, and working through my thoughts in the best way I knew how. If I didn't get to run soon, I would forget how. I had a half-marathon coming up, and in a few months, my first ever marathon event.

Did Jake run? He looked like he could have been a runner, with his athletic frame. It was another reason it didn't seem possible for him to be my bodyguard. He wasn't built like a bouncer. If someone were to attack me—like that paparazzo out in the plaza—what was he going to do? But Damien was a little bit stocky, shorter than Jake and carrying maybe an extra twenty pounds of muscle.

Damien? Where had his name come from? Now that it entered my mind, so did his image: a few inches taller than me, quiet, stern, with deep blue eyes that seemed like the deepest blue of the ocean . . . He could have been a bodyguard. I could have believed it about him. He had the attitude, the cold exterior, the ice in his veins. He didn't seem to want or make friends, but existed in his own little bubble of awareness. A smile lifted my lips. What would the twins say if they knew our mother knew their heartthrob so well? And this meant, if they came for the wedding, that they would get to meet him, too.

I sighed and draped my arm over my eyes, hissing as it brushed the stitches. My room was brightening as I lay in bed, mind racing.

Eventually, I drifted off into a restless sleep and awoke two hours later. I groaned when I read the time. Then I grabbed my phone and scrolled through my messages, frowning at the unknown callers leaving messages, and smiling at demands to call from the twins.

"We've taken Mr. Bingley hostage and will not release him except with a phone call directly from you," read Sophie's group text to Margot and me. Margot had replied with a photo of my stuffed bear, tied up with rope and with a handkerchief gag tied around his mouth. I laughed and texted back, "You still awake to arrange Charles's release?"

The answer was a resounding twofold "yes" arriving a minute later.

"Poor ol' Chaz. What did he do to you?" I asked when Sophie answered.

She scoffed. "The question is what he did to you."

"What?" I didn't follow.

"You hopped the pond—to his homeland—and left him here!"

"Oh. Well, I explained to him where I was going and he didn't want to come home. He may be impressionable, but he knew what staying behind meant." I sat up in bed and let the covers rumple around my waist as I plumped my pillow behind me.

"You're a dork," the twins said at the same time, laughing.

"Yes, I am." I fell quiet, my mind racing, and my fingers working on pulling a stray thread from the duvet.

"So . . . Dad told us about the newspaper article." That was Margot, ever gentle Margot. Had it been Sophie speaking, she would have dismissed it as rotten propaganda by our mother's haters, hardly worth mentioning.

"You talked to him?" A jolt of electricity ran through me. "How'd he know? What did he say?"

"He called this morning. His PR guy got a hold of him. You know Dad. Not much of anything," Margot said. "Stoic as ever."

"Oh come on. He said it was a deplorable attempt to discredit Mum," Sophie interjected.

"He hasn't called me. Is he ignoring me? Is something going on? How is he doing?" The questions slipped out of me, rapid-fire style.

"Don't ask. I have no idea what is going on," Sophie said dismissively.

"Margot? You talked to him?"

"I think things are going okay," she answered. "But he'll be out of town for several weeks and his cell doesn't work up there, so he has to use a town land line."

"Yeah, and he told us today he's going to Italy for some reason. We tried to get him to let us meet him there, but—" Sophie added until I cut her off.

"So he's leaving you two alone for weeks?"

"We are adults, you know," Sophie answered.

"It's true. We're nineteen now."

"We're in college."

"Oh. Right. I forgot. But what's he got to do in Italy? Why wouldn't he invite you?"

"I've no idea. Some business thing. He was rather hush about it." Margot chuckled. "Of course, it was a last minute addition, he only told us about that this morning."

"So, lots of mystery," I teased, even though I knew my father to be honest to a fault. It was where I'd gotten that trait, and the thing I loved most about him.

Our conversation ran into other news, although not much had happened in the short time I'd left. We returned to the newspaper article, and I filled them in on everything Victoria had said, but we reached no conclusion on the story's sincerity.

"And who was the inside source?" Sophie remarked. "It's not like Mum keeps someone around her who would betray her like that. Nor do you. And that nonsense about lots of people knowing about it? Come on. The whole thing is false."

"But why?" I pressed. "Why create it then? What does it gain her?"

"You're assuming Mom created it," Margot murmured. "She probably didn't—she wants good publicity, not this stuff."

"There's no such thing as bad publicity to her. Besides, it's not like it's a crime she's being charged with," I answered. "But who would have leaked it? Or invented it? It doesn't hurt her as much as it hurts me."

"Who hates you?" Sophie gave a laugh. "You don't have enemies."

"I don't know." My head pulsed, preventing any clear thought.

"You don't have enemies," Margot agreed. "It's someone who doesn't like Mom. Which, let's face it, isn't hard to find. Mom collects haters."

Sophie scoffed. "No, she doesn't."

"Let's not have this argument again." We'd already discussed to death how our mother had a penchant for insulting other high-profile celebrities, all under the guise of "telling the truth."

With regret, I ended the conversation and hung up. In the bathroom, raccoon eyes and crazy hair greeted me. "Ugh." Before I did anything else, a shower was in order.

When I had dressed, I didn't want to leave the sanctity of my room and steeled myself to open the door. *I have things to do today. Like finding a new place to live, maybe.*

Out in the hall, I stopped short. While I had been dreaming of protective, turquoise eyes, intermingled with a dark haired actor who stood staring from the shadows, the true-life surfer lookalike was nearby.

At my stare, Jake slowly stood from a comfortable looking white armchair I hadn't noticed gracing the hallway before. He tugged down his black, V-neck sweater and offered the faintest echo of his easy grin. "Hello."

Jaw working over the words I wanted to fling at him, I instead touched the stitches on my head as they throbbed. This injury was like having my own personal anger meter. Whenever my pulse rose, my head ached.

"I'm sorry." Jake's words drew my attention back to him. "I should have told you."

His stare melted me, but I crossed my arms to remain aloof. I needed to hear more than just those two words before I could trust him.

He stepped forward, then stopped. Instead of continuing, he spread his hands, palms toward me, and said, "I should have told you. But I was having fun getting to know you, and I just couldn't find a time to tell you before we got back, and then . . ." He trailed off, his gaze unexpectedly sad, and finally gave a shrug when I didn't answer. "I'm sorry."

I inhaled deeply, held it, and let it inch its way from my lungs. That was more than I had ever gotten from my mother, and she had done much worse than not tell me about a job.

"I understand if my apology isn't enough," Jake said. "I'll settle for—"

"No. That's not what I meant. That's not why I—" I broke off, not sure what to say. "It's okay."

"It is?" His eyes widened.

"Well, not really." Dropping my gaze to my hands, I used one thumbnail to scratch the red paint off the other. "It's not okay; you lied to me."

His chest lifted as he breathed deeply, straightening his spine so he rose an inch higher in the air. "I apologize. I never meant to hurt you. I hope you know that now."

"Okay." I shrugged. "I accept your apology then." I offered my hand. "Let's start over."

With a flash of his old smile, he seized my hand in his and shook it. "Nice to meet you. I'm Jake Benson, your bodyguard."

The corner of my lips twitched. "Oh? Do I need a bodyguard?"

"Have you looked outside yet?" Jake feigned concern, the skin above his nose creasing.

"No, actually." I ran a hand over my damp hair.

He smiled wryly, motioning to the window at the end of the hallway. This one, angled slightly differently from mine, had to offer a better view of the gate than mine. Not sure I wanted to see exactly how many reporters had remained through the night in order to ambush me in the morning, I slipped past Jake in the hallway. Despite its generous width, easily that of a bridle path, he felt too close. My step hesitated as I passed him, as I inhaled the hint of cedar I had detected the night before.

When I lifted my gaze, all in that fleeting moment when I passed by, he gave a genuine smile. In that moment, he reminded me so much of my ex back when we were young, when we were happy, when we had the promise of happiness stretching before us, that I forced my feet to move on. Because him reminding me of Bryan was either incredibly wonderful, the best thing that could have ever happened, or else it would utterly destroy me.

And I didn't know if I was ready to risk my heart to find out which one it was.

$$\mathbb{D}$$

My feet pounded against the tan gravel in the park with a satisfying crunch at each step. Ponytail bouncing against my back and whisking at my shoulders, an ironic smile grew on my lips despite the determined ache of my head. Doctors be darned. What did they know anyway?

Behind me the whir of a bicycle's tires threatened to overtake me, but I didn't look or change pace. Jake had insisted I wasn't safe alone, and had disappeared for an hour then returned with his bike. Apparently he was serious: he didn't run.

I couldn't expect many people who weren't already training for a marathon to keep up with me, anyway. It had taken me a few years to run like I was now.

A jitter of excitement made my step eager, which I realized when the sound of Jake's bike faded. I slowed to something more reasonable. I had missed this, even though it had only been a few days.

To distract myself, I scanned the almost empty park. Most people had headed indoors at this time of evening, while a few couples and families were enjoying the twilight. In another thirty minutes, it would be dark but for the lamps. Across the pond, a young mother helped her child feed the swans and ducks that gathered at their feet. Wildlife wasn't so wild around here. Nighttime seemed to make them even bolder.

A distant crunch of gravel cut through my thoughts. Was that Jake's bike? No, it had come from the opposite direction. Glancing to my left, I jumped to my right at the sight of a forty-pound tan dog loping alongside me. His mouth was open in a grin, tongue extending to flap in the wind, and no owner in sight. Still running, I twisted around to see if someone was chasing him down, but the three of us had the trail to ourselves.

Jake's brakes squeaked in protest. "Whose—?"

I slowed, and the dog ran up ahead, then glanced back at me with the black mask on his—no, her—face, giving her an impish expression. "Uh . . ."

Jake stopped, and I followed suit, pivoting in the middle of the rock path and searching for anyone who might own this animal. After a few solitary strides, the dog glanced back at us and padded to a halt.

When I crouched down, the fawn-colored dog raced up, nearly bowling me over in her eagerness. "Hi, who are you?" I scratched her ears, unable to keep from smiling at her happy face. My smile faded as I ran my hand down her neck, over prominent shoulder blades. In the dimness, it was hard to tell, but with my hands, it was obvious she was starving. "I think she's a stray."

"In London? Impossible." Above me, Jake still scanned the park for a possible owner.

"She's got scars all over her body—probably from fights. And she's rail thin; I'm surprised she has enough energy to run at all."

"I guess I should call—"

"Animal control?" I held out a hand to stop him. "No, don't."

"Why not?" Jake already had his phone in hand. "I don't see her owner —"

"Let's just . . . see where she goes." I shrugged.

"What?" He scoffed the word incredulously.

"Maybe her owner will show up . . ." I stood, and she jumped up at me, paws cutting into my stomach at her exuberance. Grabbing her paws and holding them, I glanced at Jake. "Not that he would deserve her back. But I hate sending dogs to the pound. I don't want to think of them getting put down just because."

Jake tilted his head at me, a tic I was learning to see as an expression of his exasperation. "And what if she follows us home?"

I shrugged and began walking toward my mother's flat. "I guess that means I have a new dog."

Jake narrowed his eyes. "And does she have a name?"

Considering her for a moment, I tilted my head at the dog with the mischievous black mask and said, "Elinor. She looks like a sensible girl."

$$\text{☽}$$

Elinor ended up having no owner, and resembled a Belgian Malinois mix, both of which I found out when I took her to a vet and had her scanned for a microchip. None was found, and apart from calling my number from the flyers and Internet ad I put up, her owner would have to put in a claim. I left my name and number with the Dog Warden, but it seemed like Elinor was mine. A minor infection from a cut in her paw required antibiotics, and she finished up her course about when I finally got my body on London time.

The morning after I'd found her, I snuck Elinor into the flat; Victoria had disappeared to Paris for who knew how long, and still hadn't returned. I'd heard nothing from her, but I supposed that wasn't unexpected. She hadn't even told me she was leaving—why should she inform me she had reached Paris or when she would return? Since I'd adopted Elinor, I'd halfheartedly been trying to find either a temporary or permanent residence. My first call to Kat had gone unanswered and unreturned, and I'd not been able to locate a reputable, dog-friendly hotel.

Without my mother at her flat, it was a wonderful place to stay. Mary had welcomed Elinor with open arms, although warned me against telling my mother about her, and urged me to find a new home for her. "I'm moving out soon anyway," I told the motherly woman. "I'll be staying with my friend, Kat. I just have to get a hold of her."

When I had reached her, Kat immediately agreed to the dog.

"Great. So when can we meet? I need to get out of here before my mother gets back from Paris."

A clunk echoed through the phone as though she had put me on speakerphone and set the phone on the counter. When she spoke, it was distant, in a raised voice, confirming my suspicions. "I can't until next week, I'll be up north until then."

"Next week is fine," I said. "I'll just hide Elinor if she gets home early."

Kat laughed her husky laugh. "Right."

"Jake said something about her being back next week."

"Oh, that reminds me." Kat hesitated, and when she spoke, her voice was near the phone again, like she'd picked it up. "Come without the bodyguard, would you?"

"Something wrong?"

"No no no." She ran the words together, followed by a hoarse laugh. "No. Just leave the bodyguard at home. We don't need him. Monday morning? *Late* morning," she specified.

Kat had given me her address and we had hung up.

Early Monday morning, as Elinor and I headed to the park for a short run, the chill penetrated deep, along with a mist that I hoped would burn off and reveal a bright afternoon sun. In the quiet of Kensington Gardens, Elinor padded along beside me, sniffing the occasional bush. It had been a two minute walk to reach the park, one past brick apartment buildings with beautiful, now-familiar façades. Since the scandal had broken almost ten days ago now, and with nothing else showing up in the media, paparazzi had disappeared, and Jake let me go out with Elinor alone. She could be an intimidating dog when her hackles rose.

Since arriving in London, I'd settled in, now gazing past the buildings around me and to the residents who lived there. Most dressed in suits or skirts as they left for the Underground in the morning, as though they were business men and women, professionals in a professional city, often toting bags on one shoulder. Out of those bags peeked their lunches and reading material, sometimes even spare shoes.

We reached the park, and Elinor paused at a rock that probably every male dog in a ten-mile radius had peed on at one time, then trotted a short distance away to squat.

In a couple of hours, I would see Kat's place, and possibly move in later in the day. Not that I had much to bring over; two trips' worth, without Jake's help. Maybe three, now that Elinor had a bed and her bag of kibble. It was a move I couldn't wait to complete.

Chapter Eight
Catching Up

"I CAN'T BELIEVE YOU'RE ASSUMING I'll be fine with Kat." I poked my spatula at the scrambled eggs in the skillet as I cooked breakfast after my run. "Isn't that like walking off your job?"

"Trust me, you'll be quite safe with Kat. I daresay maybe even safer than you would with me." He laughed. "I think the paparazzi are beginning to recognize us together."

Hand hovering over the eggs, I turned and stared at him. "Why do you say that?" Bacon sizzled from the next pan over, and my hand weathered a splat of grease as it snapped. "Ouch."

"I've seen cameras around again."

"They're losing interest in me," I insisted, more hopeful than certain. The toaster popped, and I added a slice to the plates along with eggs and bacon, delivering one to Jake across the room. He had pulled condiments out of the fridge, Worcestershire sauce, HP sauce, a variety of jams, along with ketchup, and gathered them together in the middle of the counter.

"It's the calm before a storm." Jake slathered ketchup on his eggs while I helped myself to the blackberry jam.

"I refuse to believe that. The scandal is over—at least my part in it." I sat down beside him and reached for the ketchup. "Now that it's broken, it's not like I can be surprised by anything."

His brows rose, a lock of hair falling into his face, which he jerked his chin to sweep away. "That's awfully naïve of you."

A grimace tugged at my lips. "Yeah. I know." The squirm of my stomach had nothing to do with my hunger. "I keep waiting for the next story to appear."

"Don't worry," Jake said, "it will. But why don't I drop you at the door —just to be safe?"

With a frown at his change in mind, I shrugged my agreement.

An hour later, Jake dropped me at the door to Kat's apartment, which I was pleased to discover was only a mile away from my mother's flat. Not for wanting to be near her, although I wanted to keep our line of communication open, but because Kat's flat was in a nice area of London.

Being unfamiliar with London's real estate, I had been concerned that something affordable for us had meant a dodgy part of town, one where I might actually want a bodyguard. But the address she gave me belonged to a squat and ugly three-story building in the midst of five and six story red brick buildings. It was the ugly stepsister to the neighborhood, and it might only be days before neighbors petitioned to have it knocked down.

Someone had scratched out the name "Scott" on number three, but no name was written over it. Since that was the number Kat had given me, I pressed it and waited for her response.

Jake leaned over to me. "I'll see you in the door, then I'll be back in an hour, okay?"

"Sure."

"Hello?" The voice answering my press of the button was groggy and rough.

"Kat, it's Adrienne."

"Oh, you're early!" She coughed. "Come on up, though."

Before I could argue that I was right on time, the door gave a loud buzz.

"Cheers," Jake said, pushing open the door for me.

"Right," I muttered as I passed him, strangely annoyed at his eagerness to say good-bye. "Don't sound so thrilled."

With a quick grin, he caught my wrist, pulling me against him.

Surprised, I put up my hands between us. As if far away, Elinor growled.

"I *am* thrilled. You'll be safe, I can run an important errand, and I'll catch you later." He dashed a kiss on my cheek. "Don't go anywhere, okay?"

His embrace surprised me enough that I almost fell away when he released me. "Right." Attempting to regain my composure, I turned to enter the apartment. "I won't." With a snort at his shoes, Elinor trotted along behind me.

Too confused by his actions to even begin thinking about what they meant, I headed up the narrow stairs in front of me with Elinor's head crowding my knees. Kat's apartment was on the third floor, the second down the hall, and I raised my hand to knock as it flew open, revealing a wicked grin below a mop of hot pink hair. "Morning."

I lowered my hand, smiling.

"Oh." Kat's gaze dropped to my dog. "This must be Elinor!"

Kat knelt before her, throwing Elinor into ecstasy. The dog wagged her tail, licking Kat wherever she could reach before I could stop her.

"Oh, she's adorable!" Kat ruffled Elinor's ears, laughing. "Well, come in." She stood and stepped back for us to enter.

The narrow entrance made it impossible for Kat to remain at the door and welcome us, so she walked into the living area and left me to close the door behind us. "Should I take off my shoes?" I asked as the door clicked into place; I turned the deadbolt automatically.

"No, it's all right. Just come in," Kat called from out of view.

Pulling the leash out of my hand and dragging it behind her, Elinor trotted after Kat, apparently comfortable enough to explore.

"Down this way."

I followed her voice through a door to my left. To my surprise, instead of entering a bedroom, I walked into the kitchen. "Not very open concept, is it?"

Kat smiled down at the coffee mugs she had pulled out from the cupboard. "It's a bit cramped. But it works."

"It's better than my mother's," I muttered.

Kat laughed. "I can't believe that."

A reluctant smile on my lips, I shook my head. "Okay, no. Hers is gorgeous. It's a good thing she hires someone to cook for her, or else I'd say it goes completely to waste. But this . . ." I motioned a hand to the tired kitchen cabinets, painted a shade between dismal gray and black, and the smallest oven I'd ever seen in my life. I grimaced. "At least we have a microwave."

Kat grinned, her eyes crinkling around the edges. "Glad you can be an optimist."

"Always have been," I replied.

"No milk, right? Things haven't changed that much, have they?" Kat paused before pouring the second cup of coffee.

"Please no," I muttered, thinking back to the engagement party.

"I don't know how you avoid milk. Is it really worth it?"

"Did you not see my hives at the party?"

Her nose crinkled as she poured the second cup and handed it to me. "Sorry. No." She jerked her chin toward the living room. "Let's sit out there and chat."

"Sure." I unclipped Elinor's leash, and she shook her head as if shaking off the indignity of it. Then we followed Kat into the other room.

As I settled in the couch across from Kat's perch in the armchair, I searched for something to talk about. Where to begin with a friend whom I hadn't spoken to for three years?

Kat seemed to be thinking the same thing, for after a moment of us both sipping our coffees, she said, "It's awkward, isn't it? How much happened since the last summer we met, and yet how much doesn't seem to be necessary?"

Tension eased from my body at her words. Kat's un-British forwardness was something I had always appreciated. "Wasn't it always like that, though? Don't you remember how we met?" I grinned.

"At a party. Of all ironic twists of fate, given how much we both hate parties."

"Yeah. That was the day I realized celebrity parties were boring."

Kat laughed. "Without a friend," she finished for me. "Yes. Bang on."

"Didn't you sneak over though? I mean, you were living in a nearby flat, right?" My memory of her arrival at the party was foggy. "How did you get in?"

Her grin turned mischievous. "Sort of. I was living two flats down. I was mad at my father, so I snuck out. I overheard the party, the laughing . . . and I snuck through a gap in the fence."

"Just like you. Fearless." I grinned at the image of Kat Townsend, fourteen years old at the time, sneaking out of her giant flat, probably out the window like her rebellious heart would do, and running toward music and laughter.

"We were so young," she mused. "And everyone was so pissed at that party it was easy to get in." Kat leaned back in her chair, pulling up her legs up and cocking them to one side, so she sat with her heels almost underneath her. Her black skirt brushed her knees, modest and yet sexy on her curvy frame. She sipped her coffee. "Mmm. I needed this."

I sipped my own, surprised by the depth of the brew. "Oh. This is good. Will you be my personal barista?"

"Of course." She winked. "You know my obsession with coffee is only because of you. I learned from the best."

"That is the legacy I left with you, isn't it?"

She smiled and leaned her head back against the chair. "Hard to believe we only spent a couple of summers together, isn't it?"

I nodded absently into my coffee, feeling both nostalgic and incredibly comfortable where I was. It had always been this way with Kat. We had spent only two summers hanging out, but we'd hung out every day and remained in contact over the years—until I left London, after introducing my ex-boyfriend and Victoria.

I lifted my gaze and found Kat experiencing the same kind of pleasure with hot coffee in her hands and a comfortable place to sit that I was. Despite its second-hand appearance, or perhaps because of it, the couch was so comfortable I could have stayed all day.

We drifted into the comfortable silence of friends, and my thoughts returned to Jake's comment earlier, when he had mentioned the calm before the storm. Someone out there was researching my mother, determined to find some sort of truth or to fabricate a false but believable claim against her past. But couldn't it be possible that the person behind this story was from Edmund's enemy camp? He was the one in the political spotlight. And he had known about the story before it broke. My fingers tightened around my cup.

"Adrienne?" Kat's sing-songy voice pulled me from my thoughts.

"Oh. Sorry. What's that?"

Her soft hazel eyes gleamed at me in amusement. "What's going on in that head of yours?"

"Oh, too much." I stared down into my now lukewarm coffee.

"Your mum's scandal, perhaps?"

"What else?"

"Yes." Kat tugged down her skirt to her knees and smoothed out a wrinkle. "Did it surprise you?"

A breath of a scoff escaped me. "Yeah. A bit. The media certainly surprised me. We'd gone on a walk and came back to be attacked by paparazzi." I shook my head. "I just don't understand why this story broke *now*. And who was behind it. And why it had to concern me."

Kat released a measured sigh, set her cup on the table beside her chair and straightened up again. "Adrienne, have you considered who knew you were in London?"

"No one knew. Only my sisters and my father."

Skepticism played across her face. "Then your mother knew, too."

"No. I didn't tell her." The slight narrowing of my friend's eyes and flattening of her lips told me I had missed the point. She picked at her skirt then examined the lint caught on her nail. "You think someone told her."

She shrugged one shoulder apologetically. "It's obvious."

"Is it?"

"One of the twins. Probably Sophie," she said with another dainty shrug. "You know they talk to her often."

I frowned. "I know that. But how do you know?"

She inclined her head. "That's fair." Instead of answering, she swung her feet to the ground and walked to the window, which allowed the dim London light to trickle in from the street side.

"How do you know?" I prompted when she seemed tempted to ignore our conversation.

Her head nearly touched her shoulder at my question, but she still didn't turn. "All right. The truth?"

"Always." My heart stilled. What was she hiding that she had to ask?

"Right. Always the quest for truth." Kat lifted her head, nodding it up and down at the grocery store across the street. "I've kept in touch with your family over the years."

"My family? Like . . . my sisters?" For two summers, Kat and I had been inseparable, but Margot and Sophie had had their own friends, their own tight-knit community that even I was rarely included in. "They never told me."

"Not . . . initially." Kat faced me. "I kept in touch with your mum."

Her words required several seconds to sink in. "What?"

She repeated them.

"Why? I mean, what on earth could Victoria Talbot have to offer you?"

One corner of Kat's mouth twitched up in a sardonic smile. "I found myself in a situation where I needed a mother's advice." Turning to the window again, Kat shrugged, the rest of her body unusually still as she stared down at the street below.

"And because you don't have a mother, you turned to *her*?" Disbelief pulled my heart to my stomach. "Even though you knew she wasn't someone to trust?"

Kat faced me, with a sorrow I'd never seen before present in her eyes. "She was the only one I could turn to." She shook her head as she crossed the room and stopped behind the chair she'd sat in earlier, resting her coffee cup on the top and curving her hands around it. "You don't . . ." She paused, pressing her lips together as she considered her next words. "You don't know what it's like not having a mother."

"Because my mother was so present in my life? She abandoned me!" A fire built in my chest as outrage rose.

"Wait, let me speak." Kat held up her hand to stop my tirade. "Your mum was still alive. She could be contacted, she just wasn't in your life. But my—" she broke off, looking conflicted, then swallowed and continued, "my parents are gone. Forever. I never even knew my mum. And you don't know what that's like." Her knuckles had gone pale around her cup.

I chewed on my bottom lip. Somehow, there'd been a chasm between us I hadn't been aware of before.

Kat sighed. "Your mother was there for me when no one else could be. She's why I was at her party, no one else. She's not as bad as you think she is."

Disbelief widened my eyes. "I think you and I must have had very different experiences with her, then. Have you forgotten how she abandoned us as children?"

Kat tilted her head as she looked across the room at me. "There's more than that, isn't there?"

I sucked in a slow breath and held it, staring into my coffee. I had never told a soul what had happened between my mother and me to ruin our relationship; I wasn't certain I wanted or needed to revisit it now. It had happened. That was all that had to be said.

"Are you keeping a secret?" Kat chuckled hoarsely at my answering silence.

Spurn the Moon

My coffee quivered in my hands. Secrets. Secrets and lies—how one led to the other; and how I hated both. Here I was harboring one and on the verge of the other.

"I knew something had changed in you. That's it, isn't it? You have a secret?" With a shrug, Kat claimed her seat again, this time leaning toward me. "You can keep it. I don't care. We all have some."

I blew my breath out of my nose.

"That's not what's bothering you?" Kat asked with a frown.

"Victoria's in Paris."

"Oh?"

"She left without even telling me—when I'm staying with her. I could have reported her missing, except Mary and Jake knew. Her stupid secrets. She didn't even bother to tell me there was a scandal about to break in the papers—a scandal about me!"

"I know." Kat sighed and leaned back. "She has her good qualities, too."

A disbelieving laugh worked its way free from me. "What did she do for you, Kat, to earn such appreciation?"

"I guess that's my secret," she mused, staring down into her cup as she tilted it around in her lap. The liquid touched the rim, and Kat rotated the cup so that her coffee traveled around it, dangerously close to spilling. She did it almost as though she weren't aware of it, staring down so blankly I suspected she could spill its contents and it wouldn't even register.

A buzz sliced the air, and we both jumped, Kat darting forward to avoid the coffee that had already splashed onto her skirt. With a curse, she slid her cup on the table.

"Scares me every time." Kat rose and grabbed a napkin on her way to the intercom, where she pressed a button and said, "Hello?"

"Kat, it's me," said a male voice.

"Oh, right. Come on up. I wasn't expecting you until later."

"Got in early."

The voice was vaguely familiar, but I didn't think much of it until Kat swung open the door to Damien Kerr.

My mouth fell open, but Damien was the picture of courtesy.

He kissed Kat on the cheek and spotted me over her shoulder. "Oh, I'm sorry. I didn't realize you had company."

Kat shrugged and flashed an impish grin. "She's not really company—

she's my new flatmate."

"Oh?"

There was a world to be revealed in that one word. I rose, coffee cup in hand, and made a motion as if to excuse my presence. "I didn't know you were expecting another guest," I said to Kat. "Hi, Damien."

Opening his mouth, then shutting it again, he gave me a quick nod. "Hello. Adrienne. You're looking better."

My face went hot at the memory. "Yes. Sorry to surprise you," I added. "I was just on my way out anyway. I haven't moved in yet, so . . ."

"Oh, wait," Kat turned to the table beside the front door and dug into her purse, pulling out her keychain and removing a key from it. She held it out to me. "Your copy."

I hesitated. "You know, we haven't even discussed rent—"

Kat shrugged off my words as a phone began ringing. "Oh, it'll be fine. This is under your budget."

"How do you know?"

She flashed a grin, while Damien muted his phone. "I hear things."

I rolled my eyes. "You talked to my sisters, didn't you?"

"Course." Her grin widened, and she pushed the key at me. "Here, I'll take your cup. Move in whenever—I won't be around tomorrow, but I have the day after off."

"Does that mean you'll help?"

"Lord, no!" She laughed that low, husky laugh of hers that I had seen turn men's heads. "But it means I'll direct you."

"Right. Oh, if I do happen to move in, which room is mine?"

"Oh, right. I never gave you a tour, did I?" She tapped her forehead with the palm of her hand. "Silly. I swear, I'd forget my head sometimes . . ." She almost dashed down the hallway, and Elinor bounded after her with a bark.

Taken aback at her speed, I hesitated before following.

"Yours would be the room here at the end. I hope it'll work." Kat threw open the door, revealing a room half the size of the one I'd grown up in, but which already contained a single bed with a bare pillow at the foot. A birch wood desk sat forgotten across the room from it, and a rickety lamp perched on top of it. Other than that, the only adornments were the architecture itself, the high ceilings, courtesy of being on the top floor, the exposed brick behind the bed, and the white, wood-framed window. I crossed to the glass and peered out, examining the corner view.

Spurn the Moon

A busy street corner sprawled below us, plenty of opportunity for people watching; a block or two away I could just see the edge of a bit of green —the park? Perhaps I'd walk that direction with Jake. Speaking of Jake . . . it had been almost the allotted hour already. I scanned the pavement below for him and caught a glimpse of his golden hair bobbing through the crowd at the street corner below.

"Oh, there's my bodyguard," I said with an ironic twist to my lips. "Guess I'd better get going."

"I thought you left him at home?" She cleared her throat under a pinched smile.

"He brought me to the door. Why? Do you know him or something?"

She stepped away from the window. "Yes. I . . . I've known him for a long time. My brother knows him as well." She motioned back toward the living room.

"Brother?" I frowned, following the motion of her hand as I finally put two and two together. "Your brother?" My mouth fell open for the second time in mere minutes. "Damien Kerr is your brother?"

She shrugged almost apologetically, but her expression was wry. "Who did you think he was?"

"I don't know—I thought you were dating him or something."

At that, Kat laughed, low and long, her shoulders shaking at an apparent repressed effort to keep her laughter under control. "Dating him?" she managed. "No. Not hardly."

"How did you never tell me? In all the talks we've had, you've never told me that Damien Kerr was your brother." I shot her an accusatory glare.

"It just never came up." She shrugged and glanced away.

My mind raced through the past, all of our prior conversations over the summers we had hung out, and the phone and email conversations after. We'd met halfway through my summer here when we were sixteen and seventeen, and discussed very important things like horses and books and fashion. Even though our friendship had spanned five years, the last three I hadn't spoken with her.

"We haven't seen each other in years," I said.

"I know. And really haven't spent that much time together, for being friends." Her mouth crooked into a self-deprecating smile. "Must be why you're still around."

"We were really crappy friends, weren't we?" I laughed.

Her smile turned to a grin. "We were exactly what each of us needed." She shrugged, then added, "At the moment."

"We never discussed family."

Whenever I visited London those summers as a teen, I had struggled with fitting in with my family. Victoria and the twins had created a club of three, one to which I never received an invitation. It must have trickled over, intensifying my relationship with Kat, while also making me less eager to bring up family. Now that I considered it, I didn't think I had ever asked if she had siblings.

"But the different last name?" I burst out.

"Oh, I use my mother's surname." Kat smirked. "I can't believe you thought I was dating Damien."

Numbly shaking my head, I stood in the window, as the buzzer filled the flat.

Jumping, Kat muttered something I didn't catch and turned to answer it.

After a moment, I followed her.

"—not in my flat," Kat was saying crossly to Damien when I entered the room.

Damien quelled any further words with a knowing look. "He said he'd wait outside for her."

Trying to pretend I wasn't listening, I crossed to the room and picked up Elinor's leash from where I'd abandoned it on the sofa. She perked up her ears and wagged her tail, but didn't move from her position beside Damien, who seemed to be resting a hand on top of her head. When he didn't move it, she nudged his hand with her nose. His lips twitched as he looked down at her and gave into her demands.

"Well, I guess I'd better go then." I had to step close to Damien to claim Elinor, as she wouldn't stop pestering him, and I crouched down, ever aware of his contemplative stare. "Come on, girl. Let's get out of here."

Elinor pulled on the leash in my hand, eager to get back outside, and I had to grab the wall to keep from falling into Damien.

"You're in my way," I murmured to his shiny, not-a-scuff-on-them loafers.

"Sorry." His voice was barely above a whisper. With a small smile, he stepped aside, opening the door for me before I could reach for it. "It was nice to see you again, looking better."

"Yeah." I winced, wishing he would stop mentioning the hives he'd last seen me covered with. Looking better than that wasn't a huge accomplishment.

He held the door open for us, and his stare continued to burn my skin as I walked down the stairs with Elinor, but my mind was on other things.

My name from his lips startled me, and I bumped into Elinor's side. I whirled as he came down the last flight of stairs, two steps at a time.

"Adrienne." He spoke breathlessly, but didn't seem to be out of breath at all. "I—"

"Did I forget something?"

"What? No." He shook his head, a hand lightly brushing the railing beside him. He glanced up for some reason, craning his head as if to see whether someone stood at the top of the stairs. I followed his gaze but saw no one. Seeing me, he flashed a small smile and faced me. "I had something to ask you."

I struggled to hide my surprise. "Oh?"

He took a deep breath and said, "I was wondering if you'd like to go to dinner."

I blinked at him, foot on the bottom step, and couldn't help but look over my shoulder through the window to the front door—at Jake. From where he stood, he couldn't see Damien, halfway up the stairs and looking down at me with guarded hope. "Dinner?" I echoed blankly. "You mean . . . like a date?"

He dipped his head in a nod. "Yes . . . that is what I meant. I mean, you aren't like most of the girls I date. You're far too . . . normal. You wouldn't last a day in Hollywood, you're so naïve, what with the way you reacted to the paparazzi and all."

"Excuse me?"

"But for all that," he plowed ahead, as if his words came without brakes, "I find you strangely endearing. Despite you looking like a carbon copy of your mother, you don't act like her at all. You're just . . . refreshing."

When he stopped, I found my mouth gaping open and snapped it shut. "That's kind of . . . insulting."

His cheeks began a slow burn, rising from his neck up to heat his ears. "I meant no offense."

"No. I'm sure you didn't." My own cheeks flamed as I shook my head. "It doesn't matter. No. Thank you."

"Right."

As I turned and grabbed the door to tug it open, I heard his shoes scrape against the stairs, growing fainter behind me.

Chapter Nine
The Amethyst

WHEN I LEFT KAT'S FLAT, my mind raced, thoughts of Damien outpacing any others. Distracted, I forgot about Jake's presence until I was about to push through the gate at the flat, and he grabbed my elbow.

"Adrienne."

"What?"

"You all right?"

"Yeah. Fine." I tried to form my features into a semblance of disinterest. "Why?"

"Don't you realize paparazzi have been following us for the whole time?"

Glancing behind me, I acknowledged the two men with a scowl. "Why are you following me?" I demanded. "The story is old, move on to something more important!"

In answer, they raised their cameras and clicked. Frowning, Jake grabbed my elbow and dragged me through the gate.

"What is wrong with you?"

I wiped a hand over my face. "Nothing. Sorry. I just—" I sighed. "Nothing. It's nothing."

Pushing my way into the flat, I didn't register the luggage in the hallway or the chatter of voices in the back of the house until Elinor growled.

"Oh, crap," I breathed. In the direction of the kitchen, Mary's voice carried, raised and angry, intermixing with a tone of authority I recognized as belonging to Charity Harper, my mother's personal assistant. "She must be back."

"She is indeed."

Before I could react, other than to lift my gaze to the speaker standing at the top of the stairs, Victoria was there, her eyes glittering, cold gems, and her hands on her slender hips. She wore a black pencil skirt but no shoes, and even from my position at the bottom of the stairs, I noted her pink toenails and her new tan.

"What is that *animal* doing in my house?"

Mouth working over my words, I tried to think of something to say which would save Elinor. "She——" I spoke to the dog, who cocked her head up at Victoria, tail wagging slowly back and forth, but her ears flicked back cautiously. "She was injured and I had to adopt her."

Behind me, Jake drew in a sharp breath, as if my words were the wrong thing to say.

My mother's eyes sparked.

Crap. I forgot how much she hates dogs.

"That *thing* will not stay here. Get it out."

Back straight as a board, I faced her down. "I'll have you know that this 'thing,' as you call it, has been more a companion to me than you— and she's more loyal to me than you are."

Jake shifted beside me, but I ignored him.

"And thanks, by the way, for letting me know you were leaving for a couple weeks. I mean, it's not like I was staying here or anything and expecting to see you in the morning."

Her eyes narrowed to slits, and she raised a hand, pointing it at Elinor with a marble expression of distaste. "Get it out. Or you both can get out."

My lips curved into a small smile. "Perfect. I was wondering how I was going to tell you that I'm moving in with Kat Townsend."

Although her eyes didn't widen much, her lips parted just enough to betray her surprise. Her hand fell back to her side, where it stayed for a moment before she shrugged and briefly flipped both palms toward the sky. "That's perfect, then. Agrees with both of us. Pack up. I don't want that dog staying one night in my house."

Fury rolled over me, tightening my stomach into knots and making me long to back out the door and sprint off down the sidewalk. Several miles of sprints would distract me from this burning fury. I hadn't been this angry since—

No. I would not think of that night. But how could I not? Bad things happened when I stayed with my mother, that was it. I stalked up the stairs and brushed by her, Elinor slinking by, not even daring to sniff at my mother.

☽

Under Victoria's decree, I moved out of her flat that night and fell into easy companionship with Kat as my roommate. We hardly saw each other as we lived such different schedules. I was up and out running by sunrise, while Kat slept until noon, went to work most days by two, and sneaked back inside while I slept.

As I upped my running miles and resumed marathon training, my two shadows puffed along beside me, Elinor at my heel, and Jake on his bike, but sometimes on foot dodging traffic and wasting his breath begging me to slow down. After a disastrous long run, I only let him run along with me on the short run days, when he had the chance of keeping pace with us.

A week before the race, I found myself cooking a simple roast chicken with vegetables for us on Kat's night off. She rarely stayed in when she didn't work, but today she'd complained of a headache and spent most of the day on the couch nursing glasses of Sprite over ice.

The TV was showing commercials on a low volume when I reentered the living room after basting the chicken. A pile of tabloids and newspapers perched on the coffee table, eliciting a grimace from me. After my mother and Edmund gave their official wedding date announcement to the papers, the scandal had been revived.

"You know I think there's a guy with a camera staking out our apartment," I said, pointing to the window. "I saw him when I left for my run this morning, and he was still there when I got back."

"Oh?" Kat sipped her drink.

"Yeah. Maybe Jake should meet me here?"

"He can meet you outside," Kat said firmly, reaching for the remote when her show came back on.

I exhaled through my nose. Since moving in, I'd been meeting him at the edge of the park or across the street, because Kat was adamantly against allowing Jake inside.

"Why? Not that it's a big deal, but why won't you tell me why you and Damien hate him?"

Kat muted the TV and met my gaze. "Listen, you have to watch yourself around him."

"What are you talking about?"

"He's just—" She pressed her lips together and wrinkled her nose, looking like she wanted to say something else. "You can't trust him."

"Why not? That's all you'll tell me?"

"Listen . . . " She closed her eyes, lifting a hand to her forehead and rubbing as if her head pounded. "I can't—" Without another word, she rose and disappeared into her bedroom, leaving me confused by the jumble of information before me on the TV, tabloids, and papers—none of which I wanted.

I considered myself a great judge of character. After Bryan, my ex, of course. He was the one guy that had fooled me. Jake gave no indication of doing anything but his job. Since I'd moved in with Kat, my relationship with Jake had been nothing but professional, if I could even call it that.

The doorbell buzzer sounded, interrupting me from my thoughts and bringing Elinor up from her bed and into a barking frenzy.

"Quiet," I commanded her as I rose.

"It's Damien," came the answer, and I buzzed him up.

"Your brother," I said when Kat popped her door open and returned to the living room, looking as though she'd recollected herself.

"Oh. Is he coming up?"

"You expect me to abandon him on the doorstep?" I teased, inwardly wincing when I realized that was precisely what she was doing with Jake. "Sorry, I didn't mean—"

Folding her arms around herself, she shook her head, and a knock on the door elicited new barks from Elinor, covering my apology. Kat motioned me on toward the door, and returned to the sofa.

When I opened the door, Elinor's bark turned into a happy whine. He smiled down at her, chuckling as she pushed her nose into his face while he bent to remove his shoes.

"Thought you were out of town tonight," Kat said, lifting her glass to her lips. "New York or something, wasn't it?"

"Back up, Elinor," I said, grabbing her and pulling her away so he could enter. I sent her to bed and reclaimed my spot on the sofa while Damien kicked off his shoes by the door.

"I was supposed to be, but it was canceled. Figured I'd see what you're up to." He joined me on the couch, and the old frame sagged under the weight, but he didn't comment on it.

I found myself picking at my thumb cuticle as a commercial played. Although Damien had stopped by before, I always tried to leave the room to give him time with Kat. Now though, I had to be near the kitchen for the timer. Thinking of the chicken, I rose and muttered something about checking on it, belatedly aware that I'd interrupted him halfway through a thought.

Taking my drink with me, I returned to the kitchen and spent as much time as I could basting the chicken and prepping the rest of the meal, but there was really nothing left to do. So I spent a few minutes on my phone, absently searching my social media and email accounts, checking in with friends. Fifteen minutes passed, during which I renewed my vow to ignore all social media until this scandal was forgotten. Random friend requests—from people I didn't know—and requests from high school friends I hadn't spoken to in years cluttered every one of my accounts.

"Adrienne?" Kat entered the kitchen with an empty glass. "Dinner almost ready?"

"What?" I started, looking up from my phone. "Oh, not for another ten minutes. Is Damien staying?"

"Uh . . ." She shrugged and pulled a soda from the fridge. "Ask him. He probably won't—unless you invite him."

"*I* have to invite him?"

She grinned. "If you want him to stay."

"Do you?" Confusion contorted my face.

At my expression, she laughed and called over her shoulder, "Damien! Stay for dinner?"

He appeared in the doorway a moment later. "I don't want to intrude."

"You aren't," she said. "Adrienne was just saying she'd cooked enough for four people."

I glanced at her, but didn't correct her.

"If you're sure?" He phrased it as a question, addressed to me, and I shrugged.

"Yeah, stay. We have plenty of food." I offered a tight smile, which he returned somewhat hesitantly.

When we sat down to dinner around our modest table, I caught myself examining Kat's brother. He seemed both comfortable and uneasy here, and sometimes he stared at Kat with such intensity that I wondered what he was thinking.

"So Kat tells me you're here to study at Oxford, Adrienne?"

"Oh, yes." I swallowed my bite of chicken. "Medicine."

"Really? That's a difficult course. There isn't a large medical school at Oxford, is there?"

"No, but I'm okay with that. Did you go to coll—university, I mean?"

A flicker of a smile appeared on his lips at my nearly calling their university system college, an American mistake. "I did. I studied at St. Andrews."

"Oh." I swallowed my bite of chicken. "That's a good school."

"It is."

Kat rolled her eyes and took a swig of her water. "You'll find he's quite partial to St. Andrews."

Damien's lips turned down, but I detected a hint of amusement in his eyes. "Yes, well, *alma mater* and all that."

Kat changed the subject, and our conversation turned to mutual friends of theirs.

"Oh, before I forget, I'm throwing a party next weekend," Damien said.

"London or home?" Kat answered around a mouthful of chicken.

"London," he answered with a slight frown at her apparent lack of manners. "And you're both invited, of course."

Damien was inviting me to his house party? I smiled politely and began to come up with my excuses. He still confused me, after all. He'd been so cold at my mother's engagement party, refused to get an ice pack for me, instead forcing Jake to do it. Yet every time he came over to our flat, he was warm and conversational; with the exception of the most awkward date proposal ever. "I'm not much of a party person. I'll be running a half marathon earlier that day anyway, and—"

Kat rolled her eyes. "Getting her out of the flat is a challenge. Unless it's to go run."

I grimaced and protested, "That is not true. Well . . ."

She laughed. "It rather is. You spend all day running, or else here on your computer or scribbling in a notebook. What are you doing—writing a book?"

"No." I glared at her, but my cheeks were hot, probably betraying my embarrassment. "I'm trying to prepare for classes."

At that, Kat gaped, turning to her brother, whose eyebrows started to rise before he could school them into a neutral expression.

I sighed. "I don't want to forget everything I've learned, so I'm going over last year's notes. And learning anatomy and that sort of thing. I figure it's best to know as much as possible, so—"

"You are a giant nerd," Kat said, each word coming out slow and deliberate. "And you're just perfect."

"What?"

Kat pushed back her chair and stood. "Great dinner, Adrienne. I'm beat, though. I'm going to sleep." After dumping her dishes in the sink, she grabbed her drink and slipped out into the hallway to the bedrooms. A moment later, her room door shut.

I rolled my eyes. "Has she always been like that?"

Damien smiled politely, but not quickly enough to cover up the distance in his gaze at my question. "She's always been . . . impressionable."

"That wasn't what I meant." I frowned. *Does he think I'm a bad impression on her?*

"No, I know." He folded his napkin and placed it beside his plate in a manner I found oddly formal, even though it was now a soiled piece of paper. "Adrienne, I believe you need to—"

Sounds from the hallway interrupted him, and Kat appeared in the doorway, empty glass in hand, her cool gaze directed at her brother. "Adrienne, when was the last time Elinor went out?"

"Uh . . ."

With a glance at his watch, Damien stood, seeming to read something in his sister's body language that I couldn't decipher. "I can take her. Kat, come with me?"

"I have a headache," she said, with what I interpreted as a stubborn tilt to her jaw.

His eyes narrowed in an older-brother way.

Gathering that he wished to speak to Kat alone, I headed for the door. "I'll take her. Don't worry. I'll be back in ten minutes to clean up." I softened my words with a smile. "Thanks for dropping by, Damien, if I don't see you before I leave."

When I came back from walking Elinor around the block, Damien was gone and Kat was asleep. With a satisfied yawn, Elinor stretched out on her bed and closed her eyes. Someone had cleaned up the kitchen, so I popped open my laptop to begin my nightly revisions. Instead, I ended up searching for locations to visit before school began in the fall.

$$\mathbb{D}$$

The day of the race dawned overcast and gray. When Jake and I arrived at the starting line at the park, hundreds of racers already mingled on the grass, waiting for the start. Some of the more serious participants could be seen warming up down the alleys and side streets, while others stood chatting with each other. I'd already warmed up on the way here, having gotten off the Tube a few stops early and jogged.

Since dogs weren't allowed on the course, Jake would have to take Elinor for the hour and a half while I ran, but he promised that he'd care for her well. "You're sure you can handle her?"

He gave a nervous nod. "Yeah. I don't care for dogs—bad experience as a kid—but I reckon I can hold on to the leash for a couple hours."

Nearby, people chattered with each other, friends and strangers, in typical runner fashion. Running, although a solitary sport, was full of camaraderie and friendships that could be formed quickly over this single interest. I had run many miles with people I never saw outside of those runs, but had also made lasting friendships at a race.

A multitude of merchants scattered the pavement, some trying to sell T-shirts, sunglasses, or playing music. Newspaper vendors had set up along the buildings, but they seemed to be selling more snacks and drinks than anything. Volunteers wearing bright yellow shirts passed out free water bottles and answered people's questions. Police lined the path on the main street, talking to each other, surveying the crowd, or answering racers' questions.

The three of us had found a small bubble of space near a newspaper vendor, where we could gather without being trampled.

As I sipped from my water bottle, Jake pointed to the crowd migrating toward the starting line. Numbers posted along the edge of the line corresponded to the speed of their anticipated pace.

I checked my watch. "Almost time. I'd better get up there and find my spot. I don't want to get trapped behind a thousand people." I offered him Elinor's leash, still hesitant about leaving her with him. "Are you sure?"

He rolled his eyes and snatched the leash from me in good humor. "We'll be fine."

"All right." I crouched and gave Elinor a good-bye pat, then rose and stepped toward the crowd.

"Wait." Jake grabbed my hand with his and pulled me back.

"What is it?"

He stared at our hands, shifting with uncharacteristic nervousness.

"What's wrong?"

"Nothing." Lifting his gaze, he flashed me his grin. "I have something for you."

"Oh?" Warmth spread across my middle and strings seemed to pull my lips up. *A gift? Did that mean he thought of me as more than an assignment?* I bit my lip at the thought.

He dropped my hand, digging in his pocket and emerging with a small black box. "Think of it as . . . a good luck charm. I'm sure it's not what you'd pick. Hopefully you can run with it." He pressed the jewelry box at me, an apologetic shrug accompanying it.

"Run with . . . ?" Against a black, velvet pillow lay a delicate gold pendant with a purple gemstone, held up by an even more delicate gold chain. "Wow . . . Jake, it's beautiful." I glanced up at him, but the necklace pulled my attention back down. "I don't know what to say. You shouldn't have. I really can't—" Biting off my words, I held the box steady in my hands, unsure of its meaning.

"You can." Jake gently took his gift from my hand and removed the necklace, then shoved the box back into his pocket. "Turn around." He unclasped the necklace and held it up between his hands.

My heart thudded as the pendant touched my chest. It had been a long time since I'd received jewelry from someone other than a family member. And something about this felt too fast.

"I saw it and thought immediately of you—did you know your eyes are the color of amethysts?" His fingers brushed my bare skin, tickling the small hairs at the nape of my neck, below my long ponytail.

My lips twitched. "Yes, I did. But thank you. For thinking of me, for . . ." I trailed off, lifting the pendant between my thumb and forefinger and gazing down at it. The pendant formed a figure eight, the round amethyst nestled in the larger bottom, with what looked like a small diamond above it. It was beautiful, something I would have picked out for myself. It was like he had known, and it made my middle spread with warmth—my earlier butterflies soothed and tamed, only to be replaced with lava, rippling and burning and eager to move.

"There," Jake said, his fingers centering the clasp on my neck and brushing his fingers across my shoulders, sending shivers down my spine. "Let me see."

As the warmth in my stomach spread to my cheeks, I turned to face him, releasing the pendant from my fingers and lifting my chin.

"Beautiful."

"It is."

"You are."

My cheeks warmed, and I forced a chuckle. "Come on. I've got to get going." A large clock ticked down the seconds near the start. I was risking my race standing here, and I found myself oddly okay with that. *It's just a prep race anyway.*

He leaned forward, and pressed a kiss onto my cheek. "Good luck," he whispered in my ear. "We'll be at the finish line waiting for you." He stepped back, his fingers squeezing mine. With a lopsided smile, he jerked his chin at the street behind me. "You'd better go."

"Right." His words reminded me why I was standing on this street corner, even why he might have bought me this necklace. The race contestants were moving, migrating toward the start, tightly bunched—I would have to squeeze my way in, and at this rate, it would take a mile or more before I got a good spot.

I hesitated, words on my lips that pressed to be said, but might ruin things between us. And of all things, I'd rather run a bad race than ruin what seemed to be starting between us. So I closed my mouth, cast him a quick smile, gave Elinor a quick pat and told her to stay with Jake, then turned and jogged away to find my spot in the race.

☽

The thump of the gold and amethyst necklace against my skin, warm with symbolism, carried me through the first half of my race at a quick pace. The stitch in my side hardly penetrated my brain, I was so distracted by the little jewels that warmed me and kept me light.

Racers jostled me as we thudded down the paths of London beside the River Thames. Police had barricaded any streets we crossed, so we passed through without difficulty. After several miles, I'd found a good pace partner, and now I followed the older woman in neon green leggings and the race T-shirt. Her pace was just enough to push me, to keep me running when the stitch might have made me question my pace and slack off.

But when she started to slow at mile nine, I passed her, giving her a smile of encouragement. "Keep going!"

With a pained grimace, she bent over her knees as I ran past, shaking her head.

I only wondered when I would hit "the wall."

It wasn't too far behind, I found. My step began to lag, even though I glanced at my watch every few minutes to check my pace and make sure I was on track. Sweat slipped from my brow, and Jake's necklace wasn't enough to lighten my feet anymore. Instead, my hips began to ache, weighed down by heavy legs.

At mile twelve, someone calling my name broke through my concentration. All throughout the race, spectators had been snapping photos, so I wasn't worried or surprised to see cameras pointed at the runners. Some were official race photographers, and no one would recognize me anyway, especially through my sweat-dampened hair.

Except someone had. A bunch of strangers pointed their cameras at me. I had automatically focused on them with a smile, expecting friends. Their cameras clicked furiously, and I was sure I would show up like a deer in a headlight in whichever photo they chose to publish.

"Adrienne! Have you seen the article? What do you have to say?" An industrious reporter jumped the barricade and ran alongside me, holding out something.

Stumbling away from him, I bumped into someone next to me, but without apology, for my gaze focused on the paper he held out. I snatched it, folded so that my face graced the cover. Why hadn't someone told me?

*"*VICTORIA TALBOT ADMITS AFFAIR WITH HOLLYWOOD MOGUL.*"* I stuttered to a halt in the middle of the road, clenching the paper in my hands and scanning it quickly.

"Yes, I had an affair, and soon after learned of my pregnancy. Three months later, at eighteen, I married James Talbot, who adopted Adrienne as his own. It was a mutual decision, but one I can't live with anymore. Holding on to this secret for the past two decades has torn me apart. My daughter deserves to know the truth: her biological father never knew about her."

Catching my breath was impossible. I didn't have tears to shed, not with being so near the end of this race and sweat running down my face.

But my eyes still burned. My legs started to go weak, more from the words on the page than the effort of running twelve miles at race pace.

The words zapped my strength, but fury brought it back full force. I threw the paper at his feet and forced a sneer to my lips. "Don't believe everything you read."

"Did you know?" he yelled after me.

I pumped up the volume on my headphones, lifting a hand in a wave to the media and began to run, faster this time, reveling in the ache in my calves, for it was less than the pain in my heart.

When I passed Kat at the next bend, I hardly noticed that Victoria stood beside her. My mother—the actress—smiling and applauding magisterially as I ran past, striving for the end in some race Victoria had set before me which I would never, ever be able to finish.

Chapter Ten
Dinner Party

HOURS AFTER CROSSING THE FINISH line, I sat alone on the couch in our flat with my knees bent, one hand wrapped around my legs, the other fingering the jeweled pendant on its delicate golden chain. After a quiet, yet packed ride on the Tube to the station nearest my flat, Jake had left me at the door.

Kat had swung by to change, then gone to work almost an hour ago, and I hadn't moved from the couch, where I pondered my mother's appearance at the race. Although I knew what I needed to do, I didn't know how to begin. There were things that had to be said, truths that had to be revealed. She had *promised* to tell me about news releases ahead of time. *Maybe she didn't know?*

I growled at myself and raked a hand through my shower-dampened hair. Why did I still make excuses for her? Head tilted back, I stared at the plastered ceiling. I knew she was a liar; I had known it most of my life. The moment I first remembered had been the morning she disappeared from our lives. "I'm just going out for a drink with the girls," she told me the evening before. "I'll be here when you wake up in the morning." She wasn't. And it was the start of a lifetime of times when she wasn't there. And now, although she was there in body, her heart was, as always, elsewhere.

It had taken me a shamefully long time to recognize the disconnect between body and heart, but now I thought I understood. Her heart had never belonged to me. Whereas other parents loved their children to distraction, sacrificing for them and surrendering everything for their happiness, or spoiling them with gifts when they couldn't be near, my mother hadn't. She didn't. She never would. Any gift she gave came with strings.

I covered my face with my hands, blinking against the bite of my tears and the swirl of questions in my head. Why had she even bothered to come? Had she orchestrated the media presence for this race, too? And *what* was Jake's part in this entire scheme? Had he known? It hadn't seemed like it.

Absently, I rubbed the pendant between my thumb and forefinger. Even if he had been keeping it from me, maybe it had been because he thought it would help me race better if I found out about it afterward. After all, if he'd only found out that morning, nothing could be changed.

Restless at the emotions heating my veins, I rose, wincing when my feet hit the ground. This had been harder than a simple thirteen-mile run, for I had put in more effort and raced faster and harder than ever before. It had been exhausting, but where I might have napped after a hard race before, now I was too angry and distracted to consider it.

At the window, I stared across the street at the grocery store, watching as Londoners walked in and out of the store like ants getting their meals for the evening. My stomach growled. I could go across the street, but the idea repulsed me, especially when I glanced down at our sidewalk to see someone hanging around with a camera in hand.

I didn't have the mental or physical energy to walk down three flights of stairs only to see that damned article staring back at me, not to mention the return trip up three flights of stairs. But any other take away restaurants were too far from here, and I just didn't want to deal with people. I could order in, but that felt like too much work.

Instead, I found myself in the kitchen, staring at the near-empty refrigerator, which held a small jug of milk and a half eaten bag of carrots. I grabbed the carrots and dug in. Dessert would be an energy bar from my emergency stash.

I needed answers. The media hadn't given up—which meant there had to be more than just rumors flying around. But how much more? In all my time spent reading the news reports, I hadn't bothered to search for past articles about my mother. I was either waiting for her to tell me the truth, or expecting the media to find it for me. And yet I couldn't trust the media. I had been so single-minded in my anger against my mother, I was ignoring the fact that I had the ability to do my own research.

I was setting down the bag of carrots when my phone rang, making me jump guiltily before I hobbled into the living room, retrieving it from its position perched upon the couch like a forlorn best friend awaiting my return. I was already sliding my finger across the screen to answer it when it dawned on me who was calling.

I paused, my breath stuck somewhere in my throat, before finally shoving out a terse, "Hello?"

"Adrienne." It was neither question nor greeting, but somewhere in between that I couldn't quite fathom.

"Victoria." Her name slipped from my mouth in a sarcastic return I didn't wish to stop.

"I'd like to take you to dinner. Can you be ready in thirty minutes? It's important."

"Uh . . ." Dinner was the last thing I had expected from her, and although I was starving, dinner with my mother was more likely to diminish my appetite. But this could be the best chance I'd have to ask my questions. "Sure. Half an hour. How well dressed do I need to be?"

I could almost picture her arched brows, as though I shouldn't have to ask the question of her.

"Dress. Heels. Makeup."

"Right. How about jeans and makeup?"

She was silent a moment, perhaps considering my barter. "Dress. No heels. Makeup optional. Thirty minutes," was all she answered with before hanging up.

Twenty-nine minutes later, I was watching out my window as her black Bentley drove up. A few moments later, the familiar buzz filled the apartment. Gathering the last of my energy, and trying to focus my anger into resolve, I picked up my purse and headed down the stairs in my ballet flats. A clamor greeted me, along with Charles's familiar face in a sea of cameras and faces.

I nearly turned around and abandoned Charles to the media. But his eye caught mine, and then someone I vaguely recognized as my mother's bodyguard popped into view, shoving and shouting at the cameras. I hated going back on my word—even to my mother. Not keeping promises was a reflection on me, not her. And this was a chance to ask her my questions, and get some answers. Maybe that was why she'd invited me out now.

With a muttered curse, I pushed open the door and stepped out, regretting my lack of makeup now that cameras were aimed at me. Maybe once I got a glass of wine in me, things would start looking up. It was a good thing we didn't have wine in the flat, or else I would have started already.

The men raced me to the car door, shielding me from the media with their bodies, and I slid into the car, expecting only my mother, yet finding three people.

"Hi, Sydney," I said to the teen dressed in a fluffy pink dress, which seemed to be her chosen style. "Kat, I thought you had to work."

Looking slightly uncomfortable, Kat shrugged. "How are you feeling?" She appeared almost genuine, except for the way her eyes slid from my face too quickly to study her painted nails.

"Tired," I replied. "And a bit sore."

"You did great," Kat said, a little too exuberantly. "Bang on."

"Thanks." I forced a smile as Sydney chimed in with her agreement.

"We decided to treat you for doing so awesomely," Sydney added, her eyes lighting up. She began chattering about the race, and I slipped my attention to the streets out the window as we left the media behind.

Eyes closed, I bit my lip. This was less my celebration and more a party of my mother's making. And, somehow, she had manipulated me into showing up—again. I held in the multitude of words trying to slip off my tongue, sure I would choke, and instead opened my eyes and resumed staring out the window.

$$\mathbb{D}$$

When we pulled up to a sidewalk of the London streets only a few minutes away, I frowned out the window at the orderly, quiet street. Few cars graced the road, parked outside of three and four story flats.

"Where are we?" I asked, confused. "I thought we were going to dinner."

"A dinner party," Victoria corrected, emphasizing "party" in a way that suggested she had said that earlier and I hadn't been listening.

"You said dinner. Not dinner party." I folded my arms. "Why do you insist on doing things like this?"

Victoria sighed, pulled out her lipstick from her clutch and popped open a mirror. "Go ahead, girls. We'll catch up."

The door to the Bentley swung open, which Charles surely stood behind to release us from its confines. Sydney bounded out of the car first, but Kat hesitated, catching my eye. I offered a tight smile.

"Shut the door, Charles," Victoria said calmly to the chauffeur.

With a gracious nod, he eased the car door shut. I folded my hands in my lap and squeezed them tight. Maybe she would finally tell me something worth hearing.

My mother's gaze flickered around the mirror she held up to fixate on me. "Adrienne," she heaved through a sigh, "what do you want from me?"

"The truth," burst from my lips. When she didn't answer, I added, "Why didn't you tell me?" I fought to hide the hurt softening my words, but it removed the sharp edge of my anger. As soon as the words emerged, I wished I hadn't spoken them at all.

Her forehead creased prettily as she pressed her freshly painted lips together. "Tell you what?" Her innocent expression could have fooled a room of actors, but it couldn't fool me.

"Tell me *what*?" A bitter laugh worked free from my chest. "Tell me about the interview! Why did you tell Jake that I wasn't going to be a target in the race today? Why did you let me run alone? Why didn't you tell me there would be another article of lies today? Or how you invited me to a party? Take your pick. Any of them." I knew I wasn't making sense, but I didn't care.

Her violet eyes shot daggers at me before she plastered a smile on her freshly painted red lips. "Darling, I've told you everything I've—"

"Stop it." Anger trembled through my body down to the blister on my foot.

Her eyes widened.

"Stop lying to me. By your own admission, you didn't tell me what you knew to begin with." I raked a hand through my hair and clenched it behind my head tight enough to hurt. "I'm sick of lies. Just tell me the truth."

"The truth?" She leaned in so that we were a mere six inches from each other, and an unexpected gleam of fury sparked in her eyes. "The truth is much more complicated than five minutes in a car can clear up." Throwing her infuriating smile back on her lips, she rapped on the window, and the door swung open.

If she'd physically punched me in the stomach, I doubted I could have hurt any more than I already did.

Victoria slipped from the car, and her heels tapped a gentle rhythm up the black-and-white tile steps.

"Ms. Talbot?" Charles prompted me as I stared after her, blinking rapidly.

"I'm coming." My voice sounded as weary as my body felt as I slid across the seat and emerged. "Where, exactly, are we, Charles?"

His black eyebrows lifted almost imperceptibly. "Mr. Damien Kerr's flat, miss."

Straightening, I faced him, almost eye to eye. "Are you joking? Please be joking." *I don't have the energy for this.*

He frowned, his gray eyes narrowing in confusion. "No, miss." He motioned to the stairs my mother had disappeared up, where a tall black door yawned, already cracked open as though waiting on me. "This is Mr. Kerr's flat."

"Course it is." I filled my lungs with the chilled evening air, shivering at the dampness caressing my bare skin. I ran a hand over the top of my hair again, probing the pins that I'd used to draw back half of it. The rest bounced in waves along my uncovered shoulders as I tried to ignore the goose bumps rising on my flesh. *At least the media didn't follow us here.*

"Do you think if I just stayed outside, they'd notice?"

Charles leaned on the open door, an amused tweak to his lips. "I imagine some might, miss."

Sighing, I lifted my chin to the sky. Clouds obscured the stars, and I wished more than ever for their cheerful twinkles, the reassuring solidity of their existence. The constellations remained even in the cities, if you had the right capabilities to search.

I blinked my eyes dry and lowered my chin in a nod. "All right. I guess I should get in there, then. Unless you know of someone who looks like me who could take my place?"

Charles's smile grew sad. "I'm afraid she's already inside, miss."

"Right." I began up the pavement to the stairs, drawing a deep breath before lifting my foot to press it down on the first step. All my life I had been told I resembled my mother, and I usually hated it, especially now since arriving in London. The probing eyes inside the flat raked over me in judgment, making me question my taste in classic black dresses. Was something else the current "new black"?

My musings had brought me into the stomach of a gorgeous, modern apartment that was nothing like what I had expected to belong to Damien Kerr. *I'm never sure what to expect from him,* I thought a bit sadly. *I never know what to expect from anyone anymore.*

Without guidance, I followed the rise and fall of voices, joined by laughter and the clink of glasses into a large, open expanse of a room. Somewhere in the background, a stereo played Vivaldi's *Four Seasons.*

I paused at the wide archway, admiring the room's light. An adjoining kitchen of marble and white cabinets caught my eye, utterly modern and cliché with low hanging lights over the bar, which was littered with food.

Food. My stomach rumbled and I weaved through the room into the party, ignoring the crowds of faces silently interrogating me, and headed for the platters of food.

"Thank God," I muttered at the sight. Everything from salmon *hors d'oeuvres* to mini scones to unadorned fruits and veggies. The knot in my stomach loosened in relief. Plenty of dairy-free treats to indulge in. The first natural smile of the evening pulled at my lips.

Craving carbs, I impulsively grabbed for a bread roll from the basket at the same time as someone else. My fingers grasped the back of his hand, and I raised my gaze in surprise.

"Hello," the host of the party said with a twitch of his lips. "Didn't expect to see you tonight, Adrienne."

Closing my mouth, I withdrew my hand, but he, standing on the other side of someone dressed in royal purple, grasped the bread bowl and held it toward me. "Yeah, me neither," I muttered, plucking a roll from the basket and holding it in my hands while the purple-clad woman smiled and left. "I shouldn't even eat it, but . . ."

"But you ran an amazing race today," Damien replied, helping himself to a roll and replacing the bowl in the center of the counter. "And it's dairy free."

I raised my gaze from the roll to him. "Really?"

He offered a lopsided grin. "I checked." His certainty put a frown on my lips, but he smiled in reply. "I hired caterers to bake everything dairy free."

Shocked, I blinked. "Wow. That's awesome for people like me. You have other friends with dairy problems?"

He rearranged the bread bowl on the counter. "I like to accommodate the people I care about."

What? Unable to resist the smell of the warm roll any longer, and confused beyond measure, I took a bite. My taste buds groaned as warmth spread across my tongue, an explosion of yeast and doughy goodness that made my mouth ache with longing for another bite. My eyes widened. "Oh my gosh. This is the best bread I've had in a long time."

Smiling, he nodded. "It ought to be. I hired the best caterer in the city." He leaned toward me and said in a stage whisper, "Wait until dessert. Speaking of which . . ." He caught the eye of someone and nodded. Almost immediately, caterers swept in and began to clear the counter. "Oh, don't throw anything out," he warned them. "Late arrivals might want seconds."

A loud burst of laughter cracked the air, and we both searched it out with our eyes. Across the living room, Sydney chatted with a lanky teenage boy, her smile turned goofy at the edges for him. *At least someone was having a good time.* As a caterer made to remove the bread, I snatched another roll from the basket. She paused for me with a smile.

"Adrienne, before I lose my chance," he began quietly, "I owe you an apology for the way I asked you to dinner."

His voice was so low and close to me that I knew no one but I could hear. As I chewed another bite of bread, I nodded to show that I'd heard him, but fixed him with a wary look. So much had happened since that moment, his apology almost seemed too late to matter.

"Well, thanks, but—" I stared across the room at Sydney. *Where had Victoria gone?*

"That's not an apology," he said.

Chapter Eleven
Charming Apology

"IT'S NOT AN APOLOGY?" I asked, frowning at him.

"Not at all. I said I owed you one."

A twinkle deep in his eyes betrayed his act, and understanding washed over me. I wasn't as skilled in hiding my emotions, though, and a smile pulled at my lips. "You're right. That's not an apology. At least, not a good one. Not even an acceptable one."

Indignant, he puffed out his chest like a peacock, tugging a chuckle from me.

"I am a master of apologies."

With a shrug of one shoulder, I schooled my face into dismissal. "Prove it."

His face wiped clean in seconds with the professionalism of a true actor; the world around us seemed to disappear to him. He faced me, took my empty left hand in his and enclosed it with the warmth of his own. I couldn't pull away even if I'd wanted to. "Adrienne." His solemn tone stilled the amusement in my veins, replacing it with something else, something I couldn't quite name. "I apologize for my behavior and my word choice. It was simply inexcusable, and you have every right to be angry with me. But since I'm certain we'll be seeing more of each other with your mother's approaching nuptials, I couldn't let this go any longer without issuing a most solemn apology to you. Could you possibly forgive me?" His eyes were round, blue sapphires, framed by lashes so black a jeweler could have paired them with the blackest ebony.

Where did that come from? I snapped shut my gaping mouth, dropping my gaze to his hand, still holding mine, which tingled from his touch. His thumb held the fleshy part of my outer palm, his index finger supporting my wrist in such a way I was sure he felt my pulse racing. "Uh . . . yeah." I nearly rolled my eyes with the lack of eloquence in my reply. "I mean, I'll have to consider it, but . . . you know. Sure. You're forgiven."

His face lit up with a mischievous grin, making me wonder how I could have thought him cold and aloof before. "Excellent. Can I get you a glass of wine? Red? White?"

Still smiling, I held up my water. "I'm fine with this right now."

"Oh. Of course." His face wrinkled in disappointment. "How about a plate? And I'll show you around?"

In the living room, beautiful couples chatted, laughed, and generally appeared nothing but comfortable in this environment. I nodded. *Anywhere but here.*

"Great. Here's a plate, load it up. Trust me, everything is dairy free." He smiled again, heating me from the midsection out. Shaking my head at his congenial attitude, I reminded myself as I grabbed tea sandwiches and scones—*dairy free scones?*—that he had only truly been cold and aloof at my mother's engagement party.

Damien reappeared at my side, another bottle of water in his hand, this one half full. I expected another amused smile and for him to poke fun at my gigantic plate of food, but his brow knitted, concerned. "Is that enough? I hear you were expecting dinner." He seemed to be passing judgment on someone else, not on my plate or my expectations.

Wryly, I nodded. "I think I'll survive. But you know, I often seem to be out of the loop."

"Oh?" He motioned me toward an exit to the kitchen I hadn't noticed before, instead of through the living room I'd walked in.

I sighed and walked past him. "When it comes to my mother, yes."

"Oh." His tone betrayed how he had been there before. "That's difficult."

"Experience that yourself?" The idea amused me for some reason, and I glanced behind me to judge his reaction.

His face had darkened, closing in upon itself as he hesitated. "Kat would often hide things from me." His tone darkened to the color of his charcoal suit. "For good reason, too."

"You know, she *just* told me about you being her brother." To my surprise, my words came out far more annoyed than I anticipated.

His answering chuckle was wry.

We reached the second floor landing, where voices issued from somewhere around the corner; the party obviously continued here.

"Yes. I know. I try to respect her privacy." He trailed off, and when I stopped, he didn't push past me; instead a conflicted tremor crossed his face.

"She's stubborn," I supplied, desiring suddenly to make that expression go away and recapture the easy companionship we'd had downstairs.

Looking up, he seemed to realize he was being dark, and gave a relaxed smile.

Someone emerged from the living room and headed for the stairs, passing us with a bright, "Hey, mate!"

With a cucumber sandwich stuffed into my mouth, I merely tried to chew with my mouth closed as he included me in his greeting with a nod.

"Hiya, Tom," Damien answered and headed up the next set of stairs. "Yes, she's stubborn—God love her."

My muscles ached as he led us up this flight of stairs, calves protesting and thighs screaming, but the worst was the blister under my left arch today. It had to be time to replace my shoes, although it felt like I was losing a friend to do so. After all, they'd stuck with me for the past 400 miles or so.

We were leaving the sounds of the party below—music faded, voices distanced themselves, laughter became an echo. Stress slid from my shoulders as we walked. Somehow Damien had known exactly what I needed tonight.

"It's not much farther," he said. "Just a few more steps up."

"Lots of stairs in this place," I replied. "I thought I ran my race today."

He laughed, surprising me with how easy and effortless it was. His earlier shadow was gone. "Need a hand?"

"The railing'll do," I answered, one hand on the center railing, the other holding my heavy plate. "But if I can't set this plate down soon, I'll have to stop mid-flight just to lighten it."

His grin, wide and disarming, forced me to grin in response. "I can help."

"Help me eat? Or help me carry it?"

"Both, probably. I've only eaten a roll since the party started." He glanced at his watch. "Two hours ago."

With a roll of my eyes, I continued up the flight of steps. "I'll keep it to myself then."

The stairs we climbed were white with inlaid cherry wood, with a railing of cherry wood inlaid with white marble to match. Cool to the touch, it made the house around me rise up like a statue, the shimmering wallpaper and its hundreds of gray fleurs-de-lis staring down at us. A chandelier hovered over the brief space between the spiraling banister, illuminating all three floors. As we neared the top of the house, I could have reached out and touched the lights.

"Almost there," he promised, interrupting my thoughts. "I figured we'll start at the top and work our way down."

"What?" I had forgotten why we were even walking up the stairs by this point, distracted by my soreness, my hunger, Damien's changed personality, and the house itself.

He smiled. "I'll let you eat, too, if you want."

My stomach roared. "Mmm. That might be nice."

Our final steps led us into the top floor, where a small desk squatted beside the banister. Damien motioned to it. "Feel free to sit and eat, if you like." He set down the water bottle he'd tucked under his arm, and I sank into the chair he pulled out for me. He crossed the large room and turned on the standing lamp beside one of a pair of built-in bookcases. This level was warmer than the ones below, with richer colors, almost as though Damien had started redecorating and begun here. Its warmth was as nice as a pair of strong arms around me.

Was this how Damien spent his time in London? I tried to read the titles of the books from here, but most of the print was too small. Except for one book sitting beside a leather armchair, which I read with surprise.

"Are you really reading that? Or is it just for show?" I teased him.

He followed my gaze and laughed, crossing the room to pick it up. He stared down at the cover of *Pride and Prejudice* for a moment, then flipped the edge of the pages between his fingers. It was a well-read copy; I would award him that, at least. It looked as though someone had studied it thoroughly, dog earing the pages along with multiple highlights and copious notes in the margin.

"Couldn't afford a new copy? Or studying for a test?" I questioned, jabbing a baby carrot at his hands.

"No. Well, sort of." He shrugged and scrutinized a heavily marked page. "I've read it several times recently—but it's time for me to start learning my lines."

"Lines?"

He lifted his gaze, looking over the pages to me. "I'm an actor, remember?"

"Yes, but—is there a remake in the works?"

"Isn't there always?" He cocked an eyebrow.

"True." I laughed dryly. "Very true." I crunched down on the carrot, thoughtful. "And what role do you have?" Somehow I knew the answer before he gave it.

He shrugged and tossed the book down. "Darcy."

"What else?" I waved my carrot in the air. "Of course. Millions of fans wouldn't want to see you as anyone else."

His mouth twitched into a lopsided smirk. "I actually auditioned for Bingley, but the casting director didn't think I fit."

"Bingley?" I sat back and peered at him. "I don't see that."

"Well . . . the casting director didn't either. He said I wasn't as transparent as Bingley was." His lips fell slightly, but then he seemed to brush off the comment and his wry grin returned. "He said I had too much to hide, and Bingley had to be open."

My empty hand sank into my lap as I chewed the rest of the carrot and considered how to respond. "You're not open . . . but the problem I have with Darcy is that he's a bit of a secret keeper."

"You don't like secrets?" Damien appeared at ease under my gaze, resting a hand on the top of his leather armchair.

"No." I brushed imaginary crumbs off my lap. "Sometimes I think the world would be a better place if there were no secrets."

He dropped his gaze to his hands, deep thoughtfulness in the lines around his eyes. "Aren't you a part of some secrets? Surely you have one? Even for surprises?"

"I try not to, honestly." I shrugged, attempting a devil-may-care attitude, but my heart twanged at the events of the past few weeks. "The closest thing that comes to mind right now is my mother's scandal." I bit especially hard on a new carrot, satisfied at the crack of its flesh between my teeth. "Maybe an embarrassing event in my past that I don't offer up.

You know."

As I turned my plate to better reach the other side, his gaze slid down to his well-worn copy of Austen's *magnum opus*. "It'd be nice to be at that point . . . where my only secrets were ones I had to worry about."

"You make a habit of keeping other people's secrets then?" The idea brought me to thinking of how little I'd seen him in the news. I'd been more of a story in London than he had. I shook my head. Maybe it just felt that way. After all, I only searched for my name or Victoria's in the headlines.

Damien flipped the pages of his book as though it was his script and he was searching for the right lines, but couldn't find them. "I suppose you could say that." A pained expression sparked in his eyes. "Not by choice, though."

Disappointment welled up in me for no explainable reason, and I tried to force it away. Honesty seemed like such a forgotten, undervalued trait these days. I nudged my plate away, ignoring the scone calling to me.

"Speaking of secrets . . ." Damien's voice captured my attention again. "When are you going up for the wedding?"

"Going up?" With my echo of his words, I felt a secret about to split open, sure to be unpleasant inside. The wedding wasn't for two months yet; I hadn't even considered locations or travel. "Where?"

"To Chadwick Manor. Edmund's estate?" Damien tossed his book aside and focused on me. "It's where the wedding will be held in April."

"They aren't having a London wedding? I would have thought they'd wait until summer for better weather."

He lifted one shoulder in a shrug. "It's April sixteenth."

He already knows the date. I reached for the scone. Its lure distracted me for a moment, but not enough to bite. This was just one more thing she hadn't told me. "I had no idea. I don't even know if I'm invited, really. Where is it?"

"In Yorkshire."

"Mmm." I dabbed my mouth with my napkin. "York is beautiful."

"It is. I grew up there."

"In York?"

"Nearby. Little further up, on the sea."

I tilted my head at him. The image of him riding a horse on a rocky shore, like a gentleman—like Darcy—danced before me. A small smile tugged at my lips, which he reciprocated without knowing why.

"What is it?" he asked after a moment where neither of us spoke. "Is that funny?"

"No, not really. Just . . . suits you, somehow."

"Does it? I've always been told that London doesn't suit me, but no one's ever been able to tell me where does suit me."

I chuckled and broke off a piece of the scone, holding it in my fingers in front of my lips before trying it. It felt wrong to put it in my mouth, as though my body had associated scones with a breakout of hives. I shook the thought away, and popped it in my mouth. I had to close my eyes; the explosion of flavors was so exquisite. "Oh, that's good," I muttered after swallowing.

When I opened my eyes, Damien was grinning at me, a grin so unlike Jake's quick, wide mouthed, teeth-flashing grin, that I found myself examining it instead of reacting. And as I watched, I realized why it was so different. It lingered. It was true amusement, nothing false or flitting, but true enjoyment of the moment, the situation. It felt like forever since I'd seen true amusement on someone's face.

"What?" he asked.

Shaking my head, I ripped my gaze away. "Where did you say you got this caterer? Do they have a restaurant?"

He shook his head. "No, I'm afraid not. Just a thriving catering business."

"Shame," I said around my final mouthful of scone. "I can't think of an excuse to hire them."

Damien laughed and set the book down back where it had been when we'd entered. "I'll hire them for my next party, if you'll come."

"Deal," I said, too quickly. My cheeks flamed. *Way to sound desperate.* "Especially if it's post-marathon."

"Which marathon?"

"Damien?" A voice called up the stairs, vaguely recognizable as Kat, and near enough to be on the bottom of the steps. "You up there?"

"Yes." He moved to the top of the stairs, grimacing down at his watch.

"People are starting to ask where you've run off to. And is Adrienne up there with you? I haven't seen her."

Damien glanced at me. "Yes."

There was a beat of silence, then, "Okay. Well . . . I may leave early."

A shift in Damien's weight was all that betrayed any reaction. "Right. We'll be down shortly. I'm just giving her a tour."

"Maybe I'll come up there then?"

"Yeah, of course." He motioned down the stairs, and her heels clicked on the wood as she began to climb up.

I stood from the desk and pushed in the chair just as Kat appeared before Damien. He touched her gently on the elbow, asking her if she was all right without saying a word. Instead of answering, she turned to me.

"Sorry to . . . interrupt." Her smile didn't reach her eyes.

Rolling my eyes, I retrieved my plate. "You didn't."

A flush crept up my neck, though. I'd forgotten about the tour. Really, Damien had just given me a private place to stuff my face. And, oddly, I was okay with that.

Kat carried a fresh glass of wine across the room to stand before the largest window, as big as the two bookcases which framed it.

Standing a few feet behind her, I followed her gaze to the view I had managed to ignore. The quiet street outside hinted nothing at the activity inside here. Not only the raucous party downstairs, but the secrets creating tension between Damien, me, my mother, Kat. . . Outside was picturesque London: quiet, still, beautiful. The buildings had been there since who knew when. And they had survived. Survived the changes of the street, the changes of the world around them. Survivors. Stronger for the changes, perhaps. For what had been weakened by age had been rebuilt by engineers. Probably invisible to the untrained eye, but the building had to have been reinforced, strengthened inside, like Damien's had been. Changed inside, but unchanged outside.

"Which is the one with the performer?" Kat asked, looking down both sides of the street as she asked.

"Who?" I asked, craning to see more clearly out the window.

Damien stepped over beside me, standing behind Kat to point to a tall, red-and-white brick building, singling out a flat with a baby blue door. "That one."

"Who lives there?" I prompted when neither explained.

"An interesting bloke," Damien answered, speaking to me from inches away. "He only comes out at night, after dark, wearing a black cape."

I shifted to see the flat better, brushing his shoulder. "Really?" Stories like these made cities fascinating. I could be in the house next door to the most famous person in the world and never know it.

Kat stared down at the street, silent as though she didn't hear our conversation.

"Yes. He must have some amount of money to live here," Damien said, his breath caressing my cheek, "but I think he must be a street performer . . . None of them make that much. Maybe he's an author." He seemed almost to be musing aloud, lost in a world of supposition.

I laughed. "Because they make so much money."

With a grin, he faced me, then blinked, seemingly stunned by how close we were. He held my gaze a moment before his eyes flicked to Kat and he stepped back, replacing distance between us as easily as though we were nothing but actors in a scene.

"I'd better get back to the party. I've been neglecting my hosting duties long enough, I fear." He touched Kat's elbow with his fingertips, but she didn't respond. "I need to make sure no one from the gutters has sneaked in, you know?"

I chuckled, but no one else did. Only then did I realize there was too much tension in his words for it to be a genuine joke.

He motioned toward the stairs. "Feel free to stay here with Kat, if you like. But do help yourself to dessert—if there's any left. I hear the coconut milk crème brûlée is to die for."

A pang of something like hurt stole my smile as he walked downstairs, tour forgotten.

Chapter Twelve
Whisky Night

"ADRIENNE."

I SNAPPED AWAKE WITH a start, blinking up into Damien's amused, dark blue eyes from my perch on his couch. The party had dimmed around me, and few guests remained. His fingertips lingered on my shoulder where he'd touched me to wake me.

"Sorry." I rubbed my eyes. I had rested my head for just a moment.

"No worries," he said. "But Kat's ready to go, and Charles is waiting for you."

I leaned forward, putting my elbows on my knees and drawing my hands over my face, trying to wake up. When I stared at the floor, I found myself looking at Damien's loafers. "Where's my mother?"

"She left about an hour ago."

When I looked up, Damien had an apologetic grimace on his face.

"With Edmund."

"He was here?" My voice crackled as I asked, reluctant to be used after such little sleep.

He shrugged. "Stopped by."

"Ready?" Kat's voice asked from a short ways away.

Damien's shoes scuffed the ground. I raked my hands through my hair and stood, holding back a yawn.

"Yeah. Let's go." *So much for asking my mother about anything tonight.*

"Evening, ladies," Charles greeted us.

"Hello again, Charles," I said with a tired smile.

He nodded in reply and shut the door after us.

The skies were dark, although it was already early morning when we arrived at our flat. Although yawns interspersed my slow steps, I changed clothes and walked Elinor to the park. While I let her run loose around the bench on an empty expanse of grass, I pulled out my phone and sank down onto a bench.

My finger played over my father's number. Our last phone conversation had been weeks ago. We'd been playing phone tag since then, and I missed him. And I'd never asked him about the scandal. Every time I'd considered it, my courage had failed me.

Scratching a stuck on bit of something off the screen of my phone, I debated with myself whether it was the right time to call. I shouldn't have even been questioning it. At this point, I would have answered his call if it woke me from a dead sleep, and he would do the same. Still, I hesitated. It was like something had already changed between us with all these threats of my dad not being my biological father.

Elinor sniffed around the lawn, then collapsed and rolled, wiggling her spine into the dirt and grass.

The real reason I hadn't tried to call more was simply that I was avoiding it. I didn't want my truthful father to tell me the truth. I wanted the truth so desperately, and yet I feared it. My mother's words echoed in my head, *I'll tell you what you need to know, when you need to know it.* She would never tell me anything; I'd have to find out myself.

I touched my finger to my father's number. I needed the truth, couldn't continue without it. And she would tell me nothing. It was time to start finding out for myself.

He answered after three rings, sounding as though he was stifling a yawn of his own. "H-hello?"

"Dad." My voice broke.

"Adrienne!" His smile lit up his voice. "How's it going, kid? I thought you'd forgotten me."

"I could never forget you." Leaning back on the bench, I raked a hand through my loose hair, digging at a snag before answering. "But, it's all right, I guess."

"Uh-oh." He laughed. "What's up? The race not go as well as it seemed?" There was a sense of wry bitterness in his voice, as though he had been in my place before.

"Dad . . ." I trailed off, unable to say the words.

When I said no more, Dad heaved a heavy sigh. "She's said more to the media, hasn't she? Making your life hell, isn't she?"

A tear beaded in the inner corner of my eye beside my nose, and I sniffed, looking away as though Dad stood in front of me and something elsewhere would give me strength before his sympathy. "Yeah." I tried to make my voice strong, but even that word came out weak and teary.

"Oh, hon. I'm sorry," he whispered.

If I had been standing in front of him, he would have pulled me into his arms and held me tight. He'd never been afraid to hug or kiss or show emotion. My dad, the gentle giant, the elected official, the fiercely loyal father. He was who I got my loyalty from. And now I was to believe that he might not be my father after all? That was so difficult to believe . . . impossible with my father's integrity to think I'd believed a lie all my life.

"Why does she do this?" I whispered back. "It's like she hurts people on purpose."

His breath rattled the line between us. "I know, hon."

"Why? I don't—" I sniffed, dashing away the tear as it fell, "—I don't understand her. Not at all. I just—I just want the truth from her, and she refuses to tell me anything."

"Ah, well . . ." Dad hesitated. "The truth is a bit of a complicated subject these days."

My heart thumped once and went still. "What does that mean?"

"Adrienne . . . you've been around politics all your life. What has that taught you about truth?"

"I . . ." I let out my breath, turning my free hand up in confusion. "I don't know, Dad. That you never get the entire story? Especially not from the media?"

"Well, that's one thing, yeah. But what does that say about truth?" He waited several heartbeats for me to respond, but I had nothing to add. While I stared across the park to a young mother pushing her infant in a stroller, my father continued in a pained tone, "Perhaps that there are several versions of it."

I pressed my lips together into a thin line, inhaling through my nose and holding it again. "And which version can you give me?"

"Oh, Addy." The pain in his voice had intensified. "Sweetie, I wish I knew the true story. But all I know is what your mother told me."

My breath hitched in my throat, along with something half sob and half laugh. "And what might that be?"

"I'm your dad, Adrienne. Through and through."

I inhaled a quick, shaky breath and let it out even quicker. "But whose truth is that?" I whispered.

"Mine, sweetheart. It's the truest story I know. No test result or Hollywood scandal is ever going to change that."

Elinor licked my hand, and I absently scratched her head.

"Did you . . ." I stared into Elinor's amber eyes as I spoke. "Did you ever ask her? Whether that was the real truth?"

He drew a breath as though I had stabbed him. "No."

"Why not?" My question slipped out without my permission.

He made a slight sucking sound with his lips, as though he let his bottom lip slide out of his teeth, as I had so often seen and heard him do. "Because it wouldn't have mattered to me whether her truth, my truth, and *the* truth were all the same. I learned long ago to never ask for something I wanted from her. But it doesn't matter. You're still my daughter. And nothing will change that."

Although I appreciated his sentiment, his words did nothing to quench the fire for truth inside me.

꩜

Elinor's breath, warm and clammy, began to nudge life into my fingers and my heart. A sort of fog had enveloped me after my conversation with Dad, one that I only began to come out of as I unlocked the front door to my flat.

Something cold dripped on me; I looked up into a waterfall. The skies had split open in my walk home, dumping water upon the earth and filling the gutters. It wasn't a little English sprinkle, but a deluge.

I hardly noticed that there were people approaching me, and it was at the last moment that I realized each held a camera or phone and called my name. "A comment?" "Just a few questions?" They clamored around me.

Elinor snapped her jaws when a man came too close, and he stepped back, alarm crossing his features. I tightened my grip on her leash and hauled her through the door, slamming it in the face of those behind us as she barked a deep warning.

Kat was asleep when we reentered the flat, so I grabbed a towel from the linen closet and dried Elinor before I allowed her to trot off to lap up water and curl up in her bed. Curiosity ate at me, so even though I shivered from cold, I grabbed my phone and opened the Internet browser. I put my name in the search box and waited, holding my breath, for the results. But nothing new came up. "Nothing?" I scowled at my phone for a minute, then set it in its spot beside the bed.

After a lightning fast shower, I sat on my bed with my laptop booting up, my thoughts as oddly still as my body.

I focused on the only thing that would distract me from my rapidly uncontrollable life. Both hands on the keyboard, cursor blinking, I had no idea what to type.

"Victoria Talbot—no, Richie?" I muttered to the computer as if it could have an opinion.

Elinor's eyes opened at my words, but seeing nothing unusual, she closed them again.

Starting with just her maiden name, I slogged through pages and pages of movie releases, work histories, and a million photos.

I double blinked at a picture—was that her or me? In some, it was hard to tell. Especially since, with the scandal, photos of me in connection with her had popped up like an Alaskan wildfire spreading across acres of wilderness. Only it wasn't acres of wilderness, it was the Internet, and it wasn't fire, it was me. Apparently, I was far from anonymous these days.

It all made me itch to get out of London, away from a big city with prying eyes. A small town had to be better—or better yet, a large manor. Like Edmund's . . .

I reached for my phone, scrolling through my contacts before coming across the one I wanted.

A familiar voice answered, and I cleared my throat. "Hi, Edmund. It's Adrienne."

"Adrienne, nice to hear from you. To what do I owe this pleasure?"

"Do you have a minute to talk?"

"A few, if that's all it'll take."

"Yes. I just . . ." I took a fortifying breath. "I was talking to Damien the other night at his party . . ."

"Oh, yes, you were there?"

"Yes. Weren't you?"

"Just for a few moments. You were saying?"

"Right. Well, Damien mentioned something about the wedding party going up north?"

"Oh, yes. The great migration."

I chuckled. "Is that what you call it?"

He echoed my chuckle with one of his own. "Yes, usually. My family would always go north at the start of summer, get out of the London heat. We'd spend the rest of the year in London."

"I see. Well . . . I was just wondering . . . my mother hadn't mentioned it." I clicked on an article link online. "And . . ."

"And what, dear?"

"Oh, well, I just wondered if I was invited?"

"*If* you were invited?" There was a pause of two heartbeats. "Well, of course you're invited, dear. Didn't Victoria issue the invitation?"

"I'm afraid not . . ."

"Oh, well, I'll have it arranged. You'll need a car, of course. Will you be all right driving up with your mother? Or should I arrange for separate cars?"

"Oh, whatever works. I do have my dog though—Victoria doesn't exactly care for her."

Edmund hmmmed. "Well, I'll discuss it with her and figure something out. Is that all you needed, dear? I really must run."

"Yes, it is. Thanks, Edmund."

I hung up the phone, feeling a bit like I had just won a battle. Not the war—never the war. For winning a battle against Victoria Talbot was the closest anyone ever came to winning the war against her.

☽

"You called Edmund?" Kat's voice lowered with admiration later that night when I told her what I'd done. "Impressive."

"Well, my mother won't tell me anything, but I might as well stick close and make her miserable by my asking. Maybe she'll cave one day." I shrugged and grimaced. "Maybe sooner than later. And this way, I get out of London. I'm a little tired of being the freak show."

"You know she left London this morning."

"What?"

"Yeah. Off to meet with some Hollywood chap before she starts her next film." Kat grabbed a bottle of painkillers on the counter.

Hand to my temple, I rolled my neck so that it cracked. "When is that?"

Kat shook her head with a wince as she poured herself a tall glass of orange juice. "Not sure exactly. After the wedding at the manor. She'll probably squeeze in a honeymoon before she goes, too."

"You should come up to the manor," I told her. "It'd be nice to have a friendly face."

She made a face as though she had just brushed her teeth and the orange juice was too sweet. "You'll have Damien. And Jake." She swished the juice around in her glass. "I'm sure he'll be around." Bitterness coated her words.

"What is it with you and Jake?" I shook my head slowly at her. "Tell me. Do you like him?"

"No." She answered sharply, voice chilling me. Stooping, Kat flipped a sweater hanging over the back of the couch onto the chair so that she could sit down in its place. "We used to date," she said brusquely.

"You and Jake?" Her answer, for some reason, surprised me more than it should have. I should have suspected it, and yet I hadn't. But they both loved to laugh, to enjoy life, to bend the rules.

She laughed bitterly. "Yeah. Surprising, isn't it?" A hand raked through her hair, leaving strands of hot pink candy canes sticking up in the air. "I mean, and to think I wanted to marry him . . ."

"Uh . . ." I sank down in the chair beside her. "Why don't you start at the beginning?"

"Oh, it's such a long story." She swirled the dregs of her orange juice around in her cup. "Did you know I was adopted?"

"What? No." I gaped at her. "Wait, is *that* why your name is Townsend?" She didn't look much like Damien, it was true. But part of that was her hair, dyed bright pink. "You lied to me?"

She winced visibly. "Sorry 'bout that. Just a minute." Acting as though what she'd said was no big deal, Kat tossed back the rest of her drink, stood, and disappeared into the kitchen. I heard the clinking of glasses, then she reappeared in the doorway.

At the sight of her juggling a near full bottle of whisky and two tumblers with a maniacal glint in her eyes, I almost laughed. "Really?"

"Oh, trust me, we'll be needing it." She clinked the glasses upon the table and poured a generous two inches in each. Offering one to me, she sank back into the worn couch and propped her stockinged feet up on the table, wiggling her toes. "Good thing I'm not working tonight."

"Yeah? Tired of the grind?" My words emerged grumpy. Why had she lied? There was no need to be ashamed about being adopted.

"You have no idea." A deep drink of the amber liquid disappeared down her throat without a wince. "It's a shame to waste good whisky . . ." She peered into the glass. "That's why I brought out the cheap stuff."

"Is that all I'm worth to you?"

"No." Kat shook her head, the darkness drawing her features in upon themselves. "It's all this story is worth, though." Instead of lapsing into her tale, she lifted the remote and turned on the TV. She flipped through the channels in silence for a minute. "Bottoms up," she said, glancing at me as I held the untouched drink in my hand. "Don't make me drink alone."

The whisky smelled of alcohol with just a hint of sweetness. It was some brand I'd never heard of, with a tan label on a tall, slender bottle. Drinking was never something I'd gotten into, not in college, and definitely not high school. The most I'd ever drunk in one evening was at my mother's engagement party. And I'd never, ever been drunk.

I lifted my tumbler and tilted it so the liquid touched my lips. It burned, and I winced at the slight touch.

After swallowing another gulp with practiced ease, Kat laughed. "Come on. Take a proper drink."

"How can you drink this? It's like rubbing alcohol."

Grinning, she shrugged. "It's not the best—but it's not the worst." She lifted it and considered her inch of liquid, squinting through it to the TV beyond. Glass perched on the arm of the couch, she changed the channel again. "There's nothing on."

"Usually isn't." I held my breath and took a larger drink, swallowing before I could change my mind.

As the whisky disappeared, we watched a reality TV show filled with girl drama. As Kat refilled our glasses for the second time, I tried to cover up my glass with my hand, but she pushed it aside with a laugh. "Oh, no. We're in for the long haul tonight."

"You aren't working tomorrow morning, are you?"

Kat frowned. "Morning? The pub doesn't open until eleven."

"Right. Eleven." I sat back, my third glass of whisky in my hand, determined to nurse this one for the rest of the night.

Chapter Thirteen
Memories, Words & Drink

HOURS LATER, WE HAD WATCHED a few mindless, trashy shows that failed to distract us. My head was light on my shoulders, but I tipped my drink back anyway, thankful for the numbness in my throat. Bleary eyed, I frowned at my glass. "Why are we drinking again?"

"Mmm. Men."

"Ah. Right. Specifically two men, right?" Even I caught the slur of my words, and I put down the glass, pushing it away from me.

"Jake and Bryan. That was his name, right?" Kat muted the TV and set her glass down on her thigh, rotating it in a circle as she slouched on the couch beside me.

"Yeah." I sighed. "That is his name." I made sure to enunciate each word carefully, surprised by how much effort it took.

"Hmm. What happened there?" Kat asked languidly, bringing up the subject we'd been drinking around all night.

While I squinted into the amber liquid of my glass, memories hurtled themselves against the walls around my heart. I had stopped my brain from remembering them for the past three years, determined to move on, to act like it had never happened. *Tell no one.*

"You never even told your sisters, did you?" she asked without looking at me.

"No." I shook my head. "I couldn't bring myself to tell anyone."

"Is that why you stopped talking to me?" She tilted her head away from me and shot me an oblique look, her hazel eyes wide and concerned. "Was it that bad?"

"So bad I doubt you'll believe me." I leaned forward, setting my glass down on the table with a clink. My stomach flipped: front, back, back, front. Knotting, unknotting, clenching, unclenching.

"I'll believe you." Kat's voice was quiet but determined, only the barest hint of a slur present. "After all, I know you don't lie. Not even to tell me you like my hair."

The smallest scoff of amusement squeezed out from my nostrils.

"What happened?"

Cars honked outside; a motorcycle revved somewhere. A breeze blew in through the open window, pushing the curtains aside with rough hands. A scent of fresh, spring air lifted my chest, giving me the strength to answer Kat's question.

"I came here, to London, with Bryan, when I was a freshman in college. He was a junior. He . . . wanted to meet my mom. And, I thought it was time; we'd dated long enough. I had always wanted him to meet her before we got engaged or something." I picked up the glass again and swigged a too-large gulp, gritting my teeth at the taste. "I thought we'd probably be engaged in the next few months—we'd already been talking about it. And probably married before med school. I mean, I didn't want to be one of those couples that dated forever and never got married, afraid of commitment or something."

I ran my finger over the rim of the glass, wiping away a drop of whisky. It didn't matter that we were still young—I was just eighteen, already halfway through my first year at college, and Bryan twenty when we spent Spring Break in London. I wet my lips with my tongue; they felt numb, strangely hard to control. I knew it was the effect of the alcohol, but I imagined that they were reluctant to speak these words, too.

Kat remained silent and still beside me, as if she knew I needed nothing but her presence now that the dam had fractured.

"So we came to London. We stayed with my mother." My voice had dropped to a whisper, scratchy and low as though I were suffering from a cold. "We stayed with her for almost a week; it was going great, they'd really hit it off. I had almost convinced myself that he'd propose before we left London. I had dropped hints, you know? London was the perfect place to get engaged, I told him. It would forever be a great story to tell." I scoffed. "My mother was charming; Bryan loved her—even more than he loved my dad. And Bryan adored Dad. He wanted to go into politics like Dad, and so it was like we were a match made in heaven. But . . ."

Kat shifted beside me. She refilled my glass, then hers.

"Bryan had a weakness for beautiful women." The burning began to start in my throat, this time not because of what I drank, but brought on by my words. "And . . ."

Could I say it? Dare I say it? Dare I admit out loud what I had witnessed three years ago? I had promised to take that secret to my grave, and I had done a great job at that so far. But it had been eating at me, destroying me from the inside out. Kat wouldn't judge me—and besides, it wasn't my fault, but his. I knew that, just as I knew that anyone who cheated couldn't blame anyone but themselves. I knew it, and yet I still couldn't quite believe it to be true.

"Beautiful women? Or *a* beautiful woman?" Kat's soft, probing words suggested she was following my story better than I could tell it.

My head nodded like my ponytail during a run, limpid and unsteady. "A beautiful woman." Something wet touched my cheeks. "A woman who saw him as someone to capture, to control. A woman who kissed her daughter's boyfriend. And destroyed her daughter in the process." My voice dried up. It may have been just a kiss—I didn't know if it had gone further. But one kiss was enough to ruin the already tenuous relationship I had with my mother.

Kat's hand rested on my knee, tightening so much at my words that it threatened to cut off the circulation and leave bruises. I barely felt it.

"No one would blame you for walking away, Adrienne," Kat murmured. "No one would blame you for never speaking to her again, least of all me."

Tears blurred my vision.

"No one would judge you. You don't have to go to her wedding, you don't have to be the 'good daughter' for once."

Biting my lip and squeezing my eyes shut, I nodded, but the idea of failing my duties, as well as everybody's expectations, was too much. No one knew why I acted like this with her. *Why do you care what others might think when you know the truth?* a little voice in my head asked me.

In all these years of mentally talking through this, of thinking of the words to express it in, of wondering how I might finally confess the truth to another living soul, whether friend, family, or counselor, I had never thought it would come out quite so blatant, quite so . . . honest. My mother had destroyed me. Inside out, destruction.

"Why didn't you tell anyone?" There was no judgment in her words. There was the merest curiosity, a distant thought that seemed half formed.

"I—I couldn't." It was only then I realized how truthful that statement was. Had I tried before, I wouldn't have been able to form the words. Only by seeing my mother again, by living in the shadow of her scandals, could I realize how much I needed to say them, how much this secret had changed me. And grief—a grief I had never before allowed myself to feel —overwhelmed me. I dropped my head in my hands and let the tears fall, loosened by memory, words, and drink.

$$\math{D}$$

It was only when I woke alone on the couch the next morning to a buzzing in my head that I realized Kat had never shared her story. But the next two weeks were so busy—me with running, trips out to Oxford for paperwork and flat hunting; Kat with working double shifts nearly every day—that the chance to ask again never materialized. And today, I would be heading up to Edmund's manor, and she would stay behind.

I had expected things to be awkward between us after my confession, but she acted almost as though she didn't remember hearing it at all. I didn't want to bring it up, for I supposed there was the slightest chance that she didn't remember—we had drunk quite a bit, and while I recalled it, she might not have. I wasn't even quite sure what I'd said, so guessing what she might know proved impossible.

The final pair of socks landed in my suitcase, and I glanced around the room for anything more to add. Nothing but Elinor.

She glowed now, as every morning and night she ate her fill, enough to pinch my wallet. After all, not only was she recuperating from life on the street, she was training for her own marathon.

Since we would be traveling for several hours to reach Edmund's manor north of York, we'd risen extra early and run for an hour through the nearest park. Elinor was already adept at dodging through the streets, and I was learning city running, but we both still preferred the green of the park, with the fresher air and sense of privacy it afforded. It was something like being back home, which I missed, despite not wanting to admit it to myself.

Charles was downstairs at the curb at exactly fifteen minutes to seven, as he'd promised. Elinor and I would be loaded up first, then we'd go get Victoria, who had insisted that we drive together, as if she were trying to prove someone else wrong. I suspected that she and Edmund had talked —with my invite to Chadwick Manor the subject.

Sydney had already gone up with Edmund, and Jake was to drive with us. My mother liked to travel in style and had rented a limo for the occasion, probably in order to give her more room to get away from Elinor.

An odd emotion swelled over me as I took my last look around the room. It would be six weeks before I was back. I was practically packing everything I owned: dresses, running clothes, Elinor's bed . . . We were, for lack of a better term, moving for six weeks. I supposed I could always make a trip down to London, a weekend away, or a week here and there. But I had the feeling that once I got out, I would enjoy the freedom of the country too much to return, except for my marathon a week after the wedding.

Edmund and Victoria had to have some elaborate honeymoon planned, for they were keeping it utterly secret. Knowing my mother, it would be a trip to Malta or something. Once they married and headed out of town, I would take my last chance to travel before starting medical school. And so my time to get the truth out of my mother grew short.

When we pulled up at Victoria's flat a few minutes later, I caught Charles's eye in the rearview mirror. He smiled politely, but not so politely that I thought he'd bridge the gap between employee and confidant.

"I'm going to take Elinor out for a little walk," I told him.

"Certainly, miss."

"We're supposed to leave when?"

"I'd say about half an hour."

"Right. I'll be back by then."

"Miss—"

Charles stopped me halfway out the door. "I'd suggest not straying far."

A slow, cynical smile spread my lips. "Duly noted."

$$\mathbb{D}$$

Elinor and I made a circuit, each of us finding something interesting as we walked. Truly, I loved London, in a sense of admiring something I could not understand or fully embrace. I loved the buildings, with their high windows and many stories. They had such a history, years of inhabitants and a swelling city around them. If they could talk, they would have millions of things to tell, millions of stories to relate. To think of the families that had lived inside them, the businesses that had been built up into empires or failed as start-ups. To think of what Victoria's flat would say, if it could speak, of the stories it would tell of her and me. I winced. Those stories were best left untold.

As we rounded the corner toward the front of the flat, I tore my gaze away from her building. Her door was nestled safely in the middle of the complex, unlike the one she had lived in the time I'd been here with Bryan.

Shoved into my coat pockets, my hands balled into fists. I kicked at an empty cigarette packet on the sidewalk, which proclaimed "Smoking Kills" in huge letters. As it skittered aside, Elinor dashed after it, tugging the leash out of my grasp. She ran past the box and up to the gate, where a slender woman in a long, red pea coat stood, camera in hand.

"Elinor!" I called, but she ignored me and raced up to the woman, almost as though she knew her. The woman stumbled backward, her eyes locked on the large dog charging at her, and I sprinted toward them as a vision of what could happen and the frenzy it would cause washed in front of my eyes. I called for her again, and as I did, I heard someone calling my name. Ignoring it, I rushed to the woman and grabbed Elinor's leash, an apology ready on my lips.

"I'm so sorry," I began, "she's friendly, I promise—"

"Oh my gosh—you're Victoria Talbot, aren't you?" The woman's dark eyes rounded.

"Vict—? No. No, I'm not." I smiled politely, pulling Elinor to me as she wagged her tail and panted happily.

"You are!" The slender woman raised her Nikon and snapped my picture before I could do anything but blink. As I raised an arm, a hand reached out and grabbed my wrist.

Panic rising, I jerked away, thinking it was a paparazzo or a companion of the woman's I hadn't seen before.

Elinor growled, lunging herself at the arm attached to the hand. Bared teeth sank through the black sleeve, and a curse landed close to my ear.

"Get her off!" Jake demanded as his other hand clenched into a fist.

"Elinor—" I scrambled to grab her by the collar. "Don't move, Jake. Stop moving, and I'll get her off."

Jake's jaw muscles flexed as he held himself rigid, his eyes burning. I'd taught Elinor an "out" command, but not for something like this. Still, I tried it anyway, and when it didn't work, I wrapped my fingers around her snout and pried her mouth open. Jake wrenched his arm away, his eyes fixed on the woman still snapping pictures. As soon as his arm was free, he held out his uninjured hand to the woman. "Give me your camera."

"Wha—? No." She drew back as if he had asked for her firstborn child.

"Now. Give it here." I'd never heard that tone in his voice before, the absolute fury that erased any sense of amusement or kindness from it. Suddenly I saw him as nothing but the bodyguard he'd been hired for.

"It's my camera—"

"Jake," I began weakly, but he ripped the camera from her hands and ejected the memory card, closing it in his fist.

"Hey—" She reached out a hand, but at his dark look, stumbled backward, hand up as though he might shoot her.

"Jake, come on. Let's go." I laid a hand on his good arm and tugged him away from the pale woman. "Let's get you treated."

Elinor brushed my knee, and although her feet remained on the ground, her eyes and ears remained on Jake, her hackles raised.

With eyes trained on Elinor, Jake put a hand between my shoulder blades and propelled me toward Victoria's flat. The security guard watched us through, his eyebrows glued together in the middle.

Tail stiffly held into the air, Elinor trotted along beside me, hair erect, her gaze never leaving Jake. As I glanced at her, something red glimmered on her muzzle. I winced. *Blood.*

In the safety of the black stretch limo, I instructed Elinor to lie down and stay, then motioned Jake to the seat beside me. "Sit down."

Jake glowered at Elinor as I pulled his hand into my lap, peeling back the sleeve and revealing the teeth marks below. He cursed and clenched his free fingers into the seat between us.

"I'm sorry," I murmured to him, staring at the oozing wounds. "I don't know why she did it—she must have been trying to protect me."

"I'm not a threat," he growled, his eyes locked on the dog as she licked her lips.

"She thought you were." I turned his wrist over so I could see the injury and grimaced. With a cloth from the bar, I dabbed away the weeping blood, pressing firmly on the spot which showed reluctance to stop bleeding. "You need to see a doctor."

"No. Not now. When we get up north I will."

"All right." The bleeding had slowed enough for me to see that Elinor's bite was deep, but clean. The puncture marks were in and out with no ripping, as good as I could hope. "We should at least clean it."

Jake leaned across me to the bar, grabbed a bottle of clear liquid and handed it to me.

"Vodka?" A small smile tweaked my lips. "I prefer something with a little more taste if I'm going to drink."

He met my gaze humorlessly. "Before your mother gets back."

"Right. Did you want me to pour you a drink first? This'll hurt." I tried to smile at him, but his face was a dark mask.

He shook his head. "Just do it."

I nodded and set his arm across my lap, using both hands to hold the bottle and twist open the unbroken seal. "Let's put the towel under your arm."

Jake slipped the towel from around his wound and held it under his arm.

I adjusted it slightly so that it would catch most of the vodka when I poured it and hopefully keep the limo from reeking like a bar. "Ready?"

"Just—"

"—do it?" I finished for him as I dumped the liquor over his arm.

His breath hissed through his teeth; he screwed his eyes shut and clenched his fist.

"Sorry," I muttered. "Thought it'd be best to be fast." My gaze flicked over his shoulder to where Charles stood on the sidewalk, bags in hand. "And I think Victoria will be out here soon."

He didn't answer.

"Please . . ." I trailed off and shook my head. "She didn't know it was you when you came up behind me."

"Victoria doesn't need to hear about this," Jake said, finally looking at me. His gaze slid from my face down to my throat, where the amethyst necklace lay warm against my skin. "I don't want you in trouble."

My stomach unclenched a notch, and I pressed his biceps with my fingers. "Thank you." I turned his wrist and poured more vodka over it, directly into the hole left by Elinor's canines. "Sorry."

"No." Jake drew a deep breath, inspecting his wound while I twisted the lid onto the vodka. "It's a good thing you have a dog like that." He shook his head as I slid the bottle back into its place in the bar. I snagged another towel from the bar and turned to Jake, ready to use it as a bandage.

He cocked his eyebrow in question.

"You need a bandage or you'll bleed through your shirt," I explained. "And how are we going to hide this?" I motioned to his forearm, still slowly dripping blood.

In answer, Jake began unbuttoning his long-sleeved shirt, revealing a white T-shirt underneath. "I have more clothes in the boot."

"Boot? Oh, right. Trunk. I'll get it." I peered over his shoulder, squirming around to see the rear of the car and the front of Victoria's flat. "Okay, Charles is gone. What do you want, another shirt like this?"

"Wait. Adrienne—" He grabbed my wrist as I began to slide off the seat.

I paused at the edge of the leather. "What?"

His bottom lip folded in between his teeth, but his gaze flicked over my shoulder to Elinor. "Will she attack again?"

Following his gaze, I frowned at Elinor. "I don't think so. Why?"

"Just want to test a theory . . ." He pressed his lips against mine.

"Jake—" I put my hand on his shoulder as a growl slit the air.

He jerked away from me at the sound, eyes flying open.

"Stay," I instructed her.

Lip curling, she sank back into her down position, still tense.

Jake flashed me a quick grin. "Guess my theory's bunk."

"I—" Before I could say anything else, he slipped from the car, leaving me in a mess of confusion.

Chapter Fourteen
The Heart of Yorkshire

BY THE TIME MY MOTHER came out, Jake had changed his shirt, we'd bundled up the bloody towels and shirt together, and he'd stashed them in the trunk with his luggage, while I cleaned the blood off Elinor's muzzle. When Charles began the drive, with Jake seated beside him, I still hadn't recovered from the feel or shock of Jake's lips on mine. Even though he was charming and attractive, I wasn't sure I was ready to date again. And I wasn't sure how I felt about Jake. Not to mention that he was employed to protect me.

The drive itself took an achingly long time, giving me plenty of uninterrupted time to think, for conversation with Victoria was not an art I had ever perfected.

By the time we exited the city, we had left behind all my failed attempts at conversation, as well as my desire to continue trying. I finally accepted my loss, put in my earbuds, and turned on an audiobook, staring out the window and allowing myself to fall into thought while Victoria buried herself behind a script.

Soon it was clear that my book wasn't distracting me, and so I withdrew my phone and put in the same search on the web for information on Victoria's past, again turning up a lot of nothing.

The media, even articles years old, was dodgy at best. A hint of truth had to remain in it, but which parts were true and which were lies? As always, celebrity gossip was a black hole difficult to claw one's way out of. I spent nearly an hour browsing articles, trying to look for similarities between them and comparing them to the limited number of things she'd told me, as if there would be some vein of truth threading them together.

Finally, we passed through York, and I knew Chadwick Manor neared. It was another hour before we drove down a long, bricked driveway. A pond, longer than it was wide, sprawled to our left as bricks that looked as though they'd existed for the past several hundred years murmured underneath the car. I could picture carriages and horses pulling up to the two-story high front door, permitting gusts of wind to swirl inside along with the guests in their fine silk dresses and ties.

I glanced up front at Jake, watching as he gathered his things and began to slip out of the car. *I'm just not ready, Jake,* I wanted to tell him. *I don't know what to do.* I played with the amethyst, wondering if I should return it now. Maybe I was overthinking it. Maybe it hadn't meant anything.

As we waited for Charles to open the limo door, Victoria chatted on her phone, which she had picked up after finishing her script. I now knew more about her business than I'd ever wanted to, and yet I still didn't know what she was doing. She slid out ahead of me, graceful as ever, as though she hadn't spent hours nearly immobile.

Elinor dashed out the limo after her, racing across the green lawn. Half amused, half concerned, I stepped out and stretched my arms over my head, rolling my head from side to side. It had been far more comfortable to travel in the limo versus a grimy train or a cramped airplane, except I missed the ability to walk around while traveling.

A strong, young man had come out to greet our car, and motioned two others to gather our bags as he led Victoria into the manor. I smiled politely at the men, but they spared me little notice, collecting my mother's bags before hurrying after her.

A sharp breeze of salty air pulled at my hair, whipping it into my cheeks, drawing my attention away from the looming building and to the previously unseen cliff beyond it.

A slow smile tugged at my lips. I foresaw a lot of clifftop runs.

☽

With my earphones dangling over my neck and leash in hand, I headed out the front door. This place was easy to get lost in. Just a glance at the hallway downstairs showed a maze of doors and archways.

When I emerged into the sun, a bark greeted me. Quick as a flash, Elinor was beside me and nuzzling my hand. "Ready for a run? Or have you already gone without me?"

She bounded around my feet in answer, barking that low bark of hers, tail wagging furiously, making me smile. She dashed off, but I maintained a more leisurely pace as I walked behind her, inspecting the grounds.

The even, green lawn stretched what had to be a mile from me, with not a weed anyplace. Bushes, perfectly pruned, lined the brick driveway, in between trees that had clearly been here for hundreds of years. Again, I pictured carriages and horses in my mind, drivers sitting on top of the carriages, almost like Cinderella arriving for the prince's ball.

The cliffs were behind me, but I'd inspect them another day. I didn't fancy a run along any high cliff on a windy day, even if the beach was a mere fifty feet below. It was no Dover, but I was sure they would pitch me over just as eagerly.

Where the brick turned to pavement at the end of the drive, I paused. As our arrival earlier had shown me, this wasn't a busy street, and yet the street didn't end. So instead of going back the way we had arrived, I turned to the right, tugging Elinor to my heel and beginning an easy jog.

It was nearly two miles later when we saw our first car, and another mile before the first driveway. I slowed to inspect its ornate iron toppers, where ivy was trimmed precisely back to allow them through. Glancing through the uprights as we jogged by, I saw nothing but a forest of trees beyond. Inwardly shrugging, I continued on, keeping fields and cows to my left, and a low rock wall between me and the trees to the right. It was an isolated path, the perfect horror story setting, where I wouldn't like to run alone in the dark. With my luck, I'd run into some crazed paparazzo who had followed my mother up here and mistaken me for her.

Ahead of us, the road dead-ended abruptly at a rock fence like the one I'd been keeping to my left. This one connected to the one I'd run along for miles by a wooden gate. I slowed, disappointed. I had expected a more scenic view on this jog, for the coast had to be a short distance to my right. As I began to turn, my gaze fell upon a small sign that had ivy growing up it, almost occluding it completely. With a few more steps, the words PUBLIC FOOTPATH appeared chiseled into it.

This was what I had been looking for. I bounded forward, stopping only to thread my way through the gate and release Elinor from her leash. With no cars and a private path, she wouldn't be in any trouble. As the familiar stresses settled over my body, they distracted me from any thoughts I might have about my mother.

Feet lighter than before, I bounded up the path. The fence raced alongside us, while a field full of sheep bleated in the other direction. I dodged sheep patties and told Elinor to leave them alone, racing her up the overgrown pathway to the next gate. An empty field greeted us, and we raced faster, Elinor panting and dashing forward, only to pause when she reached the next gate, which was closed. Laughing, I sprinted up to her. My ability to laugh reminded me how much of an escape running was for me.

"Thought you'd beat me, huh?" I pushed open the gate and slipped through, holding it for Elinor, who dashed forward, tongue lolling out. Thank goodness I was a distance runner, or else her high energy would drive me insane. We had run about four miles from the manor, and while she had plenty of energy remaining, the sky was darkening around us. It would probably be a wet journey home.

I slowed, reluctant to let this field run out, for the next gate looked like it led us not into another field, but a forest. When I reached it, my curiosity got the best of me, and we went through, entering the sparse woods. Thick trees reached their branches high above my head, bending under the strength of the wind. My feet picked up speed as I ran, not so much on a path anymore, for it was clear people didn't tend to make it this far. Instead, my shoes stuttered across moss and my toes stubbed into rocks. A hole grabbed my shoe once, and I crashed to my knees, slicing my hand open on a stick.

Grunting, I examined the wound, but brushed the dirt from it and carried on, slower this time. Thankfully slower. For we emerged abruptly from the trees onto a cliff a hundred feet above the shore, and it stole my breath.

"Elinor!"

At my urgent call, she halted a mere foot from the edge, gazing stoically at me over her shoulder and wagging her tail.

"Don't move," I said over the hum of the breeze, approaching the cliff slowly. The wind thumped through every molecule of my being. The waves were just audible from here, rising and crashing as the air pressed against them. I sucked in the salty sea air, suddenly eager to find a way to the shore, to run in the sand below and inspect the beach.

The thumping grew louder, pulsing rhythmically at me, as if my footfalls had a delayed echo through the woods and only now had caught up to me.

Closing my eyes, I inhaled again, allowing the wind to tug at me. A chill raced over my arms, raising the hairs.

Elinor barked. Once.

My eyes flew open, then followed her gaze behind me.

I gasped in shock, nearly backing up to the cliff's edge as a black horse and its rider charged toward us.

Elinor barked again, either warning or greeting, I couldn't tell.

The horse tossed his head, his long, wavy mane flying out from his neck, his nostrils flaring as his rider pulled at the reins, guiding him to a halt a half dozen feet away.

"You there! You've strayed from the footpath." A stern voice issued from under a black velvet helmet. "You're on private—" The rider frowned. "Adrienne?"

As he said my name, the familiarity of the voice suddenly clicked into place. "Damien? What are you doing here?"

"Adrienne?" His lips curved upward. "I wasn't expecting you." He nudged his mount forward, and the horse advanced, tossing his head and rolling his eyes at Elinor when she stepped forward.

Raising my hand halted her, and she lay on the ground, taking the opportunity to relax. "Nor I you," I answered in a half shout to be heard over the wind. "What are you doing here?"

He dismounted in one fluid motion.

"I should ask you that, as you're on my land." He swept his helmet off his head and smiled from underneath limp hair, advancing closely enough toward me that we didn't have to scream to hear each other.

"Your—" I frowned and motioned to the expanse of forest I'd run through and the cliff on the edge of the sea behind me. "This is yours?"

"It is indeed." His accompanying smile warmed me to my toes, his eyes glinting.

As I focused on them, I realized how they matched the sea behind me exactly, as if he had been born in it, and his eyes were a reflection of his home.

"How did you get here?"

I shook my reverie away. "I just arrived at Edmund's and decided to take a run." I shrugged. "Killing a little time before I call home."

Damien paused in tugging his black gloves from his fingers one by one. "You ran here from Edmund's?"

"Yes."

"Oh." He glanced back the way I'd come as if slightly disappointed. "Then you don't need a ride home."

My lips twitched. "No. I'll run, if you don't mind."

"Feel free to run here. You strayed from the footpath about a mile ago."

"Oh? I was sure the sea would have been considered public."

He smiled a bit wryly. "It's not about what anyone but the Kerrs consider public."

"Right." Staring at him with the sea at my back, I saw how someone might consider him in charge. He had an easy confidence about him, a security that came from being entrusted with an estate gifted down through his lineage.

Damien motioned to the clifftop and dropped his horse's reins as he began to walk along it. I followed him.

"So . . ." Curiosity heated my cheeks. "Are you a Lord like Edmund?"

His chuckle was almost lost on the gust of wind. "No. I'm actually untitled."

"So you're just ridiculously rich?" I teased.

His smile arced a bit unhappily. "I suppose. My several-greats-grandfather built this home. He was close to the king at the time, and was originally gifted the title of baron. Later, he was imprisoned for treason. When he was released, he was stripped of his title, but for some reason, he kept the land." Damien shook his head in thought. "I think the king liked his wife. The baron died destitute, but our land remained. And the baroness might have had a child a full year after her husband died. So through some shrewd dealings and probably some not-so-legal dealings, the Kerrs kept the land and passed it on down. Eventually to me." He clasped his hands behind him, staring down at the rocks under our feet.

"Are you all that's left? Now that your father is gone?"

Without looking up, he shook his head. "No. There's Kat, of course. And my son."

He advanced before me, as my feet scratched to a halt. "You—" I blinked, closed my mouth, swallowed, and tried again. "You have a son?"

Several feet in front of me, he stopped and lifted his gaze to meet mine. "Yes." His eyes weren't nearly as enticing right now as they had been when I thought they'd matched the churning sea below us. And now, just like the sea, they held secrets in their depths.

My jaw tightened. Another secret. Could no one be honest with me?

The wind howled at us, pushing us sideways back toward the woods.

Damien stepped back to me, hands at his sides now, either for balance, or to make himself more approachable, I wasn't sure; I couldn't read him anymore. Maybe I never had.

"I thought everyone knew. It's been made public enough."

"I don't follow celebrities," I said, barely moving my mouth.

"Kat didn't tell you?" At my shake of the head, he nodded. "Well, he's almost three, and his name is John, after my grandfather."

Waiting for him to continue, I swept the wind-loosened strands of my hair back against the rest of my sweaty scalp, and studied him. He had fallen silent, staring out at the sea. While he remained silent, my mind raced. A son? Did that mean he was involved with someone? He obviously had been, three years ago, but when had that ended? And more importantly, why did it matter to me?

Just when he opened his mouth, whether to continue the topic or change it, I said, "I've got to get back." I gestured to the woods. "Long run ahead."

He closed his mouth and nodded his agreement, but his eyes didn't leave my face as I said a hurried good-bye and called for Elinor. Then I turned my back on him and ran.

☽

Edmund arrived the next morning, early enough to join us for breakfast. Jake, Sydney, Victoria, and I sat around a too-large table, while a young man in a white shirt and black vest and pants served us toast, scrambled eggs, potatoes, sausage, and beans.

Although I had planned an early morning run, the cross-country run yesterday had taken more out of me than I'd anticipated, and I instead loaded up on the carbs and protein offered me with only slight chagrin, as my stomach had been rumbling since I'd woken at five.

I'd had to ask around to find out where breakfast would be, as well as what time, learning, along with the mealtimes, that I would have to leave my room ten minutes before each meal in order to arrive in the dining room on time. If I remembered where I was going.

"So I've had Charity call the caterer, and of course they're saying that the Alaskan salmon we want won't be available." Victoria scoffed and poked at the eggs on her plate as if tempted to blame them. Her nose curling in disgust, she took a bite of turkey bacon instead, which she'd ordered especially for herself.

"Why don't you call Dad then?" I asked before I could stop myself.

Her stare burned into my cheek as I slowly chewed the bite of toast I'd taken to halt my words.

"Excuse me?"

I swallowed. "Call Dad. He has a freezer full of salmon. He could probably expedite it over." I shrugged. "Not sure if it would be enough for the entire wedding party, but . . ."

She tilted her head, considering me with fresh interest, as though she suddenly saw value where she'd never seen it before. "That's an idea. I knew you were here for a reason."

As I flushed, Jake chuckled.

Sydney glanced between us all as my flush deepened. "Isn't she maid of honor?" she asked, tone indignant.

As my mother began to speak over her, I cast her a thankful smile. She was sweet, if a bit naïve. And a bit confused, if she thought my mother would ever ask me to be maid of honor in her wedding.

"It would be expensive to ship . . . Not nearly as expensive as buying it, of course. But we'd need a great deal." Brushing her hair back from her face, Victoria turned to Edmund. "What do you think?"

I blinked, surprised that she even bothered to ask what he thought. *It is his wedding, too,* I reminded myself, but even that didn't feel right when it concerned my mother asking something dangerously close to *permission.*

Edmund smiled blandly. "That's your department, darling. If he has the supplies and is willing to help, though, there's no objection from me."

"Settled. I'll call him after this."

"I'd wait until morning back home," I muttered with a glance at my watch. "It's a bit late there."

Victoria took a dainty bite of eggs, eyebrows arched as though I didn't understand the direness of her salmon needs. While I finished eating, I cursed myself for dragging Dad back into the relationship he'd never truly put behind him.

When I put my napkin on the table, the server appeared as if by magic to remove my plate. Thanking him, I pushed back my chair and began to rise.

"Just a moment." Edmund dabbed at his mouth with his cloth napkin. "Adrienne, do you have lunch plans?"

"Uh . . ." My words stumbled and died on my lips at the expectation on his face. "No. Not yet. Are we doing something?" I glanced back at the table, but Sydney was giving a small shake of her head, and Jake was on his fourth sausage.

"No." He smiled benignly. "I'd like to take you to lunch. I have something to speak with you about."

"Oh." My stomach squirmed. "Sure. That sounds . . . nice," I finished lamely. *What could he have to talk with me about?*

As I left the breakfast room, my thoughts followed me. And until I met him for lunch, they continued to chase me.

I reached the foyer first just before noon and sank onto the bottom step of the stairs, forgoing the several cushioned chairs and benches around the perimeter of the room. Sometimes chairs were best left for the refined. My jeans and T-shirt were fine for sprawling on the carved wooden staircase, feeling the caress of the wood under my hand, smelling the rich years of aging upon the rug before me, the lacquer on the staircase.

It was another ten minutes before Edmund appeared, which I spent watching the employees bustle around, constantly cleaning, dusting, and walking through the foyer on their way elsewhere.

"So sorry, my dear. Got held up with a phone call." He shook his head. "London can't function without Parliament. Remember that."

I arched my eyebrow at him. "And you are . . . Parliament?"

He chuckled as I hauled myself to my feet. "No. A mere pawn on the board."

Nodding at the appropriately humble response, I fell into step beside him as he headed for the front door. Outside in the drive, a car waited, with a man holding open the driver's side door, and Edmund slid behind the wheel, much to my surprise.

"You drive yourself around here?" I asked when seated beside him in the passenger seat. To my greater surprise, we pulled away alone, with no bodyguard for the first time since I could remember. Even Jake apparently didn't see fit to join us in York.

"I do. London is . . ." he shook his head as he fixed his mirror, "not worth the time and stress. But around here, there's not much point in having a driver."

The garden passed along beside us, its hedges keeping the interior from view, but the tip of a dolphin's snout peeked out, spewing water high into the sky above us. Trees quickly claimed the view of the garden as we hurtled along the drive.

"In London, I use the drive to make calls and read documents." He shrugged and glanced to the right before pulling onto the road off his property. "Here, it's a vacation." His mouth twitched into a smile. "As much as I can ever get, I suppose."

We talked about nothing much for the ride into York, mere small talk about the upcoming wedding and my studies, and, as we neared the city walls, I turned the conversation to Damien.

"How do you know him?"

"Oh, I was a bit of a second father to him. His father and I were hunting partners."

"What did you hunt?"

"Oh, deer, birds, all sorts of things. Foxes." He cast me a half apologetic look, as though I might not approve.

"Do you keep trophies?" For some reason, I'd never pictured Edmund as a hunter. Growing up in Alaska, I'd never disagreed with hunting; it was a part of life, and often a method of survival. I supposed that England had a bit of a different view on the subject, though I had never considered it.

"Not many. Though I have a few scattered about." He made a turn and familiarity grabbed me.

"Oh, the city walls." I craned my neck to look at them. Driving places in England, I was routinely surprised by the city sights, as they appeared around a corner abruptly, or in the middle of a field, a Celtic stone circle, or a relic to a bygone era set amongst modern buildings, poking themselves out as though a middle child seeking attention.

"You've been to York before, right?" Edmund steered the car into a parking lot near one of the towers to the wall.

"It's been years, but yes." I unbuckled myself and pushed open the door. "I haven't had the chance to come here since we arrived yesterday, if that's what you mean."

With a smile, he motioned to the street to the right while tucking the keys into his jacket pocket with his other hand. "There's an excellent little café down here that I like to frequent."

"Oh? So I'm not underdressed for this café?"

"No, not at all."

After a few twists and turns upon the streets, I remembered why I loved York so much, almost more than London: the York Minster. It called me like a beacon, its spire reaching high into the sky, and when we took the last turn, it stretched before us like a giant, sprawling across the ground with its characteristic circular stained glass window and flying buttresses.

I had stopped to stare before I realized what I was doing, and only when Edmund turned back to me, saying, "It's just up here, Adrienne," did I jolt to awareness. Tourists were snapping pictures of the Minster from a few feet away, and more were scattered across the small plaza, aiming cameras at the church.

It felt so inadequate to call it a mere church. As always with England, my thoughts turned to the past of the building, to the street under my feet. Who had been here, walked here, worshipped here?

"It's impressive, isn't it?" Edmund said from beside me, his voice so near that I jumped.

"Yes. Sorry. I just . . ." I half raised a hand toward the façade. "It always gives me chills."

With a curious tilt to his head, he nodded, but his gaze was not on the church, it was on me. "Yes. I can see that." He put a hand on my arm, just above my elbow and turned me slightly. "So I think you'll appreciate the café I've chosen. I've even asked them to keep my favorite table open for us."

I followed him to a small café about three doors down from where I had stopped, a suite which had to claim one of the best views in all of York. Edmund was greeted like an old friend, which he probably was, and we were led up a set of narrow stairs and back toward the front of the building, where we were seated at a small, round table in front of a window that looked out at the sprawling Minster beyond.

"Wow. This is a nice view."

While we waited for the waitress to take our order, we chatted about the Minster, about York, and about nothing in particular.

Chapter Fifteen
Under the Minster

WHEN OUR DRINKS HAD BEEN delivered, a tall glass of sparkling water for me and a tall, "Extra Smooth Bitter" for him, I finally turned my attention from the spires beyond the window and to the man in front of me.

"So any particular reason you asked me to lunch today?" I searched his face as I asked the question, assuming he'd appreciate the straight path, even though he had been anything but upfront today.

His smile was something like those I had seen Dad give when asked a question he might not want to answer honestly. "I wanted to get to know you, Adrienne. I'm about to become your stepfather, and it occurred to me, rather recently, that I've committed the rather egregious oversight of not spending much quality time with you."

I tossed back a long drink of water as I mulled over his answer. "Although you aren't going to be a typical stepfather to me, Edmund."

His gaze met mine over our drinks, his mouth quirking quizzically. "Why not?"

"Because I'm an adult. I mean, I'm pretty much independent already." I wrinkled my nose, thinking of how the past month didn't support that statement at all. "Before I came to London, I hadn't seen my mother in three years. But as soon as I'm at university, I'll hardly see either of you."

"True." He nodded agreeably. "But that doesn't make my title less true."

Title? Frowning, I inspected the bubbles in my water. "No. I guess not. But I won't see you much. And until quite recently, I haven't spent much time around Victoria. In fact, even recently, I haven't seen her much." I shook my head slightly, the Minster catching my gaze again. Only a few hundred feet away, a group of tourists lined up outside the high arching doors to enter. I'd have to visit it again soon, see if my memories of it were correct.

"That is something that we must address, Adrienne." Edmund's tone had become cool.

I turned back. "What is?"

"Well, the wedding is in a few weeks."

"Yes." For some reason, my heart began to thump, my stomach sinking. *What was he about to ask me? I don't know how much more of a part of this wedding I can be . . . not when my relationship with Victoria is still so tenuous.*

"And Victoria's brought it to my attention that she asked you to be her maid of honor weeks ago. And you have not yet answered her."

I frowned, wondering if I'd missed something over the past several weeks. "No. She hasn't. She didn't."

"Certainly it was made clear through the events at the engagement party?"

"No." A shocked chuckle slipped from me. "No, it wasn't made clear. I guess, like many things in her life, she just assumed the question was implied."

He pushed his half-drunk beer away from him and leaned back in his chair, studying me with his cool blue eyes. "Any particular reason why you and your mother don't get along?"

Plenty of reasons. But none I'll tell you. I turned over what I could tell him in my mind. It all seemed so petulant, so juvenile. The one reason I couldn't say was the one that offered the most explanation.

I took a deep breath and met his searching stare. "Edmund, I'm going to be straight with you. Mostly because I don't believe in lying, and I don't like beating around the bush." I pushed my water away so it nearly touched his beer in the center of the table. "But also because I think you need to know what you're marrying into."

He remained almost implacable, except I saw a quiver of his lips at my last words. He was intrigued, and trying not to show it.

I fortified myself with another quick breath, holding this one as I considered how to start. "You've noticed I don't call Victoria 'Mom,' surely."

He gave a single, deep nod.

"There are a lot of reasons for that, but one main reason. And unfortunately, I cannot tell you what that is." I shook my head. "Nor do I want to, to be honest."

His gaze narrowed slightly, but I met it without compromise.

"I am trying to put that behind me. And I think it would create . . . tension in your relationship with her as well." I folded my hands under the table, twisting them together as I'd seen Kat do. It did work to relieve some stress. "I don't want to be the cause of dissention among you. Or something worse. But I don't want to lie to you, either."

His chin lifted, his lips pursing out in consideration.

"So I ask you to try and understand that my mother and I have a long history together. Years which were not happy times, and which have left a significant scar upon me, and perhaps her. I don't know." I shrugged as if it didn't matter, but another grimace wrinkled my nose.

After a moment's silence, Edmund leaned forward, putting his hands on his knees and staring earnestly at me. "Adrienne," he said as though he were speaking to a two-year-old, "don't you think I've spoken with your mother about her past? Don't you think that we know each other well? Perhaps I know your mother better even than you know her?"

I considered his statement for a moment. "Better? Or just differently?"

The muscles in his jaw flexed, as though I had hit a sore nerve. "Better," he answered with ice chilling his voice.

I smiled sadly, wishing I could agree and think he went into this relationship aware. But didn't I know different parts of her that she would never share with another person? Would she dare to tell Edmund what she had done to break up Bryan and me?

While I turned it over in my mind, the waiter brought us our lunch. As he left, I spread my napkin on my lap and sipped my water, but Edmund had hardly moved except to allow the waiter to place his food.

"Don't you agree?" he repeated, as though he needed to hear my agreement.

With my fork, I pushed a piece of lettuce back onto my plate from the rim. "No, I'm sorry, Edmund." Shaking my head, I met his gaze and inwardly winced at the permafrost I found there. "I can't agree with you."

"Why not?"

"Because I find it difficult to think that someone like you would want someone like her." I shut my eyes, the words having come out wrong. What if he went back to her and demanded to know what had happened between us? What if he told her that I said she didn't deserve him? Even if it was true, it would destroy everything I'd been working for.

A sound like a scoff and laugh worked its way free of his throat. "That just shows me how much you don't know your own mother, Adrienne." He spread his napkin on his lap and picked up his fork as though the matter were resolved.

And how much I don't know you. Lips pressed together, I watched him spear a ravioli and shove it in his mouth. "So she's told you everything that might create a scandal for her if it was found out?" I asked. "For her and you? I mean, you're a politician. Her past affects you now, too."

He gave me a thin-lipped frown. "She's told me everything that matters, Adrienne. If you're curious, I suggest you ask her."

"I have." Bitterness gave my words an unintentionally hard edge.

He lifted one shoulder in a shrug. "If she hasn't told you, then it doesn't concern you."

A flash of irritation raced through my veins. "That's absolutely false."

He slowly lowered his fork back to his plate. Tension emanated from him as our relationship shifted. I had just called him a liar. "I'm sorry you think that."

A snort split the air between us as I recognized a true politician's passive-aggressive lie. "How does my past not concern me, Edmund?"

He pressed his lips together. "Perhaps you are intent on believing something that isn't true, Adrienne."

"I think the time for me being naïve and mindlessly believing what my mother says is long gone." I leaned toward him, trying to invite him to tell me the truth. "All I want is for my mother to tell me why I shouldn't doubt my past. Instead, she tells me it's none of my business. *My father* is none of my business? How can anyone be satisfied with that answer, Edmund?"

His gaze dropped from me to his plate, which he rotated in place as though selecting the best angle to eat from. "Sometimes, the truth is better left unsought, Adrienne."

"You don't know what it feels like to find out your father may not be your father, do you?" I clenched my fingers together again, tighter this time.

"Adrienne, you have a wonderful father already. He loves you very much; it's evident to everyone." He smiled with feigned kindness at me. "Sometimes it's better to accept what you have and love those you have, rather than search for something that may not turn out like you wish."

My stomach clenched. He had to know something. "Edmund, I know the truth, no matter how painful, is always worth finding out." I fixed him with a glare as I said the next word. "Always."

Head slightly tilted, he considered me. Then he lifted his drink with one hand and said, "Then I wish you luck in your quest."

I sat back against my chair, tasting defeat. "But you won't help me."

He drank deeply, wiped his mouth with his napkin, and offered a smile tinged with sorrow. "No. I can't be a part of it. I'm sorry."

"Me too," I said with a shake of my head. Disappointment had stolen my appetite, and I ate little more before telling the waiter to take it away.

$$\mathcal{D}$$

Edmund and I made small talk on the return trip home, but there was a tension we couldn't erase no matter how many questions I asked about his neighbors or his home.

That night, Edmund had invited Damien, Kat, and a few other family friends of his for dinner. We ate in one of the larger dining rooms, and the dinner felt as awkward and traditional as breakfast. Victoria and Edmund domineered the conversation with wedding talk, and I sat between Sydney and a middle-aged woman who hardly spoke a word all night. Across from me, Damien seemed to attempt to catch my eye, but after giving him a polite smile, I focused on dinner, thoughts in turmoil. What seemed a few minutes later, dinner was over. In established after dinner tradition, Edmund invited the male guests to the men's smoking room for drinks and cigars.

I looked up when Victoria and the other women rose and headed out a different door than the men, a distracted Kat following. Raking a hand through my hair, I left the table, going in the opposite direction. Outside the room, I nearly ran into Damien.

"All right?" Concern drew his features tight on his face.

"Yeah." I forced an awkward smile for him as my thoughts raced to our last conversation. Lots of people his age had children, and nowadays single parents weren't uncommon. I was being old-fashioned. And with that thought, my cheeks went hot. I wasn't being honest with myself. It wasn't that he had a son that bothered me. It was the fact that he'd been involved in a serious relationship, which he probably maintained for the sake of his son. *I'm jealous.* The realization slammed into me with the force of Elinor running full out.

"Can we speak?" He ducked his chin as if trying to catch my eye.

I tried to calm the flush in my cheeks. "You aren't joining the men?"

A faint smile graced his lips. "No. I've got to get back to the house. But . . . I'd like to talk to you first." He shifted his weight back and forth between the balls of his feet.

I shrugged. "Sure. Mind if I get Elinor first?"

"No, of course not." Damien shook his head and motioned to the stairs. "I'll be over there."

"Okay. Be right back." I walked with him to the base of the stairs, where I left him waiting. I'd put Elinor in my room tonight, for she kept disappearing over the grounds, only to show up for breakfast or dinner. *No wonder I picked her up as a stray in London.*

When I opened the door, Elinor was sprawled across the four-poster bed, all four feet up in the air, snoring. I laughed aloud, and she jumped awake, rolling over and dangling her paws off the edge of the mattress.

"Come on, lazy bum," I said, "let's go on a walk."

She leapt from the bed and across the room in several bounds. Before returning to Damien, I grabbed a jacket and shrugged it on, glancing outside to check the English weather. It, surprisingly, hadn't changed.

When we reached the bottom of the stairs, Elinor jumped at him, despite my scolding, but he ignored her, eyes on me.

I tucked my hands in my pockets and began toward the front door at the same time as he began back toward the dining rooms and kitchen. "Aren't we going out on a walk?"

His smile was warm and inviting, yet slightly apologetic. "I was thinking of the gardens."

"Oh. Sure." Shrugging, I changed direction and followed him through the maze of hallways leading to a side exit into the gardens. "You know your way around here pretty well."

"I spent a lot of time in this house growing up."

"You call this a house?" I chuckled.

His lips twitched as though he were trying to suppress a smile. "You haven't seen my house, have you?"

We rounded a corner in the hallway, and Damien led me down some stone stairs. Plaster peeled from the mauve-painted walls, exposing ancient electrical wiring. "No, I was waiting for an invitation," I managed to tease as I trotted along behind him.

He stopped so suddenly that I ran into his back and banged my nose on his shoulder. "Sorry."

"Mmm." I rubbed my nose.

"Why were you waiting for an invitation? I told you to come over any time."

Shrugging, I toed a scuff in the concrete hallway. "I didn't want to get in the way."

"'In the way'? How could you possibly be in my way?" His tone was so warm that it drew my attention up to his searching gaze.

I looked away, bothered by his warmth, despite myself. *I'm totally falling for him—and he's a father with a young child that will scrutinize our relationship— no, that will idolize our relationship until we break up and he'll be just as heartbroken as I'll be.*

"Adrienne, what's wrong?" Damien sped up so that he reached a curved wooden door a half pace before me and pushed it open to allow the fresh air of the night to enter. "Are you upset with me?"

Even though I wanted to tell him "no," I couldn't. So I tilted my head back and took in the starlit sky above. The moon gleamed tonight, and my gaze flicked to it, distracted by the way it glinted against the shiny ivy leaves along the wall.

"You are," Damien said. "What have I done?"

Holding my breath, I shook my head. "I just . . . Can I be honest with you?"

"Always," he answered immediately. He reached for me and pulled my hand out of my pocket, grasping my hand with his and drawing me further into the hedges. "Tell me what's bothering you."

I bit my lip. Admitting what bothered me meant admitting I liked Damien. And I still wasn't sure what I felt about him, or even if I could trust him.

"Adrienne?"

"I just . . ." I looked up at him. "I wish you would have told me about your son. I know it's silly, but . . . you asked me on a date and didn't bother to tell me you had a child."

Surprise smoothed the lines on his forehead. "I—" He halted, as if the words he was going to say fell off his lips, unsaid. "I'm sorry. I had no idea you didn't know." His head trembled from side to side. "Sometimes I forget everyone doesn't know about my life. The way the media splashes it around, even when they're wrong, you know they get some facts right."

"Like the fact you're a single father."

He dropped his chin to his chest, straightening his shoulders so that his jacket shifted, seeming to ripple down his arms. "Yes. That's true. Even the paparazzi gets things right once in a while. But I try my best to protect my son from all that."

At a gust of wind, I shivered, and he took my hand and tucked it into his elbow. A tingle ran through me.

I shook my head, sighing a little at myself. Was this what I had become? *I came to London to avoid an ex-boyfriend, now I've allowed my hired bodyguard to kiss me, let myself start having feelings for him, and now I'm flirting with another man. Wow. How far I've fallen.*

I forced my thoughts back to the topic at hand. I was being stupid; as soon as my words had left my mouth, I knew it, and now my cheeks were burning so I could hardly look at him. How could I have expected him to preface his request for a dinner date with the information that he had a toddler son at home?

"I am sorry—" Damien began, pulling my attention back to him and squeezing my fingers with his warm ones.

My cheeks burned hotter with embarrassment. *Come on, Adrienne. You're practically confessing a crush on him.* "No, it's—it's stupid. I shouldn't—it shouldn't have bothered me." I shrugged and cast him an apologetic smile. "Even the most truthful people don't lay out everything about themselves to everyone. I don't." *Like in instances like this, where I'd just humiliate myself for no good reason.* "And I'm pretty honest, too," I added as if it could somehow justify my explanation.

"'*Pretty* honest'?" His eyebrows arched as he emphasized the first word.

Laughing, I leaned into him, making him stagger toward the bush beside him. His hands tightened over mine automatically, and I grabbed at him to keep him on his feet.

As he straightened out, smile a slow fade, Damien kept his eyes on the ground, while I lifted mine to the sky. I never could be outside at night without stargazing.

"I just want the truth!"

Chapter Sixteen
Interrupted

THE WORDS HAD ESCAPED ME without thought and rang through the air with conviction. "Not one person's idea of the truth, or opinion of it. I want the undeniable truth. Why is that so much to ask?"

Damien turned to me, eyes wide in the moonlight, an intensity there that sliced through the night and seemed to penetrate my heart. "We're not talking about me anymore, are we?"

Tears burning in my eyes, I tried to ignore his stare and tilted my chin back, searching out the stars. I turned away from the moon, grateful when a thick cloud pushed its way in front of it. "Do you ever just lie down and watch the stars?"

"Sometimes. I don't get many chances to do so lately though."

"Yeah?" I turned to him. "Why do you work? I mean, you're wealthy without being a movie star, aren't you?"

He smiled uncomfortably. "Yes and no. The land brings in some money. But the upkeep of the estate is significant. Because of my acting jobs, and various endorsements, I don't have to host tours through the building."

"You don't want strangers walking through your property?" I teased dryly.

"Not exactly. A lot of lords do it." Damien shrugged and searched out the sky as though looking for a way to explain. "I like to come home and know that it's my home. If it takes me working hard to accomplish that, so be it."

"How much money does it take to keep your estate in good order?"

He gave me a sidelong glance. "You Americans and your interest in money."

I pursed my lips at him but let the question stand.

With a grimace, he said, "A couple of million a year."

"Million?" I choked out. "Like a couple million *pounds*?"

He shrugged. "Yes. It's an old building, with more old buildings on the land, and there are things which have to be repaired every year, and . . ."

"Wow," I muttered. "I wonder if Victoria's money will go to upkeep on this place."

He chuckled. "Probably not. Edmund has invested differently. He is one who offers tours of his home when he's not in town."

"Tours. Is that popular?"

"York is such a big destination for tourists, and a lot of them seek out ways to get out of the city. A true English manor is one of them." He shrugged again. "It's a way of life for a lot of the remaining nobility, and those with estates like ours, but my father was too private. He held out until the end—even when it almost meant our ruin."

"So you went into acting? That's hardly a shoe-in for making money."

Damien tilted his head in acknowledgment. "Yes. But I've always loved it. When I was younger, I had a very controlled life, and . . . it was an escape from that. I could be wild and crazy on set, be exactly what I couldn't be at home, and return home and be exactly what I needed to be."

"I can't picture you as struggling to remain in control," I murmured, considering him. "How did you get your big break? I know nothing about your movies—or even my mother's."

His lips twitched, but he seemed anything but offended at what could have been an insult. "Well, I had a few connections."

I pursed my lips. "Like my mother?"

"She was one of several," he mused.

"Did she help you?"

He cocked his head in that peculiar way of his before dipping his chin in a nod. "Immensely."

"Is that why you feel like you owe her?"

"Owe her?" His eyes widened in genuine surprise. "I don't owe her anything."

I pressed my lips together and looked back to the sky. The stars twinkled overhead; I had missed them while I was in London. I hadn't realized how much until now, until they burned above me, drawing my steps to slow and halt, and my chin upward to lift my face to the sky. "Is there a bench or something?"

"A bench? Sure. Are you tired?"

I shook my head. "No, I just want to lie down and admire the stars."

"Ah." He smiled and pulled me further into the hedges. A few minutes later, he stopped beside a gray stone slab with no back.

I sat down at the end of the long bench and reclined, sighing a satisfied sigh as the stars stretched out above me. I couldn't keep the smile off my lips, greeting the stars like the old friends they were. Even without looking, I knew Damien stared at me. "You're supposed to be looking at the stars," I told him.

"I am," he answered.

Involuntarily, my gaze flicked over, but he was staring at me. I pressed my lips together in mock irritation. "I am not a star."

He grinned and shrugged, but tilted his head back. "So what am I looking at?"

"I don't know what you're looking at, but I'm looking for Andromeda."

"Andromeda?"

"Yes . . . the goddess."

"Right, the 'chained lady,' The Greeks believed that her mother, Cassiopeia, bragged about her own beauty, saying she was more beautiful than the sea nymphs." His voice grew wistful as he stared up at the sky. "As punishment for her mother's hubris, the sea monster Cetus attacked Ethiopia. In order to save the country, Andromeda's father sacrificed her by chaining her to a rock in the sea. Perseus happened upon her, rescued her, and they lived happily ever after."

Somewhere during his speech about Greek mythology, I had stopped looking skyward and looked at Damien instead. I'd lost track of how many times I'd told others about Greek myths or about the tales behind the stars, but this constituted one of the few times I'd had the myths explained to me. Probably not since I could read had I had them told to me.

Becoming aware of my silence, Damien faced me. "What?"

"What else do you know?"

He laughed and motioned upward. "I know that there were forty-eight original constellations, all centering on mythology, formed by Ptolemy. Well, he was one of several astronomers who named the constellations, but his seem to be the names that stuck."

"Do you know this much about everything?"

He shrugged. "I know a little bit about a lot. But not a lot about much."

"Except acting."

He tilted his head in acknowledgment. "I do know a bit about that."

"Are you going to act forever?"

"'All the world's a stage . . .'" he murmured. He sank down above my head on the bench portion I'd left for him.

"'. . . and all the men and women merely players: they have their entrances and their exits . . .'"

"'. . . and one man in his life plays many parts.'"

I watched his lips move as he finished the line. "I suppose some play more than others," I said finally, thinking of my mother. She seemed always to be playing some sort of part, whether scripted by someone else or by herself. *She always has a script. So what is it now?*

"I used to think that Shakespeare just had to say everything in the most complicated way possible."

His words pulled me back to the present, away from my mother.

Damien cupped his hands around the edge of the bench and leaned back. "Then, when I became an adult, I realized he was actually simplifying things."

I chuckled. "Yeah. I guess you could say that."

"So, to answer your question, yes, I suppose in some sense, I will forever be an actor. And as long as I have the estate to fund, it seems likely."

"Do you enjoy it?"

He stared into the distance. "There's something both freeing and confining about it."

I remained silent, waiting for him to continue.

"To pretend to be someone else, especially when things in your life have fallen apart, when your sister is mad at you—for good reason—and when your father has died . . . Acting like someone else can let you escape even the most intense feelings by pretending they belong to someone else." He fell silent, head tilted back as the moon slipped out from behind its cloud.

"And what is confining?" I asked when he showed no sign of continuing.

Although his face was illuminated by the light of the moon, it somehow darkened at my question.

The stars seemed to fade under scrutiny of the moon, and I waited for Damien, giving him the time he needed to answer. Stubble had appeared on his chin over the day, and his throat was darkening with it.

"Well . . . there's the constriction of your life not being yours. How whenever you go out, you don't know if someone will assault you just because you played a criminal in a movie, or because they think you don't do enough for others with your time and money, or because they're ridiculously in love with you without knowing you. It's hard to tell who wants to be your friend because of who you are and who wants to be your friend because of what you do and the power they think you hold. There's no anonymity anymore. Everyone thinks they know me."

"Don't try to get my sympathy," I teased.

His shoulders shook with silent laughter. "I shouldn't, should I? You know what it's like, I'm sure. With your mother being who she is. With all this mess she created."

I shifted my arm underneath my head, crooking it so I lay on the fleshy part of my arm on either side of my elbow. "Don't be so quick to lump me in the same category as you. I spent my life in Alaska. Even if I were famous—which I'm not—it's different. People there are less enamored by fame, and it's like . . . the entire state is just a small town. No one cares, not really. I'm just another person to them, despite my parents. And my mother . . ." I sighed and shifted my arm again when the bone of my elbow dug into the back of my head.

"She didn't like it," he finished for me. "Here. Put your head here." He held my head up with a light touch, and slid toward me so that my head rested on his thigh. His hand fell away from my hair, disentangling it from the waves that tried to snag his fingers.

My heart thumped at this intimacy, but I forced myself to focus on my words. "No, she didn't like blending in. Ironically, she moved to a large city where it's almost as easy to blend in."

"Except for the large paparazzi population," Damien said with an easy smile.

"True. We don't have that at home." I bit my lip and snuck a glance at him. I couldn't tell if he was flirting, or if he would have offered the same for Kat or not. I didn't have a brother. *How* do *brothers and sisters act?*

"I should go there someday, see what it's like."

"Alaska? Everyone wants to go there someday. Pretty soon, everyone will have been there, or will be there."

"Always the cynic, aren't you?" Damien tilted his head further back and we fell silent.

If I forgot where I was, if I forgot whom I leaned against, if I forgot everything that had happened over the past weeks, I could pretend I was back home, heading out for a fall or spring run.

"You know, at home, I used to run underneath the stars all the time. All through winter. I'd bundle up and run. And my best runs were those cold winter mornings. Not a cloud in the sky. Hopefully not even the moon. I'd go out with a headlamp that I'd only turn on if I needed it. I'd have one of those flashing lights on me just so people saw me, but . . . it was better to run in the dark. The stars would give me all the light I needed. And then, if I was really lucky, and it was cold and clear enough, the Northern Lights would show up. And they'd just dance."

Damien made a small noise in his throat.

"And sometimes, they'd steal my breath. And I'd have to stop, and I could only stare. Sometimes I'd fall to my knees, they are that beautiful."

"What made you leave it then?"

I considered for a moment. "The idea of a man I'd once dated returning home." Under the sheet of night above, I didn't feel the embarrassment that I ordinarily would have with such a childish confession. "Alaska is a really big small town. Despite our size, it's easy to run into people you would rather avoid. We all go to the same stores, need the same things."

He nodded absently, and I realized he had stopped staring at the stars and gazed again at me. When I turned my gaze on him, he gave a little smile and lifted a finger to the constellation above us without looking.

"Which constellation is that?"

I was about to identify Ursa Major when I remembered his knowledge of Andromeda. "I thought you knew the constellations."

He grimaced. "Uh . . . I have a confession."

"What?" I demanded warily. "It's not another secret, is it?"

"Well, no . . . I just . . ." He shifted, his legs flexing underneath my head. He looked down at me. "I don't know the first thing about the stars."

"But—"

"I talked to Kat, and she said you liked stargazing. And that your favorite constellation was Andromeda." His leg twitched under my head. "So I did some quick research and saw what it looked like—"

Amusement tugged at my lips but I suppressed it. "And how did you know the story then?"

"Greek mythology class," he answered, his tone appropriately chagrined.

A deep laugh began in my belly and worked its way outward. "And why, exactly, did you decide that you needed to do all this?" I asked when I could talk.

His leg twitched again. "Wanted to impress you, I suppose."

Laughter crept away from me as I stilled. "You did?"

Silent, Damien dropped his gaze down to me. His expression held the barest hint of nervousness, reminding me of him standing on the stairs to my London flat, asking me to dinner.

"Well, isn't this a pretty sight."

Damien and I both jumped at Jake's voice. Although every muscle in my body had tensed, I slowly turned as my bodyguard approached. He strode up to the edge of the bench, his face a mask I couldn't read in this moonlit night. Something stubborn in me rose, and I remained reclined on Damien's lap. I felt both men's eyes upon me, as if I were the one controlling the situation, and perhaps I was.

"Can I speak with you?" Jake asked, irritation tightening his lips.

"Sure. Let's talk." I hefted myself up, leaving Damien's warmth and stepping into the night with Jake.

He strode off, his feet clipping along first the grass, then tapping on a brick path as he led me further from Damien and the oddly warm stone bench. As we walked, the sea rushed in the distance, and the sky grew darker, as though we were leaving even the moon's light behind.

"Where have you been?" I asked. "I've hardly talked to you since we arrived in Yorkshire."

A cold look on his face, Jake stopped next to a fountain of three water sprites dancing and spouting water. "Care to tell me what's going on between you and Damien?"

Flushing in sudden embarrassment, I wrapped my arms around my waist as the wind swirled around the fountain, blowing water spray into my face and making me wince. "There's nothing going on."

"Really? Because it certainly looked cozy over there."

"We were stargazing. That's it. And talking." I shrugged. "I don't lie, Jake. Remember?" The wind picked up then, turning the water's spray on me, forcing me back out of the way. "And what does it matter? You've all but disappeared since we got here. You haven't talked to me, guarded me, or anything. So I don't even know what's going on with us. Even if there is an *us* outside the job you seem to have quit."

Jake rolled his eyes and tilted his head with a huff directed at me. "If you have to think about it, I guess there isn't."

"What?" I threw up a hand in exasperation. "Let's talk about this—"

"Talk about what? According to you, there's nothing."

I almost laughed at his petulance, but caught myself before it slipped through my smile. At my smile, Jake's face darkened, his shoulders drawing back.

"Jake." I reached out and grasped his wrist before his wince reminded me that it was the one Elinor had bitten. He shook himself free and lifted a finger to point at me.

"You're choosing this ending, Adrienne, just remember that." With that, he stalked off, leaving me buried in confusion.

Chapter Seventeen
Numb

THE NEXT FEW DAYS PASSED with alarming speed, and I had nothing but miles on my shoes to show for them. My mother remained resolutely mute about my father's identity whenever I could corner her, and Dad professed not to know anything. My Internet searches failed to turn up any new information about the time when my mother was a nobody. Jake quit his job as my bodyguard for a minor movie role, a fact my mother held over me the morning after, as if it were my fault. That afternoon, she headed off to another meeting with some director, disappearing for a week. Edmund had to return to London to "deal with something important." Sydney was staying with a friend of hers for a few days, Damien had been out of town for a week, to return at an indefinite day ahead, so I was left alone at the manor with no one but Elinor and nothing but the quiet moors—along with the Internet—to keep me occupied.

Every day, rain or shine, I dragged my computer outside onto the lawn, and as Elinor gamboled about the lawn and groundskeepers trimmed the grass and tended the flowers, I sprawled on a blanket and kept an eye on the clouds, ready to run inside should they open. When they inevitably did, I rushed into my favorite sitting room, or else waited out the rush of rain in the carriageway along the mysteriously abandoned west wing, where I was guaranteed silence and privacy.

Finding answers to my past was harder than finding a moose to show a tourist back home. They always knew when you wanted to find them, and avoided you like they were camera shy.

I needed a name—a suspect—to revive my searches, and there was no one to give it.

Every day, I searched the online movie databases for casts and crew, cross searching with my mother's name in a search engine until my back and neck ached. I rented my mother's earliest movies, and purchased them when I couldn't. After fast forwarding to the end of every movie, I scrutinized the credits down to the stunt men, then performed more Internet searches in the hopes that someone's image would pop up and I would see a familial resemblance. I had taken to comparing my photo to that of James and Victoria, trying to identify the traits that I had which neither of them did—genetic traits that had to be from my father. After all that, I could only narrow it down to a rather modest dimple I'd always sported.

I spent days on social media tracking down and messaging what had to be hundreds of people. I kept a spreadsheet with names, age, contact information, where I found their names, what dates I could link them to Victoria, what genetic traits we seemed to share, and any other data I could come up with, as well as their responses to me. Few had much to offer. If anyone ever found this spreadsheet, they'd have to think I was an identity thief.

And none of it had worked. I just had hundreds of suspects and couldn't rule out anyone. I felt like a lousy detective investigating dead end after dead end, without enough evidence to scrounge up another lead.

The only escape from my constant failures was running, which I did more and more. Now, I aimed my feet toward Damien's property and powered up a steep hill. Although I ran frequently on his land, I had yet to find his home. Today, though, I was determined.

Finally, around mile fifteen, after a few circles through the woods, past modest farmhouses and lots of sheep and cows, I stumbled upon a gigantic mansion that had to be double the size of Chadwick Manor. It perched on the edge of the cliff, with what looked like less of a backyard than Chadwick Manor; a view from the choicest of these rooms had to look directly down into the water.

Gasping more from the sight than my run up the hill, I halted at the top of a grassy mound. Did anyone still live in buildings like these? Elinor dashed down the other side of the hill without pause.

Slowly, I followed toward the green hedges. It looked as though one hedge had been planted and then the middle and four pathways were cut out to plant a spouting fountain of four horses in the middle. The step-down garden crossed the entire front portion of the house, creating a grand entrance where a pale tan gravel drive snaked between the garden and the house.

It was directly out of a movie, with its brilliant green gardens and flowering fields. Making my way down the hill, curving around the trees and under the roaming hills, I lost sight of the manor more than once as I picked up a jog.

Atop the next hill, nothing lay between me and the building except grass. And a man running with his Border Collie.

The collie ran across the green, dashing ahead of the man, while a panting Elinor appeared at my side, ears tall with interest, but too tired to dash after the other dog like she ordinarily might.

She followed my slow descent down the hill, toward the oblivious man and dog. The man watched his feet hit the ground, intent on either his stride or keeping himself from tripping.

Elinor barked once beside me. The other dog's head snapped toward us, then he bolted at us, barking furiously.

A shout rang out from the man, and the dog slid to a halt, but his gaze remained trained on Elinor, who headed down to meet him, tail wagging cautiously.

Commanding Elinor back to me, I jogged toward them, gaining speed as I coasted down the hill, and she failed to return to my side. "Sorry," I called when I got closer. Elinor sniffed the other dog, whose tail wagged in welcome.

"Did you run the entire way?" a familiar voice asked, a bit breathless as though he had sprinted up to me.

"Oh." I cast Damien a smile. "I didn't recognize you. I didn't think you were back. Is this your dog?"

"Yes . . . McDuff the Border Collie."

Elinor, finding energy from somewhere, talked McDuff into playing with her.

"You like running?" I asked.

"Didn't I tell you?" He fell into step beside me while the dogs gamboled around us. Meeting the collie had infused new energy into Elinor, and she kept trying to invite him to play, but he was more interested in sniffing bushes and running ahead to the cliff.

"Tell me what? That movie stars are just like other people? They can like running too?"

He grinned. "Well, that too, but no." He gave a huge sigh. "My agent convinced me to sign up for the marathon this spring. Although I must have been mad to agree, I'm running to raise support for sexual assault victims."

I had stopped walking before I realized it, staring at him with a mixture of surprise and admiration.

Pausing, he frowned back at me. "Something wrong?"

"No." The surprise was fading, and admiration taking hold. "What marathon?"

"London."

"That's the one I'm training for then."

"Really? Excellent. Now I have someone to run with."

"Why didn't you say something sooner? We could have been training together. At least on your slow days."

He laughed. "I'm not fast. I'm certain you could outrun me."

The dogs raced each other back to us across the field. Ahead a domed, white building peeked out from behind a copse. One of those old British traditions I had never understood was making an expensive, useless building on an estate. It was a status of wealth, but it truly lived up to its name: a folly.

We headed toward it, lapsing into silence. I felt like we should have been running—we had both been on our runs after all—but it was far too comfortable to simply walk side by side.

"I'm not sure I'm staying for the wedding." The words surprised us both, coming out unprovoked as they did from my lips.

We had walked at least ten slow steps when Damien responded with a simple, "Why?"

"I just . . . You know I—" I broke off and started again. "It's pretty clear to anyone with half a brain that I don't get along with my mother. But . . . I get the feeling that she doesn't care to have me there. And why stay? I'm an adult gaining a stepfather, not a child. Whether I'm here for the wedding or not makes no difference. This is the most I'll ever live with them."

Damien listened with his head bent toward the ground thoughtfully.

"The wedding is in three weeks, and . . ." I trailed off, glancing up at the sky, where clouds were rippling across the blue above the sea. "The only reason I'm here is to try and get the truth out of my mother." Admitting that felt traitorous. I didn't care about the wedding, I didn't feel happy or sad for her. I hardly felt anything at all. "Is there something wrong with me?"

"No. There's nothing wrong with you," Damien answered before I could doubt raising the question. "You're just trying to figure out where you stand in her life, and she's not helping."

I scoffed. "You know I'm trying to find out who my father is without her. You don't happen to know—do you?" My question was aimed at him in jest, but at the look on his face, my heart went to my toes. "You don't—do you?"

Damien stared ahead at the folly, rolling his shoulders as though they were stiff.

"Damien?" The sea roared in my ears. "Please tell me if you know anything."

He raised his face to the sky, squinting into the weak spring sun. The ground was damp under our feet, but I didn't notice any of it. All I could do was scrutinize him. Finally, with a nod, he motioned to the folly we quickly approached.

"Let's sit down."

Arms tight around my ribs, trying to hold my heart in the right place, I followed, desiring both to race to the steps and prolong the moment. The dogs scrambled up the steps ahead of us, into the covered area of the pillared Greek-style building.

He waited for me to sit first, then sat and angled his body toward me, the earnestness in his gaze reminding me of sun-warmed pools of seawater.

"What do you know?" I urged.

He folded his hands in his lap, inspecting them for a moment before speaking. "Do you know a woman named Hope Grosner?"

"Grosner?" I echoed. "No. Who is she?"

"She was flatmates with your mother when Victoria filmed *Divine Mercy*," he said slowly.

I recognized the title as her first successful role, her breakout role.

"Hope was a struggling actress at the time. Since then, she's become a rather successful screenwriter. I worked with her recently, where she shared some information that might—"

"How recently?" I interrupted.

He pressed his lips together. "When I was gone last week . . . I met her."

Heart blocking my throat, I leaned away from him, wishing it would stop jumping around. "On purpose?"

He frowned. "Of course, it wasn't an accident—"

"No, I mean—" I broke off, not sure how to phrase it. "I guess I mean why did you meet her?" My fingers gripped the edge of the stone bench as I tilted forward, hardly breathing, awaiting his answer.

His smile tightened around the edges. "I knew of her connection to Victoria. It came up once before, when we worked together years ago. With this whole scandal," he motioned broadly to me and the expanse of lawn we'd crossed as if to include it, "I thought maybe it would help to ask her some questions. And I didn't want to get your hopes up if she didn't know anything."

Numbness had settled over my body. *He didn't want to get my hopes up. He didn't want to tell me because he didn't know if she'd know anything. Which means she knows something. And he has to have found it out, or he wouldn't be telling me now. Would he?* My heart gave a lurch in my throat. "Well?"

He fortified himself with a breath, reached out and took my hands in his. "She gave me a name, Adrienne."

Tears burned at the backs of my eyes. "She did?"

He hesitated, gazing down at our hands, rubbing my thumb with his. "And I know him. If you want to meet him, I can arrange it."

"Who?"

"His name is Matthew Dennison."

The name meant nothing to me. I shook my head, ice feathering out from my heart to all edges of my body. I had thought if this moment came, my mind would race, I would know exactly what I wanted, what to do, and how to do it. But instead, I simply felt numb.

☽

When I approached the manor through a steady deluge of rain, cramps radiated through my legs. The pain relieved me with its distraction, so I welcomed it. I had pushed myself harder on my return, eager to avoid thinking, eager to tire myself out and prevent my thoughts from following me late into the night, if at all possible. And still, the thoughts knocked at the back of my mind. Damien might have found my father. *My father.*

My skin broke out in goosebumps even though the rain had begun to let up. I stumbled, righted myself, and started a cool-down lap around the manor, not ready to go inside. And so it was in the garden that I found Kat pacing. A hood covered her pink hair, and her wide eyes seemed wider under the gloom as they fixed on me with a haunted expression.

"What are you doing here?" My voice barely carried over the storm, but she put a finger to her lips and motioned me away from the building.

"Waiting for you. Come on."

Before I could ask her why she was here instead of inside, she turned and began to walk away from me and the manor. Elinor, without a glance at me, rushed toward the warmth of the building, pawing at the door and nosing her way inside when it opened. I made a halfhearted attempt to call her back.

"Where are we going?" Wind rushed past my cheeks and I zipped my jacket up to my chin. Her presence had driven my thoughts out of my mind; something was wrong.

"Somewhere private," she called over her shoulder. "We have to talk."

"This isn't private enough?" She walked so quickly that I had to urge my aching body into a jog to catch up.

"No." Short, clipped steps across the waterlogged grass matched her short, clipped tone.

The rain thickened again, and frisky fingers of wind pulled at our jackets and hoods as we made our way across the grass and back the way I'd come. We couldn't be going that far, though, not unless she had a car stashed somewhere. Every step added to my aches, and soon I was shivering in a mixture of rain and my own sweat.

Kat led me confidently and silently away from the manor to the path toward the beach. I resolved to let her break the silence, not for pride's sake, but for the sake of leaving her unpressured. My mind wandered back to my conversation with Damien, but the wind and Kat's strange behavior pulled me back.

We hit the cliffs, and just when I thought she was going to stop at the edge, she turned and began walking along the top. After five minutes, and passing the only path down I knew about, I broke my promise. "Where are you taking me?"

"Away from listening ears." No humor laced her tone; it was the darkest I'd ever heard her speak.

"Are you that afraid someone might overhear us?" I had to raise my voice to be heard over the wind and rain, which crescendoed around us, and ripped my hair into tangles I knew I'd spend an hour trying to get out.

She didn't answer, and I vowed again to remain quiet. Another five minutes, and a path appeared that seemed more sheep trail than anything else. She hooked a turn and started down.

My feet stuttered to a stop. I could handle heights, but this wasn't even a game trail. As I hesitated, she slid down half a dozen feet and landed sure-footedly on a small ledge. Then she flashed a subdued smile and motioned up at me.

"Come on!" Her voice drifted back, devoid of amusement or any other emotion I could detect. "It's safe."

With a glance at my shoes, I removed my hands from my pockets and took a step of faith. When I risked a glance to see where Kat was, she had disappeared. Momentum carried me another step, then I was performing the same slide as Kat—with decidedly less grace. As soon as I reached the ledge, my heart hammering in my chest, her voice, wryly amused, reached me.

"In here."

I blinked in surprise. Kat stood in the rock. Sunlight filtering through rain and clouds offered a weak arc of light into the mouth of the cave where she stood. Rain chased me inside until I went beyond the beam of light, shaking the water from my clothing.

"It's not big, but it'll do." Kat swept an arm at the cave, but turned on a flashlight.

"You're not afraid someone might be in here eavesdropping?" I couldn't help the sarcasm dripping from my words as thickly as the rain dripping off my hair.

Stoic, Kat shook her head. "No one else knows about it."

Raking my hands through my wet hair, I glanced around for a place to sit. I selected a small outcrop of rock and perched against it, stretching out my left calf by bringing my toes toward me. "Out with it then," I said through my wince. "What's such a secret?"

"Are you . . . still seeing Jake?"

"No." A half laugh caught in my throat, and I slipped, grabbing at the wet wall to reclaim my seat. "I never was, not really."

Clothes dripping onto the cave floor, she nodded. "I owe you an explanation."

Chapter Eighteen
Kat's Secret

KAT SANK DOWN AND FOLDED her legs in the middle of the cave. The flashlight she placed on the floor beamed up to the ceiling and reflected poorly off it, but managed to illuminate the area just enough for us to see each other, casting shadows that lengthened her nose and sharpened her cheekbones.

This time, I waited for her, biting back my irritation as water dripped off my arm and splashed into a small hollow in the cave's rock floor.

"It's about Jake. It's on par with your Bryan and Victoria story."

A slow breath of stale air filled my lungs, and I held it inside as the world went still. "Okay," I said slowly. "Any of the same players?"

She frowned at me, searching for understanding. Her eyes widened when she found it and she shook her head. "No. No. Maybe I should start at the beginning."

"Wise." The knot in my stomach eased a notch. When she didn't immediately continue, I suggested, "Should I have brought a bottle of whisky?"

Her lips flickered at this, but any remnant of true humor was snuffed out before it had a chance to breathe. She twisted her hands in her lap, and began to speak. "Jake came to live with us when I was twelve and he was fourteen. His parents had both died in a car crash, and he was rough around the edges. I loved that about him. He became my idol. But he went off to school and he didn't think about me much, I don't think. Not until he returned home after a year of boarding school. I was there for the summer, going to boarding school myself, and we . . ." She shrugged. "We dated awhile. When I was sixteen, seventeen."

"You said. How long is awhile?"

"Yeah. A year or so." Now that the story had begun, the words poured forth like the rain outside the cave. "He was cute and charming, and I thought I loved him." She stared down at her hands in her lap, where her fingers lay entwined. "I pursued him. I thought we would one day be married, make babies." Her lips twisted at this. "I didn't recognize him for what he was: a charming playboy. But he amused himself with me. I didn't realize that until it was too late."

The saddest smile I'd ever seen trembled on her lips. "We went too fast. I gave him too much too quickly, and . . ." She twisted her fingers together more tightly. "I was seventeen. We'd slept together a couple of times, but I told him I wasn't ready and wanted to stop it. Later, he tried again, and when I said, 'no,' he . . . did it anyway."

The atmosphere of the cave intensified the shriek of my quick breath. Bile rose in my throat at the thought of how he had touched her, taken advantage of her. And I had allowed him to touch me. "I'm so sorry, Kat. I had no idea."

My mind raced. He hadn't seemed that way . . . he was a flirt, sure, but a rapist? Could it have been a horrible mistake? *A mistake?* I shook my head at myself. Rape was never a mistake.

"No. No one does." Kat's steely gaze met mine and hardened to flint. "Not really. Those who learned about it thought I was a liar."

"Who?"

"The police." Her voice hardened. "My father . . ." She paused and started again. "When I finally told Damien, a couple months later, when I could—could talk about it, Father insisted I report it to the police. Jake and I had broken up by then, and . . ." Trailing off, she shrugged. "I reported him, and Jake denied it. There was no evidence of anything but a consensual relationship." Her eyes shone in the pale light of the cave.

My heart ached for her. How someone could have gone through all that—being branded a liar after being so violated—and kept it all secret on top of it? It would torment me in my dreams, and it must have done the same to Kat.

"Please, Adrienne, it's incredibly important that you tell no one else about this." She fixed her gaze on me, twisting her fingers so tightly in her lap it looked like she was trying to break one.

"Of course. I won't tell." I didn't have to hesitate to promise her that. It wasn't my secret to tell.

An especially large water droplet fell from the ceiling and splashed upon my arm so hard it splattered my cheek, but I didn't tear my gaze from Kat.

She lifted her chin, but closed her eyes and lips so tightly I thought she might have succeeded in breaking a finger. "I can't bear it if others know."

I ran my fingers over my face, smoothing them up over my forehead, skimming over my eyebrows and circling them back to rest under my lashes and cover my mouth and nose. The taste in my mouth reminded me of seawater: brackish and enough to sicken me, as though I'd swallowed too much while swimming.

Tears illuminated her eyes when she opened them, glinting on her lower lashes in the flashlight's beam.

"I'm not going to be here for the wedding." Kat lifted her chin in defiance. "I can't be here . . ."

I opened my mouth to speak, to tell her that Jake had already gone, then shut it again.

Kat spoke to her hands again, her lower lip trembling. "I just can't be here anymore. Every time I come home, I . . ." Eyes closed, she shook her head, spraying water from her hood in droplets.

My stomach churned as memories of the times I had unwittingly brought Kat's rapist to her doorstep assailed me. I had been tormenting her without realizing it. Every word I said about Jake had to have ripped open her wound, every time I had walked off into the park with him had to have driven her insane.

"I just can't do it anymore. I can't keep seeing him. It's always like this, whenever I'm here."

"I understand." I hesitated. "I'll tell Victoria. She'll be fine with it. She'll have to understand. But he's quit his bodyguard job, you know."

"He has?"

"Yes. So if that's why you're going—"

"No."

We fell silent a minute, my mind racing over everything she'd told me and how I could have missed any clues. "Was this what you went to her for help about?"

Staring at her hands, Kat didn't answer immediately, but her forehead creased, and I knew she'd heard me. Finally, she shook her head. "No. It was something else."

Something you're not ready to tell me, I finished for her in my head. "Okay." I tried to smile, but found my lips too numb to respond. The minutes ticked away as the gloomy rain continued outside. When Kat stood, every layer of her clothes dripped onto the cave floor. "We should get back."

Her abruptness surprised me, but I pushed away from the wall and followed, realizing she was done sharing.

$$\mathbb{)}$$

I didn't sleep well that night. Between both Damien and Kat's confessions, my mind couldn't quiet. If I succeeded in smothering one, the other roared to life.

The next morning I dragged myself out of bed, more exhausted than when I'd lain down. Still, I postponed my morning run and instead spent the morning on my computer, searching not my mother's name this time, but Jake's.

True to Kat's word, there was no evidence of Jake's sordid past. I found nothing indicating that he had ever been arrested, or even that she had told the police as she claimed. Still, I had to trust her. She couldn't fake that sort of pain, that deep wound inside her I had finally glimpsed yesterday.

It was early afternoon by the time I dragged on my running clothes and hit Edmund's private gym for some severely overdue strength training.

An hour or so later, when I made my way back to my room to shower, I heard a screech echo through the foyer. Alarmed, I crossed the room at a run, looking over as Damien appeared with mirrored concern on his face.

"What—?" he began.

"I don't know."

We took the stairs two and three at a time, and when we reached the top, another scream sounded from our left. With a half glance at each other, we raced in that direction. I reached my mother's room a half second before him and slid to a halt.

Damien rammed into me, unprepared for my quick stop. He grasped my shoulders in his hands, his breath whistling past my ear as he gasped in shock.

White fluff fluttered around the room as though it were snowing, yet a quick glance told me it was silken fabric, not snow. From the four-poster bed hung what had once been an undoubtedly beautiful wedding dress, now immaculate from the waist up, but shredded to bits from the waist down. Beside it stood Charity Harper in a pinstripe pencil skirt and high heels elongating her already tall frame.

"What happened?" Damien breathed.

In the middle of the room, tears streaming cleanly down her cheeks in two trails, mascara perfect and unmarred, but eyes and nose reddened by emotion, Victoria released two handfuls of white fabric into the air. It caught the drafts in the air buffeted by the heat of a low burning fire in the fireplace, and floated upward before drifting down to the floor like a feather. "*This* happened. Thanks to *your* dog." She aimed the second part at me with fury unlike anything I'd ever seen on her face. I stepped back at the expression, stopped only by the solidity of Damien behind me.

Drawing in a deep breath, I searched the room for Elinor, who was nowhere to be seen. I could only imagine where she was, off in some previously-unexplored-to-her area of the manor, or outside chasing rabbits.

"Where's your dog, huh?" Victoria advanced on me, finger hovering through the air at my chest. "Where's the beast responsible for this mess?"

Damien tightened his grip on my upper arms and pulled me back against him as though to shield me from my mother. "Victoria, are you sure?"

"Of course I'm sure!" She returned to her dress, grabbed a handful and shook it at us. "Look at this!" With a furious scoff, she dashed her hand back down, what was left of the dress snapping upward on its hanger at the motion.

"Victoria, calm down," Charity said, her lilting Irish voice bringing unexpected peace to the room.

Hands clenched into fists, Victoria fixed her gaze on Charity and inhaled deeply.

"We'll call the designer and pick up another dress." Charity held up a hand to stem Victoria's objections. "No, it won't be the same, but there was that other dress you loved almost as much."

Victoria closed her mouth, reluctant consideration playing across her face as Charity continued.

"If Edmund hasn't left London yet, he can swing by on his way out of town. Even if he has, we'll have it here by tomorrow afternoon, and it can be fitted in time for the wedding. We have plenty of time."

Although my mother's eyes were still darkened with fury, she accepted the tissue Charity handed to her and dabbed her face with it. "Yes. Yes, that's what we'll do. I'm sorry. I'm just being . . . a perfectionist. Your idea will work."

I blinked. *Did Victoria Talbot—my* mother—*just apologize?*

She turned to us, standing in the doorway. "I'm sorry," she repeated. "That wasn't fair."

Surprise stole my words. As I gaped at her, Damien gripped my elbow in his fingers and squeezed slightly.

"Of course," he replied smoothly, neither accepting nor rejecting the apology on my behalf. "Of course this wasn't desirable. I'm sorry this happened. It certainly wasn't intended."

Emotion I couldn't name flickered over her face. She threw her tissue into a nearby trashcan and sank into a chair by the fire. "The whole thing has just been a nightmare." Her shoulders stooped, and Charity sank into the chair across from her.

"I know. But we'll get it all taken care of. And you'll have the most beautiful wedding ever."

Damien tugged at my arm. The motion suggested that we should leave Victoria to herself, for there was nothing we could do, and I nodded.

"Adrienne." My name caught me as I was closing the door, and I looked inside to meet my mother's solemn gaze. "Stay. I need to talk to you."

I pushed open the door another inch, certain I'd misheard. "What?"

Her answering look was both exasperated and exhausted. "We need to talk."

"Right."

Charity leaned forward and murmured something, to which Victoria replied, "Well, you can handle it. You know what I want."

Charity looked as though she might say something sharp, but with a half glance at me, bit it back instead. When she passed me, she gave me the smallest smile, one that left me unsure if it was supposed to be encouraging or condoling.

Spurn the Moon

After she left me alone in the room with my mother, I continued standing near the door.

"Come, sit down." Victoria motioned to the chair across from her, but didn't watch me cross and sit. Instead, she stared into the crackling fire, lost in her own thoughts.

Chapter Nineteen
Through the Moors

MY MIND RACED WITH QUESTIONS as though it was running a marathon at sprinting pace. This was the most time I had spent alone with her in weeks. What would she tell me now that I knew so much?

Even as I wondered, I knew it didn't matter anymore. I would find my answer without her.

What if she doesn't know? What if she's embarrassed? A little voice inside me asked. Everything went quiet in my world. I couldn't believe I hadn't thought of that before. Did she know? Perhaps my parentage was in question to *her* as well as me. Perhaps she had been with several men at the time of my conception and she honestly didn't know. But she at least would be able to tell me guesses—right? And then my mind took a turn. Kat had confided in my mother about something. Something Kat hadn't told me.

"Adrienne," she began.

"How well do you know Kat?" My words cut across her so completely that the exhaustion left her face to be replaced with surprise.

Considering me, she tilted her head. "Well enough, I suppose."

My breath caught just inside my lips.

"What is this about?" Her forehead furrowed.

"You've maintained a relationship with her while you and I were . . ." I cast around for the right word and settled on, "estranged."

She dipped her head into a nod. "Yes. We have."

"Why? What did she need from you?"

My mother blinked, then her gaze fell to the floor, where it seemed to fixate on the ornate flowery pattern of the rug. "Did she tell you how I helped her out of a sticky situation once?"

"Yes."

"So you'll know she got herself in trouble."

Trouble? My mind raced as I tried to play along. She had been in despair, surely. But could one call being raped "trouble"?

"She came to me asking for advice. What to do with it. Something that wouldn't affect her entire life." Her amethyst eyes flicked down to where my hands gripped the chair's arms. "She was woefully unprepared to be a mother."

The chair bucked underneath me. Try as I might, I couldn't force my gaping mouth to form words.

A heavy sigh wrenched itself from her body. "My advice was not . . ." She stopped, clenching her eyes shut so her silvery eyeshadow caught the firelight and gleamed. She exhaled through her nose and continued. "I regret my advice, Adrienne." Tilting her head back against the chair, she opened her eyes and stared at the ceiling as though her lines were written there. "I have a lot of regrets." Her voice twisted, the familiar honey tones gone, turned rancid. "And that is one of my greatest ones."

"What . . ." I didn't want to let on that I didn't have any idea what she was talking about, for what she knew, I wanted desperately to know. But what she knew was not what I had anticipated. *Kat had been pregnant?* As my mind scrambled, I forced my mouth to ask, "What did you tell her?"

Very slowly, she raised her gaze to mine, her eyes wet, her lips trembling around the corners. "I said to get rid of it." Her mouth turned as though she might be sick.

"And did she?"

"Yes." Tears brimmed over her lashes, spilling onto her ivory cheeks. Her face was flushing, from anger and sadness and all the emotion I was realizing she always kept in check.

"Do you know . . ." I hesitated, wondering if I could be betraying Kat by asking.

"What?"

"Who the father was?"

She seemed surprised that I would care, but shook her head. "No. Kat didn't confide in me that far. But I gathered that he would not be in the picture."

"Right." I exhaled slowly through my nose.

"I know you think I'm a failure as a mother. And, most days, I agree with you." She inhaled a shaky breath. "I don't know why you've stayed this long. I've not treated you like a daughter. I just . . ."

I didn't fill the silence that surrounded us. Nothing I said would alleviate her concerns; I wouldn't lie to make her feel better.

All of a sudden, she leaned forward and covered her face with her hands. "I'm sorry for not being a mother to you, Adrienne. I'm sorry for leaving. I'm sorry for hiding the truth from you. And for the scandal . . ." Still leaning forward, she brought up her face so her chin rested in her hands and peered at me. "I never meant to hurt you."

At first her words didn't register with me over the crackling of the fire. "You released the scandal?" It was hardly a question, and she hardly gave an answer, just a closing of her eyes and slight dip of her head.

"You weren't supposed to be here." She pressed her fingertips over her mouth. "You wouldn't have had to deal with the paparazzi outside of London . . . I thought if I left for a while and didn't give you the answers you wanted, you'd go home and ask James or maybe go to Oxford early, or do the traveling James said you were going to do." The skin around her eyes crinkled as they narrowed at me. "I didn't think that would make you stick around more."

Thoughts and emotions in turmoil, I couldn't form coherent words. All I came up with was: "On purpose?"

Her forehead furrowed. "It was all on purpose, Adrienne."

Everything. She had tried to manipulate me. She had released the scandal herself, tried to get me out of the spotlight by not giving me information and . . .

"I don't understand," I said. "That doesn't make sense."

"No." She shook her head. "It probably doesn't. Just like what I did with Bryan didn't make sense to you."

A cold hand gripped me at her words. Of all things, I hadn't been prepared to talk about Bryan tonight. "Wait," I said to her as much as myself. "Let's talk about one thing at a time. The scandal. You released it," I said, and she nodded. "Why?"

A conflicted shadow played across her features. "You think I don't know the type of person I am, Adrienne. You think I don't realize what you think of me."

A flush burned at the apples of my cheeks, but I forced the embarrassment away.

"I'm tired."

I frowned.

"Of holding on to secrets. Of fighting with the paparazzi, of so many things . . ."

I still wasn't quite following her.

"And it was only a matter of time before they discovered this. I had been talking to an old friend, and my relationship with—" She broke off, looking sidelong at me.

"With my biological father?" I prompted.

"Yes." She seemed on the cusp of something, and so I figured it was now that I could relieve her from the burden of sharing that knowledge with me.

"With Matthew Dennison?"

A sharp breath widened my mother's eyes. "How did you—?"

I both shrugged and shook my head. "Not important. Why didn't *you* tell me?"

The tension seemed to drain from her shoulders. "I told you. I didn't want the press coming to you. I thought I could control it. After all, why would they care that much? But I had forgotten how young I had been, how much they revel in past mistakes of A-listers, and what they did to get to the top." She gave an apologetic shake of her chin. "And there's always a writer doing an exposé on the sins of Hollywood. And then there was you—innocent blood, and beautiful to boot." She frowned and leaned back in her chair.

"Okay. So you've known Dennison is my father. Since the beginning?" Anger burned in my chest, slow and steady. "And why didn't you share this with me when it became clear I was going to find out by myself?" My lips tightened as I thought of how I hadn't been able to find out on my own. But surely I would have tracked down Hope at some point.

She gave me another sad smile. "I kept hoping you'd change your mind." She sighed. "I knew you wouldn't. You're too much like me."

At this comment, I turned to the fire, which now burned low behind its fancy iron grate. Even though the sweat from my workout had cooled and dried on my skin by now, these fires kept me warm, both inside and out. "And you're sure?"

"Sure?"

"About Dennison being my father?"

A breath left her mouth so quietly that I could just hear it over the fire. "Yes, sweetheart. I'm sure."

"Right. And . . . does he know?"

She didn't reply for so long that I turned from the fire to face her, and found her gazing at me with a thoughtful twist to her lips. "Not that I'm aware of."

"You never told him."

"No. I married your fa—James instead."

My head bobbed in answer just for something to reply with, for my tongue seemed to have gone as numb as the rest of my body.

"Adrienne, James loves you. And I know I acted selfishly in telling the media about my affair, but . . . he'll always be your father. No matter who fathered you."

"I know." The words came out small and distant. There seemed nothing more to say on the subject. My biological father was not James Talbot, it was a man named Matthew Dennison, and my mother had confirmed it.

All of a sudden, it became too much. I rocketed to my feet, aware of my mother's shocked gaze following me.

"I can't—" My voice broke as tears tightened my throat. "I thought—" I tried again, and my voice failed again. And with tears burning my nose and blurring my eyes, I turned and rushed from the room, unable to handle any more damned truths.

$$\mathstrut$$

☽

I spent the next day in York with Sydney, escaping my thoughts, the manor and the wedding preparations already taking place inside and out. We walked the streets, me doing everything I could to distract myself from what my mother had told me the night before. When I had woken that morning, my eyes had been bloodshot, my throat and nose raw from my tears. For so long, I had resisted the very truth I sought. And now that it was here in front of me, I felt as though I had lost my father. Almost as though he had died.

"Isn't that hilarious?" Sydney asked.

"Huh? Oh, yes." I winced, realizing I hadn't been paying any attention to her.

She continued chatting about her friends and hobbies, but mostly about how she had begun dating a boy she wasn't sure her dad would approve of.

"Not that boy at Damien's party?" I asked, putting the pieces together.

"Did you see us there?" Her face went pale, then the color of the red silk she'd forced me into at my mother's engagement party.

Shrugging, I gave a little smirk. "Yeah. You were standing there in the living room talking with him. Was I not supposed to?"

She turned away, staring into the shops we walked past. "Do you think Dad saw me?"

"I didn't even see your father, so I don't know."

"Oh."

"Why do you think he'd care?"

"He always cares who I date." She shook her head, a sullen tone having entered her voice. "He never lets me go on dates, so I've been seeing Luke secretly."

"Luke? Is that his name?"

Stopping, she whirled back to me and grabbed my arm. "Please don't tell Dad!"

"No, no. I—" I stared at her with confusion. "I—"

"He'd have a fit, and I don't want to get him concerned with everything else he's dealing with."

"But I don't understand. Just because you're dating someone? He'd be that upset? Or because it's Luke?"

"Just because I'm dating. He doesn't want me to."

"Oh. Okay. Well . . ." I shrugged. "Just promise me you'll tell him yourself."

Her eyes went wide with alarm. "What?"

I laughed at her teenage shock. "You can't keep this secret forever!"

Her lips twisted, but humor glinted in her eyes. "I can try."

"No," I said firmly, slipping my arm through her elbow. "You can't. Secrets have a way of coming out. And it's a lot better if you share them first."

With a grimace, she nodded. "All right. I'll try."

"Thank you. The last thing we need around here is another secret."

"What do you mean?" she asked, her interest piqued.

I pressed a smile to my lips. "Nothing. Nothing at all. Oh! A bookstore.

Let's go in."

When we returned home, it was dinnertime and we headed in, finding a semi-empty table. Edmund was there, but Victoria was upstairs with a headache.

Despite my nonverbal prodding, Sydney kept her mouth shut, and I didn't press the issue more. She could think about it. I had far too many things to think about myself these days. My phone buzzed in my pocket, and when I reached for it, Edmund shot me a look.

"No phones at the table, please, Adrienne."

"Right." Despite it buzzing again a minute later, reminding me I'd missed a text, I ignored it. When I left the table twenty minutes later, I had forgotten about the message. I found it when I climbed into bed after a shower. "Can you drive up to Scotland with me tomorrow morning?" Damien had texted. "We've got a meeting."

My stomach clenched, but I texted back. "Yes. I'll be ready."

Chapter Twenty
On Set

Damien collected me outside Chadwick Manor while the morning dew still clung to the golf quality grass. I shivered as he drove up in a small sports car, for my shower-dampened hair made the morning chill sink deep.

"I would have come in and got you," Damien said when I climbed into his Jaguar.

"Fancy." I motioned tot the car as I tried to shrug off my chill, but ended up shuddering, my teeth chattering.

"Thanks. But you shouldn't have been sitting outside."

"It's fine. I was ready, and why waste time?" My attempt at a grin faded quickly between my nerves at the day ahead, my chill, and my previous night's discussion with Victoria. "Now we can go get coffee, right?"

He chuckled and turned up the sports car's heat. "Yes. Coffee was never in question, though. I know the perfect café on the way."

Damien drove us down Chadwick Manor's drive, onto the shared road, and back the way I'd come up from London, on until the road became a T. He turned north and sped away from the manors, leaving the coast behind us and heading into a national park, something noted in a few street signs along the way. Twenty minutes into the drive, just when

I was beginning to wonder if he'd forgotten about the promise of coffee, we drove into a village made up of stone houses, with red-tile roofs and white, many-paned windows. He parked along the curb and shut off the engine.

"Coffee?" I reached for my seatbelt, blinking the weariness out of my eyes.

He grinned. "This is a great café. Here." He extended a travel coffee mug to me. "You'll need this."

"Oh?"

"No take-away cups here," he explained as I met him on the curb. "Unless you want to drink your coffee here . . ." He trailed off and shrugged.

"Right. Thanks." A small stone house on the curb had been converted into a little café in the front, with a large window displaying coffee beans, scales, and other antiques. Inside, a full service coffee house yawned open like a cave, the interior dark and soothing, and the mostly empty chairs forming gaps like missing teeth. Two seats in front of a propane fire were empty, as if waiting for us.

"Oh." I sighed and hugged my arms around myself. "I could just curl up here."

Damien grinned over his shoulder as he headed to the counter. "Not today, I'm afraid." To the employee, he said, "Hiya, Tom."

Tom, a gangly looking young man with straw-blond hair, gave a nod, his eyes wide in what seemed like constant surprise.

We ordered our coffees from Tom and were back on the road in five minutes, with some of the best coffee I'd ever had. Damien had been right.

"So where are we going?" I asked as we passed through fields of thistles and heather.

"Well, Dennison is filming up near the Scottish border. He's expecting us. I told him lunch, but we'll be there a bit early. We can hang out on set and watch for a bit. If you don't mind."

I shrugged. "Yeah. Sure."

A frown turned down the corners of his lips. "Have you spent a lot of time on set?"

Surprised at his question, I shook my head. "No. Why?"

"Most people are thrilled with the idea of visiting a set. Seeing famous people and all that."

My shoulders shook in a dry laugh. "Yeah. Famous people. I can't say I care about meeting any more of those."

"Oh? Am I enough for you?" he asked in a tone so serious that I turned and blinked at him. "No need for anyone else?"

I grinned when I realized he was kidding. "Oh, right. Between you and my mother, I'm good."

"All right, but don't be swayed by the dashing faces you'll see today. Just when I have you right where I want you."

My mouth fell open as I stared at him. Where had this Damien been? "You know, you weren't nearly this friendly when I first met you."

He grimaced. "Yes, well . . . there were some extenuating circumstances that night."

"Like what?" I challenged. "After all, you were so rude you had to apologize. That's more than just British stuffiness."

"British stuffi—" he began, but I cut him off.

"Don't do it. Don't change the subject. What were the extenuating circumstances?"

His nose wrinkled slightly before he turned his face away from me to glance out his window. "Some of the guests there were . . ." He shook his head.

"Are you talking about Kat and Jake?"

His head whipped around so fast I thought he might wreck the car. The front wheel went on the shoulder of the road, and Damien slammed the brakes and jerked the wheel to correct the car.

When we were back on the road, his hands gripping the steering wheel tightly, Damien spoke through thin lips. "What did she tell you?"

"Everything. Well." I took a sip of coffee that miraculously hadn't spilled. "Some I found out from my mother."

His brow furrowed, and he shot me a quizzical look. "Like what?"

"Like Kat got pregnant."

Damien inhaled sharply. "Yes. She did."

I shook my head sadly. "I wish she would have told me earlier."

He didn't answer.

"Why didn't you tell me? Warn me?"

Damien expelled his breath through his nose. "I wanted to. But Kat has always been so insistent that I never tell—especially when telling the police didn't do anything. She vowed to never mention it again, as though she meant to pretend it didn't happen."

"It sounds like she didn't really recover well."

"No. She's . . . found ways to manage, I suppose. But I don't think she ever truly dealt with it."

I frowned out the window as we drove past a low rock fence half hiding behind shrubs and heather. "Doesn't sound like it."

"No." Damien shook his head. "Let's talk about something else. What are you going to ask Dennison?"

My stomach swooped. "Um . . ."

He cast me a sidelong smile. "We'll be there soon. Why don't we figure out what you'll ask him?"

"Yeah." Grimacing, I stared out the window and sipped my coffee, despite it feeling like I was swallowing live snakes. What did I want from Dennison? Why did I feel this need to meet him? What was it I needed to ask him?

Try as I might, I couldn't come up with one decent question during the rest of the ride, except for the obvious: are you my father? And that sounded like something out of a children's book. We were way past that simple question and answer. Weren't we?

$$\smallint\hspace{-4pt}\mathrm{D}$$

When we reached the border, distinguishable from the English country only by a sign placed near the road, my stomach cramped as though there had been milk in my coffee. A slight groan escaped me.

"Are you okay?" Damien glanced at me, concern written in the lines on his face.

I nodded. "Yes. Just nervous."

He pressed a reassuring smile to his lips, put his hand over mine, and gave it a squeeze. He left it there until he needed his hand to shift, something which distracted me so much that my stomach lifted and my breathing calmed. He seemed to realize it, for he returned his hand to mine between shifting, until I closed my eyes and leaned against the seat. By the time the car stopped, I had almost drifted off, exhausted from my recent lack of sleep.

"Adrienne?" Damien's voice nudged me out of that state between consciousness and unconsciousness.

I lifted my head, looking around us. "Are we here?"

"Yes."

The nerves came back as though a cold wave crashed over me. I reached for my coffee, tilting it against my mouth, but it was empty.

Damien smiled. "We'll get you some more. It won't be as good, but . . . Dennison likes his coffee, so . . ."

Instead of soothing me, the information made my stomach squirm. He liked his coffee. As much as I liked mine? Did he like the same kind of coffee as me? My stomach tightened. If he was my father, as everything suggested he was, I didn't even know what kind of coffee he liked. Until now, I hadn't known if he liked coffee at all.

"Come on."

The sun was peeking out from behind bright white clouds when I stepped out of the car onto a temporary grass lawn of a parking lot. To the right was a long stretch of wide, low rock wall amongst the green grass with moving blemishes of white on them.

"This way." Damien pointed to the other direction, and I stood staring after him as he took a few steps. He half turned to see where I was, and halted. When I didn't follow, he returned to my side. "Do you want to do this?"

This had to be what a deer in the headlights felt like, this frightening spotlight, this terrifying feeling that if you didn't move in the right direction, you wouldn't survive to see the next minute. That need to move and yet the inability to do so. Tears burned the back of my throat, swelling it shut.

Without another word, Damien pulled me into his arms. "Hey, it'll be all right."

With my chin resting on his shoulder, my arms loosely around him, I took a deep breath.

"There you go. Just relax, take a few breaths. I won't leave you if you don't want. Not even to use the toilet."

A watery chuckle escaped me. "Great, thanks."

"Although . . ." he began, shifting in my arms. "It was a long drive. And I've had loads of coffee this morning."

I stepped back from him with a false look of irritation. "You promised."

He grimaced, but humor glinted in his eyes. "All right."

A breeze swept up around us, rustling our jackets and hair. Damien checked his watch.

"We should go?" I asked with a wry twist to my lips.

He dipped his head in a nod.

"Right." I dropped my gaze to the ground. My clogs, which I'd worn instead of my sneakers today, along with a pair of crisp khakis gave the impression that I was much more professional than I was. If I wanted to be a doctor, I supposed I'd have to get used to this idea, but I felt like nothing more than a child playing dress up at the moment.

"Come on." Damien took my hand in his, entwining our fingers together, and stepped forward.

I stared at our hands, the way his skin appeared dark against mine, his nicely trimmed nails, the way our arms stretched out, forming a link by our hands between us. Then I took a step, and then another, and our hands fell closer to the ground until I stood even with him, and I lost sight of them, but the strength his touch infused within me grew.

We passed through security without a problem, and a driver with a golf cart drove us from the parking lot into the set, driving around a courtyard of trailers I assumed were for the stars of the movie and for makeup and other such things. I watched the scenery go by in order to distract myself, but Damien's touch did that better than anything I saw.

The driver dropped us off at a large field where a tent had been set up and people in costumes had been assembled.

"What film is this?" I whispered to Damien, not wanting anyone else to overhear my ignorance.

"I can't remember the title. It's changed a couple of times. But it's a Robert Bruce film. Like *Braveheart* from Bruce's point of view."

"Ah. Could be interesting."

Damien nodded. "It's passable, I've read the script."

"Oh? Aren't you special," I teased, even though my stomach had knotted again.

He chuckled.

We stood quietly in the back of the tent for a few moments. Screens displayed what I figured was the scene being performed half a mile away across the field, and a half dozen men and women sat in a line, staring at the picture before them with large headphones over their ears, occasionally muttering something to one another.

Damien pointed to a small table set up with a full coffee pot. I shook my head.

"Which one is he?" I whispered in Damien's ear.

Subtly, he twitched his chin in the direction of a man with collar length dark hair interspersed liberally with gray at the temples, a whorl of hair on the back of his head. A baseball hat hung off one side of the chair's top, advertising for the Seahawks. I didn't follow football, but Alaska had adopted the team as it was the closest to the state, so I was at least familiar with it. I realized suddenly that I didn't know if Dennison was even American or British. In everything that had happened since I'd first heard his name, I hadn't even typed his name into a computer.

Finally the scene ended, and Dennison and the rest of the crew watching pulled off their headphones. He leaned back in his chair and clasped his hands behind his head, stretching his elbows back as far as he could manage, ending with a sickening crunch as his back cracked. He let out a little grunt of satisfaction as those around him rose and began dispersing. A couple stood chatting, with eyes that glanced at us, but I only saw them through my peripheral vision, as my gaze was locked on the back of Dennison's head.

"Ready?" Damien murmured while Dennison leaned forward as though he were going to stand.

I bit down on my bottom lip, but gave a nod.

Damien pulled me forward and with his free hand, clapped a hand onto the director's shoulder.

He jumped at the touch, then turned, and a wide smile spread over his face. "Damien! How's it been going?"

I hardly heard his next words, and tuned out Damien's reply, for I focused on a dimple in Dennison's cheek, so deep I could see it through the week's growth of beard. It was on the same side as mine.

Damien's hand tugged at me. "This is a friend of mine. Adrienne. This is Matthew Dennison."

"Matt, please." Dennison offered his hand to me, and for a second too long, I froze, staring at him, wondering if he really didn't know me, really hadn't heard of me. Then, just about when he was going to take his hand back, I ripped mine from Damien and grabbed Dennison's.

His smile faltered at the edges, the dimple flickering. He had a boyish face almost, but that could have been his round eyes, the long, lush lashes, and the sky-blue color of his irises. My father, James, had brown eyes. I had always wondered how I had lucked out and gotten those unique violet eyes of my mother, when the twins had soft brown eyes with flecks of hazel gold in them.

"Hi. Nice to meet you." I stumbled over my tongue to get the words out, belated. *He must think me an idiot.*

Damien retrieved my hand as I dropped it to my side, enclosing it firmly in his. "So how's the filming going?"

Relief welled up in me. I hadn't expected to be so overwhelmed as I faced my father the first time, but Damien commanding the conversation, and steering it away from me, gave me the much-needed time to recover. They chatted about the film for several minutes, and Dennison jumped into his work, even showing us a scene they'd shot earlier that day. I murmured appreciative comments, while he and Damien talked filming techniques that I couldn't keep up with.

"It reminds me of that one movie, what's the one? With the same style," Damien said, and for the next couple of minutes, the men tried to come up with the right title.

"Well, let's go get coffee, or lunch, or something," Dennison began. "I'm famished."

His grin was quick and ready, his laugh bubbling under the surface, but I sensed that he could change at a moment's notice. An assistant delivered him a cup of coffee, and he couldn't hide the disdain after his first sip. "Can't find a decent cup of coffee in this godforsaken country for the life of me."

I glanced at Damien, but he appeared implacable, giving me a slight smile.

"What's with this tea obsession you insist on keeping? It's the twenty-first century," he complained, motioning us forward to a waiting golf cart. "I've got a half hour before we start filming again, so let's get food."

Damien tugged me along, and I followed obediently, still a bit numb. Dennison jumped in the front beside the driver, and Damien and I sat behind. I didn't let go of him. In my heart, I didn't even have to ask Dennison a question to know the truth. His dimple, his mannerisms, his appearance, they all spoke for themselves. He had a slight wave to his hair, a cowlick in the back where, if I slept on wet hair, my hair curled the same. His lashes were almost the same length as mine, and coal black. His eyes, slightly rounder than almond, showed me where my eyes differed from my mother's narrower, almond shaped ones. His smile quirked in the same way, and that damned dimple made my throat swell shut. I smiled reflexively at him when his grin appeared, but I caught his gaze on my face a couple of times, a hint of unease entering it.

The driver took us back toward the trailers, and dropped us off at one of the smaller ones.

Dennison climbed out, turning to us and saying, "This'll give us a place to sit and eat. It's usually just me in there. I don't stay here at night. Too quiet. I drive back to one of the towns around here. Got a bed and breakfast. Of course, I'm up too early and back too late to use any of their services, but . . ." He shrugged as if it didn't matter anyway.

He pushed open the door, and revealed a small trailer set up as an office. Lunch had been delivered, and a variety of sandwiches sat on the desk, with a choice of sodas, waters, and juices nearby. A few bags of chips lay crumpled beside them, and I was surprised that a movie set didn't offer more interesting food to the director.

"Help yourself," he muttered, slipping off his jacket and hanging it across the back of his chair.

"No thanks." I shook my head when Damien offered me one. "I shouldn't."

Dennison took it in stride, swiping a sandwich for himself, perhaps assuming I was like other girls concerned about their weight. Of more concern to me was the idea of an allergic reaction at this moment in my life.

Damien opened a bag of chips and dug in, offering me one, but I shook my head again.

"So let's get down to it, then. I've only got another fifteen minutes before I need to be back on set. What's up, Damien? Why the meeting?" He leaned back in his chair as he talked around a mouthful of sandwich, untwisting the cap of a water bottle as he spoke.

Damien glanced at me, question in his gaze.

"I'm afraid this meeting is my doing, Mr. Dennison."

His eyebrows shot up as he looked from Damien to me. "Your doing?" His laugh was close to a scoff. "What do you need with me? Are you an actress?"

My mouth turned up easily at that. "No. Not ever."

"Want to direct?" His brow furrowed as he tried to piece things together.

"No . . . try again." Something started churning in my stomach, anger mixed with dread.

"I don't have time for this. Just spell it out."

I blinked at his forwardness, then smiled slightly. "You don't recognize me?"

He shrugged. "No."

"I look an awful lot like my mother."

He leaned back just enough that I noticed his withdrawal. I saw the moment it clicked, the moment he recognized me, the moment his gaze focused on my eyes. He inhaled sharply, his nostrils flaring.

"So what?" he spit out, with a hostile edge to his tone.

I held my breath for ten heartbeats. "I just thought maybe you cared."

"Why would I care if you look like your mother?" he demanded.

I tilted my head at him. "Well, since you had an affair with my mother —"

"Hold it right there, missy. I've never had an affair." He leaned forward, anger darkening his features. "You have to be married to have an affair, and I have never married."

I barely refrained from rolling my eyes at the way he announced this fact, as though the very fact that he had never had an affair liberated him from some other responsibility.

Instead I leaned forward and clenched my hands together. "Mr. Dennison, you had a relationship with my mother nine months before I was born."

His eyes rounded at this declaration. "Excuse me?"

I cocked an eyebrow, feeling sarcastic and unusually bold. "You had sex with my mother, Victoria Talbot, when she was seventeen. You were . . . thirty-two, I believe?"

He inhaled sharply, but his face turned dark with a glower. "What do you think you're going to get from informing me of this highly suspect idea of yours?"

"I hope for the truth." My voice quivered slightly, and I clenched my hands tighter together to keep them from shaking. Dennison had thrust aside his sandwich, and Damien took a swig of water from beside me, but it was slow and deliberate, almost wary, as he kept an eye on Dennison.

"The truth?" He gave a bitter laugh, tilting back in his chair, and throwing his arms out wide as if to encircle the room. "The truth? You're not going to get that listening to some crazed, fading actress."

Even though I didn't care what he thought, especially about the woman whose daughter he had abandoned, his words bruised. "Fading actress?"

"She needs a scandal like this to keep her publicity alive, sweetheart." His tone dripped irony. "She's a fool—she's an idiot to think that this is going to save her career. She's one step away from the blacklist with such a move. Does she think by telling you we had a relationship that something will happen?"

Anger and frustration began welling up in me. "Do you really think that she told me anything?"

He blinked at me, dropping his arms to the armrests and gripping them lightly. "What? Then why—"

"My own research led me here. Surely you know my mother well enough to know she's not going to share her mistakes." I nearly spat the last word at him, and he blinked as though wounded. "She has told me practically nothing. It's only the information coming from others corroborating her story that makes me even consider the possibility of this being true. You see, Mr. Dennison, I have a father. He is kind, loving, genuine, and the best father I could have asked for."

"Then what are you doing here?" A sneer pulled at his lips.

I opened my mouth to answer, then shut it, staring at him.

He widened his eyes, giving me an ironic look as if he were saying, "See? You have no reason to be accusing me of anything."

"Hoping I was wrong," I finally said. "But if anything, I can see that I'm right." Biting back my emotion, I stood. "You probably have a way of contacting either my mother or Damien. I'll let you do so should you wish to contact me. Obviously, we aren't going to get anywhere."

"Just a second—what kind of proof do you think you have that I'm your father? If that is, in fact, what you're accusing me of?"

I tilted my head to the side in agreement. "Just circumstantial."

He chuckled. "You need more than that, sweetheart." He seized his water bottle from the desk and downed the last gulp, screwing the lid back on tightly.

"Yes, I suppose I do." I studied him, lingering on that dimple, the round eyes, the thick eyelashes, remembering the cowlick in the back of his hair, and I took in everything down to the tennis shoes he wore. Salomon, my favorite brand of running shoes. I nodded my chin at them. "Do you run?"

"Yeah . . ." he said warily, lifting a foot from his seat to stare at his toes, as if to remind himself what shoes he wore. "Half marathons now. Used to be marathons."

Tears pricked my eyes. I nodded. "Yeah. Me too."

He shrugged, his sneer returning. "Lots of people—"

"Did you like science in school? English? Do you excel at languages?"

His eyes widened then narrowed in an expression of unease. "Look, I don't know where your father is, girl, but I'm not him. Looking for similarities between us, it's just—it's not—" He threw up his hands in the air. "It's ridiculous. I don't know what you hope for, but don't drag my name through the mud at this reawakening of yours. Your mother's a lying whore, and everyone in Hollywood knows that. Your father could be a hundred other guys. She's just doing this for publicity."

He tossed the water bottle toward an overflowing trash bin beside me. It hit the top and bounced out, skittering toward Damien's feet. Damien stooped and picked it up, holding it in the air in a kind of salute.

"Do you think I came here to defend my mother?" Incredulity laced my voice, overcoming all other emotion. "I'm only here because I hope to find out the truth. And despite you telling me I'm wrong, you've given me no reason to doubt what I believed when I walked through that door."

He spread his arms wide. "What do you want from me? You think I'm going to just sit here and let you accuse me? You think I'm going to tell you you're right? You're a fool to believe any word that comes out of your mother's mouth."

"And what about the mouths of her friends?" I challenged. "What about the evidence from other people that you and she had a secret relationship on set? You used—" Emotion choked me so I broke off.

Anger clouded Dennison's brow as he rocketed to his feet. "Whoever is talking is in very real danger of losing what they hold dear to them."

I stepped back involuntarily, but Damien's hand at my back halted me. I glanced at him.

"Matt, I think you have to look at this reasonably. All she's asking is if it's possible you're her father. She's not accusing. There's nothing evil going on here, just a woman searching for the truth."

Dennison scoffed and thrust his hands into his pockets, where he clenched them into fists. He jerked his chin at the door, his gaze on me, eyes darkening under the cloud of anger that made his words tremble. "Then I think it's time for you to leave, since there's nothing here for you."

I nodded. "No. Apparently not."

Damien grabbed the door, pushing it open and ushering me through ahead of him.

A golf cart waited outside, and Damien's hand on my upper back directed me toward it. I followed numbly, unable to form any reaction. What had I expected? I hadn't thought he would admit it, or embrace it, but maybe I had dreamed that a little bit. Dreamed of finding a warm reception, a hug from a father who never knew about me and regretted his lack of involvement in his daughter's life. A true Hollywood, happy ending. Was that too much to ask?

Tears stabbed my eyes, and I smothered a sob, thankful for the wind slicing across my face, stinging it with its rough embrace. I thought of Dad, and how he would always be able to cheer me up, with something sweet or silly, always inappropriate enough to make me laugh at the moment I needed it. Sometimes it was just bringing me a pint of coconut milk ice cream, or going on a midnight coffee run when I was in high school and I'd argued with Bryan, or when I missed him when he went off to college and I'd been left behind for a year.

The driver dropped us at the grass parking lot, and I blindly followed Damien out to his car, clinging to his hand as though I had gone overboard in a rough sea and he was my lifesaver. He unlocked his door, opening the passenger door for me, and shutting it after me. When he climbed in beside me, I stared numbly at the dashboard, my hands limp in my lap, utterly deflated.

"I'm sorry," he said.

I didn't answer. There was nothing to say. It hadn't been his fault; I had asked for help in finding my father and in meeting him. Damien had done exactly what I'd asked for, and exactly what I had thought I wanted. Now, I wasn't sure whether meeting Dennison had been the right thing or not. But all I knew was that I had done it. I had stood face to face with my biological father. Seeing him in person had solidified my suspicions. I knew it was true, whether Victoria confirmed it or not. I had his dimple, his cowlick, his lashes. Three distinct things, things I could have inherited from him, for I certainly hadn't inherited them from my mother. She had no dimple, no cowlick that I'd ever seen, and short lashes. Dad had no dimple, no cowlick, and short lashes. I squeezed my eyes shut, desperate for the pain in my chest to subside.

I lost track of time as we sat there, Damien waiting for something, perhaps for me to be ready to talk, but I didn't know if I ever would be. I didn't want to talk about how my biological father denied me, about how he didn't want to know me, about how he'd chucked me out of his trailer like I was nothing more than a woman off the streets.

At that thought, my tears broke loose, and I bent forward, sobbing into my hands. Damien's touch on my back couldn't soothe my tears, couldn't take the pain away, couldn't touch it. It was like I grieved the father I had never had, the father I never would have. And the sobs shook my shoulders, tearing out of my chest in ugly, wracking gasps.

Damien pulled me into his arms, pulling me across the divide between us, until my face rested in his neck. I clung to him, fisting his jacket, wishing everything were different.

I told myself to stop crying, tried to control myself. *Damien is a Brit, he's got that stiff upper lip, he won't appreciate my tears, he'll think I'm insane.* But the thought of controlling my tears made them run faster.

"I'm sorry," he whispered in my ear. "I'm so sorry. I thought he'd be more civil. I thought he'd be—" He broke off with a sigh, his lips pressed against my ear. "I thought he'd man up."

I pulled away from him so I could stare into his eyes, and found them slightly shocked at the motion. "How well do you know him? I mean, is he a good man? Should I cut my losses and run? Or should I try to convince him? What do I do?"

His expression softened, breaking as I pleaded for his wisdom. He lifted a hand, brushing a wavy strand of my hair away from my damp, flushed cheek. His gaze lingered on my mouth, as though I had the words for him to say waiting there if he could just read them. Then his gaze flicked up to meet mine, and I blinked. *He wants to kiss me.*

A sharp rap on the window made us jump, flinching away from each other as though we had been caught making out. I pressed my palms to my cheeks, dashing away tears as we both looked out Damien's window. A uniformed security guard, one of the ones we'd checked in with when we arrived, had tapped on the window, indicating with a finger for Damien to roll it down.

Damien dug his keys out of the cup holder, where he must have tossed them after getting in, and rolled the window half down. "Yes?" He frowned at the dark-skinned man. "Is something wrong?"

"I'm sorry, Mr. Kerr," he began in a smooth, low voice, "but we've been told to make sure you leave the premises. Mr. Dennison has asked you be banned from the set."

Damien's cheek flexed. "Have we?"

"Yes, sir. I'm sorry."

"Right." Stoic, Damien started his engine and threw the car into reverse as the security guard stepped back. He pulled out of the parking lot so quickly, we left divots of dirt flying out of the ground behind us.

Chapter Twenty-One
Triggered

WE DROVE IN SILENCE, WITH me staring out the window at the green hedges as we zoomed by, and Damien gripping the steering wheel with one hand, his other white knuckled on the gear shift.

I finally broke the silence with, "I'm sorry." He hadn't turned on the radio, and we'd driven for almost a half hour before I could master my tears and emotions to come up with an apology.

He glanced sharply at me. "Don't be." Although his knuckles were pink again, his face was tight with restrained emotion.

"This has been the worst week in history." I sighed toward the closed window.

"Undoubtedly."

"I hope it doesn't get worse. Tell me something happy. Distract me."

A wry smile lifted one corner of Damien's mouth. "Happy?"

"Yeah, you know, something to make me smile."

"Hmm." He stared at the road, deep in thought for over a minute.

"That hard?" I teased dryly.

"My son John," he began, "he's starting to parrot everyone. So I was on the phone one evening with my agent, and I told him I had too many responsibilities up in Yorkshire right now to just hop on a flight to LA and deal with this script problem, so I trusted him to do it right."

I tilted my head at him, waiting for the punchline.

"Well, that night, when I asked him to clean up his playroom before dinner, he looked me straight in the eye and said—"

I grinned, knowing what was coming.

"'Daddy, I have too many responsibilities to clean up these toys.'"

"A smart boy."

"Indeed." His smile was tinged with pride.

"Who . . ." I trailed off, my smile distancing itself from my lips. "Do you still talk to his mother?"

"Whose mother?"

"John's."

The gaze he tossed me was almost confused. He put both hands on the wheel, running his hands down the leather to adjust his grip. "Yeah. Of course."

I examined him. He didn't look at me right away, and his gaze shifted slowly from the road to land on me for a fraction of a moment before returning. "What aren't you telling me?"

"I thought—" He shook his head and said too quickly, "Nothing."

"Don't lie." I frowned. "Who is his mother?"

"I thought—" he began again. He combed his fingers through his hair. "I thought you knew everything about it now."

My mind ran backward as I played through the information I'd learned in the past week: Dennison's relationship with Victoria, his identity as my father, Victoria releasing the scandal herself, Kat's confession of Jake raping her, Kat's pregnancy, and Victoria's advice . . .

"Oh my gosh." I couldn't believe I hadn't realized it earlier. My stomach jumped into my throat as I gaped at him. "Kat?"

Damien's bottom lip was clenched between his teeth. "Yeah. I thought she told you."

"No. Victoria told me Kat got an abortion. Kat didn't even tell me she was pregnant." I ran both hands over my face, over my puffy eyes and down my clammy cheeks. "What happened?"

He shook his head, not in denial, but in a way that suggested he still had a hard time believing what had happened. "Jake raped her. And a couple of months later, she comes to me and says, 'I'm pregnant. And it's Jake's. And he raped me a couple months ago.'" His voice thickened, and he paused. "Fool that I was, I told our father. And he insisted Kat report the incident. Kat didn't speak to me for a month. And the police didn't believe her. Or if they did, they couldn't do anything with no proof. Jake claimed it was consensual, Kat said it was rape." He swallowed thickly. "Kat had every reason to lie."

I frowned. "Why?"

"Father was livid. How dare his daughter get pregnant out of wedlock?" He scoffed. "Dad was old fashioned about a lot of things. So am I, I suppose. But after Kat found out she was adopted, she struggled. And Jake was there ready to 'help' her deal. I knew she'd been sleeping with him." Damien's knuckles whitened over the steering wheel again. "That bastard took advantage of her pain, used her. And if she'd told Father it was consensual, she would have been cast out. Instead she told him it was rape."

I thought back to my conversation with Kat in the cave. "Do you believe her?"

He shrugged. "I don't think she lied to me. I think she couldn't hold it in any longer." He shook his head, disgust curling his lips. "But I should have done something more."

"It makes sense then that she said she won't be here for the wedding."

My words sent a jolt through Damien. "What? Is that what she said?" He stared at me so long I started looking at the road.

"Yeah, she said she wouldn't stay for the wedding." I reached for the wheel when he kept staring at me.

His face going pale, he scrambled for his phone, his eyes sweeping over the road in front of us as though looking for a land mine. His face was a taut mask of concern, his gaze flicked from phone to road and back. "What did Kat say to you? Exactly?"

"What?"

He was unlocking his phone now, eyes on it. "Tell me what she said— word for word if you can remember."

His face was the most intense I'd ever seen it, all emotion shut away as if under lock and key. His fingers moved with quick efficiency, even as he pressed a number and held the phone to his ear. He looked at me and spoke again.

"Try to remember."

Word for word? Panic started to nudge at the edges of my memory. "Um . . . She told me what Jake had done, how he had flirted with her but when she'd said no to sleeping with him, he . . ." I couldn't say it, but

Damien nodded with a "go on" expression. "Then she said she wouldn't stay for the wedding, that she couldn't be around him." I frowned, trying to remember her words. "No, she said, 'I'm not going to be here for the wedding. I can't be here.'"

Damien cursed and banged his hand, still holding his phone, onto the dashboard, his face pale. "And then what did she say?"

To avoid his searching gaze, I closed my eyes and tried to remember the exact wording she'd used. "She said, 'I can't be here anymore. Every time I come home, I . . .' then she trailed off and I remember wondering how she was going to finish that thought, but then she said she 'couldn't do it anymore,' and that it was always like that whenever she was here."

Before I finished speaking, Damien was pressing down on the accelerator, taking the next turn at double the speed he ought. "We've got to get back."

"What? Why? What's wrong?"

The tires squealed around a hairpin corner.

"Are you going to explain?" I gripped the door handle so tightly it hurt. "Should I call someone?"

He shook his head. "Not unless you know of someone she might go to when she's upset, or somewhere she might go."

I could think of nothing and said as much. We drifted into silence, broken only by the rumble of the car's engine and the growl of tires on the road.

"Tell me what's going on," I finally said when we pulled onto the motorway to York.

He ran a tongue over his lip, which seemed to be bleeding. "After the police dismissed the case against Jake, she became suicidal."

I sucked in a breath.

"She cut her wrists, but not deep enough."

My stomach had been lost somewhere along the road, leaving a hollowness there that was rapidly being filled with disbelief.

"I found her before she bled out in the bathroom," he continued. "I got her help, and she was hospitalized until the baby came. She had decided to give him up for adoption. Even chose a family."

I nodded to show him I was following along.

"I decided he should stay in the family. My girlfriend at the time agreed to feign pregnancy so no one would suspect."

"Seriously?"

"Yes." He sighed. "It was surprisingly easy. The media likes to believe whatever creates scandal and interest."

I shook away the thoughts of how the aftermath might appear, how she might be considered a bad mother to abandon a child to her ex-boyfriend.

"Kat and I discussed how it might be hard for her to have him in her life, but she had recovered so well that the doctors thought she'd be okay with it over time. She promised to keep seeing the counselors and psychiatrists, and so I adopted John." He released one hand from the steering wheel, using it to shift into a higher gear on this straight stretch of road. "Every time she comes up to visit, she struggles. She loves John, I can tell, but it goes much deeper than that. I can't tell if she regrets giving him up, letting me adopt him, or what. But she—a year after I adopted him, the first time she visited . . ."

Trailing off as we came up behind another car, Damien downshifted, then zoomed around him.

"What happened?" I prompted.

His gaze became distant and unfocused. "She fell off the cliff. She only slid twenty feet or so, and she said it was an accident, but . . ." He shook his head, readjusted his hands on the wheel, and continued, ". . . it was in a spot where she would have had to go out of her way to fall, where you just don't walk."

"You think she tried to kill herself again?"

"She ended up with scrapes and bruises and a twisted ankle. Lucky for how far she fell."

I nodded. "Luck."

He echoed my nod, overtaking another car. "Yeah. She only visited once after, for a friend's birthday, and didn't stay at the house." His hands went white. "I think he did it there. In her room." The intensity coupled with the despair in his voice made my stomach clench.

He began dialing numbers on his phone, cursing when his call to Kat went to voicemail. He kept dialing, until he nearly wrecked the car, and I took the phone from him. "Tell me who to call, and I'll keep calling," I said when he began to argue.

He listed the next name I should try, and I took over. Most answered, thinking it was Damien, and when I asked about Kat they all responded with the negative. Each answer drove Damien faster down the road until I ran out of contacts.

A metallic taste bloomed on my tongue, and I realized I was chewing the inside of my lip to pieces. I pulled out my phone and scrolled through the contacts in it, even though I knew I didn't know any of her friends, and hadn't seen her with any friends outside of me. She had to have them, but we had never gotten together with them. We had been living separate lives, me training for a race and sightseeing or chasing dead ends about my parentage, her working and who knew what else?

Why hadn't I seen the signs? She drank nearly every night, arrived home late, slept later, only to peel herself from bed and go back to work —at a bar. She was probably an alcoholic, struggling with acceptance of the things Jake had done to her, and self-medicating over the idea of her brother raising her son. A tear bloomed on my lower lashes, and I dashed it away.

My finger hesitated over her name, and then I let it descend. With my phone at my ear this time, it rang and rang, until the voicemail picked up, and I let it sink back to my lap. "No answer," I murmured at Damien's questioning glance.

He pressed down on the accelerator, whipping around another car, this time more desperate than the last.

When he had to brake hard, I winced and flew forward, hands braced on the dash. Damien's hands were white on the steering wheel, his lips thin, and cheeks sallow.

"Do you really think . . . ? I mean, is she in that sort of place now? Emotionally?"

"Your guess is as good as mine. Have you seen anything to suggest she's unstable?"

"I—" Falling into thought, I stared out my window as the fields passed us by. Green, luscious, full of stone cottages and horses and sheep; I envied them. Such a simple life it seemed. And yet nothing was ever simple, was it? No matter where you came from, people lied and people misled. Secrets were hidden in those fields. My hands turned palm up in helplessness. "I don't think I know her well enough anymore to say."

Damien considered my words before nodding in silence. "No one really knows her anymore. Not since Jake stole her from us."

Chapter Twenty-Two
The Search

THE DRIVE BACK TO THE manor stretched indefinitely long. It seemed ages since we'd left the set, and a million ages more since my run that morning. Now I only thought of Kat and where she might be, what shape she might be in, and if she might have done something as drastic as Damien thought.

A part of me couldn't believe it, couldn't believe that Kat had ever been so depressed as to end her life. Try as I might, I couldn't understand how she might think her son would be better off raised by strangers after she had just found out about her own adoption.

But then, John was different, wasn't he? Product not of love, but power. And Kat was forced to revisit that helplessness every time she saw him. What did he look like, this son of Jake? Did he have Kat's hazel eyes, or Jake's turquoise ones?

Outside the window, the scene turned from houses and city dwellings to train tracks and pastures, and the occasional village with narrow streets that we drove through.

Finally, I began to see familiar views, signs that we were nearly at the manor.

"Did anyone check the cave?" I suddenly burst out.

"What?" Instead of simply yielding, Damien stopped the car at a roundabout. "What cave?" A car honked behind us when he almost ran into our car. Damien drove on. "What cave?"

"She brought me there, for privacy, when she told me about Jake. It's somewhere on the cliff near your property. Or maybe between Edmund's and yours? Don't you know about it?"

"No." Damien shook his head, and peeled out of the roundabout at the exit for York. "I don't know of any cave on my property. Several on the beach, along with tunnels you could get lost in for days, though."

"Maybe it's not. Maybe it's on Edmund's then." I thought of how to describe it, and how I would give directions to the cave. "I don't know where. I can show you, though. I think." Eyes screwed shut, I tried to picture the path we'd taken.

"If it's along the coast, we could search for a week and still not find it."

"Then let's get back quickly—I can find my way there."

He pounded his hand on the steering wheel. "She always had a secret spot she'd never tell me about, a spot I knew she went to whenever she never wanted to be found."

"Like now?" I hesitated to ask.

The muscle in his jaw flexed as the car's engine revved and threw me back against the seat in its quick acceleration. "I hope not."

As we neared the manor, a misty rain began to fall. Through the windshield wipers, I watched it approach. With mothballs in my mouth, I tried to swallow, and found myself gasping with the effort. I longed to exit the stifling heat of the car, dash outside, tilt my head back, and allow the rain to sate me. And yet nothing would sate me now but knowledge. I had to find Kat.

"There." I pointed in the direction we'd gone from Edmund's manor to the cave. "This is where we went. Let me out, I'll start there and you can follow."

"I can't keep up with you though."

Hand on the door handle, I said, "I have my phone. And it's wet—you can probably follow my tracks. Damien, please." I had the handle half engaged when he began to brake, and fully engaged before he stopped. "I'll call you if I find her. You keep searching everywhere else."

"Adrienne—" He reached a hand out for me, catching the tips of my fingers in his. "Don't—" He closed his eyes, let go of my fingers and raked a hand through his hair, clenching it tightly, but not tightly enough to erase the worry lines on his forehead.

I gave him the most reassuring smile I could, although my heart hammered in my chest. "I'll get there as quickly as I can—it's not too far. Fifteen minutes tops, five if I don't get lost and sprint." And then, impulsively, I leaned over and kissed his cheek. "If she's there, I'll find her," I whispered in his ear. "I promise." I kissed him right in front of the ear, felt him tremble under my lips, then leaned back, and kicked the door open the rest of the way. His hand tightened on me again, and I cast him a glance.

Looking like he might be sick, he nodded and let me go.

In my clogs and khakis, I dashed over rocks and tree roots, sprinting in the direction of the cave. For the first time in my life, a life could depend on my speed, and I had chosen this day to forgo tennis shoes.

I regretted not working more on my speed instead of focusing on distance. Speed had never been my strength, but endurance. Endurance for pain, for suffering, for everything. I ran for the long haul, competed for it, and survived it. Now, everything depended on speed, and I wasn't certain I could make it.

My lungs ached, my eyes swimming as I tried to make out landscapes in the thickening rain. Refusing to slow, I raised my chin and powered on, finally recognizing a large rock near where the path down had been.

Breath coming in ragged gasps, I pushed on as fast as I dared for as long as I dared, until I reached the cliff and had to slow. Then I steeled myself, glanced over the edge, and slid down to the entrance, clutching at the falling rocks around me as my feet went out from under me and I crashed forward onto my knees.

My fingertips caught on a large rock at the mouth of the cave, and I dug in, not even wincing at the bite of rock through the knees of my jeans, but focused only on keeping myself from falling fifty feet to the base of the cliff.

Inhaling a shaky breath, I dragged myself into the cave, digging my phone out as soon as I stepped inside and turning on the flashlight.

Kat was slumped against the cave wall before me, head lolling on her chest, knees bent up to her chin and cocked slightly sideways, hands extended beside her heels as though they'd fallen from around her legs.

This had been a spur of the moment plan. Even in my run here, I hadn't thought of what to do if I found her. *Call the police, call for a medic,* a little voice inside me said. I shoved my hand into my pocket and clenched it around my phone, but couldn't find the courage to admit she needed either.

"Kat." My hoarse voice split the distance between us, crackling over the infiltrating mist. It had to be ten degrees cooler in here. The disjointed thought snapped me to attention, and, still on my knees, I scrambled toward her. My hands jammed into rocks and slipped in puddles, but I didn't care. Kat didn't stir, neither at my voice nor at my loud approach.

"Kat!" Reaching her, I grabbed at her knees, using them to pull myself up. Her head lolled to the side. Only then did I see what my mind must not have let me see before as I inspected her for outward injury. Even as I did, I knew the gravest ones remained inside.

Like me, Kat hid her wounds under layers of secrecy, but not anymore. Under the beam of my phone's light, I found the small knife she'd used to slice her wrist. Just one, as though she either hadn't had the fortitude or the strength to cut the second. I pressed my fingers to her throat. A weak thump pulsed a greeting.

"Thank God," I breathed. "Please, Kat, don't die on me. I can't let you die."

I dialed Damien's number, holding my breath until he answered on the first ring. I told him what I'd found, where I was, and to come with a rope. It had been hard enough just climbing back up on my own the last time; I couldn't imagine how we would drag her back up the cliff without a rope or pulley of some type.

While I waited for him, I lowered Kat's head to the ground, pulled off my jacket, and tied the sleeve around her wrist to stop the bleeding. Her pulse thumped, faint but steady, under my searching fingers, but she showed no signs of waking. I knelt beside her, and accidentally nudged her hand. From her palm spilled a small orange bottle, its lid off, and empty of pills. The label had been removed, preventing me from knowing what it had contained, but I feared it was nothing innocuous.

I sucked in a breath, then leaned forward and checked her pulse again. *Steady, but weak.* I leaned close to her face, listening for her breathing. *Shallow, but steady.*

"Kat?" I smoothed back her damp hair. It wasn't nearly as wet as I was; she must have been in here a long time. "Can you hear me? Can you open your eyes? Please?"

I'm pre-med; I should be able to do something. My thoughts sent new waves of despair through me, and I searched my brain, imagining myself back in the emergency room at home, where I had interned on the weekends to build up my resume. *Check her breathing, stop the bleeding. What else?* I cast my gaze around the cave, shining the light of my phone around us. *The drugs would have to be addressed at the hospital. Lay her down. Stop the bleeding.*

All I could do I had already done. *Keep an eye on her breathing. Stop the bleeding. Call for help.*

"Right!" I cursed my stupidity and called 999.

"Where is your emergency?" a deeply accented voice said. Despite my time in England, the words cut through my mind with delayed understanding.

"Chadwick Manor, Yorkshire . . ." I ran a hand through my hair. "I don't know the address."

"Okay, that's fine. Calm down, please."

"I am calm." My words steeled. "My friend has attempted suicide. She's taken some pills—I don't know what kind—and she's unconscious. She's also cut her wrist, but not that deep."

The speaker's response was garbled.

"What? I can't hear you. Hello?"

The phone went dead in my hands. I resisted the urge to throw it against the wall in frustration. *Damien's on the way. We'll get her out.*

The seconds ticked by, turning into minutes. I tried redialing, but the phone wouldn't work, and I was unwilling to move. Finally rocks skittered beside the entrance of the cave. As I looked up, I realized the rain had stopped, and Damien stood on the ledge outside the cave.

"You found us." The words escaped my mouth on a breath.

His eyes asked everything he wanted to say.

"She's alive. Steady pulse, but unconscious." I motioned to the pill bottle as he stepped inside. "She took these, I think."

My words pulled him to a halt in the middle of the cave. His eyes rounded and fixed on Kat.

"I called emergency, but got cut off. You have a way to get her out?"

Mute, he held up the end of a rope, the other side of which must have been tied off at the top of the cliff somewhere. Within minutes we had carried her out to the cave entrance.

"Should we wait for Fire and Rescue or something?" The path going up to the top, although easy enough while steady on your feet, wasn't something I wanted to try with Kat in tow, and we had just one rope, which I hoped would catch Kat should we slip and fall.

Damien glanced at his sister, then out over the edge of the cliff. He pulled out his phone and called emergency. As I returned to holding Kat, Damien clambered up the cliff for cell reception.

"They're coming," was all he said when he reentered, phone clenched in his hand by his leg. His voice was hoarse and breaking. I wanted to tell him everything would be okay, but I wasn't sure it would be. He stood in the center of the cave, barely even blinking.

"One of us should go up and meet the ambulance," I said when he continued to stand frozen in the cave.

He gave a little shake of his head. "Of course. I'll go." With another quick glance at us, he walked outside. Rocks skittered down the side of the cave, bouncing on the ground in front of the opening and jumping over the side to disappear below.

Alone with Kat again, I smoothed down her hair, checking her pulse and breathing, adjusting her head on my lap so it was comfortable. Tears of frustration pricked at my eyes. What else could I do? *Wait.*

The minutes ticked by slowly enough to be hours, but finally I heard scratching outside, and a brightly dressed man appeared, wearing a full-body harness. He gave me a smile and entered, and a second man appeared a moment later dressed the same. With their reassuring and businesslike presence, we had Kat transported onto a stretcher and up the cliff side.

Damien paced at the top, watching with haunted eyes as Kat was put into the ambulance waiting in the field. A mask of oxygen covered her face now, and paramedics swirled around her.

My hand on his arm stilled his pacing, and I jerked my chin at the ambulance when he turned to me. "Go with her."

"Do you know the way to the hospital?"

I shrugged. "No. But I'll get there. My phone can get me there—just leave me your keys."

His gaze flickered over me, then he handed them over and nodded. He looked as though he might speak, but then climbed into the ambulance without a word instead. The second paramedic shut the door, and I caught a glimpse of Damien's face, steeled against despair before it pulled away.

Chapter Twenty-Three
Confessions

WHEN I REACHED THE HOSPITAL, I was shown into a waiting area, where I sat with half a dozen other people as I waited for news from Damien. The nurses wouldn't tell me anything about Kat since I wasn't family, and although I texted Damien, I didn't expect to see him soon. So I sank into a waiting room chair and stared down at the black-and-white tile floor.

A thump startled me out of my reverie, and I blinked at a tabloid facing me. For several seconds, my gaze remained unfocused, staring at the words without seeing or comprehending. Then understanding clicked. I lunged for the paper, my stomach clenching.

ACTRESS'S DOG ATTACKS ON LONDON STREET! it proclaimed.

I gasped aloud at the claim. "What?" The fold of the paper cut a photo in half, and it was a photo I recognized, even though I had never seen it before.

Elinor and Jake. Elinor's teeth closed around Jake's wrist.

My stomach sank. And of course, they had run with the photos, claiming that Elinor was Victoria's, not mine. Elinor, my dog, was being called Victoria's. After her attack on the wedding dress, surely there was no way Victoria would ever accept her. Tears rushed to my eyes, the apples of my cheeks growing hot with my despair.

I wanted to rush home and make sure Elinor was okay, that no one had taken her somewhere or punished her. She needed food and water—and now with this news article, surely she would be ignored, or worse. But I cemented myself to the chair. Kat needed me more right now.

Shoes tapping a quick rhythm on the tiles broke through my anguish. Raising my gaze, my shoulders sank in relief to see Damien, and I tossed the paper back on the table.

"Did they tell you anything? They wouldn't let me in or tell me—"

"They've lavaged her stomach, started an IV, and are monitoring her kidney function," he recited as though he'd committed what the doctors had said to memory. He sank down into the seat beside me and bent forward, elbows on knees to prop his head into his hands.

"At least she's alive." It seemed like the only thing left to say, the only straw left to grasp.

"For now," he agreed. "She's yet to wake up. They aren't sure she will, or how many pills she ingested before we got her."

"She has to wake up," I said more to myself than to him. "She has to."

His head shook, empty of words to say; he just kept shaking, until I realized that he was crying.

"Damien," I whispered, reaching a hand out for him. My fingers brushed his back; his face dropped into the palms of his hands as he melted underneath me. Wrapping my arms around him, I offered a shoddy attempt at comfort. There was nothing to say or do as his sister lay dying in a nearby room. It seemed I was always too late these days, not quick enough to act or react. I missed my chance, not knowing when to push and when to step back. Could I have prevented this from happening at all?

As his tears dried, mine burned. When he began to pull away, tugging a handkerchief from his pocket and wiping his eyes and nose with it, my own tears clawed at the backs of my eyes, dragging their way to my lashes where my only defense was blinking.

The door swung open to the waiting room, and we both looked up.

"Mr. Kerr?" The doctor offered a smooth, manicured hand. "Doctor Nolon."

"Yes." Damien stood, and I followed suit, both of us meeting him halfway across the room in our eagerness for news.

Doctor Nolon's gaze flicked to me, and Damien nodded. "This is Kat's best friend, you're free to speak in front of her."

"Right. Well." The doctor tucked his clipboard underneath his arm and motioned to a chair. "Let's sit."

I steeled myself with a breath, closing my eyes briefly as I sank into the nearest chair. Damien sat beside me and his arm dropped heavily around my shoulders, pulling me close to him.

"What's the news?"

"She's not awake, yet," the doctor began. "But there appears to be no reason she shouldn't wake up soon."

"Could she be in a coma?" Damien asked.

"Doubtful," the doctor replied. "More likely whatever sleeping pills she consumed are working their way through her system and she'll wake on her own. It doesn't appear that she took enough to do lasting harm."

"So she should come out of this . . ."

"Yes. As far as we can tell. We'll have to wait and see whether there's any lasting damage."

As relief swelled in me so that the tears clawed their way back to my eyelashes, Damien's fingers squeezed my shoulder tightly, not letting up, as though he had to release his relief somehow.

"That's fantastic."

"Of course," the doctor continued, with a half glance at me, "I recommend getting her psychological help."

"Yes. Of course." Damien nodded, swiping his free hand through his hair with a return of some stress. "Of course."

"One more thing." Before speaking this time, the doctor consulted the test results on his clipboard. "It appears she had significant amounts of alcohol in her system." He met Damien's eyes, then shifted his glance to me. "Do you know of any problem with drinking she might have?"

"No, I . . ." Damien trailed off, glanced at me.

"I think so," I answered heavily, picking up the end of his sentence for him. "She works at a pub, and . . . she drinks quite a bit at home, I think. I never really see her drinking, but . . ." I bobbed my head to the side. "But I think she drinks a lot more than I thought."

He nodded. "She should get help for that as well, obviously."

Damien seemed to weave, and I reached for his hand, enfolding it in mine.

"As soon as she wakes, she can have visitors. I'll tell the staff to allow you in no matter the time. The cafeteria closed at seven, and you might find it difficult to get back in should you leave."

With a glance at the clock, I realized just how much time had passed. We'd been here at least two hours, and it had been early evening when we'd arrived. Coffee this morning had been so long ago.

Alone in the room again, Damien and I remained motionless, both lost in our thoughts.

"I'm sorry," I began. "I should have noticed—"

"Don't." Damien turned me to him, putting a hand on each of my shoulders and forcing me to face him. "This was not your fault. If I'd just told someone else—confided in you earlier." He closed his eyes then opened them and gave me a little shake. "It was not your fault," he said so fiercely he sounded angry.

Eyelashes brimming with tears, I lost my battle as they slowly began to fall. We'd almost lost her today. And all I could think was that I should have known she was on a downward spiral.

Damien crushed me against his chest, his arms vices around me as he buried his face in my neck and hair. "It wasn't your fault." His lips brushed my neck. "It wasn't. It could never be your fault. You saved her. If it weren't for you, she would have died."

My breath came in shuddering gasps as I sobbed, finally surrendering to the fear and emotion I'd tried to shut away.

☽

Briefly, I visited Kat before leaving the hospital. She lay in her bed, head resting against her pillow but facing the window, as still as if she were asleep. All her jewelry had been removed, including earrings and necklaces, leaving only the pink hair vibrant against her pallid cheeks. She didn't want to talk, remaining silent as long as we stayed.

Finally, I acknowledged the darkness in her eyes that I had denied until the time she'd shared the story in the cave. But now I hugged her and promised her that everything would be okay. I'd talk to my mother and Edmund and tell them that she wouldn't be attending the wedding.

She smiled sadly at my pronouncement and nodded, seeming too tired to otherwise respond.

Damien pressed his keys back at me. "I'll stay here," he said. "I'll sleep on the cot."

"Okay. I'll just come back in the morning to get you."

"That would be great." Damien followed me out of the hospital room and paused at the door. "I think she just needs some time."

"Of course she does." I shrugged. Over his shoulder, Kat remained immobile on the hospital bed, pale as the sheets. "If you need anything, just give me a call."

"Right."

I began to walk away, but stopped when he called my name. "Yeah?"

"Thank you." His eyes were soft in the harsh fluorescent light. "For saving our lives."

I frowned, thinking he misspoke, but then with a flicker of his lips, I realized he meant exactly what he said. A knot formed in my throat, making speech impossible. A nod was my only answer, then I left him there with Kat, hoping he would find out the answers to questions I could never ask.

☽

When I left the hospital, it was already dark. Finding my way through the streets under the cover of darkness had me backtracking and turning around in tiny streets, even though I used my phone as a GPS. I breathed a sigh of relief when I found the streetlights illuminating the drive up to Chadwick Manor.

My entire body ached, from my swollen eyes to my grubby toes buried in their muddy leather clogs. I wanted nothing more than to climb into bed and sleep away my problems, maybe with a drink. So I parked Damien's car and dragged myself inside, intent on following through with that desire.

Nearly as soon as I walked into the foyer, Victoria and Edmund's voices carried out from a nearby sitting room. Inwardly wincing, I tried tiptoeing by the door.

"Adrienne?"

I stopped just past the door, tempted to bang my head on the wall in frustration. Instead, I returned to the doorway and popped my head inside. "Yes?"

"That is you. Where have you been?" Victoria demanded.

Standing in the doorway, I considered how best to answer. *Scotland, here, the hospital?*

"Everything okay?" Edmund's gentler question raised a new line of thought.

"We heard about Kat," Victoria supplied when I didn't answer. She sat before the fire, in loose black pants and a silky, long-sleeved tee, the picture of casual elegance.

Edmund nodded. "Someone notified me when the ambulance was dispatched."

I bobbed my head absently in response.

"What happened?" Victoria set her drink down on the small side table wedged between their chairs. "Is Kat okay?"

A folded newspaper on the table reminded me of the one I'd found at the hospital, and I almost groaned. Another thing to deal with: Elinor's attack and the unforeseen consequences. "Yeah. As okay as she can be, I suppose," I finally said.

"I was told it might be a suicide attempt?" Edmund's words jerked me back to the current topic of conversation.

I studied him, debating whether Kat would want me to tell him the truth. "Yes."

A wrinkle creased Edmund's brow as Victoria's hand went to her mouth. "How awful," she murmured. "Have you spoken with her?"

My gaze flicked to Edmund again.

With poise, he downed the rest of his port and rose. "I'm going to check the wine cellar for that port I was telling you about, Vickie."

I blinked at the nickname, but gratitude welled up in me. I waited for him to leave the room, closing the door behind him, before sinking into his seat beside the fire.

My mother smiled faintly at me. "He's a good man. I don't know what I've done to deserve him."

I nodded my agreement without thinking.

"How is Kat?"

"She's . . . alive. That's about all we can hope for right now. She's not in a good place." I leaned against the back of the seat and raked a hand through my hair, the ends stiffened with sweat, and the roots greasy.

Victoria rose, walking to the bar. "Drink?"

I shook my head. "No, thanks."

"You sure? You look like you could use one."

"I could use some sleep."

"Yes, well . . . there was something I wanted to talk to you about this morning, but you were gone." She poured a refill of white wine into her glass. "Where were you?"

"With Damien."

"Oh?" She sipped from her drink. "And where did you two go?"

"To Scotland."

"Scotland? Why—?"

"To meet Matthew Dennison."

Eyes widening, her breath caught in a rare moment of surprise. "You met him?"

"Yeah. I met him."

"Today?" she asked.

"Today."

She gaped at me, bewilderment, confusion, and fear playing across her face. But I couldn't enjoy the display, at least not before she managed to smooth her face back to normal. When she handed me a bottle of water, I accepted with a murmured thanks.

After resettling herself before the fire, she stared at me expectantly. "Well?"

"What?"

"What did he do? What did you tell him? What did he say?"

I thought back to this morning, which felt so long ago. "He didn't say much of anything, really. He accused you of needing this scandal to keep your career alive. He said I was a fool for listening to you, and . . . he denied being my father."

"Of course he did." Victoria's face had grown flushed as I talked.

We both fell silent, me staring into the fire as Victoria nursed her wine. Forcing my mind away from that morning's disastrous meeting with Dennison, and even from the hair-raising afternoon with Kat, I recalled my last discussion with my mother, that time in her room. I had left before she'd finished telling me everything.

"Last time we talked," I began, and trailed off. A lump in my throat prevented me from continuing.

"Yes?"

I swallowed the lump down. "You were going to tell me more than I let you."

She stared into her near-empty glass. "Yes, well, you're forgiven. I overwhelmed you a little, I think."

Eyes on the fire, I shrugged. *Ask about Bryan*, something inside me nudged. "What happened with Bryan? Why?"

She sighed in answer. "As soon as I met him, I recognized him for what he was, Adrienne."

Slowly, I turned my face to hers, attempting to keep my expression implacable.

"I've known men like that, Adrienne. Matthew Dennison was one of them." She raised her glass to her lips, realized it was empty, and returned it to the arm of the chair with a frown. "They get what they want, and move on. And if something better shows up in the meantime, they'll take it. That was Bryan."

"So you kissed him to show me how misguided I was?"

Blowing air through her lips, she bobbed her entire head in response. "Yes. That was it. I know you. Well," she amended at my raised eyebrows. "I know you well enough to know you would make a marriage work for *any* reason. You wouldn't get out. And I didn't want you to marry a loser like him. He would have married you and cheated. Or left. He would have held you back and not been worth the pain."

Even though I now knew she was right, I couldn't approve of her methods. "You could have come up with some other way to tell me that."

She shot me a knowing look. "Could I?"

"*You* didn't have to kiss him."

She bared her teeth in a grimace. "True. But . . . this involved fewer people. Did you ever tell?"

"Once."

She nodded, but didn't ask the follow-up question, and we fell into contemplative silence staring into the flames, watching the logs burn down to embers. There was only one more question I had yet to have answered, something that had been bothering me since Kat had shared her story with me.

"Why did you hire Jake as my bodyguard?"

Her tongue clicked lightly against her teeth in surprise. "Why not? He's been a friend of Edmund's for some time. He needed some cash, and he's intelligent, which is half of the bodyguard job."

"That's it?"

"I suppose I could have gotten him replaced by the agency I use, but . . . I didn't see a need, honestly. You seemed to be getting on with him fine."

I searched her for hints of dishonesty, but either she was back in actress mode, or she was being truthful.

"Weren't you?" Her forehead wrinkled faintly.

"I suppose."

A log gave a pop as it broke apart in the fire, but neither of us flinched.

"It's getting late," she murmured, with a glance at the delicate watch on her wrist. "I suppose you'll want to head to bed."

"Yeah."

"But I have something upstairs I wanted to give you the other night. Come up with me?"

"Sure." Half-empty water bottle in hand, I followed my mother from the living room, up the stairs, and to her bedroom.

"I have one more thing to ask of you, Adrienne." She crossed the room to her closet, where she drew out a hanger with a garment bag over it as tall as she was. "I know you have every right to refuse me, but I hope you'll really consider your answer."

With a lingering look over her shoulder at me, she unzipped the bag, and tugged out a dress of scarlet lace with a white silk base. Somehow, this dress was familiar, although I had never seen it.

"It's the dress I wore to marry James. But altered, of course. For you."

I inhaled sharply. "Why?"

"I was hoping that you might be my maid of honor."

Staring at the dress, I raced through my options in my mind. If I agreed, I had to stay for the wedding. I couldn't very well agree to stand up beside her and then not attend. And she had been acting nicer lately, telling me what I had long desired. But was it all an act to get me to agree to be her maid of honor? I hated that my thoughts ran that way.

She seemed to sense my unease, for she left the dress and smiled. "Think about it, please. You can still wear the dress if you don't want to be maid of honor."

Lip between my teeth, I nodded. "Okay. Is this what you wanted to show me?"

"No. Actually, it was something else." She moved gracefully across the room to her cold fireplace, grasping the decorative wooden box I had always associated with my mother from the mantle. Now, she removed a key from the bottom and fitted it into the lock, opened the lid, and pulled out a bundle of paper discolored with age. Facing me, she held them mid-chest, almost to her heart, and stared down at them.

Her eyes closed briefly, as though she were steeling herself to act, and she tipped forward onto her toes, rocking back before regaining control and lifting her chin.

"These are letters." She paused so long that I almost spoke, but then she continued. "Letters that I received from Dennison when . . ." She trailed off and turned the packet of letters over in her hands. "When I thought we were in love."

I gaped at her, both hesitation and determination warring inside my every cell. She had kept letters? All this time?

"I don't know why I kept them so long. I suppose they're yours now."

She pressed them into my hands, and I closed my fingers around them. Our fingers brushed as we both held on to the letters, and I thought how this was the closest the three of us had ever come since before my existence. Then her hand fell, and I carried the weight all on my own.

Chapter Twenty-Four
Warnings

WITH MY MOTHER'S LETTERS TO Dennison clasped between my fingers, I fell asleep in front of my fireplace. My courage had failed me on the cusp of opening them, and I had stared into the flames until my eyelids had drooped shut and my chin had fallen to my chest.

When I started to wake early the next morning, after a night of convoluted dreams, the sky was still dark, the fire had turned to embers, and the packet of letters had fallen from my hands.

For several minutes, I remained in the chair, eyes heavy, my entire body aching. I reached for my phone on the table beside me and pressed the screen on, illuminating my portion of the room.

The packet of letters rested now beside my feet. The little red ribbon kept them together, but a few from the top had begun to slip, spilling off to one side. With a groan at my stiffness, I leaned forward and swooped them up into my hand, tucking the loose ones back in and squaring them up. I set them on the table beside my phone and attempted to resettle myself in the chair, but now that I was conscious, the room felt cold, the chair was lumpy, and my body ached too much to continue sitting here.

My phone had told me it was three in the morning, but I wouldn't get any more sleep now. I glanced automatically toward Elinor's bed, only to remember that I hadn't seen her when I'd come home the night before, and forgotten to ask whether anyone else had. Concerned as images of Elinor attacking Jake flashed before my eyes, I tugged on a hoodie and began wandering through the manor, searching for her. Eventually I made my way out to the garden where I had found Kat the other day.

Hugging my sweatshirt around my body, I sank onto a stone bench and began to pray. For Kat, for Elinor, for guidance. I didn't know what to do anymore, not about my mother or anyone else. Tears dripped from my cheeks, trailing down my chin, and I wiped my nose with my sweater when I had to.

Edmund found me there a half hour later, when my tears had dried and my former numbness mingled with a strange peace. Without a word, he sank down beside me, staring at the fountain gurgling in front of us.

"I spent a great deal of time here when Sydney's mother died." He nodded at the fountain. "For some reason, I thought the dolphin rather friendly."

At his words, I examined the life-sized dolphin before us. It did look like it was smiling.

"I'm sorry for the rough time you're having."

Without reply, I scrubbed away a fresh tear from my cheek.

"I don't want to make it harder, but . . ." He sighed and stared into his clasped fingers. "We must respond to the Elinor situation."

"Where is she?"

He sighed at his hands. "I had to surrender her."

"What?" Tears stung my eyes. "How could you?"

"Adrienne, we must deal with it appropriately. I cannot be seen as unwilling to follow the law. The Dog Warden must perform their investigation."

"What are they going to do?"

"I imagine they'll test to see if she's aggressive. Jake is . . ." He sighed heavily. "Jake is suing your mother, claiming the dog is hers."

"What? Why isn't he suing *me*? He knows she's mine!"

"I suspect that your mother has more money to give him."

I clenched my fists to still their trembling.

"Regardless, Jake has explained his story, now it's your turn."

"My turn?"

"There will be a press release here this afternoon. And—"

"What? I'm supposed to talk to the press now?"

"A few members of press, to clear the air. We don't need another scandal."

I shook my head. "I'm supposed to address them?"

"She is your dog. That's one thing we have to correct."

"Yes, I suppose so." I sighed, wanting to be angry with Edmund for surrendering my dog to the pound, but he was right. Even I, in my emotional state, could admit we had to do things by the law. And as Edmund left and I returned to my solitude, I resumed my prayers, this time praying to get Elinor back safely, and escape any sort of prosecution.

☽

When the sky lightened, I returned to my room and showered. I texted Damien to let him know I was on my way, but he didn't answer.

Nurses bustled through the hallway when I stepped off the lift on Kat's floor. I made my way down to her room and, as quietly as I could, pushed the door open a crack. Damien looked up from where he'd been bent over on his cot, chin resting in his hands. With a glance at Kat, who hadn't moved, he rose and headed toward me.

"She's been rather groggy," he murmured as he met me at the door and stepped with me back out into the hallway. "The doctor said we should let her sleep. Do you mind staying with her awhile? I've got to go and pick up John. He wants to see her."

"Her—your son?" I winced as I misspoke, but he smiled and touched my arm with a hand, walking me toward the elevator and away from the nurse's station as we talked.

"Yes. He was very upset to hear about Kat. The nanny says he had nightmares and keeps asking for her." Wrinkles appeared above his nose, and he inspected the state of his shoes.

"Right." Not sure what to say, I halted and lifted his keys into the air. "Here. You'll need these, then."

Facing me, his features tinged with exhaustion, Damien leaned forward and kissed me gratefully on the cheek. "Thanks. Did you at least get some sleep last night? You look dead on your feet." His eyes narrowed, scrutinizing me.

At his concern, I gave him my best attempt at a good-humored glare. "Yeah, you don't look much better." I raised a hand to his hair, and patted it where it stuck out in disarray, making him grin a shadow of his old slow grin. "I got a few hours. I had a nice chat with Victoria and Edmund."

"Uh-oh."

"Did you happen to see the paper?"

Damien grimaced. "You mean Jake's newest method of torture?"

I was relieved I didn't have to explain. "You think he released the photos?"

"Did he have control of them?"

"Yes."

He tutted. "Then of course."

"Yeah, well, Edmund gave her over to the Dog Warden, apparently."

"When?"

"Last night, I guess. He told me about it this morning."

With a distant expression, Damien raked a hand through his hair.

"I guess after I visit Kat, I'll go by the pound, or wherever you keep confiscated dogs. See if I can't find her and convince someone she's harmless." I made light of it, but my heart ached at the thought of being too late.

"Good idea." He hid the key in the palm of his hand as he spoke, sticking his fist into the pocket of his tweed jacket, but all the time, his gaze remained intently on me, as though my soul were bared before him.

"Yeah. Maybe." Lip folded in between my teeth, I sighed through my nose, and watched a couple of nurses chat at the station nearby. One of them pointed at the computer, then reached for a patient chart.

Around us, the craze of nurses had slowed down, as if morning duties were trailing off, and they were returning to their desks to write up reports, or else going home. The clock read three after nine; I dragged a hand through my hair. "You'd better go if you're going to pick up John."

Following my gaze to the clock, Damien grimaced. "Yes, I should. Listen." He paused, half turned away from me. "Don't worry about Elinor. I'm certain everything will work out."

I nodded and watched him disappear onto the elevator before returning to Kat's room and letting myself inside. The gentle hum and incessant beeps of machines greeted me, along with Kat's barely perceptible breaths. A chair already perched beside her bed, and I claimed it as quietly as I could, but within a moment, her eyes flickered open and she smiled tiredly at me.

"Good morning," I said. "How are you feeling?"

She shifted, digging for the controls to the bed in the crevices of her mattress.

"Need help?" I began to stand, but she shook her head, and I sank back down.

She found the controls and pressed a button to raise the top half of the bed. "I thought Damien would be here."

"He just left." I paused. "To get John."

Eyes widening slightly, Kat pressed her lips together, looking even paler than before. "John, huh?"

I nodded. "He heard you were ill. And apparently was very upset."

"And my brother thinks it's a good idea to bring his son here?"

"I think he wants to see you. And I think that means a lot," I said as gently as possible.

Her head shook atop her neck like a marionette. "I am not so sure about that." The sorrow in her voice cut me, at once injecting me with pain and guilt as I realized how selfish I had been all morning long.

Unable to look at her without allowing my pain to show, I walked to the window instead, contemplating what I should say to a suicidal girl who never wished to wake up. Finally, I turned back. "I'm so, so sorry, Kat. I can't—I haven't been a good friend to you. Not at all. I should have listened to you more, I shouldn't have—"

Kat cut me off with a roll of her eyes. "Adrienne, don't take this the wrong way, but nothing I did had anything to do with you."

I bit back the rest of my words, sandwiching my bottom lip between my teeth, and feeling tears smart behind my eyes.

"I wouldn't have told you more than I did even had the stars aligned. There was nothing you could have done . . ." She sighed as though she was too exhausted to say more.

"I'm sorry. Still. I should have noticed. I never should have stopped talking to you. I should have just listened. I don't . . . I don't know." I twisted my fingers together in my lap. "Maybe I could have been a better friend, that's all."

Kat's hand twitched on the pillow as if she would reach for me, but thought better or simply didn't have the strength to lift it. "You were a great friend."

"Were." The emphasis was all mine, and it was bitter.

Her lips twitched this time. "Are. Always have been. It's not you that's messed up. It's me." Her gaze drifted away. "It's always been me."

"Damien told me everything. I think."

She picked at the controls for her bed with a fingernail.

"Why didn't you tell me the rest of it?"

"You mean John?"

I shrugged.

"Mmm." She was so still and unmoving that I almost couldn't tell she was breathing. "You only want the truth. And sometimes the truth isn't—I can't—" She raised her eyes to the ceiling. "Some of us deal with the truth differently than you would."

I frowned. "What do you mean?"

"I can't explain . . . I don't . . . Admitting it to myself . . . that I needed help . . . I gave up John. He's not my son. Not anymore."

"How—how can you believe that?"

She stared hard at the bed controls. "My birth parents aren't my parents."

"Do you think he'll never find out?" I pressed, unable to help myself. "Secrets have a way of emerging at the worst times."

"They do, don't they?" she mused, her empty gaze slowly lifting to mine.

I sank back against the chair. Why did I keep pressing? Obviously she felt bad enough about the way things had happened, and now . . . she was recovering in the hospital, and I pressed her in her guilt, trying to convince her that my way was the right way, that everyone should tell the truth because it was the truth.

My stomach turned. Restless, I rose and crossed to the window, staring through the glass, hugging my arms around myself as I shivered. When would I find enough truth to be satisfied?

"I know I should tell, but . . . I can't bear to see them. John loves me because he doesn't know the truth. And I still have nightmares about . . . him." With her free hand, she folded the sheet and rubbed the two sides together between her fingertips. "I'm tired, and I can't sleep. I'm afraid I'll wake up to him again, and then when I wake up, it's reality and he's around all the time."

I didn't know what to say, and so I said nothing.

A heavy silence had invaded; both of us were stolen by our thoughts, and the minutes ticked along as though we were outside of them.

Finally she turned haunted eyes on me. "What do I tell John?"

I pushed myself away from the window and returned to the chair, collapsing in its frame like I weighed a ton. I had thought my life a tribute to honesty. But it was no great example, just a mockery.

Kat answered for me, pursing her lips and shaking her head. "There will never be a good time, will there?" She picked at the hospital sheets, and we resumed our silence, our waiting. "Sometimes I wish . . ."

"What? What do you wish?"

She smiled sadly. "That I'd never gone through with it."

Only because of my conversation with Victoria did I know what she meant. And tears stung my eyes. I couldn't help her. Nothing I could say would change anything. The truth clenched at my heart, an icy claw desperate as though I had sunk through thin ice, and tried to claw a hole through it with my fingernails for a breath. I was drowning when a gentle knock on the door returned air to the room.

Damien stood in the doorway with his hands on the shoulders of a young boy. The boy had a mop of dirty blond hair that fell down into one eye, so much like Jake's that my stomach clenched. Still, I fancied I could see the family resemblance between this boy and Damien, even though I knew it wasn't possible; I scrutinized him for a likeness that couldn't exist. Slender, tall for his age, with long fingers and delicate cheekbones, he scanned the room with a confidence I didn't expect from any child under three years old. He was his father's son. And it was that thought which made pity swell in my chest, spreading up my throat and choking me with regret.

At the sight of him, Kat readjusted herself in the bed, casting a large but tired smile across the room. Despite what she said about not being able to bear seeing her son, her eyes lit up at the sight of him, just as his hazel eyes darkened with concern. Suddenly I was imagining Kat after childbirth, gazing at the child in her arms with pride, cherishing him. But it hadn't begun that way. And it certainly hadn't ended up that way.

"John, this is my friend, Adrienne. Adrienne, my son, John." Over John's shoulder, Damien smiled at me, his eyes aglow with paternal pride. "John, can you say 'hello'?"

"Hello," John said politely to me, his voice high and boyish.

Damien leaned down and whispered something in his ear, then John dashed across the room and nearly leapt into Kat's bed. He nestled up beside her, turning his round, hazel eyes on her with adoration.

"Are you sick?" he asked her quietly.

Kat didn't answer right away, but pressed her lips together as John burrowed in next to her. She slipped her arm around his thin shoulders, hugging him against her.

I didn't wait for her answer, but rose and moved toward the door to give them privacy. Damien cast them an encouraging smile and joined me out in the hallway. In his smile there was tenderness and just a touch of fear.

Side by side, we walked in silence for a minute, then Damien asked, "So have you decided to stay for the wedding?"

A pair of nurses hurried down the hall toward us. My mind raced along with them. "I guess. I've got too many loose ends to tie up here before I can leave."

His mouth quirked. "Loose ends?"

"Elinor for one." I lifted a shoulder. "The only thing waiting for me in London now is the marathon. Kat probably won't be returning to the flat this summer, so I guess I'll have to cancel the lease, or—"

"I'll take care of all that."

"I'm sorry." I couldn't help but apologize again.

"For what?" He sounded genuinely confused.

Sniffing, I dashed a look around for a box of tissues. Reading my mind, Damien snagged a box from a nearby nurse's station and held it out to me.

"Thanks," I mumbled.

"What are you sorry for?" he repeated as we walked down the hall. We turned automatically through the halls, following the circular path as it had been set out.

From inside a room a few more nurses emerged, talking in low voices. One cast us a distracted smile.

"That I didn't catch on she was in a spiral of self-destructive behavior," I said through a bitter half scoff, half laugh.

He slipped his hand into mine. "It wasn't your responsibility. It never has been." His breath left him in a slow ache. "And it's taken me years to realize that it's not my responsibility either, as much as I wish I could fix it all." He sighed, his attention captivated by the view of sweeping green hills beyond the town from the hospital window. "That way I could fix her, or make her get fixed."

Grateful for his touch, I dropped my gaze to our joined hands. There was strength there, strength I hadn't noticed before, paired with a deep calmness that went far beyond my comprehension.

"I finally had to recognize Kat makes her own destiny; even though others may affect her life, she chooses her path. We all do. And there's little I can do about that, except make sure I affect her in a positive way. And that's all any of us can do." He took a deep breath, his chest expanding at the effort of stretching his lungs to their capacity. "I'm going to leave soon. For awhile. I don't know how much I'll see you before then."

My heart stilled in my chest. "Why?"

He stopped and took my other hand in his so that we faced each other. "I'm going to find Kat a center to get better at."

"Oh." I stared down at our hands, my thoughts in turmoil. "Where at? Same place as before?"

"No." He sighed. "They're full. And they're a bit too close to here." He dropped one of my hands and tucked my other in his arm, resuming our walk and pulling me close to keep up. "So I'm going to take her south. There's a good one outside of London, and . . . I think some additional sun will do her good."

"Right." I squeezed Damien's arm with my fingers reassuringly. "It will." When he glanced over at me, I smiled. "You're a good brother, Damien. You'll get her better."

He blinked rapidly and turned his face away.

Chapter Twenty-Five
Promises &
Surprises

ON MY WAY HOME FROM the hospital, I stopped at a local animal shelter in York and explained the situation to them. They wore looks of disapproval when I admitted my ownership of a "vicious dog," and I was told I would have to make contact with the Dog Warden and wait to find out if charges would be pressed.

"I'm sorry, I can't tell you what will happen," the woman behind the counter told me, leaving me unsure whether she didn't know, or whether she just wasn't allowed to tell me.

"She might be put down. If she's deemed dangerous," the other woman said.

My stomach swooped, twisting midair, and landed in a tangled heap near my feet. "Can I see her?" I knew the answer was probably no, but I had to ask.

"I'm sorry. She's not here, and I can't give out any information about an open case."

I left my contact information with her, knowing I wouldn't sleep well until everything got settled.

When I left York this time, the city had lost some of its magical luster. At the manor, I was greeted by the unsmiling faces of Edmund and

Victoria, along with a half dozen members of the press. Wincing at how I'd managed to forget about this, I spent the next fifteen minutes accepting Edmund's instructions on what to say, then answering questions from the press, trying to avoid any form of lying while still being open.

After they were dismissed, I dragged my tired body up the stairs to my room with the intention of a good, long bath. Instead, I opened the door to my room and found the bed occupied by two bodies that lifted my heart from my feet, making it flutter in amazement.

"Margot? Sophie? What are you doing here?" I flew across my room as they climbed off the bed, and wrapped my arms around both of them at once.

Margot's grin widened as Sophie began to explain.

"Did you really think we were going to miss Mum's wedding? You should know us better than that," she said.

"We wanted to surprise you," Margot added in her calmer voice. "Thought you'd be up a bit earlier, though."

"Well, you did. You really did."

They exchanged a smile.

"Gosh, I can't believe how much I have to tell you. Has it really only been two months since I've seen you?"

"I *know*." Sophie launched into an explanation of their summer so far, how they'd barely managed to keep this visit a secret, and how excited they were to get a new sister.

I showered while chatting with my sisters, the door cracked open, only the shower curtain between us. They sprawled across my bed, Sophie flipping through an entertainment magazine, Margot reading what looked like a travel book.

When I stepped out with a towel under my arms and on my head, the twins looked up from their position on the bed.

"Don't you have a dog?" Margot asked. "I expected to see her."

"Yeah, well, don't." I glowered and unwrapped my hair to towel it off. "Unless you go to the shelter, or wherever it is they keep confiscated dogs."

"What?" Margot's book lay forgotten on the bed, one hand over the top of the open pages.

"Oh yes." Sophie's kohl-painted eyes wide with understanding, she nodded. "You had to surrender her?"

With narrowed eyes, I examined the younger twin. "Do you follow all the tabloids?"

She grinned. "I know who to talk to."

"Clearly. Who told you in this case?"

"Sydney."

The towel in my hands drifted to my waist as I straightened. "Really?"

"Oh yeah. Where is she, by the way? I thought we'd see her right away. Instead we see this delicious blond man . . ." She trailed off with a mischievous grin.

Mouth open to respond about Sydney, I changed words as she finished speaking. "Jake? He's here?" The only way I was going to get Elinor back was by convincing him to drop the charges, and maybe not even then.

She grinned. "Yes, is he available?"

I glared at her. "Don't—just don't even think about him. Where is he?"

Sophie's eyebrows arched high in unexaggerated interest, but Margot frowned at me, always quicker to catch on to subtleties.

"Are you finally interested in someone else?" Sophie squealed. "Oh, I'm so glad!"

"No," I said sharply. "And if you're smart, you won't give him a second glance. Looks aren't everything you know."

Sophie's smile faded at my words, and, with sinking shoulders, she murmured, "I know."

"Sorry, I—he's not a good guy. Please stay away from him."

"Well I hardly think he was trying anything with us." Margot swept her hair over her shoulder. "He was just being friendly. Trying to show us around. We were about to take a tour before you got here."

"Please don't. Not from Jake." I balled the towel up in my hands, knowing they needed to understand to keep far away from him. "Anyone else is fine—even the stable boy—but avoid Jake. Like the plague," I added at Sophie's skeptical expression, lips pressed together disapprovingly. "I can't tell you why, Soph—it's not my story to tell." I cursed inwardly. Here I was, withholding another secret. And was it worth it? Should I tell them? Even if it meant losing Kat and maybe Damien in the process? I sank to the edge of my bed and covered my face with my hands.

"Addy?" Margot murmured. "What's wrong?"

"Kat's in the hospital," I said into my hands.

"What?" It was Sophie speaking this time, and her scrambling on my right to sit up beside me and get closer.

"She tried to kill herself." My voice broke.

"Oh my gosh," Margot murmured, her hand going to my shoulder.

"Is she okay?" the twins both asked at the same time.

"Physically, she'll be fine." My mind turned over everything I had learned over the past week, and everything I couldn't tell them about Kat and John and Damien.

"What happened?" Margot urged.

I bit my lip, not sure how to continue.

"Does she not want us to know?" Margot reached for my hand and took it onto her lap, holding it in both of hers.

"She doesn't want anyone to know," I said through a half laugh, half sob. "Obviously people know she's in the hospital, but she doesn't want people to know why." I raised my gaze to Margot's, appealing to her for understanding.

After a brief contemplation, Margot nodded. "Of course. We respect that."

"We do?" Sophie asked, always up for more gossip. But this time, she asked it in such a way that it sounding teasing, as though Margot wouldn't always be allowed to make the big decisions for them.

We both smiled in Sophie's direction, and she pouted prettily. "That's all right. We won't ask you—we'll find out some other way." She winked.

"You know I'd tell you if I could, Soph." I opted to refrain from warning her about poking her nose into this business. She'd not listen to me anyway, and it would make it more "forbidden" and interesting to warn her against it.

Her face relaxed into honest sympathy. "I know. I know it kills you to hide anything." She winked again, then drew me into a hug that Margot joined from the other side, creating what they had always dubbed an Addy-melt, as I always melted into their embrace.

☽

By almost all accounts, I had achieved what I had come up to Yorkshire to find. The lingering question of how I should answer my mother's question to be maid of honor kept me rooted to the spot, though. I couldn't deny that I hoped my mother would continue her ever-so-slow change in behavior. *She apologized to me*, I reminded myself. *She's never done that before. She's starting to change. I just have to stick through this summer and let her see I'm not running away again. See that she matters to me.*

As the days ticked by, I crossed them off in my mental calendar, visiting Kat every morning, dragging my sisters to York and other nearby towns after that to avoid Jake, and wishing that Elinor and Damien were able to join us. But Elinor was still in doggy jail and Damien had hardly left Kat's side, except to start making arrangements with a hospital.

My morning runs were no longer the peaceful escape they had been, sans Elinor, and on one of them, I found Jake pacing along the clifftop. Today, I clutched the amethyst necklace he had given me in my hand and headed toward him.

As I jogged over, my feet felt oddly weightless. By the time I reached him, he faced the water, hands shoved into his jacket pockets. I slowed, ambling up to him, and began my own inspection of the sea.

"I thought you'd be out here," he said, just loud enough to carry over the sound of the wind and the waves crashing on the rocks below.

"You were looking for me?" His words sent my blood racing again. "After what you've done? What are you even doing here? I thought you got some big break."

His glance at me was contemplative, and I noticed an intelligence there for the first time that I hadn't seen before. Or perhaps it was just that I knew who he was this time, for real. I knew the truth instead of the lies he projected for me to see.

"What's your game?" I demanded when he didn't respond. My fists clenched at my sides, and I crossed my arms to cover them; the act brought a faint smile to his lips.

"We're all playing the game, Adrienne."

"You forget. I don't play games."

"Sure you do," he answered with a shrug that came too easily. "We all do. Isn't that what you and dear ol' Damien were talking about?"

"We're all players on the stage of life?" I remembered my chat under the stars.

He inclined his head to the side in agreement.

Wordlessly, I extended my fist to him, dropping the pendant from my fingers when he cast me a confused look.

"Ah." A nod dipping his chin down, he reached up and seized the necklace.

Withdrawing my hand, I tightened my arms around my ribs again, for the morning chill was setting in, and thick droplets of sweat sent a shiver rippling over my skin. The sun peeked out over the ocean now, a low eye in the sky.

"I can't believe you took everything out on Elinor." I shook my head. "She didn't do anything wrong."

"I'll be permanently scarred!" he complained, pulling up his sleeve to inspect his arm. "Lasting damage."

I scoffed deep in my throat. "They could kill her. Does she deserve that?"

He lifted one shoulder in a careless shrug.

"I could get in trouble. Maybe go to jail. Do I deserve that?"

"I think your mum and Edmund will carry some influence there. But that's up to how you play the game." His eyes twinkled, and he winked at me, as if he didn't consider that a real possibility, or completely didn't care. "I'm going to leave. I've given up my position here."

"Victoria didn't fire you?" I asked dryly, unable to keep the bitterness from seeping into my words. "I thought you'd already quit anyway." I knew I should tread carefully with him, as he alone had the power to withdraw charges against Elinor and me, but it turned my stomach to even consider it.

"No. She wouldn't dare. Not with my lawsuit pending." He smiled as though he'd won his hand, and it set my heart rate monitor buzzing at me, notifying me of my heart rate entering a higher zone.

I worked my jaw around to avoid clenching it, chewing on the words I wanted to say and the ones I would say. "So you think you just get to run off, scot-free. Again?"

"Again?"

A forced smile on my lips set his to frowning. "I hear stories, Jake. Stories that would make most women—and people in general—run from you."

"Oh," he said in understanding, and his face darkened. "Stories. Are you sure they're true? You sure you know who to believe?"

"As certain as I am that I stand here next to you."

His jaw clenched, a furious flush climbing his neck. "I told her that accusation would never go away. And now she's convinced you, too." He stooped to the ground and picked up a round rock, turning it over in his hand as he rose. The flush slowly left his cheeks, returning them to his natural hue. "Be careful who you believe." His eyes caught mine. "And what you think you know."

"Why is that?"

He considered the rock, holding it up for me to see a rugged, black heart shape inside a white circle of stone. "Thankfully, what I learned was that unless you have proof," he swung his hand back, then thrust it forward, letting the rock go at the apex, "it doesn't exist, and it's not true." The rock soared through the air, out past the edge of the cliff and arced down, down, down to the water below. Its landing was lost over distance and the roaring of the wind battling my heartbeat in my ears. "That's what I learned when someone insisted on spreading lies about me."

I wanted to scream at him. I had proof. I believed Kat—not him. Jake had to be lying; I couldn't believe that Kat, dear, sweet Kat, would lie about something like this. But Damien's words, unbidden, came back to me now: *Kat had every reason to lie.*

Now, standing in front of Jake, I had to choose sides. In a court, he would have been innocent. Innocent until proven guilty. And this was a case of he said, she said. A case where neither person was a reliable witness. I ran a hand over my hair as Jake continued.

"All you have is a girl's tale of unrequited love and heartbreak."

I couldn't tell if he was joking or serious. "You're saying she accused you because you broke up with her?"

He lifted a shoulder, his lips pressed together in something like disgust. "A pretty story to evoke sympathy, eh?"

"Why would she lie?"

"I don't know. She was always a bit unstable, wanting attention. Perhaps the same reason she dyes her hair bright pink?"

"You're a bastard."

Shock widened his eyes. "I don't need you to believe me. I know I haven't done anything wrong."

Fury pushed a scoff of disbelief out of me. "Are you trying to say it wasn't wrong to treat a girl like you did?"

"I don't know what story she told you, but once she found out she was adopted, she changed, Adrienne." He gazed at the sea once more, then back to me. "She was hanging all over me, desperate for attention."

"That's your story? It's *her* fault?"

"I'm not proud of my relationship with Kat. Things would have been a lot simpler if I had never touched her." He shook his head, confusion creasing his brow, his words laced with honesty. "It's nothing personal, it's just the truth. I thought that was what you wanted, after all?"

Digging deep down into my gut still left me empty of replies.

"Sometimes the truth isn't simple," he said.

The wind whistled past my ears, sweeping away every possible response.

He turned his back to the sea, his turquoise eyes intent upon me as if he could read the heartbreak and confusion there. Pressing a smile to his lips, he leaned forward and brushed a kiss on my cheek. "I'm sorry things couldn't be simpler for all of us."

And he left me there, my cheek burning at the touch of his lips, wishing for things to be different, and in the end, stooping to the ground and grabbing a fistful of dirt, rock, and sand to scrub away the feel of his lips from my skin.

Chapter Twenty-Six
Past & Present
Choices

AFTER MY CHAT WITH JAKE, my muscles were so taut it took a half hour's run to regain my stride. By then, my anger hadn't faded; it was merely replaced by aches in random places, which ate at me as much as my frustration did. Usually running helped prevent me from being overwhelmed, but today, reflecting upon Kat's suicide attempt, Elinor's dilemma, Jake suing my mother, and my disastrous meeting with Dennison, running drained my energy. Everything was falling apart. I shouldn't have even come to Yorkshire. Nothing good had happened on this trip.

My depressing thoughts had carried me back to the manor, but I wasn't ready to go in. Instead, I wandered to the lake in front of the manor, where I crumbled down on a stone bench and sank into a deeper state of even more depressing thoughts. What if Kat didn't recover? What if Jake did something awful to her? What if—

A bark sounded somewhere behind me, turning my thoughts to Elinor. What if Elinor got put down? Leaning forward, I dropped my face into my hands. Things could still get worse then. Much worse.

The bark sounded again, nearer this time. I forced myself not to turn and look. It was probably McDuff, Damien's Border Collie, even though it sounded an awful lot like Elinor's bark. *I have to be hearing things. I just want it to be her.* Just when I lost my battle in keeping my gaze averted, something collided into the side of my knees with the force of a sack of flour.

A furry fifty pounds of dog followed, a low joyous whining filling my ears. "Wha—?"

Nails scratched at me as a fawn-colored dog tried to climb into my lap, barking and practically singing with joy.

"Elinor!" I managed to extricate my hands from our tangle of limbs and held out my arms to her, pulling her into my lap as she dragged me off the bench and to the soggy ground below. Licks and whines surrounded me as I wrapped my arms around her and struggled to hold on to the lithe, wriggling body. She surged repeatedly at my face, her tongue flashing, tail wagging, and body trembling out of sheer joy. "How —? Where did you—?" I couldn't finish a sentence in my relief, and it was a full minute before I thought to search for her deliverer.

A tall, dark haired male in a striped polo shirt strode across the lawn toward us.

At first glance, I thought it was Damien, but as he neared, I saw this man was taller, older, and a bit more out of shape. He inspected the grass at his feet, as though checking for holes in his path. When he lifted his chin, I recognized him immediately, and it was the only person that could have torn me away from Elinor's side.

I raced Elinor across the lawn to my father's side, his grin welcoming me into his arms. The force of our impact nearly knocked him off his feet, but we staggered, arms around each other tight.

Finally I pulled away to look up at him. "Dad, what are you doing here?"

He grinned down at me, brushing my hair back from my forehead as he had done when I was a little girl. "Figured I'd come for the wedding." He bobbed his head to the side. "And make a little salmon delivery." He shrugged. "Your mom asked."

"Right." An overwhelming sense of relief was flooding through me. "I thought you were in Galena or Italy or somewhere?"

He grinned, and his extra white teeth were made shocking against his tanned skin. "I was. You've lost track of time. I've been home since then."

"But I thought you were staying in Europe?"

"I am in Europe." His grin turned to a smirk, and I returned it with a roll of my eyes and a playful shove against him.

"Well I wasn't told you'd be in England!"

He pulled me against his chest. "I wasn't supposed to be, but my trip to Italy turned out . . . useless. The person I was supposed to be meeting left early. So I decided to come—"

"For the wedding?"

"—to see you," he finished at the same time, smiling.

"Awesome." I stepped back to look up at his face, memorizing the dark beard, the soft brown eyes, the receding hair line with hints of gray streaks just beginning to appear, and beamed at him. "I'm so glad to see you. Where are you staying?"

"Here." He squeezed me tightly again before letting me go. "Your soon-to-be-stepfather appears to be a generous man."

"Isn't that a little awkward? To stay with your ex-wife and her soon-to-be-husband?"

He shrugged. "We haven't lived under the same roof for fifteen years. I think we can put the past behind us."

Elinor barked, chasing the shadows around our feet.

I frowned. "Did you bring Elinor back?"

"Elinor?"

"My dog."

"No. This is the first time I've seen her. There was a dark haired young man, though, who seemed to point her in this direction."

Damien. A smile tugged at my mouth.

My father smiled back. "I can see that means something to you."

Cheeks growing hot, I watched Elinor race away from us, stretching out her legs as she dashed toward the cliff. I finally had Dad by my side, and I could ask him anything I wanted, now that I'd found out the truth about my birth.

"Why'd you come, Dad?" I finally settled on asking. "To your ex-wife's wedding?"

He chuckled, his hands shoved into his pants pockets. "Oh, I don't know. Because my three daughters are here, watching their mother remarry, and I like to think that, somehow . . ." His lips fell as a shadow crossed his face. "Somehow we're all still a family."

Fine lines creased around his eyes that hadn't been there the last time I'd seen him, along with puffy circles underneath, which suggested that he either suffered serious jetlag right now, or else he hadn't been sleeping well for another reason.

"I know you have questions, Adrienne. And I missed you. I was nearby, had the time . . ." He shrugged. "Do I need more excuses to see my eldest daughter? Actually, all my daughters?"

"No." I smiled warmly and slipped my hand through his arm. "No, you don't ever need any excuse to drop in on me. I hope you know that."

He pulled my head toward him with a hand over my ear and planted a kiss on the top of my head. "Oh, honey, I'm relieved to hear you say that."

"You are?" I pulled away only to look up at him and frown. We were almost at the clifftop now, another dozen feet to go, and our feet slowed. "Why?"

Halting, he grimaced, staring out over the sea. "I heard you met your biological father."

The world seemed to still around us. Although the sea still churned below us, and the wind ruffled our hair and clothes, time seemed as though it was giving me a chance to come up with something worthwhile to say. And yet all I could come up with was, "Yeah. I think I did."

Lips pursed, Dad nodded.

"And he was, quite possibly, the biggest jerk I could expect."

Dad's arm went weak as tension bled from his shoulders into the ground below us. "What?" He sank down onto the rocky grass on the clifftop.

A sound halfway between scoff and sob slipped from me. I sat down beside him, and it took me a few tries to answer. "He's a jerk. And he denied everything. I'm not even sure it's him, but . . . it makes sense if it is." Then, sitting together at the cliff on Edmund Chadwick's property, I filled my father in on the meeting with Matthew Dennison, and watched his face flush with anger.

"Are you upset with me for not letting this go? For wanting to know the truth when you never cared?"

"Oh, Addy." He sighed and slipped his arm around my shoulders, squeezing me against him. "It wasn't that I didn't care, it just never mattered more to me than you did."

Frowning, I opened my mouth to speak, but he continued.

"I never asked because I was a bit of a coward, you see. I was pretty sure, at least for a while there, that I might lose you if you suspected the truth. But the first moment I laid my eyes on you, when you were bloody and wrinkly and cone headed—"

I rolled my eyes, having heard that before.

"—I knew I'd love you forever, no matter what hell you put me through. It didn't matter to me if I was your biological father or adopted father or something in between." He gazed at the horizon, his voice growing distant. "I've always been your father in my heart, and I didn't want the truth to get in the way of that. For either of us."

Leaning over my crossed legs, I picked up a jagged rock that had been digging into my palm.

He cleared his throat and continued. "Even as a politician, I've tried to seek the truth and instill that truth in you. This . . . this was the only time I've willingly accepted a lie and pretended I didn't know it was false. And it always ate at me. I suspected, but I never had the courage to ask, to press your mother to tell me. I knew, if I did, she'd leave me forever." He crossed his ankles out before him and leaned back on his hands. "In the end, it didn't matter anyway. My hold on her wasn't strong enough. Not even after your sisters arrived."

I turned the rock over in my hands, clenching my fist around it until its corners bit into my fingertips and palm.

"But we had some really good years in there," Dad mused, as if to himself, as though he had forgotten he talked to his daughter and not a friend. "And I guess that's why I just kept pretending, hoping that she could, one day, come back and find it again."

I frowned at my clenched fist, not quite sure what he meant anymore, or what "it" meant, at least. But he lapsed into a silence that I couldn't find it in me to break, and eventually, feeling crusty with dried sweat, I said good-bye and, calling Elinor to me, headed off to take a hot shower.

Emerging from my bathroom, I found the twins sprawled across my bed, in what was quickly becoming their M.O.

"What are you doing here?"

Sophie flashed a quick grin. "Hanging out."

"What's wrong with your own bed?" I rubbed a towel over my hair.

Margot tossed a stuffed bone for Elinor, who raced after it, nearly bowling into an antique secretary desk, making all three of us wince.

"I see you've made friends with Elinor," I remarked when she trotted back with the bone, tail high and proud.

"Of course," Sophie agreed.

"Can I ask you something, Adrienne?" Margot threw the bone for

Elinor again, who scrambled across the wooden floor to snatch it between her jaws.

Sinking down at the foot of the bed, I shrugged. "Sure. You know me, I'm an open book."

Margot took the bone from Elinor and paused, turning it over in her hands.

"But first," I said, "why don't you tell me how long you've known about Dad coming here?"

The twins exchanged a fleeting grin, and a flurry of conversation slowed only after they'd shared the little amount they knew about our father's plan. But he wasn't *our* father, was he? He was *their* father. I stood and crossed the room, where I sat before the fireplace, stretching out my legs and crossing them in front of me. Sophie followed, claiming the chair beside me.

"So, I've something to ask you, Adrienne, if Margot's never going to."

"Yes?"

"Why won't you tell us why that blond guy—Jake or something—is off limits?"

Staring into the fire, I sighed. "It's not my place to tell. I wish I could, but . . ." The desire to tell the truth warred within me with the desire to respect Kat's wishes. The twins, although they were my sisters and I loved them, were awful at keeping secrets.

"Is this another Bryan thing? Where something horrible has happened, changing you forever, but you refuse to tell us?" Sophie showed her characteristic turn-on-a-dime temper switch, which reminded me of a certain someone else when she didn't get her way.

"Another Bryan thing?" I repeated slowly.

"That's your story and you still refuse to share it," Sophie said.

"Why does it matter, Soph? He cheated on me. We broke up. That's it." Even though I had confessed it to Kat, I didn't want to go through it again. Not without another bottle of whisky, at least.

"She's right, Adrienne," came Margot's more matter-of-fact tone. "The only thing about never lying is that it makes you one of two things: either the worst liar ever when you do lie, or else the best liar there is because no one expects it. You happen to be the former."

Wide eyed, I stared at her.

"The only lie you've ever told is why you and Bryan broke up."

How could I ever have considered Margot less like our mother than

Sophie? For once, I wasn't sure: tell them about our mother and Bryan's kiss or keep telling a lie?

"I never lied. I omitted." My hands trembled as I reached the decision. "But you're right."

Confusion etched the twins' faces.

"That's as good as a lie." I crossed my legs, staring into my hands as I twisted my fingers together in my lap to keep them from shaking. "But it's one I'm going to keep telling."

Sophie fell back against the chair with a huff while Margot sighed into the fire.

"I'm sorry." Rising, I felt like I ought to say more, but I couldn't. I couldn't be responsible for the destruction of Victoria's relationship with the twins. She deserved her own chance to mess things up with them, without my help. Maybe she really was sorry, and to bring it up now, after keeping it secret for so long, would just hurt everyone all over again.

Chapter Twenty-Seven
Hen Night

TWO DAYS BEFORE THE WEDDING, the five of us women went to York together, leaving the men at the manor heading to the gentleman's room, in what I imagined would be an awkward time of drinking brandy and smoking cigars. Edmund, along with Damien and Lord Callum, the other groomsman, headed off after an early dinner, and insisted on Dad coming along.

Dad, ever the politician, accepted the invite with the grace and poise his job had taught him, saying he'd be pleased to join them celebrating the upcoming wedding. I sensed that only I detected his tempered enthusiasm.

Victoria had excused herself early from dinner in order to deal with a last-minute question from her wedding planner, but all the rest of us girls waited in the foyer for her arrival. Everyone else had changed clothes after dinner, but I'd taken Elinor out for a bathroom break instead, then returned her to my room, careful to lock the door and double check it. Now we had been in the foyer for the past ten minutes, awaiting Victoria, as was the custom. Along the wall near the front door stood a man in a suit with hands clasped behind his back, as though he had nothing better to do.

"I haven't gotten my nails done in weeks!" Sydney bounced on the balls of her feet and inspected her cuticles.

I smiled faintly at her, while Sophie began picking at her nails, and Margot moved off to examine one of the paintings hanging on the wall.

"Do you have the nail polish?" Sydney asked, and Sophie patted her purse in answer.

"So sorry, girls, got tied up. Is the car here?" Victoria swept down the stairs, dressed in a long flowing skirt and sandals, while a large purse dangled from her arm.

"Of course, madam," the man said from the doorway.

Victoria paused before us, a queenly expression on her face as she took in her three daughters and future stepdaughter. She looked as though she might speak, but bit it back. "Let's go, girls." She swept to the door, which the man opened as if part of a choreographed dance.

Sophie and Margot linked arms on the way out the door, while Sydney followed after. Steeling myself, and giving one last glance down the hall where the men had disappeared, I trudged along after, and was the last to climb into a long, black limo Victoria had rented for the occasion. I wondered at her lack of other friends. She had not told me about any other bachelorette party, but I wouldn't know if she'd had one already.

While I sat back in the corner, listening to Sydney, Margot, and Sophie chat and laugh, my mother was doing the same. She stared out the window mostly, watching the scenery go by as I watched the interactions between my sisters. They were more similar than the rest of us, I found myself thinking; a thought which lumped my mother and me together, a pairing I wasn't certain I warranted.

Not an hour later, we ended up at a small nail salon in York, which had three seats available at a time, one for pedicures and two for manicures.

"Bride goes first!" Sydney chirruped when we stepped in, motioning her almost stepmother on.

"Oh, you're a doll, Sydney," Victoria said, warmth blushing her cheeks. "But I should let you girls go first."

The cliché "age before beauty" ran through my head, and I barely kept my tongue. Doubtless, that would not be a sentiment well-received.

The twins glanced at each other, then Sydney and me. "We can—"

"I'll wait," I said with an easy shrug, thinking of the book I'd stashed in my purse on the way out of my room earlier that evening. "I don't mind."

"We'll draw straws. Pick numbers," Sophie suggested with a smile.

"Oh, it's fine." I turned to Sydney. "Why don't we go and get everyone coffee?"

Her expression cleared, a tinge of relief lighting up her gray-eyed gaze. "Yeah, sure."

With what I hoped was an honest smile, and trying to ignore the pang of guilt at the thought that I had been living in my own little world lately, I headed back out into the street. "I think there's a little coffee shop this way. Maybe get you a scone?" I teased, recalling our first meeting.

She blinked as if she didn't know why I would say that, then understanding dawned in her eyes, and she smiled sadly. "Right. Scones. My weakness." She shook her head down at her sandaled feet. "No. I'm supposed to be on a diet."

"A diet?" Surprise made my eyebrows collide into my forehead. "You don't need to be on a diet."

She frowned. "I do if I want to be an actress."

Right. Only a matter of time before Hollywood gets to her. She's so much like the twins. "Well, I don't think you need to diet. I think you're beautiful."

She turned to look at me so fast that she put a hand to her neck as though she had popped something. "You do?"

The expression of wonder and delight on her features was marred only by a hesitancy to show just how much my words meant to her.

"Well, yeah."

A frown threatened at her lips as if I hadn't delivered my line convincingly enough. "But you're so pretty, you can say that."

"Sydney, you're beautiful. Surely your dad tells you that all the time?"

She shifted her purse on her shoulder, hooking one thumb on the strap to hold it closer to her body. "No. Not since I was young."

"Well, you are. And don't let anyone tell you differently." We reached the coffee shop and, as my hand touched the door, I realized our mistake. "Crap, we didn't get anyone's order."

Sydney leapt to attention and dug out her cell phone. "No worries. I'll text Margot."

The answer she received two minutes later was from Sophie, however, as Margot was having her nails done and had passed it on to her sister. As we waited for the order to be filled, I said, "You know, Victoria can be a perfectionist. She *is* a perfectionist."

Sydney stared out the window at the passing pedestrians, but I could tell by the glaze over her eyes that she wasn't seeing them.

"And she puts that on everyone around her." Outside, a mother pushed twin boys in a stroller past the shop. I cleared my throat, considering how best to phrase what I felt she needed to hear. "You have to be careful how much you let her opinion mean to you. Because, in my experience, she'll never find anyone to be good enough, including herself."

Slowly, Sydney's head bobbed into a nod, her eyes gradually finding focus. Before she could speak, two of our coffee orders were called, and soon the other three followed. A couple of minutes later, with all the coffees in hand, we returned to the nail salon. On the way, we passed the mother with her twins in the stroller, one of whom had a streak of chocolate ice cream on his forehead. Sydney pointed at it with a fingertip and giggled, making me smile and think of John.

A little while later, I sat next to Victoria as our nails were done. Sydney reclined in the pedicure chair a short distance away, and the twins had disappeared somewhere, to get ice cream or dessert, I thought I'd heard.

Victoria was staring at her unvarnished nails pensively. "I've given an interview, Adrienne."

All my attention focused on her words. "Okay?"

"I thought you wanted to know when I did that."

"If it concerns me, yes." In the bright lights of the salon, Victoria's wrinkles were evident. She had few of them for her age, helped no doubt by modern medicine, but, for once, I could freely see them.

"It does." She frowned at her bare nails, yellowed slightly from the nail polish that had been removed.

I held my breath for a moment before speaking again. "How much does it concern me?"

"Well, let's say it's how I met your father. And how I got started in Hollywood."

"What—what do you mean?"

"Adrienne, do you want to hear all this here? I can't really speak about it in public, you know. It's an exclusive. I'm not supposed to say anything at all until it breaks, and then only what I've already confided to the papers."

"I—"

"I'll tell you—if you want. I owe you that much. And more."

Unexpected tears pricked my eyes. "Yeah. I'd like to know before it all goes public."

She nodded, her gaze traveling to the salon workers as they returned from gathering more tools for our manicures. "Come to my room when we get home. I'll fill you in."

"Thank you."

When we got home after a leisurely dinner and dessert, it was late, but with a questioning glance at my mother, I understood our meeting was still on.

I changed clothes quickly, let Elinor out and returned her to my room, then went to my mother's suite. Before knocking on the door, I hesitated. She was willing to tell me everything that she'd said in her interview. Could it be possible that she was really listening to me? That she was really, truly, finally trying?

Hoping and praying that to be true, I knocked.

Her honey smooth, "Come in," answered my knock, and I entered.

Dressed in a robe of red silk, she smiled at me, tightened the sash, and motioned to a chair before a modest fire. Atop an antique table, a bottle of white wine with the cork half sticking out of it rested in a large silver goblet of ice. Two wine glasses stood beside it, waiting to be filled.

"Sit down. Have a drink."

Thinking of my night drinking whisky with Kat, I grimaced and said wryly, "Am I going to need it?"

She cast me a curious look, her lashes sweeping up and down as she took me in. "I don't know. Better safe than sorry, I suppose."

"Right." But with my mother, it couldn't hurt, so I poured us each a small glass and sat. "Let's get started." My stomach churned at what she might tell.

"Well," she said, sitting down and taking her drink in hand. "I promised to tell you what I said, right?"

"Yes."

"You know how I told Charity to release the information earlier."

"Yes, but I don't understand why."

"Why?" she asked blankly.

"Yeah. I mean, was it because you're marrying a politician and wanted to cleanse the past?"

"A bit. But what I said in my interview was true: I'm tired of this secret. Do you know how hard it gets to keep secrets?" She took a sip of her drink.

"I try not to keep them, honestly."

She laughed lightly. "I forgot—Miss Honesty is sitting next to me." This time when she said it, it was with a hint of admiration, not mockery.

"Yeah. Well, there are worse traits, I guess."

"True. Much worse." Her smile faded as she seemed to search for her thoughts in the fire. "You know, I admire you on a lot of levels, Adrienne. I don't know how you turned out as well as you did. Well, actually that's a lie. It was all James."

Allowing her to muse for a while, I swirled the pale yellow liquid around in my glass, not interested in drinking its overpowering sweetness. "So what's in this interview?" I finally prompted.

"Well, let's start with the beginning. I told them all about my relationship with your father. Your biological father."

The question of why it mattered to anyone but me and those directly involved floated before my closed eyes. Regardless, it was out there; my mother was a public figure, and so was my father. I could expect no privacy.

"What did you tell them?" I asked.

She smiled faintly. "I . . . I'm not proud of all this, Adrienne. Teenage pregnancy is nothing to be proud of. And it changed my life . . ."

"I know."

"What you don't know is why I did it."

"I assume you didn't plan to get pregnant." I scoffed.

At this, she sighed. "That wouldn't entirely be accurate."

"What?"

"Hollywood operates a little differently . . . I needed leverage." She tilted her head to the side. "Or I thought I did."

I gaped at her. *Maybe I should have started drinking.* "You wanted to get pregnant in order to have leverage over Dennison?"

A weak smile made her appear older and more conflicted than I'd ever seen before. Her usual confidence and grace had sunk out of her. "I said I'm not proud of it. I was young; I thought I had to climb the ladder by sleeping with people. And if I was pregnant with the man's child, I could maintain a relationship with someone who held a lot of power." She closed her eyes, for once looking tormented by her past actions.

"You screwed up. It doesn't have to forever follow you around."

Facing me, her expression grew wistful. "That's extraordinarily naïve coming from you."

I flinched.

"Anyway. I got pregnant. And when I told him the news, he insisted on an abortion. I countered with demanding his next lead role after I terminated the pregnancy." She gave a delicate shrug. "We compromised. I told him I wanted the role next year, or I would tell him I was underage when we started sleeping together. He couldn't prove otherwise, and he was already rumored to be interested in younger girls. That was the last thing he needed—it could blacklist him. I was risking being blacklisted already, but I didn't really have much to lose at that point. He had everything to lose." She wiped a fingertip over the lip marks on her wine glass.

"Why next year? Why did he agree to that, I mean? Wouldn't it be obvious you weren't going to terminate the pregnancy then?"

A glint of her old confidence reentered her gaze. "Ah, well, I told him that if he offered it to me now, it would be too obvious that he was only giving it to me because we slept together. Neither he, nor I, really wanted that appearance. So I told him a few lies, like how I was going to audition and try to make it on my own until I cashed in on my lead with him. Instead, I went home, married James, had a quick little honeymoon, and did some plays and modeling before I started showing. I was lucky—I didn't show quickly at all. I was probably six months before people could really notice anything. Good genetics for you, you know. James always trusted me. Never doubted that our little honeymoon baby was two months early."

"Biology isn't everything." I scoffed. "It doesn't matter all that much sometimes."

She shrugged. "I'm not excusing what I did. I hope you realize that. I . . . I've been a selfish prat, really. But having you here, seeing the woman you've become, Adrienne . . . And seeing the closeness between Edmund and Sydney . . ." A single tear traveled down her cheek. "It makes me wish I hadn't missed out on so much of your life. I'm sorry. And I hope, one day, you can forgive me." She swiped at her cheeks with one hand, one after the other. She set down her wine glass to free both hands and ran both index fingers under her eyes.

Questions swirled within me, a vortex of events lacking explanations. "Why did you leave in the first place?"

Victoria leaned forward, covering her face with her hands. For the first time in my life, I witnessed my mother's shoulders shaking with true grief.

Chapter Twenty-Eight
Rehearsing

I DIDN'T TRY TO HUG my mother or even pat her shoulder. I couldn't—not until I had the answer I had so long waited for. Instead, I downed half my wine in one gulp as she gathered herself. I grimaced, the sticky sweetness of white wine coating my tongue and teeth and overwhelming my senses.

"I don't know," she finally continued. "I was so selfish then. I was not in a good mindset, and I must have been a horrible mother even while I was there." She sniffed loudly and searched the table next to her. She stood and crossed to a nearby table, grabbing a box of tissues and returning to her seat before continuing. "I hated Alaska. I hated how responsible James was, I hated how much history I had there, how small it was, how confining!" She straightened and blinked away her last tears, inhaling a deep breath and dabbing at her eyes. "I just . . . I felt like I was drowning there. I was never meant for that life, and I tried to make it work. And I suppose I thought, if I left, James would find you a better mother, one that was worthy of him and you girls. Even though I hated my life, I knew it was pretty sweet."

I turned my wine glass around in my hands, staring into the small bubbles clinging against one side. "Did you have post-partum depression?"

"What?"

"You know, depression after having the twins?"

Eyes wide, she raised her gaze to the ceiling as if thinking hard. "Perhaps."

"Thanks for not killing us then."

"What?" A shocked laugh escaped her, and she looked at me as if unsure whether laughing was the right thing to do.

I shrugged. "Well you know, the whole Andrea Yates case and that sort of thing. You could have wiped us all out. Instead you just left us with a very capable father."

"Dear Lord," she muttered into her near empty glass.

A grin tugged at my lips. "Never thought of that?"

"I don't . . . No, not really. But I *was* depressed. And getting away . . . leaving, well, it helped to some extent. It certainly didn't fix me. But I was older, a little more experienced." She fell silent, slouching down in her chair and curling her hands around her wine.

"Do you regret leaving us?" My voice came out small, aimed at the crackling flames instead of the woman I had longed for a relationship with for so long.

"Every day," she whispered, her voice breaking. "I wonder how my life would have been different. How much happier I could have been being a mother, instead of this constant battle climbing the ladder."

"Well, the perks of being a movie star are pretty nice, right?"

"Even perks grow old." Victoria's gaze became distant. "Don't you ever wonder why so many actors get pulled up into drugs and alcohol abuse?" She lifted the wine glass as if she included herself in that. "Humans just aren't meant to deal with the kind of pressure Hollywood puts on them."

As I turned to my drink, my lip curled at the edge, and my stomach flipped. I set it down beside me, now that it was warm from my hands and the heat of the room anyway.

Victoria watched me do it, sad resignation on her features, as though she watched me prepare to leave her. "I can't ask you to forgive me. I know I'm unforgivable. I'll spend my lifetime trying, and certainly failing, to make it up to you."

"You're not unforgivable," I told her firmly, but I stopped short of granting her forgiveness.

She sat before me, her shoulders stooped and sorrow written on her features. I hated that I suspected her of playing a part, of stringing me along right now, simply for her own desires. I wanted to think she'd changed, wanted to believe she saw her mistakes and wanted to avoid repeating them. But something inside held me back. She hadn't yet earned my trust. And I knew I would spend the following months, and even years, doubting everything she said and did.

"I'm sorry," she finally said. "I asked you here to tell you what I told the press."

I shook myself from my reverie. "Right. Hopefully not all that?"

She gave an apologetic smile. "No."

"So what did you tell them?"

"Well, I told them about my relationship with Dennison, how it started on set and—"

"Do they know who it was? Did you say Dennison's name?"

She folded her lip in between her teeth. "Yes. From my story, it was evident whom I had a relationship with."

I sighed. "So everyone's going to know."

"I'm sorry. I couldn't hide it, and . . . There's something else, Adrienne."

"What?"

"Dennison has been rumored to be interested in younger girls."

"You already said that."

"The police might be investigating him now."

I leaned forward and put my elbows on my knees, propping up my head as I absorbed the information that my biological father might be imprisoned for sex crimes. Against underage girls. My stomach flopped and my throat tightened. I was suddenly glad I hadn't drunk much, or else it would be coming back up now. By sheer willpower, I refocused my thoughts. "Why now? It's days before the wedding." I gave a helpless little scoff that might have been a laugh or a sob. "I just don't understand your timing."

She sighed. "Originally I thought the story would revive interest in my wedding. And it has." Her voice grew distant again. "I just didn't expect it to be so pervasive. I didn't expect them to focus on you so much. But I couldn't hide what Dennison was anymore."

I shrugged as if pretending it didn't matter meant it didn't matter. But the truth was, this was the only reason it made telling the media right.

"I'm sorry for all this." She swung a hand toward the fire as if it was the problem.

"You've had a big impact on my life, you know?"

She closed her eyes, and two tears squeezed their way out from her lashes. "Yes."

"And it hasn't been good."

She pressed her lips together, her entire faced screwed up against my words.

I inhaled. "I want that to change."

Her eyes flew open, her expression filled with unguarded hope.

"But I can't trust you yet." My voice cracked. I cleared my throat and my voice gained strength. "You can't talk to media about me first, then fill me in later. I need to know before. I need to know when something concerns me—and not the day it breaks. I want the truth, even when it hurts. Because it's going to hurt more coming from some stranger meddling in my life than it will coming from you. That's your mistake, Mom. Your mistake is not trusting me—and Margot and Sophie and even Dad—to deal with the truth appropriately."

Blinking away her tears, she nodded with her lip still between her teeth.

"I do forgive you," I continued.

Her eyes widened slightly with hope, then fell at my next words.

"But I haven't forgotten. You have to regain my trust. Or else our relationship is doomed. And the way you need to do that is to be honest with me. Okay? Don't lie to me, don't cover up anything for me. When I ask a question, tell me the truth, or tell me why you can't answer it. And it better be a gag order," I added, my tone turning so wry that it elicited a giggle from Victoria's lips.

"Right. That may be the case sometimes."

"And I understand that. But I think I deserve to know about my past, and my origins. And if something is going to thrust me in front of the media, prepare me for it, please."

Running her fingertips under her eyes, she nodded, her hopeful expression evident even with her hands half covering her face. "Okay. I can do that."

"I hope so." I straightened in the chair and glanced at my watch.

"Have you opened those letters I gave you yet?"

I cast her a sidelong glance. "Not yet."

She nodded as if it was the answer she had expected. "Take your time.

The only thing that's still true about them is your father's signature. Maybe not even that."

Perhaps that was why I hadn't yet read them. Because I was realizing that biology wasn't everything, and sometimes the past should stay in the past. "I guess I should go to bed."

"Running in the morning again?"

"Yeah." I looked around the chair to see if I'd forgotten anything, but I hadn't brought anything in. "Should I take the dishes down to the kitchen?"

"No, I'll take care of it. Thank you. Oh!" She lifted her gaze from the fire to me. "One more thing."

"Yes?"

"Jake's dropped the charges against Elinor. He's decided to not sue either."

"Really?" Relief flooded over me. "Why? How?"

"I don't know. But we were notified earlier today."

"Thank God. What an answer to prayer."

Smiling faintly, she nodded. "Yes. I figured you would want to know."

"Yeah. Thanks." Feeling a hundred pounds lighter, I headed to the door. When I reached it, her voice trailed after me.

"Be careful on your run."

Her words pulled at me, making me pause in the doorway and look back. "Sure."

For a moment, it seemed she might have something else to say, but the expression fell away, and she nodded. "Good night."

"'Night." I walked away wondering whom I left in the room behind me, for she certainly wasn't anything like the mother I'd known. And yet tomorrow might show a different mother, and the next day yet another.

))

I had waited for this wedding to arrive for so long the rehearsal dinner seemed almost anticlimactic. I wanted everything to be over, I wanted to put this all behind me and move on: go to school, get a job, start a life.

Damien was supposed to be back tonight, after taking a week to get Kat settled down south of London. It was a good place for her, he said, with enough distance to offer some solitude, and yet close enough for him to offer support. I missed them both, and was strangely nervous about seeing him again. The last text I'd gotten from him had arrived a few hours ago, telling me that he was home and he'd be over shortly.

Spurn the Moon

Now I stood in front of the mirror in a crimson, floor-length gown, with my hair lifted off my neck and heels adding four inches to my height. Victoria insisted I wear a string of pearls James had given her, and a strange sense of nostalgia pushed at the edges of my world. Although I wouldn't wear her old wedding dress until tomorrow for the wedding itself, when I gazed at the woman in the mirror, I didn't see myself. I saw my mother, years before, in a dress that might have been pushing out the seams around the middle. The only difference was the scar on my head, just peeking out from my hairline.

Giving a sigh, I turned my back on the mirror. It was time to head downstairs to face the event I was simultaneously dreading and anticipating.

In the hallway, I had to focus on not tripping over my heels and entangling myself in the yards of fabric swirling around my ankles. I was so distracted I didn't hear the familiar voices arguing around the corner until I was almost upon them. I couldn't make out what they said, but the twins appeared to be having a standoff of some sort.

"I think we should ask," Sophie insisted.

"Just leave it be," Margot said more softly, but as firmly.

Their heels gave muffled taps on the carpet as they began walking away, and soon a third pair joined them, these ones crisper but still dull, like men's dress shoes, on the stairs.

My heart leapt into my throat.

"Hel—oh my gosh," Sophie said, and three sets of tapping shoes fell into one as the twins halted at the top of the stairs.

"Hello," came a deep, familiar British voice. "Is Adrienne up there?"

With a smiling glance over her shoulder to me, Margot replied, "I think she's right behind us."

"You're Damien Kerr," Sophie continued as if neither Margot nor Damien had spoken.

"Yes, I am." Damien's tone dripped with wry amusement. "You must be Sophie and Margot."

Hurrying to the top of the stairs, I didn't have to picture the shock on Sophie's face—her hazel eyes were round and her mouth was forming a circle as she came face-to-real-life-face with the person whose image had decorated her wall most of her teenage years.

Margot grinned at me.

Skin hot, I hurried up to them, and promptly tripped on the hem of my gown. Barely managing to catch myself on the stair railing before I went crashing into my sisters and pinned Damien like a bowling ball, I lifted my gaze to his.

From twelve steps below, Damien's alarmed eyes accosted me.

My face burned.

"All right?" he asked, hands half up as if to catch me.

A strange giggle escaped from me. "Yes."

He shot me a bemused look. Sophie turned her expressive, amused eyes upon me, and my face flamed into an inferno under her scrutiny.

"Come on, Soph, let's go." Margot took her sister's arm and began leading her down the stairs past Damien. "It was nice to meet you."

My stomach hollow, I watched the twins disappear even as Damien climbed the stairs separating us and joined me in the hallway.

"Nice weather for a wedding, huh?" I offered when neither of us spoke after a minute.

He chuckled. "I thought it was going to be awful, but it's turning out fine, isn't it? A bit of damp, but . . ." He trailed off with a lifted shoulder under his coal-black suit.

"But it's clearing up nicely." Smiling, I leaned onto the railing overlooking the foyer.

"It is," he agreed, stepping up beside me.

"And how was the weather down south?" Below us, a couple of hired help for the weekend crossed the room, chatting and carrying silver trays.

He sighed and leaned on the rail. "A bit darker."

"Hope for improvement?" I asked as the two women disappeared through one of the doors.

Gaze distant, he shook his head. "I hope so. Nothing to suggest that yet, though."

I faced him, cocking my hip against the railing, and inspected him from head to toe. He wore an ecru shirt under his black suit, with a tie that matched my dress. His hair fell in perfect waves on his head, and his cheeks were smooth from a fresh shave. Everything about him exuded masculinity, professionalism, and maturity. For the first time, I could see him on the red carpet, and the idea created mixed feelings.

"I think I owe you an apology. And a thank you," I said.

"For what?" He tilted his head.

"Thanks for Elinor. That was you, wasn't it?"

He smiled faintly. "Yes. I would have returned her personally, but . . . I met your father, and decided he could do the honors."

"You were there then?"

"I was." His smile broadened. "Your father seems like a good man."

"He is. How did you manage it? To get her released? And I got a voicemail saying all charges were dropped too—how—?"

"Let's just say I called in a favor. And explained the situation."

"A favor with whom?" I paused, studied him and said, "Do I want to know?"

Chuckling, he shrugged. "Jake and I . . . reached an agreement."

"Oh." Hugging my arms around myself, I grimaced. "Victoria said something about Jake dropping the suit, but she didn't elaborate. What happened?"

He unbuttoned his jacket. "I blackmailed him."

"You what?"

Hand falling down to his sides, he sighed heavily. "The thing you have to understand about Jake is this: he loves money more than anything else. I'm convinced he dated Kat because of her money."

"Okay."

"I won't give him money, not for what he's done. But I have no qualms about contacting every future employer he ever has and telling them exactly what he's done."

Silence fell, and my mind raced. I debated asking if there was more to Jake's story than just his assault on Kat, but something stopped me. Another person bustled across the foyer, this time a young woman I recognized as a maid of Edmund's in her modest black and white uniform.

"Well, I'm still sorry," I said finally.

"Why?"

"I've felt a little bad about how I've treated you."

He shook his head, perplexed.

I grimaced. "Maybe it's not apology worthy, but I feel like I owe you an explanation before . . ." I hesitated. Perhaps I had been reading this situation wrong. Perhaps I had been reading *him* wrong.

"Before something happens between us?" He smiled when I raised my gaze to his. "Adrienne, I don't think you're dishonest enough to hide anything. You're not a Brit."

I frowned, wondering if I should be insulted.

"No, no, no, that's a compliment. Brits are notoriously closed-lipped and avoid all semblance of upfront conversation. That conversation we just had about Kat? *That* was a British conversation. It gets exhausting sometimes."

"Oh. So, it's good?"

He laughed and reached for my hands, pulling them into his. "Adrienne," he began in a solemn tone that raised goosebumps on my arms, "you can tell me whatever you want. And you can keep whatever secrets you want."

"Oh really?" I teased.

He shrugged. "Well, I don't recommend a few, but . . . I won't ask you about any of them. Tell me if you want, when you want." He frowned down at our hands. "If there's one thing I've learned from Kat, it's to not force someone's confidence."

"You didn't," I said without thinking.

He sighed, shaking his head, and seemed unable to speak.

"Well, if you won't accept my apology about my own actions, how about I apologize for my sisters'?"

He laughed.

"My mother?" I grinned, my nerves pulsing as he ran a thumb over the back of my hand.

"Now you're becoming British, apologizing all the time."

"Ah well, we can't all be perfect."

"You're pretty close."

A flush heated my cheeks and made my hands go clammy in his. "What?"

"I don't date a lot, Adrienne. And I get turned down even less." He avoided my gaze, staring down at our hands.

"Does that make me special?"

"Worth fighting for," he replied solemnly, looking up from under his lashes at me.

My throat grew tight. "Well," I began, and stopped to clear it. "Well, if it helps, since I got here, someone has kinda distracted me from all my troubles."

"Here? Yorkshire?"

Flushing, I glanced down to the foyer again, but it was empty and served no legitimate distraction. "Do I have to spell it out?"

"I wouldn't mind hearing it." A slow smile spread on his lips, and his hand lifted as though to reach for my face.

A laugh bubbled up in me. "Oh? You wouldn't? What if it's not you?"

Hand freezing half lifted, the smile slid from his face, his cheeks turning to marble.

"I'm joking," I added, terrified he might not think so.

"I hope so," he murmured.

I tried to read him, but finding his face a mask, I pulled away and crossed my arms, scoffing. "This is why I hate actors. You can never tell if they're being honest with you or just feeding you a line."

A flash of amusement lifted the corners of his lips. "I find the best actors are the ones who aren't actors at all."

"In other words, liars."

"Not necessarily." His lips relaxed into a smile. He reclaimed my hand, pulling me toward him, as his other hand slipped around the back of my neck, careful not to mar my makeup or hair. "Adrienne, you're beautiful. Inside and out. And that's God's truth."

Any fight slid away from me, and I stepped into him, slipping my arms under his jacket to circle his waist. My cheek brushed his as I dropped my forehead onto his shoulder, with a fleeting thought of my makeup and the photographers downstairs, and how I should do anything to avoid messing up my appearance. But all I could think of was how I wanted to kiss him. With a shuddering breath, I lifted my head and faced him, fresh words ready.

At the sight of pale freckles scattered across his nose, I forgot what I was going to say. He half turned, his lips parted and an inch from mine, and suddenly nothing I had to say mattered as my heart thumped its way into my throat. His hand encircled my waist, and my head tilted back in response to the touch of his fingers on my skin. My lips parted, and then he was leaning down that slight distance between us, covering my mouth with his.

As far as first kisses went, it was better than my first kiss with Bryan, way better than my first kiss ever, and probably the kiss I'd spend the rest of my life chasing after in some drug addict's quest for a new high.

Chapter Twenty-Nine
Results

WE MADE IT THROUGH DINNER without betraying ourselves. Sure, there may have been a few more smiles in each other's direction, but Damien wasn't considered a good actor for no reason.

Had it not been for Damien, I would have looked for ways to escape the party as soon as possible. Between the tedious, long-winded rehearsal; the photographers who draped themselves all over the room to get the perfect shots; and the dinner party that included far more than just those in the wedding, the night seemed never ending.

After dessert, when people were enjoying conversations loosened by drink, and the photographers were packing up to leave, Damien disengaged himself from the crowd that had followed him all night and leaned over the couch beside me. "Come on. You look tired. Let me walk you upstairs."

I threw him a smile and glanced at the others, but they were all distracted by their own activities. Some played a game of cards, others drank and watched the card game, still others were chatting so animatedly that no one noticed us as he snuck me out of the room.

We wandered through the house and ended up outside in the east garden, all without Damien's hand leaving mine. As we reached the fountain, he seemed to withdraw. Although he didn't drop my hand, I felt him retracting from me, as if there were something between us that kept him from embracing me.

"There's something I have to give you," Damien said, his tone uneasy. "And I may have overstepped my bounds in doing this. If I have, I hope you'll forgive me."

Dread welling in my stomach, I stepped back. His hand fell from mine, leaving me cold. "What is it?"

A glint of white teeth flashed as he chewed on his bottom lip, examining me, then he dug a hand into his inside suit pocket and produced a legal-sized, white envelope, which he held out between us. "I tested Dennison's DNA for you, against yours and your mother's, to see if you're related."

My hand halfway outstretched to take the envelope, my body went numb and mind blank at his words.

"These results arrived earlier today."

"I have to sit down."

Concern on his face, Damien hastily put his arm around me, guiding me to a nearby bench. "I'm sorry," he murmured, crouching down in front of me. "Was I wrong?"

I stared at the envelope he still held in one hand. "I don't know. But . . . have you read the results?" I tore my gaze from the white rectangle to his face.

He didn't meet my eyes, but focused on my hand in his. "No," he said after such a long pause that I expected the opposite answer. "I wanted to. But . . . Kat talked me out of it."

"Oh." A wry smile parted my lips. "I guess Kat's got a good head on her shoulders, then."

"I think she does. Hopefully she'll pull out of this, too."

We fell silent, our thoughts traveling independent paths, each impenetrable to the other.

The envelope had somehow entered my hand, and both its weight and the texture of the paper rubbed foreignly against my fingertips. Like with Dennison's letters, I couldn't decide whether reading it and getting it over with was better than setting it aside and facing the truth later.

"Why didn't you ask me?"

He grimaced and took the seat beside me. "I'm sorry. I thought you might say no, and this way, if I did it . . ."

"It'd be better just to ask for forgiveness than permission?" The irony in my tone directed his gaze to mine with an apologetic shrug.

"Yeah. Suppose so. I tested it anonymously, by the way. No one knows the samples were yours, Victoria's, or Dennison's."

I nodded my thanks to that news. "I don't know what I'm supposed to do, Damien." The statement slipped out of me.

He put an arm around my shoulders. "You don't have to open it now. Later. Never."

Head shaking, I slipped a finger under the flap. "I've put off too much for later." I thought of the letters I had yet to open. "I have to know. What if I'm wrong? What if my mother is wrong?"

He didn't reply, just squeezed my shoulder.

Out of the envelope, I removed two sheets of paper. One was a cover letter I ignored, instead shuffling to the next page, a list of the genetic markers tested under the left column. Down the next column under the title of "mother" was a list of numbers, sometimes one, sometimes two. In the middle under "child" was a similar list, followed by a third column titled "father." After that, a "parentage index," with a low number given to the second decimal place.

Running my gaze down the center column, my eyes flicked between the left and right columns, comparing the numbers. From my lab work at school with DNA, I knew how to read these results; I didn't need to read the lab's summary to understand what this told me. Tears stung my eyes as the papers wilted in my hand.

Damien squeezed my shoulder, and I melted into him, burrowing my face into his neck as I cried.

"I'm sorry," he murmured over and over again.

When I picked myself up from his shoulder, I stared down at the crumpled papers in my hand. "What am I supposed to do?" I hiccoughed and swallowed. "Am I supposed to just pretend I don't know? Pretend that he isn't related to me?"

"I can't tell you what to do." Damien let me pull away from him, let me rise and pace in front of the fountain. "You wanted to know the truth. Now it's up to you what to do with it. Nothing has to change."

Nothing has to change echoed in my mind, until my mind answered: *it's too late. Everything already has.*

Into the morning, long after I'd showered off the party and my tears, I sat in the open window of my room, inhaling the fresh sea air off the water, allowing it to be a balm to my soul. Yawning, I turned from my reverie, and my gaze traveled to the crackling fireplace, and from there to the mantle, where the letters, still tied in their quaint little red bow, waited for my fingers to untie them. The stack of letters caught the soft glow of the embers and seemed to light themselves on fire.

$$\mathbb{D}$$

The next morning, Elinor and I raced each other on the hills and the clifftops, avoiding the arriving guests and hired help as we dashed through the trees. I knew I should take it easy, begin my taper for next week's race, but I couldn't seem to stop once I got started.

Even though it was still early when we returned to the manor, I was immediately whisked away to shower and be prepared. The beautician gave me a withering glare complete with pursed lips as if I were inconsiderate to have spent my mother's wedding morning doing something for myself. I refrained from reminding the man that I had little to do this day except look pretty, which was his responsibility.

Despite his complaints, he had me finished hours before the wedding, and then told me to stay impeccable until the ceremony, as if I were a flower girl that couldn't be trusted.

"You look gorgeous," Margot assured me as I peered in the mirror for a final time. "Absolutely beautiful."

Curling my lip at my reflection, I examined the twins instead. Although they wore matching scarlet dresses, their hair had been done starkly different, with Margot's hair flowing down her back in soft curls, while Sophie's was straight, and swept back into a loose side bun.

"Where did you get this dress?" Sophie asked, tilting her head at me, and trailing a finger down the slim shoulder strap. "It's gorgeous."

"Uh, it's our mother's old wedding dress."

"What?" Margot and Sophie asked together.

"Yeah. Mom's got a great eye for detail. She had it altered with the red lace for me to wear."

The twins exchanged a look.

"Really? You must be the favorite daughter," Sophie said.

I chuckled. "I don't think so. Just the oldest."

"Hmm." Margot stepped back, considering me from a distance, as Sophie lifted the flowing, red-lace skirt.

"It's really gorgeous," Sophie admitted, her tone dripping with reluctance.

"It is," I agreed. "It's absolutely wasted on me."

Margot grinned a slow grin. "No, I think we know someone who will appreciate it very much."

"Oh yes. Do tell us all about you and Damien," Sophie teased.

My cheeks began to burn.

"Yes, you, the self-proclaimed, shy introvert with no aspirations toward publicity of any kind—" Margot began.

"—Unless you make some amazing medical discovery—" Sophie said.

"—Or save a breed of dogs from extinction," Margot said.

"Or head up a new women's shelter," Sophie added, and they nodded at each other in complete agreement as I rolled my eyes.

"You are dating one of the biggest stars in the world." Margot gave me a raised eyebrow look that suggested she had expected more from me.

"He is not." I put a hand on my hip.

"He's not?" Margot's eyes lit up innocently.

"But you *are* dating him," Sophie said, grinning.

"Yes. I guess. I think. I mean, we've kissed." My cheeks had to be bright red now. It never got easier discussing these things with my sisters.

Margot laughed as Sophie said, "Tell us!"

"Oh good Lord," I began. "Is nothing in this world sacred?"

"First kisses? No." Sophie shook her head vehemently, making me laugh and bringing a grin to Margot's lips. "What was it like?" Mockingly, she lifted her hands to cup her face and stared at me with her wide hazel eyes.

"Come off it," I said through a giggle. "You're a dork."

"Well," she said, dropping her hands and spreading them out in front of her instead, "I don't stop until I get what I want, so, you'd better start thinking of how to share."

As she and Margot led the way out of my room, I released a little sigh. I'd gotten a stay—for this and for everything else. But it would only last a few days at most. Chewing the inside of my lip, I crouched down to give Elinor a quick stroke, then whispered for her to be a good girl, and followed my sisters from the room that, sometime during the last few weeks, I had begun to consider a refuge.

Chapter Thirty
The Wedding

THE STRING QUARTET WAS PLAYING. Guests had arrived and were already seated; they only waited on the wedding party, which lacked a bride.

In a few short minutes, my mother would lead all four of her daughters down the aisle in the British tradition. I would walk first, followed by the twins, who had insisted they walk together, then Sydney would bring up the rear.

As our wait for Victoria lengthened, the manor seemed to tighten around me, and I stepped outside for some fresh air.

Chatter from their direction reached me, and I scowled faintly at the guests waiting in the garden only to see Damien heading over. Apparently groomsmen in England acted as ushers for the wedding, and I hadn't seen him since earlier this morning.

I spared him a smile before gazing up at the sunny skies. It was an uncommonly pretty spring day, one which Victoria had probably called in favors for, if she had that kind of power.

"Something wrong?" he asked.

"No," I answered. "Just getting some fresh air."

He stood beside me in silence for a moment. "Nervous about the cameras?"

I glanced past him into the rows of filled chairs and shook my head. "No." I paused and exhaled a deep breath. "Just exhausted by everything."

He slipped his hand into mine. "Everything will be fine."

From beside the wedding aisle, a camera pointed in our direction, and I bit back the instinct to scowl at it. Today it was allowed to take photos; professionals had been paid to take them.

Turning my back to the camera, I faced the hedged garden adjacent to the lawn the wedding had overtaken and, as I did, a flash of dark hair caught my eye. I straightened, craning to see the man who had disappeared so quickly.

"What is it?" Damien asked.

"I thought I saw—" I dropped his hand and strode after the figure, taking the right-hand turn into a clump of decorative hedges. Ahead of me a blue-suited man disappeared around the corner of a triangular hedge, and I followed.

Around the corner, waiting at a small fountain of a young female centaur pawing at the water, was Matthew Dennison.

My feet carried me halfway across the green before my head stopped me. "What are you doing here?" My voice was cold, high, but determined. "You don't belong here. By your own admission."

He dipped his head in acknowledgment. "I know. I'm sorry about that. You . . . caught me by surprise."

Chin lifted, I examined him. Same dark hair I saw every time I looked in the mirror, minus the gray streaks, but the same dimple . . . and same shape of eyes, again accompanied by the shrewdness I had noticed before.

"What do you want?" I kept my voice calm and open by force of will.

His right hand went into his pocket, and it moved there as if playing with something. "When you and Damien met me, I was surprised. I hope you realize that."

I glowered. What did that matter? Didn't how he acted when he was surprised show his character more than anything else he could have done? Everything about him irritated me. Anger boiled up in me from my toes to my scalp.

"Well, I'm sure you can understand that I've got a lot to lose should you—" he curled his hand casually through the air "—decide to talk."

The way his eyes narrowed on mine, while he continued to feign disinterest, sent a shiver down my spine.

He knows. He knows about the DNA test. About to speak, I stopped and looked at Damien. After a moment spent wondering if I should dance around the issue, I figured blatancy would be best. "How did you know about the test?"

His face descended into wrinkles, on his forehead, around his lips and between his eyes. "What test?" His words came out cross and annoyed. "I'm here to—"

"About the test results. The DNA test." I didn't wait for him; I was done waiting for him.

"What?" His pale face couldn't be faked. "You tested my DNA?" He seemed to be trying to gather his anger and fling it back at me, but he only succeeded in gaping at me like the fountain behind him. A sudden spurt of water jolted words out of him. "How dare you."

"How dare I?" My fingers twitched beside my thighs. "How dare *you.*"

Words balanced on his lips, but he managed to pull them back and close his eyes, breathing deeply and regaining control with such effort that I doubted he often restrained himself at all. "Listen, Adrienne." His eyes fixed on me, dark and observant. "I know you think you've discovered something, and maybe you have. I don't know what you think you've found out, and results could have been mixed up, you know. But, if you keep these results quiet, I'll . . ." He shrugged, pulling his right hand from his pocket with a rectangular object in it. "I'll make it worth your while." He flipped open a leather-bound checkbook. "A hundred grand? Will that suffice?"

Indignation rose in me, followed quickly by disgust. "Is that why you're here?" I demanded, stepping forward and lowering my voice. "You're here to buy me off? Did Edmund put you up to this? Is that what this is about?"

"Edmund? Chadwick? No—no! No, not . . . buy you off, just . . . make it worthwhile to stay silent." He spread his hands casually, his blue suit rippling on his arms as he did. He wore the suit well, and it made him into a distinguished older man. In another life, maybe I could have admired him as my father.

The thought stilled my anger, replacing it with something like pity. "Why would you do this? Why would you think that all I want from you is money?"

"Well, isn't it?" He frowned, looking genuinely confused.

"No. I don't want your money. I never did."

For a moment, relief eased the wrinkles on his face, smoothing them away like a steamroller. Then they returned, deeper. "You're not pressing charges? You can't, you know. There's nothing criminal about my relationship with your mother. She was legal."

I had the overwhelming desire to step back from him, put distance between us. Everything about him repulsed me. How could I be staring at my father? "I'm not pressing charges. Although . . ." I thought about Kat and Jake. "If I could, I would."

Music swelled over the hedges. I straightened, facing him with the remainder of my strength and courage. "I sought you out because I wanted to know my biological father. I'm sure—I hope—this relationship between us was as much a surprise to you as it was to me. I want to believe that you would have had the decency to help the woman you got pregnant, no matter her age, but obviously not. I don't know why I thought that, especially given that you never sought me out." I stopped, fisted my hands and continued. "I wanted to know who you were, to see if we could have a relationship. That's it. Family is important to me. And whether you like it or not, and you clearly don't, we're related. Nothing's going to change that." I considered him, and slowly added, "But that doesn't mean we'll be family."

A blank gaze was all I received in answer, and I shook my head, pain warring with disbelief and anger. "If you ever feel like manning up and taking the responsibility you should have taken two decades ago, then look me up. Otherwise, don't bother. And certainly don't assume that you can buy me off."

Dennison stood before me, his unruly hair flopping down into his eyes, a streak of steel glinting in the sun. A breeze off the ocean swept in, rustling the leaves of the hedges around us and tugging at his jacket. He reminded me of a lost little boy, and pity and revulsion swirled in me.

Head shaking slowly from side to side, I stepped back, away from this man, my blood. He had nothing to offer me. I didn't care for money, and I never had. But he didn't know it, because he didn't know me.

Now I turned my back on him. At the edge of the small square we stood in, Damien waited for me. He had obviously heard a great deal of the conversation, for his jaw was set in anger, and his eyes shot unspoken insults at Dennison. But he said nothing and simply held out a hand.

And without checking over my shoulder to see what Dennison was doing, I returned through the garden the way I'd come.

☽

Damien slipped up front to his seat right before my mother led all four of us girls down the aisle. Aware of the half dozen cameras primed and recording in my direction, I tried to school my face into a picture of joy appropriate for my mother's wedding day.

The music of the string quartet filled the air as the minister spread his hands and pronounced them husband and wife.

Sydney beamed beside me, her smile straining across her face to her ears, while Damien smiled from across the aisle at me, his eyes warm and such a deep blue they almost appeared black. I couldn't help but smile back at him, my heart lighter than I had imagined it would be on this day, given the circumstances.

The guests, nameless faces in the crowd to me, stood and clapped for the bride and groom as they descended the elevated stage and walked down the aisle, now together. A distant thought of what Victoria and Edmund's future together might hold pecked at my mind, but I shoved it away. This was not the time to dwell on what might be, but only what was.

I followed their path down the aisle, and reached the spot near an archway of roses where the receiving line would begin and people would be funneled into the other section for dinner.

"Congratulations, Mom," I said when it was my turn. "I'm happy for you." The words were easier to say than I had imagined they would be.

Curiosity smoothed Victoria's forehead as her lips parted. "Thank you."

"I hope you've found joy."

Victoria pulled me into a quick embrace, pressing her lips against my ear. "I know I'm leaving for our honeymoon, but I hope I will get the chance to see you while you're in England? More than just the occasional holiday?"

"Yeah," I said as she pulled back. "I think that'd be okay."

Her lips curved into the most honest smile I'd ever seen on her face, and it made her seem ten years younger. "I don't deserve you, Adrienne." She held both my hands in hers and stared down at them, folding her bottom lip between her teeth.

I shrugged.

"Maybe I can try, though." She smiled when I remained mute,

uncertain how to respond. "In the meantime . . ." She leaned forward and whispered into my ear, "I think you've chosen a good man this time."

My cheeks heated. "Oh?"

"Yes." She straightened and gave a subtle nod of her chin. "You're a wise woman. I have no doubt you'll go far." She lifted one shoulder in a shrug. "With or without me."

Damien's hand touched my lower back, notifying me that people pressed on behind us, and I gave her a tight smile of thanks. There would be time later to talk, to share our lives with one another.

"Don't go too far," she called after us. "We've pictures!"

I groaned, and Damien grinned at me.

An hour of posing and smiling until my face hurt for wedding photos followed. When we finally rejoined the party, it was well under way, and we played catch up. We all danced, Damien leading me to the floor, Sydney dancing with her groomsman, as Edmund and Victoria danced their first married dance together in the spotlight. It was all awfully traditional, I found myself thinking. And horribly unexpected from my mother.

Hours later, after toasts and dancing and chatting, I began dreaming of escape. Damien was a step ahead of me, taking my hand and leading me out of the fray.

"Anyplace in particular you'd like to go?" he asked.

"Hmm." I tightened my hand in his, leaning my cheek against his shoulder as we walked. "Oxford?"

"Oh? Moving on to the reason you came over?"

I nodded absently. With all that had happened, university had been far from my mind. But I couldn't live off my mother forever. The idea brought a tired smile to my lips.

"Well, I've been thinking about getting a flat in Oxford."

"What?" I peered up at him, amusement twitching my lips. "You have? Since when?"

He shrugged. "Since you mentioned it."

"When?" I pressed.

"A minute ago." His eyes danced in the moonlight.

I laughed and slipped my arm around his waist. "Perfect."

"I mean, we'll have to discuss how serious we are." His teasing manner had disappeared. "After all, I do have a son to think about. And I don't date casually. I hope you're okay with that."

A small laugh broke through my smile. "I'm okay with that. I love kids, and . . ." I hesitated, not wanting to say the words on my lips. "And I think we have a shot."

He glanced down at me as if aware of the words I hadn't said. "But I actually meant right now, you know. Anywhere you'd like to go?"

"What are my options?"

"Anywhere," he answered.

Thoughts invading again, I considered his offer for a moment. "I actually need to go to my room."

"Oh." He seemed disappointed but he rallied. "Of course, you're tired."

"No, well, yes, I am, but . . . just for a minute."

He nodded, and we walked through the large house in near silence, too exhausted to talk. At my room, I pushed open the door and waved Damien inside. Elinor welcomed us with a leisurely stretch and a happy tail, and I took my time greeting her, deep in thought.

Dennison's visit had solidified my decision. Now, as Damien sank into the chair in front of the empty fireplace, I rose from petting Elinor and kicked off my heels.

"Oh, that feels good," I muttered. I tossed them in the direction of the closet, and from his chair, Damien gave a little laugh.

"You know those are probably worth more than your computer?"

"Couldn't care less," I replied, smiling. "They pinch my feet."

His answering smile looked as tired as I felt. The weeks of preparation leading up to this day had made my bones weary. Now that it was over, there was more to be done.

Hand on the mantel, I ran it down the carved marble, cool to the touch. Inside the fireplace, a setting of kindling, logs, and tinder waited to be lit on fire. And next to the nicely tied letters on the mantle sat a box of matches. My fingers found the letters, and when I picked them up this time, they felt lighter than before.

Damien shifted, rubbing his knee with his hand. "What are those?"

"These are letters my mother gave me." I turned them over in my hands. "When she admitted her affair with Dennison to me."

"She gave them to you?" His tone had turned sharp from shock.

"Yes. She said I could keep them, get to know my father as she knew him once."

"And you read them?" He had mastered the surprise in his voice, and it was quiet now, a murmur that didn't press me.

"No." Holding the letters from Dennison with both hands, I knelt before the fireplace in the altered wedding dress my mother had worn to marry my father James. "And I don't think I will." I clutched the letters a moment longer on my lap before setting them on top of the stacked logs in the fireplace. Then I lit a match and held it to the corner of the envelopes. Under my watchful gaze, the flames took hold and my mother's past burned.

When I stood, Damien was behind me. He slipped his arms around my waist and kissed my cheek. "Too late to go back now," he murmured.

Nodding, I agreed. "Yes. It's time for new beginnings. So let's go."

"Where?"

"Anywhere. Where memory can't follow."

Epilogue
The London Marathon

THOUSANDS OF RACE PARTICIPANTS SHOWED up in the London streets the next weekend, milling under the shadow of buildings both ancient and new.

Even though the past sixteen weeks of my life had been directed at my running this race, butterflies soared to life in my stomach. I used a Porta Potty for the eighteenth time, then made a slow warm-up jog around the nearest block, searching for Damien.

In the week since Victoria and Edmund's wedding, I had returned to my empty London flat and lived alone, Kat never far from my thoughts. I spoke to her every day, for as long as she would endure me. I refused to let her disappear on me or withdraw into herself. I could never return to the way things were, but I could work to make the future better.

At a fence post, I paused to stretch and texted Damien, 'Where are you?'

When I finished with my other quad, Damien's response came through with a ding. 'At the start. Meet me here?'

'Be right there,' I answered, finishing up my stretches. When I reached the start, I headed toward the pace setter I would follow for the next three hours, hoping to find Damien along the way.

"Adrienne!" My name being yelled from the sidewalk drew my attention out of the crowd and back to the sidelines, where I found the object of my search striding toward me. My greeting smile died on my lips when he didn't return it. My gaze fell on his hands, which clutched a newspaper.

"What's happened now?" Dread knotted the wings of the butterflies together in my stomach.

"Are you sure you want to know?" He held the paper so the cover was folded upon itself. "Or would you rather find out after the race?"

Lips twisted into an ironic smile, I reached for it. "Might as well read about it now."

He hesitated in handing it over, and we both held the ends and stared at each other. I read the concern in his eyes, his willingness to tell me, but his desire to shield me. "You said you didn't need to know everything anymore."

His words sent a shiver through my veins and made me hesitate. But the compassion in his expression made me certain I wouldn't be going through whatever this was alone.

"I think I'll run better if I know, rather than wondering." I tugged the paper from his hand and opened it, curiosity overtaking me.

Matthew Dennison's face greeted me, half covered by his outstretched hand, paired with several photos of young girls with black rectangles across their eyes. An unnatural chill settled over me.

The headline read in huge block letters: OSCAR-WINNING DIRECTOR ACCUSED OF SEX WITH UNDERAGE GIRLS.

A flailing pulse in my stomach suggested the death throes of my butterflies as their wings tangled together.

The article told me nothing I couldn't have expected: that many child actresses had come forward over recent months, claiming he had groomed them while they worked with him. The investigation must have already started when I'd met him. No wonder he wanted me to stay silent with my DNA results, desperate to avoid any proof that a hint of this was true. His youngest victim was a fourteen-year-old.

I came to the end of the article and couldn't stop staring at the words. He was worse than I'd imagined. And yet a large part of me wasn't surprised at all.

"Are you all right?" Damien's stare weighed me down.

Forcing a shrug, I refolded the paper. "No. But I will be."

"Sure?"

"Yeah. I hope this means Dennison will get what he deserves in the end." Thinking about Kat and what she'd had to face, I slipped my hand into Damien's. "And maybe I can help. Somehow. I still have the DNA results."

"You think we all get what we deserve?" Damien stared into his water bottle as he spoke, surely thinking about Kat and Jake, too.

Nearby, a small group with cameras began chattering excitedly and one pointed at us.

Giving his hand a couple of quick pulses, I nodded. "Eventually, I think we do." I tugged him into the crowd of runners lined up for the race, away from the cameras. "And we have an entire marathon to devise ways we can help give him what he deserves."

Damien's lips flicked. "I like that idea."

A huge clock ticked down the seconds from ten. Fingers of excitement caressed the crowd, which already pushed forward like horses in a gate.

"And sorry, but I'm not waiting for you." With an eye on the cameras approaching to get a shot of Damien Kerr, the movie star, I grinned wryly. "And you can deal with your paparazzi on your own today."

The starting gun exploded at the same time as his burst of laughter. With a flash of a smile at him, I took off, racing down the streets of London with the freedom that only running allowed.

Would you leave a review?

Did you enjoy this book? Please consider leaving a review. Indie authors, like myself, thrive upon the reviews of readers like you.

It doesn't have to be much, just a rating and a few words to say what you liked (or didn't like) about it. I treasure each and every review written, whether it's three words or three hundred.

Simply head to Amazon and search for "Spurn the Moon" or "Kelsie Engen" and click on <u>Spurn the Moon</u> in the search findings. Scroll down to the beginning of "Customer Reviews" and there will be a button for you to leave a review of your own.

And thank you for reading and reviewing <u>Spurn the Moon</u>!

Acknowledgments

I must first acknowledge my Lord and Savior, Jesus Christ, for giving me the desire to write and the determination to do so. I'm not sure if I can write the "ability" or "talent," as that's so subjective and it's a writer's prerogative to constantly doubt every word she writes. But it is He who put writing on my heart and urges me on when the days seem insurmountable.

And to those treasured beta readers and reviewers who took the time out of their lives to read my words (sometimes quite rough), and to give me their honest opinions: thank you. You make this writing journey an exhilarating ride.

About the Author

Kelsie Engen grew up in North Pole, Alaska, where the long winters taught her to love reading and writing of all kinds. Now she edits and writes all day long, escaping the subzero temperatures by delving into previously uncharted worlds.

She still lives in Alaska, now with her husband, children, cats, and dog, all of whom create a million distractions to getting her next book written. (But she wouldn't trade any of it for the world.)

Where to find her:
www.Instagram.com/KelsieEngen
www.Twitter.com/KelsieEngen
www.Facebook.com/KelsieEngenAuthor
www.Pinterest.com/KEngenAuthor

Other Titles by Kelsie Engen

Short Stories

Finding Home (Available on Kindle)

Emma Chesworth is a happy wife to an NFL player. But that all changes in one moment when her husband unexpectedly asks for a divorce.

Supporting her four-year-old daughter, while grieving the loss of her marriage, Emma throws herself into restoring a dilapidated, Victorian home. Nothing about this job promises to be easy, and Emma is soon sure she's bitten off more than she can chew.

Yet in exploring the home, she comes across some of the previous owner's belongings, and in there is something that might just hold the key to both her relationship with her ex-husband and the new financial troubles she finds herself in. Until it disappears.

Finding Home is a family tale "wrought with highs, lows, pain, and joy."

Bernadette & the Stranger (Kindle and paperback)

"The stranger hadn't moved from where she'd left him, not that she'd expected him to, but his chest rattled every now and then, evidence of life that scared her as much as soothed her."

When Bernadette Laurent suffers another loss in her life, she abandons humanity and moves to the island that her father left her. There she finds the solitude she hoped for. For awhile.

One day a storm rolls in, depositing a man in a lifeboat upon her shore, and thus destroying her island sanctuary. In this stranger, Bernadette finds more than she bargains for, including a ticket home--if she is brave enough to take it.

Anthologies

From the Stories of Old, "The Bear in the Forest" (Kindle and paperback)

In this international collection, new life is given to fairy tales, both classic and obscure.

Mythical creatures put the fairy in Fairy Tale. Mermaids, selkies, and ocean guardians experience the best and worst of humanity; sisters encounter an unusually friendly bear; a brave bride meets a silly goose; and a spinner of gold sets the record straight.

Urban fantasies modernize classics: a Frenchman learns the truth about magic, his past, and his girlfriend; a girl sets out to find love but receives a curse; and today's naughty list makes Old Saint Nick not-so-jolly.

New worlds bring a fresh sense of wonder! In the future, a young woman fights for her people and herself; a bastard son finds acceptance in a world ruled by women; and a farmer's wits win the heart of a frosty king.

Discover unexpected twists on old favorites, and fall in love with new tales and worlds to explore!